Acclaim

"REVERIE is a charming, witty, and heartfelt story of one woman's journey to find herself. This book will tug at your heartstrings as Ms. Taylor expertly weaves together themes of faith, forgiveness, and second chances." – Latisha Sexton, bestselling author of *The Grump's Bodyguard* and *Bram Baxter Marries the Wrong Sister*

"The concept for REVERIE drew me in immediately — travel, amnesia, second chances, and mysteries which never let up—who is who? Will they, won't they? What is the truth? Set in fun locations with high stakes and providence, readers of this genre will enjoy the journey." – Nova McBee, author of the *Calculated* series

"REVERIE is an emotional rollercoaster of a romantic thrill-ride you are NOT going to want to miss! I held

my breath the entire time and couldn't put it down." –
Chelsea Bobulski, author of the *All I Want for Christmas*
series

"Drew Taylor creatively crafts fiction inside of fiction,
forcing the reader to question everything, while inter-
mittently enticing us all to fall for more than one book
boyfriend. Her approach to romance from the Christian POV and the fact that—hold your pearls—Christians
have bodies and would like to use them, is not only
written thoughtfully, but also with realistic depictions
of sexual desires in line with God's design for marriage
and sex." – B.R. Goodwin, author of *Forget me Knot* and
the *Sugartree Romance* series

Reverie

DREW TAYLOR

DAYDREAMS & DISASTERS
BOOK 1

Taylor Made PUBLISHING

Paperback Cover and Dust Jacket Design by Melody Jeffries Design

Case Laminate Design by Callie McLay

Edited by Leah Taylor

Proofread by Alicia Whitaker

Dedication

To all the girls who transpose mundane life into romantic reverie—make reality better than fiction <3

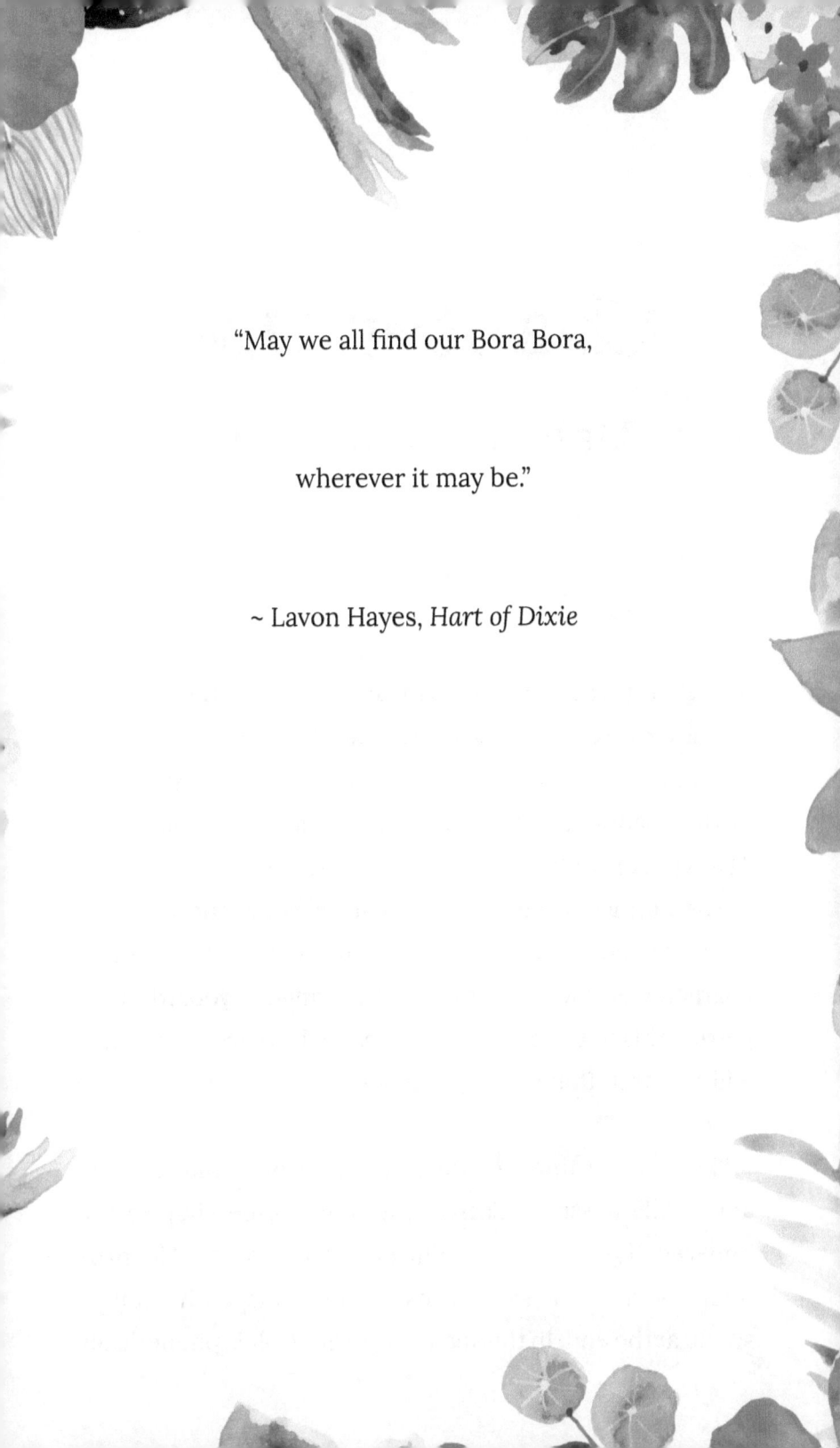

"May we all find our Bora Bora,

wherever it may be."

~ Lavon Hayes, *Hart of Dixie*

Chapter One

ME IN HINDSIGHT ~ APRIL

"To tattoo or not to tattoo?" Bulging biceps with roses, thorns, and ivy inked in black over tanned skin infiltrate my thoughts in intimate detail. In the middle of the chaotic, twisted flora and thistle is a simple cross. The words *Beauty in the Bramble* weave around the cross.

The warmth rising up my neck answers my question, and I type "tattoo sleeve on left arm" into Noah Ashley Ashton's character profile using my clunky orange keyboard. If I'm getting this hot over my imaginary book boyfriend, readers will go feral. Romance consumers love a tatted-up male lead.

"Esme Lorraine Jenkins," Crazy Colt hollers from across Main Street Coffee, the only coffee shop in the one-red-light town of Whitney, Mississippi. He pronounces my name *es-may* instead of *es-me*, with a long e sound at the end. In this instance, Crazy Colt is phonetically and culturally correct, but my parents have called me *es-me* since day one, so that's my name. "Cut out that there typin' on that loud keyboard of yours before I do somethin' we both gon' regret."

I open my mouth to shout an apology when a man with a deep, throaty voice talks over me.

"Can it, Colt. You're creating a civil disturbance," Sheriff Vincent Hodges commands from the high-top bar by the register. He's a tall, tanned, certified bad-to-the-bone law enforcement officer who has a jail cell with Colt's name on it. Metaphorically, of course. His K-9, a black Doberman named Ares, sits at attention, his cropped ears perked as he glares menacingly at Colt.

"Her clankin' is a civil disturbance," Colt retorts, running a hand through his thin, graying hair before pulling at his well-worn T-shirt. I think he's already slipped some of his moonshine into his morning coffee, and a hundred bucks says Sheriff Hodges will be picking him up off the street tonight. My heart goes out to the old man, but he refuses any and all direct help. As a community, we do what we can to make sure his needs are met, but at some point, people have to learn to stand on their own two feet.

Just like I had to after the accident nine months ago.

Rising from my chair, I hold up my precious, brand-new keyboard. "Sorry, Colt. Look. I'm putting it into my bag, okay?" I slip it into my pink backpack, mourning the feel of the large keys beneath my fingers and the stimulating sound it provides. I guess I'll only get to use this bad boy at home. I should have known others wouldn't appreciate the sound of it like I do. It grounds me when my head is too full.

"Thank yer, Meme. How's ya mama and 'em?" Crazy Colt goes on talking as if he didn't just threaten to smash my new keyboard.

I take to giving the whole coffee shop—which also includes a former student of mine who works as a barista, Grannie Bertha, and a few others—a run-down of everything that happened over the last afternoon and evening. *As if I hadn't talked to this same group yesterday morning.* I fight to keep from rolling my eyes, but a smile slips through my annoyance. I love these people and this town.

With my fun keyboard gone, I get back to brainstorming using the bland laptop keyboard.

After the new year, when I decided to write the story swirling around in my head, I began to profusely study. I've spent the past three months deep-diving into the inner workings of the romantic comedy when I wasn't grading papers or lesson planning, but my devotion to devouring the genre serves as my biggest teacher. It's a proven fact that women melt over tatted men with flirty personalities who have eyes only for their women.

I do.

Deep down all women want to be made to feel important, special, and unconditionally loved by a man. *Their man.*

And my man is fictional—the *best* kind.

The character of Noah Ashton set up camp and brought coffee to slow roast over the fire inside my brain a few weeks after I woke up from the coma. That was almost a year ago, and even then, I knew I had the perfect male character to lead a romance novel. It still startles me how loudly he speaks to me. And he does it at the darndest times like while I'm washing dishes, doing laundry, driving, taking a shower, and the likes. Always when I'm lost in daydreams while completing mundane tasks. He never talks when I'm actually sitting down to brainstorm.

It's nothing new, really, talking to the man who lives only within the confines of my neural pathways. I'd secretly always wanted to write a novel—which means I've always had imaginary people in my head—but it wasn't in the cards for me, so I settled for teaching books to high schoolers. A small-town girl from the middle of nowhere isn't cut from the same cloth or blessed with the same resources needed to be successful in this line of work.

At least that's what I used to think.

Not anymore.

I lost three years' worth of my memory from the accident that broke some of my ribs, punctured my lung, and pushed me into a coma, which changes a person intrinsically. Waking up thinking you're twenty-three when you're really twenty-six is like trying to clear the blurry sleep out of your eyes, but no matter how many times you blink and rub, you still can't see straight. It forces you to reevaluate the meaning and purpose of life. I asked myself questions like: *What does it mean to truly live moment by moment?* and *Does life only start after I get married and have kids?*

After taking the doctor's recommendation and integrating myself back into my normal life as best as I could, I realized my memories probably weren't coming back. But I wasn't upset.

I was empowered.

I would write a dang book.

And I would start living my life despite my singleness.

I had fictional men to fall in love with. They tended to be better than the real thing, anyway. Lane Burtram taught me that lesson.

But back to my new life's purpose: novel writing. Noah was already speaking to me, so all I needed to do was craft his leading lady. I easily decided she would be me. It's only fitting I make my first female character based on myself since I know myself best. Plus, amnesia seemed like a good trope for me to write about since I've experienced it—am experiencing it. I even used my real name, Esme, since I'm publishing using a *nom de plume*, Lorraine E. Jenkins.

Lorraine is my middle name, and Jenkins my last, so it's not that different. But it provides enough separation from who I am versus who my author persona will become. Hopefully that will help any criticism I receive not to puncture my heart. *Too much.*

Exiting the character profile, I open up a new document while I take a deep breath.

It's time.

After almost a year, I'm sitting down to write the story that's been percolating inside my head. For good luck, I run my finger over my cross necklace a nurse gave me right before I left the hospital after my accident. The elderly lady slipped it into my hands while my parents checked me out. She told me I should always cling to my faith, and though I've wavered time and time again, I remember her words. The silver cross is a wink from God, letting me know I will be okay, even when I'm not.

God's provision on my side, I think of the story on my heart. The fated insta-love and he-saves-her tropes with flirty banter and unexpected depth is ready to be written. I understand from research that insta-love isn't popular. But I wish people understood that loving someone is a choice you make, and some people make choices quicker than others. I've read thousands of stories online of people who met and were married within a month, and guess what? They're still married and in love. I'm a firm believer of the power of fate, love, and choice, and so I'm taking a risk with my debut novel and demonstrating those concepts.

My female main character, however, has her doubts that a love like that can happen. Because as fully as I believe it can happen, I'm a bit of a hypocrite. Whirlwind loves happen all the time, but not for me. Unless I'm writing myself into a fictional world.

Taking a deep breath, I rub my hands together then tuck brown strands of hair behind my ears, preparing to type the title of the book into the first draft: *Forgetting My Vacation Fling*.

"You writin' one of *those* books?"

I jump in my chair, throwing my hand over my racing heart. Bertha Simmons hobbles from behind me and helps herself to the empty chair across from me.

"You scared me half to death, Grannie," I exclaim in exasperation, staring wide-eyed at the Black woman who insists the town call her Grannie. I don't mind it because she genuinely is our wise, old sage. Grannie is a moth drawn to a flame when it comes to poor, lost souls. She houses them at her inn, making sure she shares the love of Jesus with them before they inevitably leave.

"Should always expect the unexpected, Meme, dear." Grannie sighs, sinking into the wooden chair and resting her cane between her legs. She closes her eyes and leans her head back, that dark gray hair of hers going nowhere due to how gelled she's got it in that signature bun of hers.

"But I was in the zone."

"Writin' a smutty book?"

I open my mouth in shock before closing it and replying. "No! What in the high heavens gave you that assumption? Do you read those books?"

"*Forgetting My Vacation Fling?*" Grannie opens her dark brown eyes and pegs me with a stare that says she might call my Pawpaw, the pastor, later. "Sounds like a title I'd pick up off the dollar store shelf, dear."

Lost for words, I stare at her as she only shrugs and waves over the barista, my former student, Katie McBride. "Katie, dear. What do you think of when you hear the book title—"

"No, no, no!" I wave my hands as if that's going to stop Grannie from saying those next words. *As if.*

"*Forgetting My Vacation Fling?*" Grannie finishes. I scowl at her while Katie flicks her eyes between us, probably wondering how she should answer or if this is a prank.

Katie scratches her neck before fiddling with her blonde, straight hair. "Uh..." She glances at me. I give her a pleading look. *Do your old teacher a solid, huh, Katie?*

She laughs and drops her hands, then shrugs. "Sounds like a book Miss Jenkins would tell us we're too young to read."

I groan into my hands as Katie buoyantly walks away. "Fine, Grannie. You're right. But what am I supposed to do? People like those kinds of titles."

We could play around with that, my little author, the familiar, masculine voice in my head speaks.

I mentally swat at the flirty man. *Not now, Noah.*

According to my research—and a bazillion books to prove it—readers enjoy titles that showcase a book's trope. I think it's a little cringeworthy, but to each their own. I need to reach a market and gain a readership before I smack them with my unhinged ideas for what a romantic comedy *could* be and how much heart can be interwoven into the spaces between humor and happiness.

Slapstick is great, but it's even better with angst and depth.

As my Pawpaw would say, "*Who'da thunk it?*"

"Here's a word of advice for you, dear." Grannie stands and moves to place her wrinkled, warm hand on my shoulder. I meet her gaze, hanging on to every word out of her hot-pink-lipped mouth. "Let the world roll around in the same ole muck. Don't be afraid to create somethin' different."

"Thank you, Grannie." I place my hand on top of hers. "Truly."

"Love you, Meme. Keep me updated on that story of yours. I'm readin' the latest Ashton Ashley novel with my book club right now, and I can't wait for the day we get to read yours."

Gulping down the anxiety that rises like acid when I think of my townsfolk reading my book, I stand to hug Grannie. She teeters away with her cane, leaving me to my thoughts about creating new things and standing out in life.

At twenty-six—well, twenty-seven in a couple of months—I never imagined I'd move into a homey camper across from my parents' place, but here I am. All because I hit my head in a jet skiing accident, which set me back in time, effectively shaking up my world. I'm still teaching English at Whitney High School even though I took the first quarter of the year off to give myself more time to heal, but I utilize every free moment available to me to work on writing. I hope to make it full-time one day. School lets out in just over a month, and I plan to complete this first novel over the summer come hell or high water.

I felt the Lord's undeniable call—as I did before the accident—to write romance stories that unashamedly bring Him glory and honor while staying true to the human experience. To show humans in all of their nuanced successes and faults as they navigate an emotion so crucial to our existence: love. Even more, to portray reality in a way people can accept.

Through fiction.

I'm not sure how Esme and Noah are going to accomplish those things, but I trust God's guidance as He directs my pen—er, fingers. I'm typing this draft.

When I told my former therapist about my novel idea and how strongly and vividly I could see it playing out, she suggested it could be a memory, but I don't think so. If it were a memory, it would have come back by now and I would *know*. I would feel it as if the events happened to me, not as an outsider looking in.

No, this story is simply a tale of enduring love, and honestly, it's a reflection of the love the Father has for His own. He has loved me so well despite my constant questioning, fit-throwing, and doom-spiraling of despair as I've tried to piece my life back together after the accident. He wants me to share the message that love—true love—is ultimately given and received through Him alone.

Losing three years of my life has taught me a lot, but most importantly, I've learned to live with open hands. Because only the God who gives and takes away can decide my fate. I'm mere mortal flesh who withers and wastes. He is enduring. Eternal.

"Oh, you sweet fictional version of me," I say to my blinking cursor, "you're going to have a beautiful character arc."

And then I type my first sentence from her point of view: *A thousand smiles can't hide the darkness underneath my face.*

As I stare at the sentence, something doesn't sit right. It's too dark for fictional Esme. She's upset about being cheated on and left at the altar, yeah, but she realized it was a good thing he was out of her life.

I delete it and try again: *When I look at him, it's the same feeling I get when I watch sun rays reflecting off of raindrops.*

Reading the line over, I groan. It's too much too soon. Intense and all-encompassing despite the happy vibe. The couple hasn't even met yet!

One more time: *Not even the blisters on the soles of my feet could ruin this moment of pure bliss.*

I delete it all again. Nothing is sitting right.

I knew from the off-set the story starts on a beach. I chose to use Bora Bora to pay homage to the place that siphoned my memories. But now what? My outline says to introduce the characters in their ordinary lives, but how?

Fictional Esme is from a lively college town up north called Juniper Grove, Mississippi, and Noah is from the town that neighbors Juniper Grove: Hartfield. They meet while vacationing in Bora Bora, which is funny because they lived thirty minutes apart from one another the entire time.

Esme is there because she was left at the altar—which apparently happened to me and is why I was on a honeymoon alone when I lost my memories—and Noah is there to write a book (because who doesn't love a male romance author lead?).

I even have the meet-cute planned, which involves an almost-kidnapping. Even though I am writing a rom-com, I can't seem to stop myself from going dark in not-so-subtle ways.

I have *all* of that figured out, but what did the two of them do before meeting on the island? What was ordinary life like for them? Their day to day? Why is the mundane so difficult to imagine?

In reality, for me, from what I can remember up to twenty-three, where a black hole sucks time until I'm waking up in a hospital bed, I led a predictable, boring existence. I wasn't happy. Not really.

But what was Noah doing? Because all I can think is that Noah Ashton's full-time job is being hot, making women swoon, and writing words that will melt even the hardest of souls. Noah Ashton doing something mundane? *Ha.*

Noah? Give me a little bit of something, please?

Silence. Of course he doesn't answer when I need him to.

"Ugh." I throw my head back and run my hands through my oily, straight strands.

"You okay, Meme?" Mrs. Gloria asks from the table behind me. I turn to address the elderly woman. Her kind, light eyes and shiny, white hair bring a smile to my face. Laugh lines paint a picture of a life of happiness and joy. I hope I age as gracefully and beautifully as she has.

"I'm good, Mrs. Gloria."

"You were mumbling to yourself again."

I blush. "Sorry, Mrs. Gloria."

"Don't apologize, Meme. You just sounded perturbed."

"More like frustrated," I reply. "Struggling to figure out a few things for this story."

Mrs. Gloria smiles. "Anything I can help with? I'm a good listener if nothing else. We used to meet and chat over recipes before your accident."

A familiar pang of memories forgotten churns in my stomach. "Thanks, Mrs. Gloria. But I'll figure it out. Let's meet up later in the week to talk about our recent kitchen explorations?"

She nods her head, a mile-wide smile overtaking her face, and then turns her attention back to her grandkids.

In my head, the story has already written itself, and I'm itching to skip to the falling-in-love story beat. It's going to be flirty, reckless, and everything I'm not, because the Esme of the story is a version of myself I wish I could be.

In reality, I'm a woman of prescribed order, so I have to write the beginning first. No one told me it would be this hard to download the story from my head to the screen.

I look at my well-worn copy of *Days in Dothan* by one of my favorite romance authors, Ashton Ashley, tucked in my open bag. Can I write a story that well? With the angst and the tension and the depth? While still maintaining humor and romance?

"God?" I tilt my head and stare at the high ceiling wooden beams just for the heck of it. "I didn't make up this calling from thin air, right?"

Just write.

The words are seared into my vision, and I smile. I'll get to the meet-cute by the end of Chapter Two, anyway.

Something to work toward.

Excerpt from Esme's Novel

Swimming with sharks wasn't on the agenda for today, but neither was going on my honeymoon to Bora Bora alone. Yet, here I am. Staring out at shark-infested waters and contemplating throwing myself to them even though I don't technically see any.

Hey! Maybe the hidden sharks will do me an immense favor and unalive me. Death by a hungry shark sounds much better than five more days on this god-forsaken island, drowning my sorrowful worries in strawberry vodka shots and shrimp. Which, trust me, does *not* taste as good coming up as going down.

I'm only here because I paid for half of this stupid honeymoon, and my parents are of the old-fashioned Southern mindset that women should be married off by the time they're twenty-one. *Ha, here I am, continually breaking the mold by being unmarried at twenty-six.* When I told them I didn't want to go on my honeymoon alone after Ryan never showed up at the altar, they practically shoved me out of the house yelling, "It'll be good for you to reevaluate your life. Besides, maybe you'll meet someone new."

I'm my parents' only hope for grandchildren as I'm an only child, and I've never liked disappointing them.

At least they don't blame me for the absent groom.

I *think.*

That text message he sent me still shouts in my head.

> **Ryan:** Esme, I'm sorry. I can't do this. I'm in love with someone else. - Ryan

I hate how he always signed his name on text messages.

Hot sand burns the soles of my feet as I shuffle across the white beach, looking out into the crystal blue ocean where stingrays freely swim alongside humans, yet I haven't dared to step foot into the salty water. The sun is brilliant and bright; it would ruin my eyes if not for my big black sunglasses.

I loathe the sun.

I crave gray skies and teary clouds. Maybe the occasional clap of thunder and bolt of lightning. A massive, raging hurricane branding my name would be sufficient and up to par with my macabre mood. Anything other than this soft, salty breeze against my sun-kissed skin, beckoning my spirit to shift the slightest degree toward the happy setting.

Day two of my spouse-less honeymoon, and my lips itch to twitch upward at the beauty around me. But no. *Ryan*

has another woman he loves. I wasn't enough for him. And
he just had to wait until our wedding day to come clean of
his two-month affair.

No amount of vibrant flora, luscious fauna, and mesmer-
izing sea creatures can divert my thoughts far enough away
from the fact that I'm now a twenty-six-year-old woman
who has been cheated on and stood up at the altar.

I down the Mai Tai in my hands before waving down a
resort employee to take the glass away from me. "And a
refill, too, please," I shout as the young Polynesian woman
dressed in khaki shorts and a tucked-in light blue polo
with *Forever Summer*—the resort name—embroidered on
the left chest nods and rushes off.

I browse for an open umbrella and chair to occupy and
wait for my third cocktail of the day, which is not normal
for me, *but when in Bora Bora...*

People are everywhere. Couples in love. Children
sun-drunk. Adults drunk-drunk. And an overall vibe of vi-
vacious carelessness.

It's almost enough to make me crack a smile, but I don't.
Because I can't afford to be careless. I have a job teaching
high schoolers the beauty of literature awaiting me back in
Juniper Grove, Mississippi. I have hearts and minds to in-
fluence. A life to get back on track. A new living situation to
consider since I'm no longer moving in with Ryan. *Hunting
down a new husband for myself so I can live up to my parents'
and the entire South's societal expectations.*

Finally, a chair frees up, and I walk the short distance, dodging humans, and shimmy out of my swimsuit cover. A high-pitched whistle coming from the chair beside me draws my attention.

"Do that dance again, *muñequita*." A Hispanic middle-aged man with a bald head waggles his brows, and I fight the urge to gag in disgust as he licks his lips. My gaze snags on the tattoo on the side of his neck. Is that a pentagram? With a *heart* in the middle of it? Disturbing isn't the right word to describe the sight of that.

Discommoding. Ominous.

"Uh, no," I state plainly, not bothering to hide my disdain. I'm a feisty woman as it is. Couple that with alcohol? Better watch out. The world is mine to conquer.

The man stands, taller than I expected him to be. His slimy smile sends shivers shuddering down my spine. "Don't be like that." He grabs my forearm, yanking me against his chest. I try to squirm away, but he's stronger than he looks, and I grow ice-cold in the middle of this balmy summer island when he whispers against my ear, "I have a knife in my pocket. If you scream or try to run, I will not hesitate to use it, *muñequita*."

Breath catches in my chest; my body is a statue.

I sober up real fast.

"Good girl." The man wraps an arm around my waist and shoves against the back of my legs with his knee. "Walk. And smile. Don't even think about calling for help. I need you."

Help. I should call for help.

God, help. If You care, help. Please help.

He could be bluffing about having a knife.

Or not.

Fear grips its dark tendrils around my neck, and my mind runs through a million possibilities of escape.

As I take step after step with a pasted smile of horror upon my face, I imagine myself throwing my body away from his fingers digging into my waist. I would punch him and kick him down after that and then run and scream until every eye was on me. I would point at him and yell that he has a knife.

Yes. That's a good plan. *I can do it. I can do it. I can do it.*

Courage swells within me, and right as I decide to spin out of his arms and punch him with the force of a thousand Bora Bora suns, the man falls face-first into the blistering, white sand as gasps ring out from beachgoers around us.

I'm frozen once more as I eye the guy who tried to take me away squirming to his feet. A bronzed and broad-shouldered wall of a man steps in front of me, muscles rippling across his back as he raises his fist and punches the other man square in the nose as soon as he struggles to his feet.

The guy who attempted to take me stumbles backward before running away, holding his nose. A resort worker approaches us after he runs away and starts inquiring if everyone is okay and what happened.

I'm silent and stunned as the stranger who stepped in to help me turns around, revealing the most handsome, concerned face I've ever seen, stealing my breath for a whole other reason. I don't know who this man is, but my soul leaps and dances and preens under his intense gaze. I have the urge to reach toward him, to cling to him forever. Safety seeps into my bones as my eyes flick down to his silver cross necklace.

"Are you okay?" he asks in a raspy, breathless voice, running a hand through his dark curls. His entire arm is tatted in a symphony of bramble and buds. I manage a nod, and he turns to the resort worker. His voice is thick like honey, slow, and Southern. "That man was trying to take this woman against her will, I think."

The beautiful stranger eyes me for confirmation, and I nod once more. My mind has done a one-eighty, and the kidnapping attempt is the furthest thing from my thoughts as I stare unashamedly at the sexiest man I've ever seen in my entire existence.

He and the resort worker discuss the details back and forth. This man must have been watching the entire scene play out from afar because he tells it exactly as it happened.

Minus the knife.

"He said he had a knife," I finally blurt, coming to my senses and wishing I would have said it sooner. The kidnapper guy is no longer in view as he's blended into the crowds of people on the beach and boardwalk.

The stranger curses, and immediately, he and the resort employee work together to get the police on the phone. The next few hours are spent in a whirl of questioning, describing, and doing lots of paperwork. By the time the police let me and the man whose name I've learned is Noah Ashton go free, it's well past lunchtime, and my stomach is eating me alive.

And despite my show of bravery and courage that was rudely interrupted by a Justin Baldoni lookalike hero, I'm a little frightened to leave this wall of a man's side until the creep who tried to take me is apprehended.

Noah must sense that.

Once we leave the police municipality of Bora Bora and step foot back onto Forever Summer Resort, Noah asks if I'd like to accompany him for lunch.

"That would be nice." I smile a smidge too widely at him, sticking close by his side as we walk on the boardwalk of the resort. We pass person after person, and fear saturates my blood every single time I spot a middle-aged balding man. *But I have a punch worthy of a thousand Bora Bora suns,* I remind myself. *And I have now acquired a Noah Ashton.*

Noah must take notice of the inherent fear I can't seem to shake. He runs a hand through his luscious-looking black curls, mussing them before he speaks. "I know we are strangers, but I promise you I'm safe. I'll provide references if you wish. Would you want me to take you back to your bungalow and order food to be delivered there?"

We pause, and I meet his eyes. They are warm and hazel with golden flecks. His smile is genuine, laugh lines appearing as it grows wider. "That won't be necessary," I state, grinning at my luck to meet such a handsome man on day two of this unwanted solo honeymoon. "The references, I mean. Lunch at my bungalow sounds like a date."

"A date," he reiterates, his smile somehow growing bigger. Noah offers his large hand to me, and I take it, feeling utterly safe with the man towering over me, acting as my fortress. As we begin to walk toward the bungalows overlooking the ocean, I sneak another glance at my rescuer.

He was shirtless when he stepped in and saved me from the guy, but now he dons a classic white T-shirt taut over his well-defined chest. His waist tapers into massive legs that could rival the trunks of Mississippi white oak trees. Noah is a wall. Beautiful, broad, and brick. Donald Trump would approve.

"Like what you see?" he asks, catching my gaze. I immediately shift my eyes away, heat creeping into my cheeks.

Very much. "Thank you for helping me," I say, ignoring the comment until I decide if I'm going to flirt back. "I promise I was about to attempt my escape, but I was worried about it."

"I didn't know if the two of you were together, but the interaction didn't look friendly from where I stood, so I just kept watching. When he started dragging you off, something didn't feel right, so I decided to intervene just in case something nefarious was happening." He pauses, then says, "I'm glad I could help. No woman should have to experience a man in that capacity."

The unspecified *type* of treatment we both imagine that man had in store for me sends a wave of nausea over me, but I take deep breaths and settle myself. I change the conversation as we approach the bungalows. "That one is mine." I point to number twenty-one.

"Serendipitous. Mine is that one." He points to the bungalow across from mine. A fresh layer of safety coats me, and I grin.

"It's like fate."

Chapter Two

SEE ME AGAIN ~ LATE JUNE

T he old coffee machine sounds like it's dying with every gurgle and hiss, but it will brew the enchanted liquid needed to help me get through the current Shakespeare reading assignment for my master-level online college class. Some detrimental memories I lost were the years spent obtaining a master's degree. I've begun redoing every literature class I took, and as always, I'm grateful to the woman I was: a meticulous note-taker who filled the by-lines and color-coded with a legend for reference. A small part of me wonders if I'll ever get that rigid streak back, but then again, when you almost die and lose three years of life, rigidity sounds like a prison sentence. I still prefer order to chaos, plans to spontaneity, and structure to going with the flow, but I've loosened up a bit. At least according to my best friend and sister-in-law, Sam Jenkins.

Speak of the raucous devil...

My camper door swings open without so much as a light tap masquerading as a knock, and in sweeps a summer tornado of short, blonde curls and curvy hips reciting Shakespeare. "'Things base and vile, holding no quantity / Love can transpose to form and dignity. / Love looks not with the eyes, but with the mind, / And therefore is winged Cupid painted blind. / Nor hath Love's mind of any judgment taste; / Wings and no eyes figure unheedy haste.'"

"A *Midsummer Night's Dream!*" I shout as if I'm a contestant on a game show.

Sam grins, high-fiving me. "Right you are. Two points, Gryffindor!" She slaps me on the rear before stealing the daisy coffee cup from my hand.

"But I'm Ravenclaw."

"Were. Before the accident. Come on, you know that." Sam winks, reaching into the small cabinet above the kitchenette to grab another mug. "You've re-tested several times over the past year and you've gotten Gryffindor each time. Accept your new fate, Meme."

But my heart will always belong to Ravenclaw. "I guess it shows how much I've changed over the past year."

"It really has almost been a year, hasn't it?" Sam muses as she pours our coffee, handing me mine black in a sunset-orange mug that reads *Shakin' Up the 'Speare* and features an image of the Bard himself wearing yellow sunglasses and tossing up a peace sign. It was a gift from Sam after her first performance with her Shakespearean theater troupe based out of the neighboring city and state's capital, Jackson. Sam's that kind of person; she gifts people for coming to her performance instead of expecting flowers. And yes, I always bring flowers regardless.

"The most stab-me-in-the-back thing you could have changed about yourself is taking your magic bean water black." She pours creamer into the daisy cup and stirs before throwing a pouty expression my way. "I mean, seriously. We used to mock Ethan so hard for this very thing." She gestures to my coffee, and I lift my brows before taking a sip and humming with pleasure. But I don't miss the way her face falls a little. "I miss those moments."

Knowing Sam might murder me if I attempt to apologize for my missing memories for the thousandth time, I let her have her moment of sadness and then continue our conversation. "Guess my brother somehow rubbed off on me."

"Methink'st thou art a general offense." Sam hip-checks me lightly as she maneuvers around to the burnt-orange couch that can also serve as my dinner table and bench seats when I fold it out. "But I'm glad you came around to the color orange. It's truly superior."

"Yes, that is still a mystery to me." I remember hating it. When I woke from the coma and doctors were asking me all kinds of personal questions, I answered that I loved the color orange before remembering I once thought the color made me feel like I was putting my brain in sport mode. I changed my answer to pink, but over the past year, I've fallen in love with the colors of the setting sun. "But the color brings me comfort instead of jostling my mind."

"I couldn't tell," Sam jests, her brown eyes scanning my small space filled with various hues of oranges, pinks, reds, yellows, and blues. It's chaotic and warm. And completely opposite of my former palette set to earthy neutrals alone, though I still have my beloved houseplants. The current vibe is a blend—an earthy, desert chic.

I think about life and death a lot, and the accident was a wake-up call for me. I can't remember where I was in life at twenty-six, but from what everyone tells me, I was too cautious, safe, and controlled. Timid and anxious. I was well on that path at twenty-three, and I'm trying not to live that way anymore now that I'm pushing twenty-seven. I grab my best friend's hand, not bothering to mention my internal thoughts. She's heard me spill them a thousand times. "I want to be the version of me I'm writing about in my novel. Bold. Flirty. Speaks her mind. Fun."

Sam smirks. "Try and try, Meme, but never forget that you are who you are. And who you are is lovely in every sense of the word, my friend." She pulls at my ponytail, that innate sadness crossing her full features once more. "I think you're plenty of fun. Even when you doubt yourself, overthink, and choose to play it safe. I liked who you were before the accident, and I like who you are now."

Yeah, so fun. I spend my days with an imaginary man living in a fiction world I'm creating. Which was my goal for the summer, but still. I don't go out unless it's for groceries or to write at the coffee shop. Sam usually comes here to hang out, though occasionally I visit her and my brother in Jackson. And then I have supper with my parents most nights of the week. *I'm just the highlight of the party for one.*

The couch buzzes, and Sam tugs her yellow phone from her back pocket.

"Hello, my hunk of a husband," she coos, and I groan, rolling my eyes. I can't remember their wedding, and sometimes, it still shocks me that they're married. It will forever gross me out when she starts talking in the language of a lover to my brother, though I am supportive and over the moon about their marriage.

Oh, sweetheart. We would have them beat. We would excel *in the language of lovers. I speak it fluently.* Coffee dribbles down my chin as I fight to contain my laugh at the fictional man's nonsense. Noah's voice is always alive in my head, and he says the most inappropriate things at the most inappropriate times.

Sam tosses me a concerned look, but I wave her off.

I move to my makeshift desk area by the north window of my camper where I can look out and see a green, grassy field with wildflowers blowing in the light summer breeze across the two-lane highway past the treeline. At the south end of the camper sits my parents' house across their front lawn. Enough distance to have my space while still allowing me easy access if I need them. My parents like to hover, so after the accident, when I was ready to start taking some space to figure out who I was and who I was becoming, we agreed to this camper lifestyle so long as I stayed on their property. I love the life I've curated for myself, and I wouldn't move out of my camper for nothing, short of getting married to a man, but ultimately, I've had a problem caring too much about letting others down, and it's the hardest of all to confront when it comes to my parents.

Turning on my computer, I hunt down my old notes on *Romeo and Juliet*, the next Shakespeare play on my latest list. Sure enough, I find a file labeled with the play's name and click on it. Another list of folders pop up, each numbered before the file name to keep them in the formation I wanted.

I shake my head and puff out a breath of air. I really was organized to a fault back then. Scanning my tiny space and noticing the piled dishes in the sink, sticky notes full of plot ideas covering a wall near the door, and clothes tossed haphazardly on the rocking chair, I realize maybe I could use a teensy bit more of that desire to be tidy. But then again, at least I've loosened up some, and regardless of what Sam preaches to me about how I'm good enough the way that I am, I know I can stand to untie the uptight knots even more.

Sam hangs up the phone before bouncing up, rocking the camper with her movement, and trudging toward the door. "I hate to do this, but I need to leave. Ethan said he's not feeling well and is heading home from work. I should go check on him."

"No worries. Give him a hug for me, and let me know if I can bring anything over later after my meeting."

"Meeting?"

I smile and shimmy my shoulders, relishing in the news I have for her. "It's the reason I invited you over today. Well, that and to help me with Shakespeare, of course."

Sam raises her dark blonde eyebrows and motions for me to continue.

"I'm meeting with a literary agent at Main Street Coffee later." I can't contain the girlish squeal, and neither can Sam as we hug one another.

"I'm so happy for you!" She claps her hands before covering her open mouth. "My best friend is going to be a best-selling author!"

I blush and wave off her words. "It's just one meeting. Besides, I still haven't written the ending even though I've been working on it for two months. I've only had more time recently since we are out for summer break." *A lot of time. Endless time. It's consumed my existence. And I'm fully in love with a fictional man.*

"I didn't know you created a pitch."

My embarrassed-at-the-praise blush deepens. "I didn't. I've been posting vague snippets about my book on a new author's social media account for the past month because I know that's where I'll find a readership, and it kind of blew up. One reel with the blurb of the book went viral. The agent saw it and reached out to me. I looked the company up, and it's a legit business."

I looked it up enough to know the agent eerily looks like my male main character, though a little more put together than I imagine Noah to be, but how could one really tell from one photoshopped picture on a website? The company isn't huge, and they only represent Southern authors.

And they represent my all-time favorite romance author—Lucy May.

Maybe I'll get to meet her. I hold back a squeal at the thought.

"Are you famous?" Sam asks in all seriousness, already whipping out her phone and pulling up the app. "What's your handle?"

I shake my head. "No! I've only got like three thousand followers." I'm kind of nervous for people I know in real life to follow my page. Not because there is inappropriate content, but because this book is personal to me. It's a testament to the woman I wish I could be instead of the bland, boring, boxed-in life I've lived. It speaks to the type of passionate love I wish I could experience, the type Lane said was irrational and unreal.

But Sam's my best friend, so I tell her. "It's @authorlorraineejenkins."

"And you're just now telling me this?" Sam's eyes bulge out of her head as she scrolls through my account. Then her screen goes black and she shoves the phone into her jean pocket. "Okay, I've got to go, but schedule me in for dinner tomorrow because unless I'm vomiting and forcing Ethan to clean it up, you're telling me everything."

I laugh and agree, and then see her out, halfway hanging out of my door and waving as she drives off in her silver Honda.

I've been shoving the meeting from my thoughts ever since the agent, Nikhil A. Prewitt, reached out and asked for it a week ago. (Yes, I chuckled at the fact his last name is the same as my female character.) I can't allow myself to get too hopeful only to crash and burn. As much as I enjoy teaching, I want to be a full-time author. It's a torch I've carried for a long time, but I was always too scared to light it up. Failure isn't an option in my book, and my parents would have a heart attack if I quit my steady job in education due to the unpredictability of the publishing realm. They've ingrained in me that stability is the most important thing to have in life outside of God. It's a little contradictory if you ask me, because God calls us to trust Him. That's it. Trust in Him. Not in stability.

However, I know they're not entirely wrong. God calls us to trust Him alone, but He doesn't call us to be ignorant and readily set our lives to flames.

But as I've told them, God has given me this story to write, and I have to trust that He will provide everything I need at every step of the way. I'm almost twenty-seven and can make my own decisions. I won't quit teaching yet (because I'm not ignorant), but the moment I can remotely afford a basic living off of my books, I will light my torch and carry it high. Because I trust God not to let it catch everything around me on fire. Even more so since He kept me alive during that Jet Ski accident last year, which has been the sole driving force in me being able to stand up to my parents regarding this authoring gig.

I forgo reading Shakespeare for today since the meeting with the agent and all the possibilities it brings to the table are too front and center in my head now. Instead, I make another pot of coffee and sit down to hopefully edit another scene (because I'm procrastinating the ending) before I need to start getting ready.

The blinking cursor on the screen reminds me I'm at *that* scene—the first kiss between my beach-going lovers. I didn't write yesterday to avoid this moment, opting to spend my day reading first kiss scenes instead, but I have to power through. Just as I did when I wrote the scene originally.

Here's the thing: I've only kissed two men before. The first was my college boyfriend, Lane Burtram. The second was Bryan, the ex-fiancé that I forgot due to amnesia, which is good because he stood me up at the altar. Supposedly, according to my family, he suddenly claimed he wasn't ready to get married, so I took my honeymoon alone to get some space from the town and their pitying looks. My family has no idea what happened on the island other than what the officials told them, and so their next memories of me after getting on the plane are hovering over my unconscious body on a hospital bed in Bora Bora.

Their stories feel like just that—stories. Not real. Not like it actually happened to me, though the scenario is a great reason for fictional Esme to be in Bora Bora. I changed the guy's name to Ryan, to be polite. And added a cheating layer even though infidelity was never mentioned to me as a reason he called off the wedding.

Ultimately, there are no hurt or sad emotions at the name Bryan. No memories of taking my honeymoon alone. It's all a tale of a dead version of me. I guess, for which, I'm thankful. I'm not married to a man who didn't want me (which, yeah, stings just a smidge due to the notion of the concept). I assume I kissed him if I was going to marry him, but outside of that logical conclusion, I don't remember ever kissing a man besides Lane, and those memories still feel a little too raw due to my amnesia. I dated him for two years while I was in college, and I don't want to dwell on the way his kisses always made me feel warm inside.

Or the way I thought I loved him.

Or the way he told me that my idea of love and romance was too grandiose for any normal, real guy to live up to.

Which resulted in him breaking up with me on Valentine's Day of my senior year of college at Juniper Grove University.

What a—, I have to cut off Noah's voice in my head, but I smile anyway. At least my fictional boyfriend has my back.

I scowl at the screen, knowing the only options for me to write this scene effectively are to keep it non-descriptive and PG clean, relive the way Lane kissed me while telling me the hard truth that human men can never measure up to fictional men, or to pull from other books I've read.

Number three, my lord, I mentally say in the voice of that masked guy from *Shrek.* I crack my knuckles and do what God has commanded.

Just write.

I finger the cross necklace around my neck. I guess the first thing on the first kiss editing checklist is to make sure I've set the scene. My head conjures up a romantic sunset, a candlelit beach dinner, and...

Mangos?

Listen as I guide you, my little author. First, I place my palm on your cheek...

Excerpt from Esme's Novel

"Favorite color?" Noah asks as we sit on the edge of my bungalow's deck, soaking in the sun. He's trying to take my mind off of the attempted kidnapping earlier today while we wait for our late lunch to arrive. He's asked me first-date-type questions, and with that vibe forming between us (and the fact he saved me), I'm having *thoughts*. Sexy savior complex type of thoughts.

I shut them down, grimacing at the water. It would be one thing if I just thought he was hot, but there's something else lurking beneath the haze of attraction. Something... oceans deep. Too foreign to explore.

"Pink. But like, pale." I respond, eyeing the man who has at least seven inches on my five-foot-five frame, even while we are sitting side by side. "And yours?"

"Orange."

I cease kicking my feet in the ocean, tossing him an incredulous look. "That's the worst color in existence."

He feigns hurt, bringing one large hand to his chest. I *really need to stop focusing on his hands...*

"Dang, girl. You're brutal."

I shrug and resume kicking my feet. "It's truly awful. So loud. Bright and in your face."

"I like bright and in your face," he croons in a sultry way that nine out of ten is not supposed to be taken that way. Or maybe it is? This Noah guy is the flirtiest man I've ever encountered.

"Favorite book?" I ask, positive he isn't a reader. It should turn me right off from his good looks, and then I can get my crap together and go back to sulking over getting left at the altar by a cheating man and reckoning with almost getting taken—

"*The Joy Luck Club.*"

Once again, my feet stop their mindless splashing. I choke out, "Amy Tan?"

He raises one dark eyebrow, a smirk pulling at the corner of his full lips. "Yes?"

"You read books? Classic books? Books all about women and their familial, cultural struggles?"

"And why does that shock you so much, Esme?"

"Look at you." I gesture up and down, perusing his stellar frame shamelessly.

"I'm hot so I must be illiterate?" He crosses his arms in a challenge, biceps flexing. He asked me when we got back to my place if he could strip his shirt off while we lounged on the deck, and I told him I'd be comfortable with it.

I needed a little sugary-sweet eye candy to pick me up after the past week I've had. *The afternoon I had...*

"I don't make the rules."

"That's a hasty generalization, Meme. You're hot and obviously a reader since you asked me that question. We can be hot readers together."

I try not to focus on his eyes taking a once-over or the fact that he used my nickname without knowing it is my nickname, but I'm sunburned, so the heat on my face can be attributed to that. "Females have to be literate. It's trendy to be a voracious reader."

He drops his arms and pulls one leg up from off the edge, tucking it underneath him as he manages. "So you only read because you feel feminine society says you must? Aren't they all about the erotic, anyway? Is that what you read, Esme?"

My face burns so intently that the sun gets a little jealous it couldn't do the job as effectively as Noah. "No. But if I did, you'd judge me, right?"

He shakes his head, loose black curls bouncing. I ache to find out if they're as silky as they look.

"You're lying," I state.

"It could be... fun." He winks and places his hand over mine, his fingers sinking in the spaces as my hand flattens against the wooden deck. *Oh, mercy. Lord, give me strength...* "But, I don't encourage that, Esme. You should know that right off the bat. Sex is sacred between a married man and woman."

My brain is short circuiting. *Who is this man?*

"Well, I don't," I brilliantly articulate, staring down at our intertwined fingers. His hand looks like it's eating mine for dinner, and I think I'd let it happen. I've never felt this way about a man before. It's new. It's invigorating. It's *dangerous.*

My skin tingles with interest and desire as I move my gaze from our hands, up his tanned, sculpted forearms, and finally, my eyes snap to his face.

His stupidly gorgeous face.

Maybe I don't need strength to withstand. Maybe I just need to *live* for a week. Maybe I need to be reckless and make forgivable mistakes.

I can have a vacation fling. I'm single. I'm sad. And he saved me. Quite frankly, I don't want this man to leave my side until I know the perpetrator is caught. I shiver once at the thought of that guy finding me again. *Thousand Bora Bora suns,* I think, as if tricking myself into thinking I can deliver a good punch is the way to make it happen.

"Are you single?" I blurt before I can change my mind. I wait with bated breath for his answer.

Noah's responding smile is wide, crow's feet forming at the corner of his pretty hazel eyes. "I am. Are you?" His finger caresses one of mine.

I don't have the courage to tell this beautiful man I was cheated on and forgotten at the altar like something old and discarded, so I merely nod, returning his smile and getting lost in his eyes now that I know I have full permission to. The depth of his eyes, which can't seem to decide on blue, brown, or green, beckon me in. *I want to jump.*

Should I be worried about being alone in this bungalow with a stranger? I should be. Why am I not? Did his hotness break me?

No, his heroism touched me.

And where I had an off-putting feeling from the other guy immediately, with Noah, I feel safe. Protected. I can't explain it; it just... is.

I eye his cross necklace, the emblem sitting right above his chiseled pecs. Yes, he must be a Christian. I'm safe. In *all* ways.

"How old are you?" I ask.

"Twenty-eight. You?"

My heart dances even though I command it not to. "Twenty-six."

Noah stares at me with a look I can't quite name—disbelief? Fear? But also, joy?—and then his phone dings beside him. "Our food is here."

I move to stand, but he stops me. "I've got it. You stay put and relax." Noah's voice is like the bass in the band, somehow rumbly and smooth simultaneously. He takes on a focused look like he's prepping for a battle. It dawns on me he's keeping me here in case it isn't our food.

What a gentleman.

I swoon a little as he stands and walks through the doorway back into the bungalow. I lay down on my back and breathe. It's my first moment alone since Noah stepped into my life acting like a real-life hero. I thank God for having Noah in the right place at the right time, and tears begin spilling from my eyes, rolling into my ears. They flow harder as my body decompresses, allowing every moment of frozen fear to come to the surface in the form of salty tears and full-body shakes.

God and I haven't been on the best of terms. Why did He allow Ryan to cheat on me? Why did He allow me to get left at the altar? *Why did I not listen to Him sooner and leave Ryan after he told me that I had too high of expectations for any man to reach in terms of romance?*

I pretend that the last question doesn't exist. Because if it does, I'm ultimately to blame, not God.

My life plan was going as I wanted.

Go to college.

Get a job teaching.

Find a good man.

Marry him.

But somewhere along the way, I started to dread teaching. I desired to write, to tell gripping romantic stories. I craved romantic gestures and butterflies in my relationship that had come to be a little... well, stale... regardless of the glorious way in which Ryan kissed me.

"A good man" no longer felt like enough.

Ground-level romantic expectations didn't do it for me.

I wanted burning red love. A love that would simultaneously set me aflame and hold me tight. Just like in the novels I read.

But Ryan did a marvelous job of convincing me that was not achievable for any man no matter how much he loved a woman, so I planned to meet him at the altar anyway just to be told he wasn't going to be waiting for me.

"Do you want to eat out here, or inside the—" Noah stops talking as he looms over me, concern etching into his features. He kneels, wiping wetness from my face. "I'll set up lunch inside. Take as long as you need, Esme."

With that, his handsome face disappears from view, and a new round of tears—ones of gratitude and disbelief—takes over.

Because so far, it seems like Noah Ashton stepped right out of a romance novel. And I think I might want to have this week with him, even if it ends in burning flames. The feelings he calls to surface within me are bright and new, and I want to see how we fit, even if it's just for this little slice of summer. Something tells me he might be worth it.

***

"She reads smut and she cooks," Noah teases, gripping the edge of the island bar in the middle of the kitchen as if he's trying to stay upright. He groans, tilting his head back as if he can't wait to taste my food. He stayed after our late lunch. We went for a swim, talking about nothing and everything, went grocery shopping for food this evening, and now, we are enjoying a sunset dinner on the deck of my bungalow. A meal that I cooked out of sheer appreciation for this magnificent specimen of a man.

He only left to shower and change, and while he was absent, fear nestled into my soul, and I kept the door locked and a kitchen knife in my hand until he came back.

I don't know how I'm going to make it through the night. My "thousand Bora Bora suns" maxim is no longer cutting it the more I dwell upon what almost happened to me out on the beach.

"I don't read smut," I state, swatting his hand away as he attempts to steal a mango slice off of my fish taco. I don't understand how this man makes me feel terribly at ease. It might be scarier than the kidnapping attempt to be honest, but I'm here for it. All the way. One hundred percent, pedal to the metal. I decide to jump into the depths of his eyes.

It's Bora Bora, after all.

On top of making me feel like I've known him for a lifetime instead of half a day, Noah has done the impossible tonight. He's made a button-down Hawaiian shirt and a pair of mid-thigh khaki shorts runway-ready. *As long as he's the one walking.* I chose a pale pink flowy sundress, which matched the pale pink in his shirt.

Noah leans against the kitchen counter. "I know, sweetheart. It was a joke. I'm glad you don't; I want my future wife to be fully consumed with *me.*" And as if he didn't imply what I think he did, he carries on. "What do you read?"

I shrug, gathering my plate and glass of Orange Julius. Noah told me earlier that the drink was a favorite, so I had to blend it up for him. "Classics. British literature because I—" I cut myself off from mentioning that I teach it. I've shared things about myself with this man, and we do know each others' first and last names and ages, but I take pause because I'm not that irresponsible. How much of my personal life should I tell this stranger?

"You what?"

"My profession requires that I know a great deal about British literature."

"You're not going to tell me what it is you do, are you?"

I grin, stretching my neck to look into his eyes as he stands at his full height. "Nope. I'm undecided how much of my personal life I should share with a hot, strange man. Ted Bundy was a looker, you know."

Noah laughs, a rich and delectable sound. "Fair enough. I'll go at your pace. Though by that accent of yours, I can tell we are from the same region of the United States." He winks, and I turn my head so he can't see my smile.

Conversation slips away as we both stare out at the setting sun; the sound of the waves lapping against the deck promises peace and tranquility. I beg and plead that it's not lying to me.

The flame of the candle between us on the small black table dances in the whispering wind, and I meet Noah's gaze above it. He smiles, and I blush, looking away once more and admiring the flames of the tiki torches instead.

This is what I wanted. Someone who sets butterflies fluttering in my stomach with one glance. Something Ryan did at one point, but as our relationship progressed, and he blamed the lack of passion on me for wanting the impossible, they died. Words like daggers, until not a single fluttering insect remained.

So why didn't you leave? The signs were there. I ignore the small voice beckoning me to face the facts. Instead, I think of how Noah could star in a romantic comedy.

Even the thought of Noah's name has the insects flapping and begging to let loose. When I glance in his direction once more, he's wearing an incredulous smirk. I raise my eyebrows, and he scoots his chair around the circular table until he is right by my side.

Noah's so close that I smell his cologne. It's warm, sweet, and spicy, much like his personality. A warm finger slides along my jaw until he hooks it under my chin, tilting my face to his. A few more inches and I'd know if he tastes as good as he smells. *And by golly, I bet he does.* "I do want to know you, Esme Prewitt. And I'm planning to make it my mission if you'll let me."

The heat coursing through me feels as if the flame from the candle has set me on fire, but I square my shoulders. I'm here. Single. And I've decided I don't want this man to leave my side. Even after the creep who attempted to take me is apprehended. I'm going to hold Noah close these next five days.

Because I can.

Because I deserve some fun after Ryan's humiliating exit from my life.

Because this guy might have stepped straight from the pages of a novel even though I've only known him for an afternoon. Heck, maybe he'll be my living proof that real men can live up to fictional men. *They had to be inspired by someone.*

Regardless, we'll part ways and never talk again once we leave the island, so what's the harm in having a consensual island fling?

"I'm a tough shell to crack, but you can try." It's a lie. I have no doubt Noah will know my blood type by the end of our time here. I'm too much of a people-pleaser to not answer his questions eventually, but I'm going to hold out as long as I can.

Just because it will be wildly amusing and a turn-on.

Something I haven't had in a while. Even Ryan, in all of our time together, never made my body feel tingly like *this*. And now I recognize the need to be careful with my sexual feelings and thoughts surrounding a man, something I haven't had to do before. With Ryan, I only felt like this after a successful date night and lots of kissing. But with Noah? One glance at the man sends me into a tizzy.

New. Thrilling. Deliciously dangerous.

And coupled with the sense I've known him forever...

Oh, God, help me.

I don't believe in past lives or reincarnation, but I believe in predestined, orchestrated events, expertly woven by the hand of the Creator of the universe.

"And so it begins." Noah's face shines with enjoyment of a challenge as he scoots back to his place across from me before taking a huge bite of his fish taco. His eyes roll into the back of his head as he slouches against the chair. I watch him savor the food I cooked, a warmth blooming inside my stomach. "Esme. This is the best fish taco I've ever eaten."

"Really?" My voice reflects the wideness of my eyes. There's something about a man appreciating the food you cooked.

"Really, really."

"So you are properly thanked for saving me from Creepy Guy?"

A mango piece slides down his chin, and without thinking, I reach across the table and wipe it away with my thumb. And then I lick my thumb, mango flavor exploding on my tongue.

I'm rewarded with wide, blazing hazel eyes...

That flick to my mouth.

I bite my bottom lip and look out to the calm ocean, noticing the array of colors painting the sky as the sun dips below the waters. Then a head of curly black hair and a tanned face with perfectly sculpted cheekbones occupies my vision as Noah squats beside me. One of his hands rests innocently on my knee while the other is gripping the corner of my chair. "Esme, sweetheart, you can't do that and expect me not to want to kiss you. Now I don't want to come on too strong here, especially after what you went through today, but baby, you're making it mighty difficult. Exploiting this chemistry between us and such."

My stomach swoops and soars at his words. I've never felt desired like this. It's not weird, though part of me thinks it should be. No, it's *hot*. And I think I'm going to burn my tongue instead of waiting for this to cool off. "Too bad I don't kiss on the first date."

"I walked you to your bungalow earlier today and had lunch with you. After saving you, I might add. I believe this is at least date number three."

"I don't even know your middle name," I retort, though I know and anticipate exactly how this conversation ends. Nerves hum most anticipatingly. I'm dying to know how this man kisses. Will it be tame and bland like Ryan? Or will it cause me to forget Ryan's name, at least for a little while?

"You said you're hesitant to give away personal information."

I run my tongue along my top lip. "I did." *Oh, this is my new favorite game.*

A rumbling sounds from Noah's throat as he stands, taking my arm and pulling me up with him. He tugs me flush against his chest, bending his head down while I rise on my toes to get a better look at him.

"When do you leave, Esme?" He draws closer, and I tilt my chin up.

"Five days."

"And you definitely need me near just in case that awful excuse for a man comes around again, right?" Closer.

"Yes." The word escapes as a shaky, *wanting* sigh.

Noah tucks a flyaway behind my ear, his palm coming back and cupping my cheek. His arm snakes around my waist as his forehead touches mine, a look of wondrous disbelief in his eyes. "Why does it feel like I've known you a thousand lifetimes?"

My soul cracks, and something golden shines through the dull gray. It does feel that way. Ever since I locked eyes with him after he intervened earlier today. Something inside me recognized him. And he feels it too. "Maybe this is what they call fate."

Noah's breath kisses my face, and the smell of mangos invades my senses. I rest one hand against his heart, feeling it beat, beat, beat to the rhythm of my name. *Es-me. Es-me. Es-me.*

I run my other hand along his forearm, up his bicep, until my fingers sink into his curls. And yes, they are as silky and perfect as they look.

Noah's lips are whispers from mine, but I don't lunge at him like I'm aching to. The build-up, the anticipation... It's the best part. I only get to kiss this beautiful, anomaly of a man for the first time once.

Don't let it go too far, Esme...

"Esme..."

His lips press against mine for long seconds before the hand on my back shoves me further into the contours of his body. He coaxes my lips apart, deepening the kiss, and the taste of mangos once again explodes across my tongue. His fingers feather down my neck before he lightly pulls at the hair at the base of my head, eliciting a surrendering moan from the depths of my soul.

I finally understand what the authors of romance novels mean when they describe a first kiss as electrifying. My body is vibrating under his touch, his kiss. It buzzes and hums, lighting me from the inside out. And I know if I opened my eyes, the sunset would somehow be brighter and more beautiful than ever before.

Kissing Noah is not vanilla.

It is a five-layered cake made with exotic ingredients that wax and wane on your tongue.

And I think I finally understand what it means to be *alive*.

I think my heart has stumbled into its home. But I can't bring myself to admit that.

"Ashley," he says breathlessly, his light eyes searching mine as if he can see the most intricate parts of me. "I'm Noah Ashley Ashton."

Chapter Three

A FAMILIAR SOUND ~ LATE JUNE

Standing outside Main Street Coffee, the local coffee shop inside of a vibrant red brick building on the corner of, you guessed it, Main Street, I smooth down my brown plaid pleated pants and check that my boobs aren't showing through my deep vee white blouse. Only the peek of a crease, so I'm good. I take a steadying breath before squaring my shoulders, clutching my leather satchel, and reaching for the glass door. I eye the blueberries painted on the glass pane, leftover from the town's annual Blueberry Jubilee a few weeks ago, as I open the door.

An arm intricately tattooed with woven briars and roses pushes from the other side.

"Oh, sorry. I—" My words trail off as I take in the tall, buff man who resembles a wall if I'm honest. He's just so... massive. But when I reach his face, I gasp, my satchel sliding off my shoulder as my hands rush to cover my opened mouth. *No wonder his tattoo looked familiar.*

This man is identical to my male main character, Noah. He sports dark, curly hair, though his hair is more tame than I imagine Noah's to be. He has entrancing hazel eyes that look like they're glittering, but his irises are a deeper green than Noah's. The tanned skin, pointed nose, and a chiseled jaw that's covered with a five-o-clock shadow, however, is one hundred percent my leading hero.

He is *not* from Whitney, Mississippi. That's for sure. The town would have tried to set me up with him as they have done with every single man around my age, which there aren't many. Only Sheriff Vincent Hodges, Jay McBride, and Luke Benson, to be precise. I grew up with Luke and Jay, and I have no interest in them because they both are rodeo boys, and I want nothing to do with horses or bulls. Those massive monsters terrify me. Respectively, they have no interest in me because my nose is always stuck in a book, and well, we all survived middle school together. Outside of sharing a few dances with both guys at The Wild Whitney a few Saturday nights out of the year when I'm coerced out of my camper by Ethan and Sam, we don't talk that much. Sheriff Hodges, at thirty-seven, feels a little too old for my nearly twenty-seven, though I don't look down upon the women who like their men older. It's just not my taste.

And the town knows better than to try and pair me with Bryan again. I shudder.

I often wonder why Bryan chose to stay here instead of moving back into Jackson with his family after he left me at the altar. It's like he's lurking around the edges of town, waiting for something, though I don't know what.

"Are you okay, ma'am?"

His voice has depth and richness as it echoes in my soul. It's exactly how I hear Noah in my head. Glancing at his tattoo until it disappears behind his rolled, black sleeve, it's a mix of ivy and briars with roses and thorns. Just like Noah, only on the other arm. *I wonder if he has a cross underneath that sleeve of his.*

"How is this real life?" I murmur, bewildered at this encounter. My emotions are jumbled; this man is like Noah jumped right out of the pages.

"Excuse me, ma'am?" the man asks, his tone perplexed.

I snap out of my trance and pull my gaze back to his face as heat crawls up my neck over my brassiness to stare at this perfect stranger. And I do mean *perfect.* "I'm so sorry; it's just you look exactly like how I picture a character in a book I'm writing."

This stranger's smile is brilliant, and it dawns on me who he is. "Oh, really? Are you Lorraine E. Jenkins by any chance?"

"Yes." I shake my head, rushing my next words. "Well, it's Esme, actually. Lorraine is my middle name. I'm using it to publish my book. And you are..." I trail off, waiting for him to fill in the gap even though I know exactly who this handsome stranger is. I need him to talk so that I will stop rambling about my name.

"Nikhil Prewitt." He shoots out a large, veiny hand. "But I go by my middle name, Ashton. I'm a literary agent and the owner of Prewitt Publishing."

A broad smile sweeps across my face, mirroring his. I slip my hand into his and give it a firm shake. *I'm shaking hands with my book character!* If the book ever becomes a movie, this guy has to play Noah. Or Justin Baldoni. But I think this man in front of me fits the bill more perfectly than my beloved Baldoni boy.

Hold your horses, Esme. Book deal first.

Though a small part of me wants to swoon, I must remain professional because my book's future is on the line. That's more important to me than a cute—okay, fine, molten hot—man who resembles my MMC.

"It's so good to meet you," I state. "Shall we go inside?" *Shall? Really?* I mentally facepalm myself and blame my recent Shakespeare deep-dive.

"We shall, my lady." Ashton tips a faux hat before backing against the open door to let me walk through first. I scramble inside, mumbling under my breath and reminding myself to be cool, not a bumbling, awestruck woman. Just because he *looks* like he stepped out of a book doesn't mean he *did*. Because as Lane once told me, fictional men don't exist in real life.

Ashton follows me to an open table toward the back of the building against an old, open brick wall. Main Street

Coffee is a small but cozy place with its solid wooden tables, metal chairs with cushioned seats, dimmed fairy lights, and pothos plants vining out along the walls, mixing with English ivy. The counter is located in the middle of the room, and after setting our stuff down, Ashton leads us to order.

"Hi, Miss Jenkins and Miss Jenkins' guy-friend. What can I fix up for y'all today?" Katie McBride, the young barista who graduated last year from Whitney High School, asks through a wide, toothy smile. She side-eyes me, asking a million silent questions through her transparent face. My students always pester me about tying down a man, and Katie is most definitely going to be taking a picture of me and Ashton and circulating it around the high school, which means the whole town will know soon. That's what I get for recommending we meet here instead of me going to his agency in Tuscaloosa.

"I'll have a twenty-four-ounce iced Americano. No room." Ashton looks at me to order.

"Oh, I can get mine." I say, waving him off. But as he insists with a smile and a nod, I finally order. "My usual. Thanks, Katie."

He lifts an eyebrow at me, a subtle mirth filling those green-flecked eyes. I shrug, and a melodious laugh bubbles from his chest.

Yes, very cool, Esme. Nonchalant. Chill. "I come here frequently."

"Like every day," Katie pipes in. I toss her my teacher look, but since she's no longer my student, it doesn't have the same effect. She grins and winks.

I'm as cool as that forbidden phrase associated with cucumbers people no longer like in romance books (according to my research), so I shrug nonchalantly. "The book won't write itself."

"We will have that right out to you," Katie says with a high-pitched, amused tone as she eyes me once more, a smirk playing on her lips. She jots down the orders on our respective cups before Ashton pays and then we make our way back to our table. I feel Katie's phone camera trained on our backs as I embarrassingly blush my way to our seats.

Finding my words as we sit, I ask, "So, were you leaving earlier or something?"

"I was stepping out to take a phone call, but then I ran into you. I'll call Branda back later."

Branda. Sounds like my hot future literary agent is a taken man. At least that makes focusing on him for work purposes easier. He's not my fictional boyfriend come to life.

"Ah, okay." I reach into my satchel and pull out what's done of my manuscript. "I brought what I've completed with me."

I hand over the thick pile of papers held together by a large pink binder clip. Sitting on the edge of my seat and fiddling with my necklace as he thumbs through the stack, I interject, "As I told you via email, I'm almost finished, but

I'm still trying to figure out the ending." I frown. "It's like every part up until the end has been a vivid dream. Then, the story simply falls off into a black hole."

Ashton presses his lips together before setting the manuscript down and folding his hands together on top of it. He stares at the papers with knitted brows. A beat of silence. Another. Another. The only sounds are light chatter among customers, the whirring of the espresso machine, and the shuffling of feet across the wooden floors. I notice Gloria Smith's three grandkids under five years old are smacking on sandwiches a few tables over.

Is it hot in here, or...?

"Say something." My voice is mousy. I laugh nervously and plop my elbows down on the table, covering my eyes with my hands. "Please."

"I haven't read it yet, Miss Jenkins."

"Esme, please. You're not one of my students." I remove my hands and scrunch my nose. "And I know. But this silence will be the death of me." And quite possibly my career as an author. Because I don't think I could handle him hating my manuscript. Not after I've attached myself so completely to it. In a way, it's healed me. It's allowed me to escape. *And Noah is my perfect man, which this guy looks identical to.*

"I love the premise. I wouldn't have reached out for this meeting otherwise." Ashton's eyes flash with amusement before dimming to something a little more melancholic. "I'm curious about the ending, though. Do you have an inkling of an idea for the direction you'd like to take the story?"

I crack my knuckles to give me something to do with my hands. "I mean, there will be a happily ever after, of course. I just don't know how it unfolds for them. The rest of the story came so naturally, and now there's a big blank space."

Ashton raises his brows. I'm learning they're quite expressionistic. "Is this your first experience with writer's block?"

I spurt a laugh. "I'm barely a writer. How can I be blocked?"

"It happens to everyone."

Shaking my head, I deny it. "No. I just need to get closer to the ending. I've got to tell the story up until the ending to decide how the ending happens."

Ashton hums in agreement. "That's a good idea. How long do you think until you have the completed manuscript?"

"At the rate I'm going through edits, I'll most likely have it finished within two weeks." If the ending reveals itself, that is.

Patience, sweetheart. Give me time. I start at the sound of Noah's voice, which sounds eerily like Ashton's, in my head when the man I envision him looking like is sitting across from me. Ashton doesn't notice, thank goodness.

Katie approaches wearing that same gossip-spreading smile pasted as she sets down our coffees. "Enjoy. Let me know if y'all need anything else."

"Thanks, Katie," I reply, using my friendly teacher voice and leveling her with another stare. She grins wider and walks away. There's no chance of me getting out of this meeting without the whole town talking. *Why, oh why did I pick this location?*

"What inspired the story?" Ashton asks, his voice intense. "You've shared on social media that you were on vacation when an accident happened, leaving you in a coma and waking up with amnesia. Does that have anything to do with the story you're writing?"

"I'm not sure if it's directly connected or not. I just know when I woke up, I had this image of a man I'd never met before at the forefront of my mind." I leave out mentioning once more that he looks just like said man. "That was it. The rest of the story started coming to me in bits and pieces, and my therapist suggested it could be a memory. However, it doesn't feel like it belongs to me, you know? I think it's the Lord putting a story on my heart to tell. I've always wanted to be a writer."

"How can you be certain it's not a memory?"

Ashton's question strikes me. "I guess I can't be certain it's not, but I feel like I'd know. It's all fiction in my head. I still wake up and think I'm in my early twenties instead of my late twenties sometimes. That's more real to me than this random guy and story taking up space in my brain."

I'm insulted, my little author, Noah pushes back, but his tone is light, feigning offense. I fight off the smile while he says, *I'm not some rando dude in your head. You've crafted me with care and precision, and I...*

I continue my *other* thoughts, ignoring Noah droning on about how he's real enough. "Besides, nobody can verify the story or the man. I'm sure I would have told my parents about him. Definitely would have told my best friend, Sam. There's no record of him amid the pictures I took on my phone while in Bora Bora. No texts, no number. Noth—."

I pause in my speech, wondering why I dumped all of that onto this stranger. But before I can succumb to embarrassment, he hums, nodding his head as if he understands.

"You haven't shared the details about what happened to you to cause the amnesia. Why is that?" Ashton narrows his eyes as if he's deep in thought before he runs a hand over the dark scruff on his face.

"I—" I trail off, transfixed on the brick wall behind Ashton. Every time I focus too long on trying to recall what led to the amnesia, a blanket of sadness covers me. I only know what the doctors told me; I have no idea what led to that fateful moment. And why is he pressing me about this? We don't know each other like that. Though I'm frustrated, I continue with gentleness to not stir trouble. "I don't think I'm ready to share about it. That moment, though I can't remember why, feels intimate and a bit gutting if I'm being honest. When I try to think about it, it's like something inside of me is ripping. Though, I can say it was a Jet Ski accident. I just don't know how or why it happened."

Snapping my gaze back to Ashton, his expression resembles someone offering condolences at a funeral. He's opening his mouth to respond when his attention is pulled to someone behind me. I turn around to find a mid-sized, stocky man with slicked-back brown hair hovering over my shoulder.

The forgettable ghost from my past that won't go away.

Bryan.

An unexpected shiver runs down my spine, and I straighten as if my body is on high alert.

"Oh, hi," I state with a tight smile. "It's good to see you, Bryan."

I glance around the coffee shop, and the few townsfolk secretly eyeing me and Ashton have made their gazes non-conspicuous.

"Hi," he says in a voice that grates my nerves. I don't recall everything that happened between us, only what my parents, brother, and Sam could recount; they didn't like him much, apparently. I'm sure there are things that only Bryan and I know about, but I don't care to fill in the gaps with a man who left me standing at an altar on our wedding day just a week and a half after my birthday.

Bryan waves one hand awkwardly, then starts pulling at his mid-sized beard. Everything about this guy is mid—his voice, his stature, and his personality. We've spoken here and there over the past year, and with every encounter, I cringe harder at the pre-amnesia version of me who was going to marry this man. *What was I thinking?*

He continues to stand there silently, his eyes darkening for a split second before they return to their usual glassy look. I swallow, discomfort blanketing my shoulders as I shift my attention between him and Ashton. Ashton stands, takes a step around our table, and holds out his hand. "Hey, man. I'm Ashton. Can we help you with something?"

"Uh, no. Just saying hi to my fiancée." He takes Ashton's hand, and I watch amazed at how Ashton's hand dwarfs Bryan's.

"Fiancée?" Ashton asks, arching that thick eyebrow and glancing down at me. His tanned face pales two shades.

I shift in my seat. "Ex. He left me at the altar before I went and got myself a big dose of amnesia. Guess that was for the best." I attempt a laugh, but it comes out breathy and shaky with nerves over this public encounter.

Bryan winces, yanking his hand away from Ashton's. "Well, Bryan. I think the woman is uncomfortable around you, so I'd appreciate it if you would allow us to continue our meeting in peace."

Bryan shrinks back, but there's no trace of an expression outside of his tight jaw. It's as if he's indifferent to the fact that I'm having coffee with this runway-model-looking man.

I, however, care greatly that Ashton is standing as a brick wall between me and Bryan. It's male-main-character energy. My heart rate has spiked, and I don't need a mirror to know a pink blush is blending into my cream, freckled face. This has got to be the hottest thing that's ever happened to me. *Men really help women out like this in real life? It's not just a thing of romance novels?*

"Uh, right. Yeah." Bryan awkwardly turns around and heads toward the counter. Ashton sits back down and sips his coffee while I stare at him in disbelief.

"You were going to marry that guy?" Ashton's voice is full of incredulity, that eyebrow of his rising once more. Ashton, unlike Bryan, is animated.

I stifle a laugh at the same time relief seeps into my skin. "Yeah, I guess the old Esme planned to. He did us a favor leaving her at the altar. Even if it did end with amnesia."

"I agree." He snickers, pushing back in his seat. "Now. Where were we?" He thinks for a second, fixing his face back to business. "Ah, yes. Fateful moments. Well, Esme. I like you. If your manuscript is as interesting as your personal story, I think we will do great work together."

"Thank you, Mr. Prewitt." A genuine smile breaks across my face.

He laughs, his features relaxing. "Ashton, please. I helped you shake your stale cracker of an ex. That's personal name type of stuff."

If I would have sipped my coffee, it would be all over Ashton right now. I've gotten to know Bryan a little over the past year, and what I came to terms with in the span of several uncomfortable encounters, Ashton deduced from one. "You did not just call him that." I can't stop the boisterous laugh, and I throw my hand over my mouth to stifle it. When I gain my composure, I lean across the table and whisper, "My best friend, Sam, refers to him as a bland bag of vanilla wafers."

He mocks offense, those eyebrows rising high as his dark hazel eyes widen. "Tell her from here on out he must be referred to as stale crackers. Vanilla wafers are delicious."

"Noted." At that moment, I realize he has leaned in, too, and his eyes are alight with an air of playfulness. So far, I've seen the business side of Nikhil Ashton Prewitt, and now this side. I don't think he intended to show me this side, but who knows? Maybe he's one of those people who doesn't chameleon themselves. Maybe he is who he is regardless of whether he's working, on a date, or talking to his friends and family. I can respect that greatly. I value honesty.

He must notice our closeness because he audibly swallows once before looking over my shoulder. "He's gone."

I haven't moved an inch, trapped in his eyes. "Good."

His eyes flick down to my chest. I have the urge to cover myself, and I briefly wonder if I've made a mistake coming here. But his wide eyes rise to mine as he asks, "Where did you get that necklace?"

"Oh, uh—" I bring my hand to the cross emblem, leaning back under his intense stare. "A nurse gave it to me after my accident back in Bora Bora."

Ashton tilts his head ever so slightly before pulling at a chain around his neck. "I have one, too."

The uneasiness prickling at my senses vanishes, and I audibly exhale at the sight of the silver cross necklace that is identical to mine. What are the odds? "Well, would you look at that. It's like fate."

Ashton hums, a small smile twitching at the corner of his lips, before abruptly standing. "I'm going to read through what you have, and I will reach out about another meeting when the manuscript is complete. I live in Tuscaloosa, Alabama, and it's a three-hour drive to get here, so I should be on my way back home." Ashton pulls a card from his wallet. "Here. Just in case you accidentally lose my number."

I drop the card into the front pocket of my satchel, a little taken aback. I don't know why I thought he lived closer even though his company was based in Tuscaloosa. "Thank you." Then I add, "You drove all this way just to meet me?"

He nods, a small smile tugging on his full, pale pink lips. "I like to show my future authors that I'm committed to them and their craft. Plus," he shrugs, "I can go to Bass Pro Shop over in Pearl before I leave."

Chuckling, I say, "There's the real reason."

"What can I say? I'm only a man."

Yes. You are all man. Hot, bookish man, I think while sweeping my gaze across his broad shoulders before chastising myself and remembering he was talking about calling a woman named Branda back earlier. But I am intrigued by the ease between us. I don't talk to hot men so openly. Ever.

Clearing my throat, I rise from my seat. "Regardless if it was me or Bass Pro Shop, I'm glad we could meet and you could rescue me from my ex. I'm not good at getting myself out of conversations with him because I feel a tad guilty that I forgot the time we were together."

"Never feel guilty for that," Ashton says gently, a softness overcoming his chiseled features. "He left you at the altar. You owe him nothing."

Tears push against my eyes, but I hold them back and nod, cursing my mom's gift of cry-over-anything genetics.

Ashton offers his hand. "It was a pleasure to meet you, Esme. I look forward to reading this story."

I shake his hand, enjoying the warmth and firmness of his grip. "I hope you like it." Anxiety settles in my chest, and a million questions race through my mind. I hear the Enemy's voice stirring doubt, and I counter with a quick, silent prayer for the Lord to battle it for me. Aloud and through a forced smile, I say, "And if you want, we can set up a Zoom meeting or something next time so you don't have to drive all this way."

Ashton shrugs. "We'll see. I like traveling."

And with that, he leads us out of the coffee shop and disappears around the corner of the parking lot while I slip into my old, beat-up Toyota.

I white-knuckle the steering wheel as my brain shuffles and repeats the encounter with Ashton, analyzing every detail against my book character, Noah *Ashton*. His looks, the tattoo, the silver cross necklace...

There's no way...

My phone buzzes, and I check the incoming message from Isla Grimsley, the owner of our one dance studio,

Whimsical Whitney Dance Studio. We don't talk often as her work keeps her busy and she's about ten years older than I am, but on occasion we rendezvous back together for coffee and catch ups.

Isla: Jay said that his little sister said that she saw you in Main Street Coffee with a man and that y'all were cozy. Care to spill? ;)

I groan, dropping my forehead to my steering wheel. "Stupid small towns."

Excerpt from Esme's Novel

I wake up to the smell of something burning.

Snapping my eyes open and thrusting myself out of bed, I race out of my room and into the—

There's a shirtless, oversized bronze man with mussed dark curls and a tattoo sleeve on his left arm flipping a pancake in my bungalow kitchen. *Wildest dreams do come true.*

Memories from last night crash into me like the ocean waves against the edge of this hut at high tide. Noah Ashley Ashton, who gave me his middle name right before kissing me senseless out on the deck. Noah Ashley Ashton, who swept me off my sandaled feet and into those capable, muscled arms God blessed him with. Noah Ashley Ashton, who I did not ask to rewire my heart in the course of a night, laying me down on the hammock attached to the roof before he attempted to climb in after me and got us all twisted up in fabric, rope, and each other.

Somehow, the contraption ejected me first, and I hit the rug underneath it with a thud. Noah followed soon after, but thankfully, I'd crawled out of the way in time.

We lay on our backs, roaring with laughter. Every time I thought I might be done because my abs ached, we'd turn our heads toward one another and the fit would start all over.

That lasted well into the night, broken only by kisses, conversation about anything and everything except our personal lives, and the occasional light snacking while sitting on the deck watching the stars shine for the two of us. At some point, we fell asleep, and I think Noah might have tucked me into bed.

But that memory is a little hazy, and I'm also not entirely sure I didn't dream that part.

All in all, last night, I promptly forgot about being a rejected bride because of this wonder of a man. At least in comparison to the ones I've experienced.

"Good morning, sweetheart." Noah's deep voice snaps me out of my midnight-memories stupor.

I realize I've been staring at him this entire time. He waggles his brows before tossing the pancake into the air with the frying pan. It flips effortlessly and lands right back in the pan before he places it back on the gas stove. I'm glad he knows how to use that thing. "Like what you see?"

"Very much so," I hum as I wrap my arms around my chest, clinging to the oversized T-shirt I put on sometime after the hammock incident last night. (And yes, I'm wearing cotton sleep shorts underneath. We kissed and cuddled last night, nothing else. I woke up alone, though I was surprisingly sad about that. All of *this* is new to me.) Once I'm right beside Noah in front of the stove, I add, "That pancake looks delicious."

"You mean I look delicious," Noah retorts, flipping the pancake once more. "Take a bite out of me."

A thrill runs down my spine, and I learn that innuendos—at least the way Noah says them—take my mind spiraling to places it probably shouldn't go. When I kiss him, it's different. I'm in the moment, enjoying the innocent bliss of the magical sensations, and could kiss him until I die. But when he says remarks like *that*, my mind conjures *other ways* to find new sensations. Ones I won't allow myself to explore because of my beliefs. I redirect. "Nah, the hammock did that well enough last night."

Noah's laugh is rich and hearty, and I want to bottle it up and take it back to Mississippi with me. Pull it out when I need a boost of serotonin or simply want to *remember*.

"Did you sleep on the sofa last night?" I ask.

"I, uh, slept on your floor." His voice lowers and he catches my gaze. "It took all my willpower not to crawl into bed with you." My eyes must betray my concern because he quickly adds, "Just to cuddle. You looked unbelievably soft and warm, and I wanted to hold you all night. But I know that could have led to more."

My heart hammers in my chest, but not from fear.

From wondrous desire. A concept I didn't know I could actually experience with a man.

And thankfulness.

Because had he not had the discipline, I know good and well I would have thrown those Christian morals of mine right out the window. Island Esme needs a tighter leash. Or maybe it's just Noah. I've never battled *want* like I did last night with him. Like I am right now. It's new. It's glorious. And I know I can't give in to it.

But I can kiss my vacation fling. As long as I remember my boundaries and trust that he has his. Once more, I eye his necklace. He's a flirt, but I think we are on the same page. But it's best to make sure.

I rise onto my tiptoes, place my hands on his shoulders for stability, and kiss his flirty mouth long and slow, savoring the minty taste from his toothpaste. "For the record," I whisper against his hypnotic lips, "I wanted that, too. But thank you for choosing the floor instead of ravaging me. Is this us setting that boundary right here and now for the rest of the week?"

He hums *yes* against my mouth and then breaks the kiss, turns his attention back to the stove, and finishes cooking breakfast. I set to work preparing the table out on the deck. I set the white plates out, procure the silverware, and light a candle. Then, I take a moment to close my eyes as the morning sun caresses my skin and the salty ocean breeze wraps me in a hug. I can't believe I'm here right now, and I'm not mad or sad or angry. I'm...

Utterly happy. Content. At peace.

My responsibilities are at bay.

I'm free.

Authorities still haven't caught the man who tried to take me yesterday, but with Noah here, it doesn't matter. Creepy Guy was probably fibbing about having a knife anyway.

Footsteps echo from behind me, and then Noah's arms loop around my waist, his chin resting against my shoulder as I lean back into him. "I think this is as close to heaven as I can get on earth, love."

Love? I don't let the word root in my mind. And Noah tenses, which leads me to believe he didn't mean to say it.

We stand there in silence as he slowly relaxes, melting into me as that four-letter word evaporates into the salty air.

Noah is some earthly version of heaven, sent for reasons unbeknownst to me. I don't know what it is about this handsome, funny, coy, and kind stranger, but he makes me feel like we've known each other for eternity, though I hardly know anything about him at all outside of our likes, dislikes, and random stories from our childhood that we exchanged last night.

Once more, a burning smell wafts from the kitchen. I turn in his arms. "Noah, I think you're burning our breakfast." He sniffs the air and bolts inside.

He returns minutes later with two plates of pancakes, bacon, and eggs. "I don't know how to use a gas stove. Never had to use one growing up. We always had an electric."

I shrug as he sets the food on the table. "Can't be too difficult. We didn't use one, either." I run inside to grab orange juice from the fridge. Something I had on hand for mimosas even before our grocery run yesterday. But this morning, I don't feel like drinking the day away. I want to indulge in every moment I have with this man and this newfound free feeling. I plant myself back down at the table with Noah and examine my plate. "Want me to whip up more Orange Julius, or do you want to just drink the juice?"

He grins. "Regular OJ is fine, sweetheart. Just sit down and eat with me." Noah shoves a forkful of pancake into his mouth. "You're right. This pancake is delicious. I'd take it over me any day."

***

"**N**oah! You're going to get us killed!" I scream against the sounds of the jet ski crashing against the ocean surface. My body vibrates and bounces as he conquers wave after wave, the salt water misting my skin just so the sun's rays can lick it dry. I cling like a starfish to Noah, and I briefly wonder if he can breathe with how tightly I'm squeezing his torso.

Bare torso.

With sun-kissed skin and meticulously defined muscles.

I've learned Noah Ashton enjoys being shirtless whenever he possibly can be.

And I'm not complaining one bit because I am Island Esme. And I quite enjoy admiring God's handiwork on this human.

"What?" Noah shouts, turning his head to the side.

"Slow down!"

I can't hear Noah's deep laugh as much as I feel it rumble against my chest, but he obliges my wishes and the jet ski slows to a manageable pace before coming to a complete stop.

"Am I too much for you, sweetheart?" Noah stands, the jet ski rocking as he maneuvers to sit facing me. I scoot back to give his long legs room, but instead, he grabs under my knees and lifts my legs around his hips, tugging me closer.

His bold declaration of desire sends a tremble through me as I lose myself in his hazel eyes, admiring the flecks of gold shining through. "Admittedly, you might be." I grin as he rolls his eyes. I continue my train of thought. "But, I think I can withstand the force of nature that is you."

His fingers mindlessly massage my thighs while he contentedly looks out across the sprawling ocean. I follow his half-moon gaze, thinking about nature and God and purpose. Though God and I haven't been on the same page lately, and I often wonder if He even hears or sees me, I'm mesmerized by His intricately created beauty around me. The ocean sparkles and dances as if it's celebrating our arrival at its center. I can see the island off in the distance, but we're so far out it feels as if the world belongs solely to us. As if God created this scenery—this moment—just for Noah and me.

"You mentioned fate before," Noah says, turning his attention back to me. "What does that mean to you?"

I inhale the salty air, contemplating my answer. Fate can mean a myriad of things to different people. It's serendipitous. Ordained. Constructed. Mystical. Untouchable. Maybe fate is made up of minuscule pieces of everything, the mundane merging with majesty. But ultimately, it's out of our control. Which has been the source of my beef with God lately. I exhale slowly, then respond. "God. His will. Whatever He has predestined to happen." *Such as being predestined to marry a man who doesn't believe in top-tier romance*, I think to myself bitterly. But if I spend time ruminating, which I have done on occasion, maybe the almost-marriage wasn't God's doing at all. Maybe it was all me, though it stings to admit. Ultimately, Ryan leaving me at the altar just might be the mercy of God in action. Soul-mauling mercy, but mercy nonetheless.

Noah hums as if my answer satisfies him. "It really frees you up, you know? Living like you believe God's plan will unfurl exactly as it should and when it should. That's the hope I cling to even when life doesn't go the way I planned it."

"I—" The words fall off my tongue. It should free me up. Right? Living life as if I have no control and being completely okay with it. I've always prided myself on my adaptability and easygoingness (though those two qualities most likely stem from my people-pleasing tendencies). Yet—I look down at my hands as Noah takes them in his—I often live life clenching my fists and refusing to free my plans. As if I'm terrified whatever I currently have is the best it can ever get. Just like with Ryan.

"Esme." I meet Noah's soft gaze. "Your pretty brown eyes are dark. Dump those tumultuous thoughts on me, please."

I laugh breathlessly, amazed he can even tell I'm deep in thought. Ryan would have never noticed. He never picked up on my subtle mood shifts. "I know I believe God is in control, so I wonder why I struggle to open my fists and surrender my plans. It's like He has to pry my fingers off the agenda I've carefully crafted for myself." I pause, briefly wondering if I should tell him about Ryan and why I'm here. I've always valued honesty, so I take a fortifying breath before spilling the reason.

"There was a man named Ryan. And he cheated before standing me up at the altar. This is supposed to be my honeymoon."

I brace myself for Noah's repulsion, but it never comes. Instead, he squeezes my hands as if telling me to continue. "Though it hurts because, despite everything, I did love him, I'm glad, ultimately. He was never the man I was supposed to marry. He was the safe choice for me. A man who had a stable, well-paying job, wasn't from my hometown, and had the same values and goals as me."

Noah nods, and I let everything out, knowing deep down this moment would eventually come for us. "He wasn't, though. And I knew that at least six months into our relationship. He never understood me. He was bland and vanilla and boring. Was always too focused on work and his friends. We had a standing date night for crying out loud!" I laugh at the ridiculousness, putting my hands over my face to hide my embarrassment that I let a man like that hurt me. Some girls may want that, but I'm not one of them, and I should have never compromised. I drop them back to my lap to speak again. "I can't believe I didn't have the willpower to end it sooner. Before I was the one getting cheated on and left. I didn't want to disappoint my parents or hurt him or disrupt our lives in such a grand way."

"But maybe if you would have, you wouldn't be sitting on a jet ski in the middle of the Pacific Ocean with a spicy, citrusy, and thrilling man such as myself." He winks, and I shake my head, laughing. I tend to do that a lot with this man, laugh. Noah once more takes my hands and places them around his waist, drawing us closer. "In all seriousness, I'm sorry that happened to you, but I will never apologize for the situation bringing you to me. In fact, I have to give credit to the sleazeball who attempted to run off with you, as much as that grinds my bones to do."

His lips are inches from mine, but neither of us moves in. We stay like that, searching each other's souls and burying ourselves in the comfort of *home*. "It truly does feel like fate—God's plan—meeting you," I whisper, lifting one hand to play with his wet curls. "Even if it took an almost-wedding and an almost-kidnapping."

"I was on my way to talk to you when that sorry man tried to make off with you," Noah reveals. "I'm glad I got to play hero. Saved me from coming up with a non-creepy hello to say to the woman who had suddenly captured my entire existence with just one sassy toss of her brown hair." He tucks a strand behind my ear, lingering. "Thank you for trusting me with your story."

LOVE AT FIRST SIGHT.

The phrase appears in capitalized, italicized, bold letters inside my head. But no. That doesn't happen, right? Attraction at first sight. Lust at first sight, which admittedly, I'm doing too much of and should reel in now that I know what it feels like at my ripe age of twenty-six.

But love at first sight? Surely not. Love has to be built. Trust has to grow alongside it. It takes time.

Can two people truly know they're meant for one another with one look? One night spent talking? One morning spent jet skiing together?

Is it just the damsel-in-distress rescue weighing on my heart? The drugged effect I feel by being here on this island, miles and miles away from Mississippi and my responsibilities and my demons?

I jerk back, realizing I'd been *petting* Noah. Both of my hands had found his hair. His cheeks. His shoulders.

What has gotten into me? I don't do physical touch.

"Come back here." Noah's voice is a notch above a breathless whisper as he wraps one hand around my head and tugs me toward him. His lips press against mine, and clarity seeps in through the soft contact. No. If I hadn't been confronted by that other man, and Noah had approached me anyway, I know my soul wouldn't have let me rest until I knew everything there was to know about him. His voice, his smile, his eyes, and even his smell... They call me like a siren's song.

Deepening the kiss, I pour every emotion I'm experiencing into his lips. I think when most people kiss, they lose their minds. But when I kiss Noah, the world finally makes sense, and I want to live in this placid lucidity forever.

The Jet Ski continues to bob up and down, and Noah and I pull apart. "I like your necklace."

Noah's hand instinctively rises to the silver cross, his eyes traveling back to Mississippi as he looks off in the distance. "Thank you. It was a gift from Grandpa before he passed away. Said it would always guide me to love just like it did for him and Grandma."

"That's beautiful." I place my hand over his. Noah's gaze shifts back to me as he dons a soft, heartachingly beautiful smile.

Noah kisses my forehead. "I come from a family of romantics. What can I say?"

***

"So, I told you why I'm here alone. What are you doing in one of the most romantic places on earth by yourself?"

Hiking was not on my to-do list today after a morning of chaotic jet skiing, but Noah insisted that we see the view of the island from the top of an extinct volcano. I'm sweaty and a bit breathless, but Noah is graciously letting me keep the pace.

Plus, being away from the resort settles me. It's a moment of knowing without a doubt I'm safe since the police still haven't caught the guy.

"You wouldn't believe me if I told you."

I scoff. "Try me."

"All right," he says before grabbing my hand and stopping us. He tosses my water bottle from the back of my bag to me as he grabs his own. "I'm here because I'm doing book research."

"Like, you're writing a book?"

He grins, amused, before lifting his shirt and wiping a sheen of sweat off his face. "Hot guys can write books just as well as they read them, sweetheart."

Excitement takes over. "Tell me everything! I've always wanted to write a book."

As we continue to climb, Noah tells me all about his career as a contemporary romance author. He says his whole family is in the publishing business in one form or another, but he's the only one who has written books.

Three books, to be precise.

Two are published with one in the editing stages. And he's currently drafting another that takes place in Bora Bora, which is why he is here.

"You take your career seriously, huh?" I ask, stepping over a pointed rock. Noah is right beside me, helping me trek as I need it. However, he doesn't answer immediately, so I stop.

Noah walks a few paces ahead of me before turning around, beads of sweat rolling down his face. "Are you coming?"

"Are you going to answer my question?"

Noah's shoulders slump, a flash of uncertainty flickering across his expression.

"It's okay, Noah," I begin, already walking toward him. "You don't have to—"

"I've never been in love before."

His abrupt confession glues my feet to the terrain. "What?"

"My last book was criticized rather harshly. Reviewers said they had a hard time connecting with my male character because he felt distant and aloof, even as he confessed his love for the heroine."

"You? You're the king of romance. You could give lessons on the art of flirting. Trust me, I've been on the receiving end of it lately. Ten out of ten. Five stars. Would recommend."

That statement earns a chuckle, but Noah still looks downtrodden with his slouching frame and long face. "You're right. I'm great at flirting. I'm great at romance. But love? The kind built between a woman and a man that's meant to last a lifetime? I fear I've never experienced it. At least the real kind. The kind that doesn't leave or fade away even after death. The kind my grandparents and my parents have—even when the other half of them is gone to be with the Lord. I want the kind of love I *want* to choose. A *person* I want to choose."

I gently caress his arm before moving to place my palm on his face, forcing him to look me in the eyes. "Noah Ashley Ashton, you might not have experienced that type of love before, but I have no doubt you are a capable and worthy man. You deserve a love that stays. One that doesn't fade away into the recesses of memory."

Water drips from Noah's chin, and I can't tell if it's sweat or a tear.

"Thank you, Esme. You deserve that, too," Noah whispers, his fingers brushing across my cheek. We stand there as moments—maybe eternities—pass, touching each other's face and staring into one another's soul. But then a gust of wind sweeps through, rustling branches and ushering dust particles into our eyes. We break apart, finishing the rest of the hike in a comfortable silence.

As we reach the peak of the mountain, I know there's no universe or dimension in existence where I go back to Juniper Grove, Mississippi, and pretend that Noah Ashley Ashton—contemporary romance author Noah Ashton—doesn't exist.

"How have I never read your books?" I muse as we over-look the island, boasting a vibrant floor of green with daz-zling specks of color throughout. The sun is high above us, casting diamonds into the ocean out below. We sit on a huge, jagged rock, his arm around my waist and my head leaning against his broad shoulder.

"Probably because the second novel has a sucky love interest." Noah kisses my forehead, and I'm glad to see he's joking about it now instead of letting it weigh him down. "But the one I'm writing now? Based here in Bora Bora?" Noah pulls me closer. "I think I might get it right." He pauses, asking me if I catch the meaning behind his words, and my chest aches from the beat of my heart as frissons rack through my body. Yes, I want to say. I hear you loud and clear. But I can't bring myself to admit it aloud. It's not possible to fall for a vacation fling. Noah and I are reveling in the reverie of it all. It's a fever dream.

But it feels a whole lot like forever...

Letting me off the hook from responding, Noah asks, "You'll read them now, won't you? When you get back to wherever you're from?"

His tone rises at the end, hinting for me to tell him. When I pull away to look into his eyes, my heart thumps wildly while every other part of me feels absurdly safe. And just like that, the doubt-switch flips.

This safety is *different.*

It's   not   a   cautious, this-is-the-best-I'll-get-so-I-should-settle type of safe.

It's a soul-securing type of safe. The type of safe where you know he would save you before saving himself. The type of safe where you can trust him enough to fall asleep in his arms. The type of safe one only finds in their metaphorical soulmate. It's a thing of romance books. And he's the leading male in my world.

They do exist. Men like that. Ryan was wrong.

And I was a fool to believe it all this time.

"Yes." I breathe the word. "I'm going to read every single book you've written when I get back home to Juniper Grove, Mississippi." He's earned yet another personal fact about me. This one could lead him straight to my doorstep when this vacation fling is over.

I'm starting to hope it does.

He grins wickedly. "Goodness gracious, girl. This just gets better and better," he says in an exaggerated Southern accent. I playfully elbow him, but he continues. "Fate, indeed. I'm from Hartfield, Mississippi."

"Thirty freaking minutes from me!" Astonished, I rocket to my feet. He moves with me, a grin the size of Alaska painting his face. Excitement and terror collide together, thundering in my ears as my heart pounds.

"Esme, I hope you don't mind this"—he gently tucks fly away strands behind my ear—"but I have every intention of never going another day without talking to you."

I swallow, shivering pleasantly under the intensity of his stare. I don't know this man, not truly. He's measuring up to be better than all the book boyfriends I could ever imagine. Have I gone clinically insane?

Could this transpose to real life back in Juniper Grove? Or Hartfield?

This whole time, we've lived thirty minutes from one another.

I've lived thirty minutes from my dream guy.

And so far, he is everything I want.

Any time we are around others on the island, or we are interacting with the staff, he is immensely respectful and considerate. He saves women from potential kidnappers. He is funny, kind, flirty, and just so lively. He speaks of his family as if they are his lifeline. He writes romance stories.

He drags me out of my comfort zone and pushes me to live without even having to try. He's infectious. But not like a disease. No, he's infected me with realness. He's showing me passion is a real thing, not just something found between the pages of a novel. He doesn't even know that minute by minute, he's encouraging me to let loose and open my fists. And I kind of like who I am with him. Could I spend the rest of forever with a man who is so seemingly perfect? Who healthily pushes my boundaries?

Wait. Why am I thinking forever after two days? Is it because of what he said about talking to me every day? That's just talking. That doesn't mean it leads to forever.

Right?

Right?

"Esme." The sound of my name snaps me out of the spiral, and I meet his golden eyes, so bright they rival the sun. "What's your middle name?"

The innocence in his soft gaze, the curious tone of his voice, and the feel of his calloused palm cupping my cheek crack open the gates to my heart. Just a fissure, but the pressure is building with every receipt of authenticity Noah delivers to my hardened unconsciousness.

"Samantha. My name is Esme Samantha Prewitt. I'm a high school English teacher, but lately, I've had thoughts of quitting to write down the stories constantly swirling in my head."

The most lovely, authentic smile I've ever seen on a human stretches across his face. "Esme Samantha Prewitt," he muses. Then he tucks a strand of hair behind my ear. "How did the Lord see fit for me to meet a woman like you?"

But all of this could fade when I start demanding too much, I want to say, but I stuff it down and enjoy the time I have with him. Because regardless of these feelings, when we go back home, we won't be the same people. Island Esme is meant for the island, and if we start dating, our passion would sizzle quickly like mine and Ryan's did.

Chapter Four

It's Just Pretend ~ early July

Nothing will ever satisfy quite like chips and queso from El Mariachi on my birthday.

I crunch down on a corn chip loaded with gooey, hot, white cheese while Sam and Ethan bicker over who gets the last chip from their bucket. I sometimes wonder if their marriage survives strictly on arguing and making up, but when I see the tender way my brother looks at my best friend—okay, gag moment—I know they're perfectly happy, and bickering over stupid things like chips keeps the romance alive.

"Give me the chip or I won't vote for President Marshall's reelection," Sam warns, narrowing her blue eyes at my brother.

Ethan snorts. "Oh, really? Who will you vote for then?"

"I will abstain," Sam says, crossing her arms and snubbing my brother.

"You admire his wife too much and want to see four more years of her. Of them together. You ate up their campaign trail romance like you've eaten all these chips." Ethan laughs then breaks the last chip into two pieces. "Here, babe. 'Cause I love you."

Sam giggles, and I roll my eyes. Sam and I will be voting come November, and we'll be voting for our favorite political couple. Hayden Marshall is a powerhouse of a woman; I was glad when President Darcy Marshall announced that she'd become the new Secretary of State when the previous one had to step down due to health concerns halfway through the President's term.

"Speaking of politics," Dad chimes in. "Have you guys heard about One Love Organization's recent kill? As if what they did in Japan a few years ago wasn't bad enough..."

"Oh, hush," Mom swats the air. "That's just conspiracy. The Prime Minister of Britain was old and died of natural causes."

Ethan leans in closer to Dad and loudly whispers, "I'm with you Dad. That's a cultish organization if I've ever heard of one. Did you know they kidnap women to offer them up as sacrifices?"

"Ethan," Sam hisses under her breath. "Stop talking about kidnappings."

I make eye contact with everyone at the table, but right as I open my mouth to question their absurdity, Mom speaks up. "How's the book coming along, Esme? You've been so secretive about it with us. We only see the little snippets you post. Heard back from the agent?"

The table quiets at Mom's squeaky words. Though my parents have been vocal about their support for my authoring endeavors, especially now that I've caught the eye of a literary agent, it's still unfamiliar territory for all of us. It's drastically different from the ten-year plan I had in place, but that was before I mentally lost three years of my life.

"Well," I begin and then pause to take a sip of sweet tea. "It's only been a week since I spoke with him, and I told him I'd need at least a couple of weeks to finish my draft."

Mom nods, then she gets that look on her face that tells me she's going to do that thing where she frets over my stability: knitted brows, a twitch in her lip, and hardening eyes. "You're still going to teach this year, right? I support your writing, but I just want to make sure you have a secure income. That has to be your first priority, sweetie."

"Yes, Mom." I release a small, unnoticeable breath to calm myself. "I still plan to teach come August." I open my mouth to add that my book is a hobby, a side project, but I snap my lips closed. That's the old me, the one who would belittle my love of writing. The one who would shrug off my unspoken ambitions to become an author.

Not anymore.

That's my woman, Noah interrupts. I bite my tongue to keep from smiling. Ever since meeting Ashton, I have a clearer vision of the man inside my head speaking to me.

I hear the deep rumble in his voice, which sends chills rippling down my limbs.

Dad, always the laid-back one, pipes in before Mom has a chance to respond with questions about how I'll juggle teaching and writing a book. "Who is the company again? The one wanting to represent you?"

"Yeah, I don't think you ever told us *his* name." I don't miss the emphasis on "his" Mom adds, bringing her lemon water to her mouth.

"The agent is with Prewitt Publishing." I avoid saying Ashton's name right off the bat so Mom's flying fingers don't start searching for him and find out he's an attractive male around my age. Mom spits out her drink, sending the spray spritzing across the table onto Dad. Dad's eyes widen by three sizes, and he's too shocked by something else to care that he's covered in Mom's water.

"Prewitt?" Dad asks, his voice elevated.

I nod, my brows furrowing. "Yes. Is something wrong with him?" I did more research on him and the company after meeting with him, and I found nothing that raised a red flag. In fact, I learned that Ashton represents another one of my favorite romance authors, Ashton Ashley, who inspired Noah's middle and last name in my story. (Also, I was watching *Gone With the Wind* at the time.) I vaguely wonder if it's Ashton writing under a pen name because there are no pictures of Ashton Ashley when you search the name, and I plan to find out if he'll tell me.

Because if it is...

Holy smokes. The guy is a serious romantic, and I don't know if my heart can take working in such proximity with him when I feel like I know his soul from his stories. He wrote my all-time favorite novel, *Days in Dothan.*

"No, not at all, baby," Dad says, grabbing a napkin and finally wiping off his face. I don't miss the look of concern he sends Mom's way, however.

"What is it?" I ask again with more force.

Ethan and Sam exchange glances, and I feel like I'm in one of those "Who's gonna tell her" moments.

"They're a publishing company strictly for the South? Based out of Tuscaloosa, right?" Ethan questions as if he already knows. But something is still off. Moments left unuttered.

"Yes," I say slowly, wondering how my brother, who hasn't picked up a book since high school, is aware of a small publishing company. "Which is why this is a huge opportunity for me."

"Yeah, it is!" Sam lifts her hand for a high-five, but her smile doesn't reach her eyes. But I'm unable to press any further because, at that moment, Bryan and his parents walk through the door and spot us. My spine stiffens.

"Oh, hi," Bryan's mom, Sandra, says as the trio approaches the table. Bryan is an equal mix of his parents. He's got his mother's short and stocky frame while parading his father's sharp facial features.

"Hey, Sandra," Mom says through a tight smile before addressing Bryan's dad. "Dave."

My dad only nods his head in greeting. Ever since their son left me at the altar, my parents aren't friendly and welcoming like they typically are with others—even strangers. I have no recollection of any of it, and I think my parents try to protect me from any sort of pain I might feel if I did suddenly remember. I don't blame them, but I do wish they'd understand that I'm not the same person. Even if I did begin to recall events of the past, it's been one whole year of rewriting my life already. I don't think I could ever go back to the woman I was pre-amnesia.

"Where's your boyfriend?" Bryan asks, cocky sarcasm lacing his voice. *Weird. He's usually expressionless.* I've never felt the desire to slap someone as much as I do at this moment. The audacity of this mid-tiered man, to barge into my favorite restaurant on my birthday, and suggest I have a boyfriend!

But wait...

What if...?

Every set of eyes turns to me, and I make a split decision to play into Bryan's assumption just to get him off my back. *Adiós, Bland Box of Crackers.*

The way Ashton stood up and stepped in for me at Main Street Coffee replays like a broken record in my head, and I think he wouldn't mind if I used him at this moment. He was adamant that Bryan stay away from me because he made me uncomfortable.

After sipping my sweet tea for sugary courage, I square my shoulders and ready for the eruption to commence. "He is on a work trip right now." I pause, eyeing everyone carefully at the table. Sam's jaw is dropping, Ethan is clenching his teeth, and Mom and Dad are working overtime to take deep breaths.

Then the questions amalgamate and ring out.

"Girl, who is the man who took your attention off of writing for two seconds?" Sam leans back in her chair, crossing her arms and waggling her eyebrows.

"I want to meet him," Dad and Ethan bark out at the same time.

"I'll be," Mom says, breathless, holding a hand over her heart. "Why did you keep this from us, sweetie?"

Because it's all a farce and I'm a big fat liar, and oh... He's my potential literary agent. Let's not forget that one.

"It's still new." I shrug and occupy my dirty, lying mouth with another cheesy chip.

Bryan is sulky, back to his blank expression and sagging shoulders, but his parents seem fine enough. "Well, we should get seated," Sandra says, ushering her crew away as we all wave and mumble goodbyes. "Oh, happy birthday, dear!"

I thank her, then meet four sets of eyes staring at me.

"Awkward," Sam sings out, leaning back toward the table. "But Meme. Girl. I'm a little butt-hurt you didn't tell me."

Guilt swirls in my stomach, and I quietly blurt, "I lied."

"Huh?" Ethan asks around his straw as he sips his sweet tea.

"I'm a big ole liar," I say, sighing into my hands as I hang my head. "Bryan saw me meeting with the agent, and he surmised we were dating. I decided not to correct him just to keep him off my back."

I lift my head just in time for Ethan to burst out laughing as Sam elbows him. She's grinning, though, despite herself.

"You had to go and get a fake boyfriend because you can't get a real one," Ethan guffaws, wheezing with laughter. I level a stare at him, but that sends him over the edge with a roaring sound that garnishes the attention of those around us.

"Quiet, Ethan," I bark out. "You're going to ruin the ruse. I want that man to just stay away from me."

"Okay, okay." He throws his hands up though he can't wipe that stupid teasing grin off his thickly bearded face. "I'll only play along because I never liked that Vanilla Wafer man."

Now I'm the one smiling as I recall Ashton's insult. "We can't use Vanilla Wafers because they're actually good. We have to use stale, bland crackers."

That starts round two of laughter from the table, and even Mom and Dad join in, though Mom's laugh is silent as she fights to not let it loose like the proper Southern woman she is.

"What's the ruckus?" Pastor Larry of Whitney Baptist Church, the only church in our tiny town, approaches the table with his wife, Veronica. But I call the duo Pawpaw and Meemaw.

"Hi!" I spring to my feet and wrap Meemaw into a hug before Pawpaw noogies the top of my head. I quit asking him to stop a long time ago because it was a hopeless request. "Glad y'all could make it."

"Like we'd miss our Pumpkin's twenty-seventh birthday lunch." Meemaw sits in the empty chair next to me, straightening the lapels of her floral dress. "I'm paying, by the way."

"Don't have to tell me twice," Dad replies, earning the look from his father. It's proper etiquette to at least deny the offer once before humbly accepting, but Dad has never been one to turn down his mom's offering to treat any of us. He knows it's her love language—to spoil us through gifts.

As we settle in for my after-church birthday lunch, my phone vibrates. Ashton's name flits across my screen, causing a blend of nervous excitement to overwhelm me. I make a scene of pretending my phone is vibrating and that there's a call I need to take. The family is too busy mocking my momentary fake boyfriend situation to care, though Dad and Mom seem to be watching me with a strange expression. A mix of concern, a million questions, and... fear? I smile at them and stand to "take my call."

I wind around the heavy wooden tables with horses and riders carved into the back of them, pass the bar of draft beers, and slip into the single restroom just to take a breather and have the freedom to react however I need to to Ashton's messages.

> **Ashton Prewitt:** I know it's Sunday (don't worry, I'm not texting in church), but I just finished your draft and was wondering if you've made any progress on the last third of the book. If so, would you mind emailing me a copy?

I squeal. That's a good sign, right? That he'd text me on a Sunday. That he'd want to finish my book after church? And then message me for more?

My fingers fly over the screen.

> **Me:** I'm not finished, but I have written up to the climax of the story. However, I'm still trying to figure out what it should be or how it should go. But I will send you what I have as soon as I get home! *orange heart emoji*

Crap. I meant to press the smiling emoji.

> **Me:** So sorry! I meant *smiley emoji*

Three dots immediately appear, and his response doesn't take long to come through.

> **Ashton Prewitt:** You're an orange heart kind of woman? Orange feels a little... loud, don't you think?

I release my breath, thankful that he isn't being weird about the mistype.

> **Me:** Pre-amnesia me would have chosen pink, but there's just something about orange that calls my name. When I watch a sunrise or a sunset, I feel like heaven is smiling down on me. There's something comforting about it. It's not loud, it's... warm.

> **Ashton Prewitt:** Here's to sunsets and warmth. *orange heart emoji*

I giggle like a schoolgirl, biting my bottom lip as I begin to type out a series of orange emojis, but a knock at the restroom door snaps me out of the daze I found myself in. I stare at the message I was about to send, laden with orange hearts, sunsets, orange swim shorts, coral, fire, notebook, and—oh my gosh—peach emojis.

Holding the backspace button down until all that's left is a blinking cursor, I flush the toilet even though I didn't use it and then wash my hands, wondering what in the world came over me to try and send something like that to my potential literary agent when all he was doing was saving me from embarrassment over a mistyped text. Talking to him comes as naturally as breathing.

I exit the bathroom and my phone buzzes in the back pocket of my jeans.

> **Ashton Prewitt:** If you need help brainstorming the ending, I may have some ideas. Say the word, and I'll make the drive.

> **Me:** We can do a video chat! I don't want to inconvenience you. Plus,

I hesitate, wondering if I should tell him that I used him today as my fake boyfriend. I continue my text.

> **Me:** We can do a video chat! I don't want to inconvenience you. Plus, I might have used you as a scapegoat today. My ex-fiancé, Bryan, (remember him?) showed up to lunch and asked

> about you in front of my family. I may have said we were dating. Don't worry, I told my family the truth after Bryan left.

Seconds pass by, and I grip my phone tightly as I stare intently at the message thread. Dots finally appear.

> **Ashton Prewitt:** Bass Pro Shop? Remember? Don't rob me of a trip, Esme. And you can happily use me if it keeps Box of Bland Crackers (trademark pending) away from you. I saw the way he makes you uncomfortable, and no woman should have to deal with that. He left you, plain and simple. Like him. Get it? He's plain and simple. Ha.

I sit down at the table, still memorizing the text. He typed back a whole paragraph! What guy does that? I laugh, reading over the text one more time before responding.

> **Me:** You're kind of really cool, you know that? Then let's plan for Friday or Saturday. That way you have time to read what I send over today.

> **Ashton Prewitt:** I'm sure I'll have devoured it by the end of the day. How does Tuesday sound?

My heart thumps in my chest, and through shaky fingers, I type.

> **Me:** See you then!

I set my phone face down on the table, fighting but failing to hide my mile-wide smile and a wicked blush.

What is it about this guy?

I've met him once and have only chatted with him a few times over text about book updates. But this time? It bordered on flirty. At least, I think it did. Right? I'm not crazy? *Man, I need to get out more. Date. Even if it's just for fun.*

The self-talk helps. I have a new mission: figure out who the Branda woman he was talking about at the coffee shop is. I can't assume it's his woman. Because if this man is available to me, I might take the leap regardless of whether he's my potential agent or not.

Though... I don't want him to think I'm flirting with him just to get a book deal. But he's flirting with me, right? *Or maybe he's just a friendly guy*, my brain retorts.

I continue to wrestle with my attraction and my morals, but honestly? If we both air it out and decide business can be separated from pleasure, then why not?

If I've learned one thing from losing three years of my life, it's that the time we have on this earth is short. Make every moment count and live it in joy to the fullest while bringing glory to God. We were created for nothing less.

Which means if I have a chance with this man, I should take it.

A throat clears, and I glance around at six sets of curious eyes.

I cough, taking a guzzle of sweet tea. "So that was the agent."

"And?" Mom demands, a little too jumpy if you ask me, but she's excited for me.

"He wants the rest of my book. I've got to buckle down and finish it. We are meeting again on Tuesday." While the pressure to finish weighs on my shoulders like a loaded barbell when I'm doing squats at the gym, I work well under tight deadlines.

Sam squeals, eliciting half the people in the restaurant to look our way. Unlike Mom, who seems a little too on-edge for happiness, Sam is elated.

"What's going on over there?" Buddy, the old owner of Whitney Hardware, shouts.

I'm about to shout back for him to mind his business, but Ethan beats me to the punch. "Our Meme is going to be a famous author!"

Groaning, I sink low into my chair. Buddy Smith and his wife, Gloria, stand and walk toward the table. Shortly, more families who attend church are joining and offering their congratulations.

"Well, would you look at that," Branson Grant says, patting Ethan on the back. Those two are peas in a pod. His wife, Cathryn, wrangles her three-year-old boy while firing off questions I don't have answers to. Thankfully, another interruption occurs, saving me from further humiliation. I'm going to murder Ethan when we get back. I hadn't planned to tell anyone anything until I signed a contract.

The entire staff of El Mariachi appears, holding a deep-fried ice cream with a lit candle on top. Everyone begins to clap—and I'm talking about everyone in the restaurant—so I join in as they sing "Feliz Cumpleaños" to me.

Warmth replaces the malice in my heart as I look upon the smiling faces of my family, both blood relatives and those who I've known since diapers. Twenty-seven is going to be my year. I feel it in my spirit. Everything will change.

The owner, Paulo, wishes me a year full of blessings before the staff disperses and I wave to my townsfolk family, many of whom I saw at church earlier, and say my thank yous as if they didn't sing to me during our discipleship class this morning.

And as we're leaving, I overhear Sam whisper to Ethan behind me, "Do you think she'll remember him?"

I freeze, and Ethan runs into me. "Meme, what are you—"

"Remember who?" I demand as I spin on my heel, rogue thoughts of Ashton being someone I should remember flitting across my vision. The coincidences are too... coincidental.

"Oh, uh," Ethan searches for words, but Sam fills in for him.

"Bryan, of course," she says through a tight smile. I want to question her further, but the couple steps around me and bolts for Ethan's truck.

Excerpt from Esme's Novel

Noah stands on a pedestal in the middle of the room in nothing but his cross necklace, braided brown bracelet, and bright orange swim trunks that do a stellar job of highlighting his bronze skin.

He's flexing his arms, his head turned off to the side in a lifted tilt, looking as proud and smug as ever that he was the man voted to be today's muse.

I bite my bottom lip and try not to remember that twenty other women, primarily of the elder category, are ogling him alongside me as we paint his sculpted figure onto our canvases. I've never been much of a painter, but when Noah suggested we attempt the class today, I shrugged and said, "Why not." I'm Island Esme, after all. Bold. Brave. Trying new things. Such as wild vacation romances.

Regretting the decision to do this activity as my face flames from drawing his sculpted body, I make the impromptu decision to give him an orange superhero cape to match his swim trunks. Grinning, I lift my brush from the color palette on the stool beside me and get to work.

I add the cape, which I label with his hero symbol: NAP. Yes, he is now Noah Ashley Prewitt (it will be funny to see how he reacts to me giving him my last name). His superpower? Naps! And boy, oh boy... he cuddles some type of way. It might secretly be a power of his.

Swatting the thoughts away, I examine the canvas.

I only have one thing left to paint onto him.

And if I want to get them right, I need to have a closer look.

Setting my brush down, I walk toward Noah, who senses me and motions to the studio director that he is taking one of his allotted breaks from posing. His white smile is brilliant as he runs his hand through those silky black curls. And I reflect upon how those curls feel caressing the bare skin of my neck and shoulders when he kisses me there. *Heaven have mercy*, I plead. *This man will be the unraveling of me.*

When I'm close enough, he grabs my hips and pulls me in for a deep but audience-appropriate kiss.

I swear I hear a younger woman's disgruntled sigh from somewhere off to the side, so I snake my arms around his waist and enjoy him a little longer.

"I'm going to have to beat these women off of you with my paintbrush," I jest, sliding my fingers down his chest. I still can't get over how touching him like he's mine comes naturally. Instinctively. As if he were made for me to touch him. "And you might have to reassure some of the men in the room that you aren't after their ladies."

Noah chuckles, kissing my forehead. "I think I just made it very clear where my affections lie, sweetheart. Your hands alone belong on this body. Whenever you'd like to put them on it." He winks, and I feel that familiar tightness in my stomach. These comments he makes... They're so bad. *But oh so good...*

I hum as my mind derails from the PG-13 level thoughts, preening under his gaze. It's adoring and smoldering. I've never met a man who could simultaneously look at me as if he wanted to cuddle me and devour me at the same time.

No, Esme. Get control of your thoughts. He's not yours to think of that way.

I came over here on a mission, anyway.

"I'm almost finished, but I need to add your tattoos." As I stare at his tatted arm, I'm nervous. Tattoos are personal. His look like there's a story to tell, and while I'm starving to know every detail, I don't want to push too far. "Can I see them?"

He steps away from me, and without hesitation, he holds out his left arm for me to analyze. I trace the intertwining tendrils from the top of his shoulder down to his wrist, real-izing it's made of briars and ivy. Roses with larger thorns are interspersed throughout the jumbled briar patches, and on the inside of his bicep, right before the crease of his elbow, is a small cross.

It's intricately stunning, and it reminds me of how beautiful things bloom from the bad. A Bible verse about how God makes everything beautiful in His time comes to mind, and a small smile tugs at my lips.

Noah speaks in a whispered voice. "I got this tattoo when I was twenty after my mom lost her battle with cancer. I can't believe it's been eight years without her."

My heart falters as I stare into his haunted eyes.

"She used to always say that there is beauty in the bramble." Noah smiles sadly, and I match his expression, taking his large hand in mine. "Every time she said those words, this is what I thought of." He looks at the tattoo. "So after the Lord called her home, my siblings and I got matching tattoos to remind us of her." He grins more fully, crinkles forming in the corner of his eyes. "I'm the only one who got a full sleeve, though. Used to joke with my brother and sister, saying it made me the favorite child. I could picture Mom rolling her eyes in heaven."

I don't know his mother, but I imagine she had so much love to pour out onto this man for him to be the way that he is today. I wish I would have known her. "Tell me more about her. About your entire family." His hazel eyes glow, but then he glances around the room, and I remember we are in an art studio with other men and women, who are anxiously waiting to get back to work painting the Greek god I have the privilege of now knowing one shade better.

Noah kisses that tender spot underneath my ear. "How about over an early dinner?"

I only hum in response, my eyes fluttering close as he lingers. He chuckles. "I'll take that as a yes."

As I pull away from him, our intertwined hands the last to break apart, I whisper words I had no intention of saying until they were falling off my lips. "Yes. Always yes."

***

Two more days of heaven.

Noah massages my feet as we soak in our swimsuits inside the oversized jet bathtub overlooking the ocean. I play with the rose-smelling bubbles as the salty evening air encloses around us while I drone on about the past.

Noah gave me every morsel of information about his family that I hungered for over our romantic candlelit dinner at one of the fancier restaurants that serve Mediterranean classics. My favorite thing was when he spoke so gently and lovingly about his grandmother, who is, according to Noah, the scariest and sweetest woman to ever grace this planet. After dinner, we walked back to the bungalow as he asked question after question about my life and family.

The interrogation is continuing.

"When did you know you wanted to try and write a book?"

I pop a bubble and shrug. "I really don't know. I've always loved stories whether they were told or written or shown. It's why I majored in English while getting my degree in secondary education. I thought it'd be the perfect job for a woman who's obsessed with story."

"But you're discontent."

"Yeah, I am." I release a long sigh before sinking further into the hot water. "I want to tell my own stories now. Not just teach high schoolers about other people's."

"I could help you with that, you know," Noah offers with a playful grin on his handsome face. I admire all the laugh lines, knowing he has lived a wholesome, happy life. "I'm published and all."

I splash him. "I have a hard time accepting help or hand-outs. I want to do it myself, you know?"

"Sounds reasonable." Noah's long leg shifts against mine, and I know he must be uncomfortable in this bathtub with me. It's oversized on my end but not for his massive frame. "Would you consider joining a writer's group I'm in?"

"Maybe. Tell me about it."

He sits up taller. "We call ourselves the Southern Writers Association. It consists of three guys and two women. We could use a third female to balance us out."

"Hm. I could consider it. But that would mean I'll see you again once we leave the island." Sufficiently flustered over the thought of *after Bora Bora* with him, I start to stand. "Want to go cool off in the ocean?" I suggest, my voice rocky. He nods, and we get out and take a few steps onto the deck.

Before we jump in, Noah's face grows serious and he says, "Esme, you have to realize you're worthy of an earth-shattering love. And more than that, if you want to write a novel, go write the best novel you can write." He kisses me wildly and breathlessly, then he whispers, "I have every intention of sticking on your side like a starfish for the rest of my life," before shoving me into the ocean under the glittering stars.

He jumps in after me, and I latch onto his back, making him keep us both afloat while I trail salty kisses across his shoulder, up his neck, and behind his ear. He growls, swimming us toward the ladder to get back onto the deck. But he doesn't climb up. Instead, he grips the ladder with one hand while pulling me to his front with the other. I wrap my legs around his waist as my arms drape around his neck, effectively clinging onto him like a barnacle.

"Esme." My name is a plea on his lips. His hazel eyes sparkle to the beat of my heart, and the thought that I have to leave him in the span of two days is too much to bear. I shove the reminder far away as I draw his mouth to mine.

It's a kiss full of stardust and midnight colors. A kiss that echoes through time and imprints upon one's soul.

His fingers dig into my back as his lips move achingly slow against mine, savoring and tasting and exploring. He hazily murmurs my name, pulling away from my lips just to rest his forehead against mine, salt water from his drenched curls dripping down my face. "Esme, I love your soul. I love your desire for passion. I love how you want to please your family. I love your hesitation and your wild abandonment. I love your heart. Esme, I love you. I didn't fully understand that word until you. My readers were right. The male characters I wrote were not ones in love with a woman. Because now, I know what it feels like."

I'm silent, hearing the words while I read them in his eyes. Feel them in his grip. Before I can respond, he continues. "I don't care if it's too soon to tell you that. Genuine, earth-shattering love is deeper than a feeling. It's a choice, as my mom used to say, and I choose to love you. You're the only woman I've ever *wanted* to choose. Stay with me when we leave this place. Make a life with me in Juniper Grove or Hartfield or wherever else you want. Meet my family. I want to meet yours. And when you're ready, Esme, sweetheart—" Noah pauses, removing his hand from my back and cupping my face, wiping at the liquid streaming from my eyes as it merges with the ocean water already there. "Marry me. Pencil me in. I *will* be waiting for you at the altar. Let me love you well for the rest of our lives."

"Noah, that's crazy!" I gasp, but I can't stop laughing. Laughing because yes. I want to say yes. I want him. This. Forever. "People just don't fall in love over the span of days."

He grins against my lips. "Sweetheart, just as two people can instantly become friends, they can also instantly love. I clicked with you, and we've been building a romantic friendship all week. I've dated women in the past for months and never could bring myself to say those words. But you?" Noah exclaims, shaking his head while disbelief shines in his eyes. "If I'm honest, I wanted to tell you that I loved you that first night. I just... *knew*. Would you prefer it if I worded it a little differently?" He nibbles my bottom lip, proving we are, in fact, miles away from the friendship line.

When I don't answer immediately, Noah pulls away, but only far enough to where he can look me in my eyes. "Esme Samantha Prewitt, will you do me the greatest honor of being my best friend for life?"

Tears mix with the water in my face as I live in this suspended moment of disbelief. How is this real? How is he real? Have I gone bonkers? Lost my mind?

If I have, I'd rather not get it back.

But he doesn't know me. Not really. "Noah, you don't even know the real me. This woman you've been with, she's—" I pause, searching for words that will break into his bones and make him understand I'm not right for him. "She demands too much. We have this fiery chemistry now, but what if it dies? What if it was never love? What if what we have fades away and is lost to memory of time as it has in the past for you? What if one day I decide to tell you I want more romance in our relationship and you walk away? You're like a fictional man, Noah. You're not real. You're too perfect."

Noah's laugh is strangled and disbelieving. "Esme, sweetheart. You think I'd ever turn away your request to be more romantic? I write the genre, baby. I'm all for inventing new ways to woo you." He presses his lips together, a firmness flickering across his expression. "If that sorry excuse of a man who cheated on you and left you at the altar ever told you that you demand too much, then he's the one with an issue. Not you. Esme, you are easy to love. Every laugh, smile, kiss, conversation... Every moment with you is easy. As natural as breathing. Don't you want that forever? I do. I don't say those words lightly or without intention, Esme. I haven't known love in the past because I think God was waiting to bring me to you. So that I could choose you. And that's how I know what we have won't fade. Because every day, I'm going to choose it. You. Us."

My heart pounds hard enough it could be mistaken for an earthquake with the way I'm shaking. He's saying all the right words, and I think I'm ready to jump to the insane asylum with what I want to say.

But Noah continues. "I know I have so much more to learn about you, so please, take me to school, Miss Prewitt, because I want to learn. I want to do it every day by your side. I want to learn your soul." He places his hand over my heart. "Your mind." He moves his hand to cup my face. "And every inch of your body." He kisses me and mumbles, "There's no one else for me, Esme. I've never been more certain of anything in my life. Believe me when I tell you that. And I think you feel it, too. Heck, I'll even take your last name as you suggested on that painting of yours."

The grandest smile I've ever smiled stretches across my face as I make my decision. Unlike Ryan, when I felt uneasy and unsure, I am ready and more confident than I've ever been. Noah, I think, brings out the real me. Maybe Island Esme isn't totally who I am, but I'm also not the woman I was when I first arrived here. Not anymore.

"Yes, Noah Ashley Ashton, I'll take your last name. But I'm not penciling you in. I'm writing your name down with a Sharpie."

Chapter Five

Nothing Lasts Forever ~ Early July

With every ding of my phone, I experience whiplash from the force of my head snapping to see if it's Ashton messaging me back. I texted him to confirm our meeting tomorrow, but honestly, I wanted a reason to talk to him as I sit at my desk in my camper and contemplate the ending of this novel.

> **Bryan:** Would we be able to go out for dinner tonight? Just the two of us? I'd like to fill you in on my side of things from our wedding day. - Bryan

My stomach knots.

That is the *last* thing I want to do today.

But the person deep inside of me who longs for peace and placidity—and who has never had a long enough conversation with Bryan to find out his side of the broken engagement—whispers to give him a chance to explain.

Especially since I have no strong, hurt emotions over the scenario like he might have.

> **Me:** Yeah, sure. Where should I meet you and at what time?

He doesn't hesitate to respond.

> **Bryan:** How about Gunnar's. It's where we used to always eat when we were dating. 7pm. - Bryan

> **Me:** Sounds like a plan. See you there.

No, my little author. Stay here with me. Make some more coffee and slip into the ratty pajamas you like so much. Let's write the end of the story. I'll guide your hands, sweetheart, Noah says, his deep voice a seductive coo.

I snort. *As if. I've been begging you for a week to tell me the happy ending.*

My fictional boyfriend goes silent.

Bryan doesn't respond, either, and I put my phone back down as I stare at my manuscript, pushing thoughts over how tonight will go far out of my head. The cursor blinks, blinks, blinks as I contemplate three different endings I've drafted for my book.

In draft one, Esme gets amnesia on the last day in Bora Bora via a jet ski accident, just like my real experience. Noah stays by her side and helps nurse her back to health as she falls in love with him again.

In draft two, Esme gets amnesia after returning back to Juniper Grove when she's in a car accident driving to Hartfield to visit Noah. Noah finds her on the side of the road, brings her to his house, and nurses her back to health and she falls in love with him again.

In draft three, I lean into the suspense side of things a little more. The guy who tried to kidnap Esme returns, and while in an altercation with him, Esme is knocked down and hits her head on a rock. Noah knocks the guy out and rescues Esme again, staying with her in the hospital, but when she wakes up, she's forgotten him. In this version, I think I'd have the two of them stay in Bora Bora to retrace their steps to try and help her get her memory back. I do wonder if this version is a little too dark for a romantic comedy? I guess it's all in how I choose to write it.

Each results in a happily ever after because readers will riot if my main characters don't end up together, but something still isn't sitting right, and I can't pinpoint the problem.

Noah hasn't been any help at all.

Hopefully, Ashton can help you when you see him tomorrow, my mind helpfully reminds me, and I swear Noah growls in the recesses of my brain. I grin and get a little heated thinking about a Noah versus Ashton showdown, and that's when my phone buzzes once more. I'm not as quick to grab it because it could be Bryan, but when I pick it up, Ashton's name lights up my screen.

> **Ashton Prewitt:** Main Street Coffee again? 10am?

Dinosaurs stomp around in my stomach as I bite my bottom lip.

Me: Unless I'm sick, captured, or dead, I'll be there!

After I hit send, I reread the text, grimacing. *Why did I say such morbid things?* This man knocks me all off my game.

Not that I had any to begin with if I'm being truthful.

Ashton Prewitt: Block out a lot of time. We've got much to discuss.

My heart thumps in my chest.

Me: Is that a good thing or a bad thing?

Ashton Prewitt: Great things about the book. You're a phenomenal author. See you tomorrow.

A thrill runs down my spine, and I allow myself to bask in the warm glow of the feeling for all of one minute before I tamper it down, locking it up inside a vault labeled LITERARY AGENT AND NOTHING MORE.

I wanted to throw caution to the wind on my birthday, but afterward, I thought about it. I need to focus on my career, and trying to date my literary agent would be a huge mistake. Ashton Prewitt is off-limits.

And his slightly flirty personality is just that. A personality. He's also stood on business in our conversations. I'm mistaking kindness for flirtiness, a mistake many women have made. I can't fall prey to that, so I will toss away my romantic notions.

Though it's safe to admit I've developed a teeny tiny crush on this man.

Okay. *Fine.* A little more than teeny tiny.

Gosh, I'm feeling the whole early-twenties thing at this moment. I'm now twenty-seven, but I feel like a teenager with a massive high school crush on the popular guy. Or the way I felt when I pined after Lane. He was one of the coolest guys on campus, and I dreamt of meet-cutes between us every time I'd see him out and about.

But then our meet-cute actually happened when we were placed in a partnership for our U.S. History class. And the rest, is, in fact, a scar-filled history as he made cut after cut to my core beliefs about love.

And that's when it hits me, the reason I think I was going to marry Bryan. Lane made it clear to me that true, passionate romance doesn't exist in real life. That real men don't have the emotional capacity to meet a woman where she is, not like men written by women.

Lane led me to believe I'm meant for the Bryans of the world. The safe choices. The passive choices. And I guess I believed him because I was going to marry Bryan.

Do I still believe that? Is that why I'm hesitant to date anyone and end up talking myself out of any possibility of a romantic relationship?

A knock on my camper shakes me from my thoughts.

I open the door. "Hey, Mom. Want something to drink?"

Mom takes a few steps and plops down on my couch with an exhausted sigh. She runs her hands through her short and thin honey-color hair, the same color as mine. "Yes, please. Coffee would be appreciated."

I set to work starting the old, gurgling pot. "Are you okay?"

"Your brother drives me mad sometimes." I turn to look at Mom, and she's laid up, massaging her temples. "I think he does things just to get a reaction from me."

This is going to be interesting.

"Well, what'd he do?"

"Bought a new truck. Again. His third one this year!"

Yikes. Even I think that's excessive. But my brother has always appreciated deals and new, shiny things. "Mom. We've talked about this. It's his life. As long as he's not asking you for money, there's not much you can do."

Mom groans, throwing her hands in the air before they slap down to her lap. "I know, Esme. But it still bothers me that he is so careless with his money at times. And Sam! I can't imagine how she feels about it."

She probably encouraged it, I think to myself, but I don't share that with Mom. Not while she's letting off steam.

Mom has always been my best friend despite our differences. She has given up her whole life to raise me and Ethan while being the best wife she could be to Dad. So, I'm her person. I don't mind it at all; I love her and will always be a listening ear for her.

"He can afford it, so we might as well let him. I know Sam doesn't mind."

"Yeah, you're probably right," Mom says, shaking her head and crossing one leg over the other. "Sam has always understood his mind in a way I can't for some reason."

"She's good for him." I pour two cups of coffee, handing one to Mom before sitting down beside her.

"Will you please tell me more about this book you're writing, Esme? I didn't want to pester you too much, but I want to know what kind of story has you so entirely captivated."

Taking a sip of my black coffee, I ready myself. I'm glad Mom is interested in my book, but I'm also anxious to share this story. Every time someone else puts their eyes on it, I have to remind myself that feedback and critique are positive things. I stand and move a few feet to sit at my computer where my manuscript is currently pulled up.

I start at the beginning.

"It's a story about a vacation fling that turns into something rich and deep between a male character named Noah Ashton and a female character named Esme Prewitt. I used my name since I'm publishing under Lorraine E. Jenkins." I laugh nervously, turning to my side to see my mom's face since I'm about to mention Prewitt Publishing again and my family had such a strange reaction the first time. But her face is already as white as a ghost. I continue anyway. "I thought it was funny that Prewitt Publishing reached out because I used that name for the female character."

"Can I read it, Esme?" Her words are choked, barely above a whisper, like she's fighting for her life to hold back tears.

"Mom, what's wrong?" I twist to my side to give her my full attention.

Her mouth opens and closes as she finds whatever words she wants to say. "I just..." She trails off before trying again, tucking her graying hair behind her ears. "I'm proud of you. For writing a story that you believe in and for already securing an agent."

My chest warms though something still feels off. "Thanks, Mom." I return her tight smile. "But it's not a done deal yet."

"It will be." Mom's voice is soft and sure, but her eyes are far away. "I need to go find your father, but send me a copy of what you have written when you get a moment."

I nod, thankful she's supporting me in this capacity. "I will. But, Mom," she stands to leave, "is something else wrong?"

The sorrowful smile of someone who has just received the news that they have lost someone near and dear to their heart crosses her face as she gently shakes her head before exiting.

"What was that?" I ask myself aloud and then call Sam.

I know she knows something by that off-the-wall comment she made at El Mariachi about remembering someone, and I will get it out of her if it's the last thing I do. Something is off.

She picks up after three rings. "Hey, Meme. What's up?"

"Drop whatever you're doing and get over here. I have five hours until I meet Bryan for dinner."

There. Luring her with a steaming mug of gossip tea.

"Be there in twenty," she shouts before hanging up, the sound of banging pans silencing.

***

S am wouldn't budge, but now I know, without a shadow of a doubt, that something is off.

She told me that out of respect for my parents, she wasn't going to talk about what was going on. But she did say she'd talk to my family for me and tell them that she thinks it's time I knew.

I asked her what I should know, but she only offered me that same sorrowful smile my mom did.

Now I'm sitting at a table at Gunnar's Hamburger Joint, a place I enjoy now and apparently used to enjoy often with Bryan. I'm fifteen minutes early and still reeling over whatever it is I'm missing from my memory that my family has chosen to hide from me.

I don't like the deceit, and quite frankly, I'm mad.

Yes, I lost the memories, but they are still my memories. I trusted each of them to tell me everything. *Everything.*

Whatever is missing is serious. I can tell by the sorrow etched on their faces. And does it have anything to do with Prewitt Publishing? Or just the name Prewitt in general?

Was my therapist right? Am I writing down a memory of some sort in the form of fiction? Am I narrating what happened in Bora Bora before the jet ski accident?

I can't believe I'm asking myself this, but is Noah Ashley Ashton—

Ashton.

Ashton Ashley.

As in the contemporary romance author Ashton Ashley that is published by Prewitt Publishing. The name I switched to make my male main character's name. Who is an author. And whose family is in the publishing business.

"Oh, God." I whisper His name in a disoriented plea as I piece together what's happening in real life and unravel the fictional world I created.

One that might not have been so fictional after all.

My head is spinning like the tilt-a-whirl at the town fair, and I'm about to stand and reschedule with Bryan when he walks through the door, wearing his typical khaki pants and a tucked-in flannel shirt.

"Hi," he says in that grating, monotone voice of his. I'm going to have to practice an immense amount of patience with him tonight, but I will find out what happened on his end. Because whatever it was might lead me to whatever truly went down in Bora Bora.

"Hey, Bryan. Thanks for inviting me out tonight."

He sits down across from me, flagging down the waiter.

Once we've both ordered, our sweet teas are brought to us, and we've entered into idle chatter about his work and the hot summer weather, I steer the conversation to the topic at hand. "So, Bryan, I'd love to know what truly happened last year. All I know is that you left me at the altar. I deleted all traces of you from my phone and social media, apparently."

Bryan closes his eyes and takes a breath, his bushy eyebrows knitting in the center as a dimple forms there. "I wasn't ready to get married. I freaked out on the day of our wedding, and I bolted. I sent you this text message." He holds out his phone to me, and I read the text.

> **Me:** Esme, I'm sorry. I can't do this. I'm not ready. Go to Bora Bora without me and enjoy yourself. I'm sorry. - Bryan

I stare at the date, which is exactly one year from today. It would have been our anniversary. The now-familiar sense of unsettlement undulates around me. It happens more often than I'd like, the feeling that I've somehow jumped through time. There are marks of my presence in years gone by, but I have no recollection of them. No emotional attachment to the stories told to me about my life.

"So you left me at the altar because you were scared," I reiterate. The idea he did such a thing frustrates me, but of course, I don't feel the pain, hurt, and betrayal I'm sure I should be experiencing.

"And though I'm a year late, I want to tell you I'm sorry in person, and I'd like to ask for your forgiveness. I was immature and selfish. There are things..." He trails off as if he's contemplating telling me something. And his tone is different. He sounds regretful. With a tinge of hope.

"I forgive you." The words flow easily. It's not like I am harboring hate for his actions. And I'm glad to know his reasoning, no matter how ridiculous it sounds to me. He had six months of engagement where he could have left, but it is what it is. "Did I ever respond to your text?"

The waiter delivers our food as Bryan fidgets with the sleeves of his shirt. How is he wearing long sleeves in June?

This guy is odd to me; what was the other version of me thinking, wanting to commit my life to him?

But then I remember I think I found the answer to that question I often wondered about. I was settling because my expectations were too high.

"You did send one more text. The day before you were supposed to come home."

"Can I see it?" I ask, moving to sit on the edge of my seat.

Bryan shifts his eyes from me to his burger and then finally to his phone lying face down on the table. "I deleted it."

"What?" My tone is loud, causing other diners to glance in our direction. I wave a hand, forcing a smile to let the onlookers know everything is fine. "I'm sorry. Do you remember what I said?"

Bryan swallows, clearly uncomfortable. I'm about to demand an answer when he finally speaks up, his voice darkening, "You said something about how you were thankful that I left you at the altar and that you'd found the love of your life because of it."

My heart races against my rib cage, preparing to beat right out of my chest. My palms are sweaty as I slap my hands down on the table and rise from my seat. "Did I say who? Did I send any pictures?"

Bryan shakes his head, leaning back and folding his arms across his chest. "No. That was the last time I'd heard from you before your parents found out that you were in the hospital in a coma from a jet ski accident."

I want to scream, but I clench my teeth to hold it in.

Noah must be real.

And he—he somehow stole my heart.

No wonder I feel a connection with Ashton.

He's the last person I was with, and now, I need to know everything. I need to know who that man is to me. He must remember. He found me. He—

I start hyperventilating, and the overwhelming scent of greasy burgers stirs my stomach.

"I've got to go, Bryan. I'm sorry." I stand all the way and push my chair in. "Thank you for telling me the truth."

"Esme, wait!"

I spin on my heel. He's on his feet with one hand reaching out to me, a hairbrained look in his eyes. It frightens me a little, if I'm being honest. "Give me another chance, please? I promise not to repeat my previous mistake, and I will be more romantic for you. More unplanned date nights, I promise. Let me show you who I really am."

Did I hear that correctly?

I told him he wasn't romantic enough? Planned date nights like Ryan in my novel? My head spins, reality and fiction blurring.

Was I the cause of him running away from me?

A small part of me wonders if it would be wrong to say no. If I should give him another chance. If he will be upset if I say no.

But then I remember Ashton's—Noah's?—words. I owe Bryan nothing. Regardless of what I demanded of him, to use Lane's words, he didn't have the decency to call off the wedding until the day of.

I can't stop the miffed laugh. "No, Bryan. Just... No."

He clenches his fists, his eyes becoming blaring red alarms to run. A hazy image of Bryan grabbing my forearm too tightly as I tried to run resurfaces, but I don't give the potential memory another thought.

I bolt. As I quickly walk out of the restaurant, balmy summer heat wraps around me like a blanket. I race to my truck, and once I'm inside with the door firmly shut, I scream.

I beat my hands against the steering wheel and shout at God for answers while salty tears create rivulets down my cheeks, soaking my yellow T-shirt. My parents knew. They knew I met a man in Bora Bora, and they kept this from me. From him.

And what was with that memory of Bryan? Was I—?

I gulp, knowing it's no use to try and remember whatever *that* was. I don't want answers to that.

I want answers surrounding Prewitt Publishing and Ashton and Bora Bora.

A knock at my window yanks me from my fit. Crazy Colt waves and motions for me to roll down my window. Knowing I won't get the old man to leave me alone until I comply, I set to work manually lowering the driver's side window. I work to keep my voice even. "What do you need, Colt?"

"I don't need nothin', but yer might." He offers me his flask through the window. I huff in disbelief before rejecting it. I smell the moonshine on his breath. Maybe I should take it to make sure he doesn't consume anymore tonight.

"No, thanks, Colt. I don't drink while I'm upset." I wipe at the steady flow of tears still pouring from my eyes.

"Always helps me with the pain," he says in a forlorn voice.

It piques my interest, and I shake the fog in my head away. "What causes you pain?"

Colt's blue eyes crinkle in the corners as he looks up at the night sky. "Losin' yer other half, Esme. Issa pain no human escapes from." Before I have a chance to respond, he throws back the contents in his flask and staggers off. I make a mental note to text Sheriff Hodges when I'm home.

God, protect him, I ask, even as my tears pick up once more. Poor Colt. We all knew he was sad when Gigi died five years ago, but he's never moved on. Judging by what he told me tonight, I don't think he intends to move on. My heart hurts for him, and it hurts for me. It hurts for all the confusing, aching loves that have existed and will exist in this messed up, fallen world.

Hey, sweetheart. It's going to be okay. I'm here. Noah gently caresses the neural pathways in my brain.

"Shut up!" I scream. "No you're not! You're fake! Ashton is real!" Silence follows.

Pulling up Ashton's picture from Prewitt Publishing's website, I cry harder. He looks as I pictured Noah in my story. All this time, I've been writing about him. About us.

Hiking on Bora Bora. Jet skiing. Swimming. Painting. And so many kisses and conversations lasting early into the morning.

No wonder he wants to represent me, an insignificant, unknown author.

I mean something to that man, and I want to know exactly what it is.

I want to remember. The real. Untethered from fiction inside of my brain.

My hands shake as I type a message to Ashton. Before I can think better of it, I press send.

> **Me:** Can we meet somewhere a little more private tomorrow? Maybe High River Catfish House in Jackson?

I want to be outside the prying eyes and listening ears of Whitney for this conversation.

> **Ashton Prewitt:** Sure, that's not a problem. Why the change?

> **Me:** Because I know who you are. Who you really are.

Ashton's response doesn't come until I've stopped the crying jig and have made it back to my camper. It took everything inside me not to march to my parents' place. But I need to talk to Ashton first. To figure out what's real. I don't trust my parents not to lie to me again.

And Sam. Ethan.

My heart turns to dust. This betrayal is bone deep.

I read Ashton's latest message one more time before crawling into bed and crying myself to sleep. He knows. Whatever it is that I don't know, he knows.

But I know one thing's for certain.

Nikhil Ashton Prewitt is Noah Ashley Ashton.

Ashton Prewitt: I'll see you tomorrow.

Excerpt from Esme's Novel

I'm bringing myself a husband home from Bora Bora.

And not just any husband—THE husband. Because for all of Noah's flirty, mischievous, and playful antics that simultaneously put me on edge and awaken my soul, he's the one I want. The one I need. The one I *choose*.

My bookish boyfriend—future husband—come true.

Whatever awaits us back in Mississippi, we will tackle it head first. As a team. Nothing will come between us. Not if we choose each other every day as we grow in love and trust.

"What do you think about this plot point?" Noah asks. He's sitting lazily on the deck, his feet splashing in the water while he types on his computer. I've warned him a million times that he's going to lose his laptop in the ocean, but he only smirks and says, "I'm good with my hands. You'll find that out soon enough."

Naturally, I look to the sun and blame it for the red blistering my face. "You can't say stuff like that until we're married, Noah."

He chuckles. "So I am too much for you?"

"I just don't need *thoughts* occupying my head."

Surprisingly, Noah sobers us. "Of course. I'm sorry, Esme. I sometimes think before speaking and let the flirt get the best of me. Forgive me?"

"Already forgiven, thank you." My heart swells with respect for this man as I watch him resume his typing.

I'm sitting at the table on the deck, far from where the water could consume my notebook. I've started writing story ideas down at Noah's prompting. He says I need a place to put them to sleep until they're rested enough to wake up and develop.

He's the cutest soul underneath all of his hot man energy.

I set my notebook down on the table and pad across the wooden deck until I'm sitting next to him, fingers trailing up and down his spine. I love that he loves being shirtless. And that he's going to be my husband soon. "I'm listening," I prompt.

Noah launches into his idea, and I lose myself in his animated speech. He is enamored with storytelling and the art of crafting a novel. And he's brilliant at it. I haven't told him this, but ever since he told me he had books published, I immediately downloaded every one to my e-reader. I couldn't wait until I got back to Juniper Grove. I've started reading in the wee hours of the morning while he sleeps soundlessly on the floor beside me, still too much of a gentleman to give in to my desperate pleas for him to fall asleep beside me just so we can cuddle. He says if he wakes up in the middle of the night holding me, he might not be able to control himself. And while I love his intentions, it's driving me mad knowing he's right there next to me but so far away. But I respect his boundaries just as he respects mine with the double entendre jokes. Ultimately, I don't know what I would do if he wasn't the one holding back. People widely talk about how a man struggles with this stuff, but I'm here to say women do, too. Self-control is a fragile thing.

But back to his stories. He writes with heart, telling love stories with depth and truth. If he hasn't been touted as the next Nicholas Sparks—better than Nicholas Sparks—he should be. He might not have ever experienced real love, and I can see where readers found flaws in his male main character of the second book, but overall? Noah, whether he believes it or not, knows how to transpose the idea of love to the written word. I guess some people didn't have enough depth to them to realize it, and I hate that those critiques have impacted him and made him believe for even one second he didn't understand love.

"Noah, you should consider taking your books to a publishing house. You deserve all the recognition for your talent."

He sets his laptop down and scoots it away from the edge before patting his lap, indicating for me to take a seat on the throne that will be permanently mine as soon as we get back to the States and announce our engagement. After we meet each other's families, we plan to have a small ceremony before moving me to his house in Hartfield. We talked about every detail last night between spicy kisses, fiery touches, and heated stares.

An outdoor ceremony in my parent's yard.

My pastor will perform it after we go through a little counseling.

And we will have orange poppies as our flower.

Because it's become my favorite color as I've watched sunset after sunset while in the arms of Noah Ashton.

"You just want to be able to boast about how amazing your husband is, huh?" He nuzzles my neck. "You can do that anyway, sweetheart. I don't need a publishing house for my books. They're gaining traction, and I make more money publishing independently anyway."

"But your family is in the business," I state.

He shrugs against me. "Maybe I'm a little like you. Want to pave my own path."

I laugh as he starts tickling me, causing me to squirm before jumping into the ocean. The cool, salty water caresses me, but I still prefer Noah's arms.

Breaking the surface, I realize he's jumped in after me, and I swim to him, basking in the light of this untethered joy. "I love you, Noah. And I can't wait to continue to fall in love with more of you with every day that passes. Until death do us part."

Noah's responding expression—the softness of his hazel irises, the crinkles in the corner of his eyes, and the one dimple on the left side of his untamed smile—tell me that I'll never know another love like this.

It took all of five days, and I'm jumping off a metaphorical cliff with him.

Five days, and he's so effectively rewired me to believe passionate love is not only real but that I'm also worthy of it. That instant love isn't a bad thing. Sometimes, souls find solace in one another. And that is something beautiful and worth celebrating.

A simple work week, and I'm already thanking God for Ryan leaving me at that altar. His plans truly are higher; I will never understand how this came to be.

But understanding it doesn't matter.

Because I will never go back to the woman I was before.

And it's as clear as day that this teaching gig is over.

It's time to tell my story.

One of an almost-kidnapping and a spirited awakening.

Speaking of, "Do you think they'll finally catch the guy who tried to take me after we leave?" Though I do think about the creep occasionally, Noah has distracted me so well that I've hardly had time to be fearful. With him by my side, nothing or no one can touch me.

Noah's face hardens. "I hope so. But I'll be glad to have you back safe and sound." He kisses my temple, black curls flopping against my eye as he presses his forehead against mine. "In my arms. Where you'll forever stay."

"Where do we want to honeymoon?" I trace the creases in the corner of his eye before dragging my finger down his cheek. "I've always wanted to travel to Alaska. One of my favorite singers, Fable Fox, is from Crescent Cove. She speaks highly of the place in her interviews. And I hear it's magical."

Noah hums against my lips. "Crescent Cove, Alaska, it is then. I've seen you in the sun. I'd like to see you in the snow."

"I don't do cold well," I warn as I kiss the tip of his nose.

I hear the deep hum in his throat. "I'm banking on that, sweetheart."

***

Noah and I spend the rest of the day leisurely packing, swapping story ideas, taking pictures, and participating in the occasional tickle sessions that turn into make-out sessions. Noah is always the one stopping us before things get out of hand, and I respect him all the more for it.

By the time the sun begins to lower, creating a golden path along the ocean, we're packed and ready for our last sleep in Bora Bora.

But I'm not ready to sleep just yet.

"I've got a surprise for you. Bring your notebook." After he picks up the black notebook from the table, I grab Noah's hand and lead him out to the boardwalk connecting the bungalows over the water, including the one across from me that belongs to him. One he's hardly set foot in since we've met.

Noah's rich laugh sings to me from behind as I drag him until his long legs fall into pace with me. "Where are we going?"

I side-eye him. "Mr. Author. Do you not know the meaning of the word 'surprise'?" He chuckles, shaking his head lightly and causing those silky black curls to bounce. *Oh, we are going to have beautiful babies.*

"Do you want kids?" I ask, realizing I haven't talked about that with him. There's a lot we haven't talked about, but that's what counseling with a pastor is for. Though I know in my soul there's nothing Noah and I can't work through. We choose each other.

"Lots of them. A baseball team."

My heart leaps. "Good."

We exit the boardwalk and start shuffling through the sand. Pausing, I slip my sandals off, and Noah does the same. Like the perfect gentleman he is, he holds my shoes for me as we walk hand-in-hand down the white beach, deep in conversation about how we want to raise our future children until we reach the docks.

A guide awaits us there, just as I'd asked.

"Esme Prewitt and Noah Ashton?" he asks through a thick accent.

"That's us," I say, smiling up at Noah. "Ready for our last adventure out on the seas?"

Noah wraps his arms around me from behind, resting his chin on my forehead. "We have so many adventures ahead of us, sweetheart."

Giddy, I gesture for him to hop into the small boat before following after him. Our guide, an elderly man whose name is Fetu, tells us all about the local culture of the area. He is native to the island, and he comes from a long lineage of explorers.

Noah is entranced, his tongue touching his top lip as he viciously scribbles in his notebook while listening to Fetu's stories.

Our painting instructor was Indigenous, and as we chatted while Noah continued to model, she connected me with Fetu so that we could get off the resort and experience real island life. I knew Noah would love the chance to experience something richer than a resort for his book research.

Through our communications, Fetu told me there would be a cultural celebration tonight filled with their traditional dancing, tattooing, and giving thanks to their ancestors. It seemed like the perfect opportunity to show Noah how much I've come to care about him and love him.

The stars glisten overhead, casting diamonds into the ocean around us. I listen half-heartedly to the conversation happening, taking a moment to silently thank God for His blessings. If someone had told me I'd fallen in love with a man I'd only known for five days, I would have laughed in their face and told them they didn't know me at all. But it turns out I didn't know myself well enough. Didn't know what I was capable of. I told Ryan as much when I finally responded to the text message he sent me on our wedding day. I told him I was thankful he left me at the altar because I met the love of my life. So, while the pain of what he did still lingers like a week-old wound, I recognize it's more because my pride was hurt.

I should have left first.

But I believed I wasn't worthy of a bookish love.

That's over now.

We arrive at another part of the island—one that tourists are not typically welcome to. Smoke rises into the dark, navy blue sky, and the sound of beating drums and chants in a language I don't know how to speak float to meet us at the edge of the shore. An excited energy hums in the air as Noah hops out of the boat and takes my hand, our bare feet splashing in the warm water. We follow Fetu through a clearing in the trees, and I'm awestruck at the ceremony underway.

The locals are dressed in what Fetu calls their traditional attire. He says it's made of natural fibers, and I stand amazed at how they've crafted beautiful skirts and tops out of material like beaten mulberry tree bark. They welcome us into their space, celebrating us, our engagement, and our love. Many couples tell us how they were arranged in marriage, but that didn't stop them from choosing one another. "No matter how two people come together," Fetu says at one point during the night, "it's the choice to remain that's important."

We spend the rest of our time learning traditional dances, learning local lingo, and celebrating our engagement. It's a night I swear to never forget, and well, Noah's going to have one heck of a story to write after this.

We wave as Fetu departs, leaving us back on the beach of Forever Summer Resort. The smell of mango and coconut still sits in the air as smoke clings to our clothes; the high of the midnight hour lifts us and carries us back to my bungalow in a whirlwind of laughs, recounting Tahitian words, and starry-eyed gazes.

"This is going to be our lives, you know?" he asks, though it sounds more like a wonder-filled statement. "Traveling for first-hand experiences so that we can write the best novels that we can."

My stomach leaps and flips at the thought of exploring the world with Noah by my side. "You forget I'm a teacher."

He kisses my forehead. "We will work around your schedule until you no longer have to teach. I believe in you, Esme. If you want to make authoring your full-time career, I know you will achieve it."

With my heart swelling in size, I stop him right outside of the bungalow, giving him a slow, deep kiss. "Noah, thank you."

"For what, sweetheart?" His hands run through my wind-blown hair before caressing the bare skin of my shoulders, sliding underneath my spaghetti straps. His touch sets me aflame, but I need to tell him.

"For bringing me back from the dead. My whole existence feels like a black-and-white film. But you"—I cup his cheek with my hand, enjoying the feel of his scruff—"You are in screaming technicolor. You show me what it means to be cherished and loved and desired. Noah, you've taught me what it means to dream and live passionately. You've changed me, and I thank God He brought me to you and has used you to wake me up."

"Esme." My name is a sacred oath on his lips before those beautiful, love-filled hazel eyes triple in size as he looks behind me. "Esme!"

Suddenly, Noah shoves me, and I find myself rolling on the wooden boardwalk, splinters lodging into my arms and thighs, as he lunges at a dark figure.

My blood runs cold.

As he falls to his knees, Noah screams a guttural sound that will haunt me for the rest of my days. I scramble to my feet and dash to help Noah, but the dark figure steps into the stream of moonlight, and my blood ices over.

It's *him*.

The man who tried to kidnap me.

"Esme, don't—" Noah wails as he forces himself to his feet, stumbling a few times before he gains his balance. His hand clutches his side, and I don't like the way his white T-shirt is growing dark as liquid drips from the area.

"Noah!" I howl his name, which causes our attacker to turn on his heel. Noah dodges his attack and runs to me, fear and determination warring in his eyes.

"Go inside, Esme," he spurts as the assailant approaches from behind, putting a gleaming silver dagger to Noah's neck. My world tilts on its axis, breath catching in my throat. No. No. No!

"Give me the girl," the man demands in a low, growling voice. "And I'll let you go."

My response is immediate. "I'll go!" I screech the battle cry, my heart racing against my chest as I reach for Noah. "Let him go and I'll go with you!"

A feral grin crosses the man's face as Noah shakes his head, causing the knife to nip into his neck. Blood trickles down from the wound, and I beg him to stop. "Stay still, Noah! I'm saving you!" *Let me save you,* I cry. *It's my turn to save you.*

Tears saturate my vision, but I walk with unbridled determination toward the man as I beg God to send down lightning or thunder or anything. *Anything! God, save him!* "Let him go!"

Noah mouths three words, "I love you," before he rails backward into the attacker, sending the two of them stumbling down to the ground.

I run, knowing Noah's too wounded. He needs my help.

But when I get to the brawling men, Noah's broken scream cuts through the silent air.

"Get out of here, Esme! Call the police!"

Right. I can do that.

Just as I dig my phone out of my dress pocket, the attacker breaks free from Noah and lunges for me. White hot pain blooms in my chest as I'm shoved to the ground, the assailant landing on top of me. Every ragged cough and breath is laced with pain as a wheezing, rattling sound escapes my lips. Wet, thick liquid runs down my chin.

The attacker grabs me by the hair and slams my head against the boardwalk before Noah pulls him off me.

Splitting pain pierces my skull, sending waves of nausea over my body as I tense and freeze. My vision begins to blur as I will myself to keep my eyes open.

But it's no use.

And as my eyes flutter close, and I fight against the piercing pain in my chest, I watch as Noah delivers a groaning punch to the man, violent curses and monstrous screams echoing in my head. Then, there's a knife at Noah's throat.

I scream, but no sound escapes.

As the darkness closes around me, I claw at it, begging it to let me give a message to Noah. To let Noah know he's going to win. He has to. Then I'm going to be okay. We will be okay. We will survive and get married like we planned.

I have faith in you, Noah.

Help him, God. Don't take him away from me.

Chapter Six

You'll Remember Me ~ early July

My foot creates a chaotic rhythm as it taps, taps, taps on the wooden floor, my anxiety rising with every fleeting second.

It's eight minutes until ten, and Ashton will walk through that door at any moment, carrying with him the loaded truth of the night I lost my memory back in Bora Bora. My bones ache, knowing he is somehow involved, and while I'm desperately seeking the truth, I'm terrified of what I will learn. Afraid of what it means for my future.

For my book.

The fish house is dead as I figured it would be this time of day. There are a few older couples gathered together at one of the round tables, but I have a tiny square table in the back room. The smell of fried catfish is concentrated, and it stirs the nausea that's been settled in my stomach since I woke up this morning. I usually love the smell, but

I'm too on edge to enjoy it. Maybe I should have chosen a different location like an outdoor park or something. Then again, anything outdoors in the city of Jackson stinks to high heaven with construction fumes and marijuana. Not like the fresh air of Whitney. But there wasn't a sliver of a chance that I'd have this conversation with Ashton with snooping eyes and ears. Even when you think you're alone in Whitney, you're not.

Ashton appears from behind the stretch of wall separating the two dining rooms. He's wearing casual but preppy clothes—orange shorts that hit just above his knees with a white collared shirt. He immediately spots me, his expression a twist of pain and pity. It reminds me of a recurring dream I've had, one where that look on that same face mingles with unadulterated horror. I've always wondered what caused my character Noah to wear that face, and now I'm scared I might find out.

I'm going to be sick.

Ashton must be Noah. He has to be. From the way he looks to his mannerisms, he is like the man in my novel. It's not merely coincidental that I used the names Ashton and Prewitt. *Or Ashley, for that matter, if this man is more than a literary agent.* He has to be the guy I woke up from a coma dreaming about and decided he was just that—a dream. Because nowhere in my family's history did they mention a Noah or show me pictures of a man who looked like him. It was all just a vivid dream.

Until it wasn't.

Until he was running into me through my town's coffee shop's door with piqued interest in my debut novel.

What secrets are my family harboring?

Ashton stands behind his chair, waiting with bated breath for permission to tell me everything. For me to say something. To prove I know him.

"It's you." My voice is barely a whisper.

He nods as he sits, tugging at his shorts. He looks at old wooden walls decorated with lures, fishing poles, and mounted fish. Then he looks down at his folded hands resting on the table. And, finally, he settles on me. Taking a deep breath, he leans forward on the table and folds his hands. "We have much to discuss today, Esme."

His formal tone surprises me, but what shocks me even more is the desperation he's attempting to hide. It's in the slight quiver of my name on his lips, in his whitened knuckles as he squeezes his hands. It's in his run-through curls that were tamed the last time I saw him. It's in the heaviness of his slightly swollen eyes that signal a night as rough as the one I had.

I'm silent as I wait for him to start discussing whatever it is we must. Realizing I'm not going to respond, he continues, "My name is Nikhil Ashton Prewitt, and I really don't know how to tell you this." Ashton leans back, running a large hand through his messy curls.

The round table presses into my stomach as I take a turn leaning in, anxious for him to say what I know he's going to say. "Do we know each other? From my past? From Bora

Bora? Are you..." I hesitate. I can't believe I'm going to ask this. *Never in a thousand lifetimes...* "Are you the man from my novel? Noah?"

I hate the anxiousness in my voice. It's hazardous. Pleading. Needing. Which completely matches this man's energy in this moment.

When Ashton shakes his head emphatically, my heart stops as confusion strangles me, and I question with force, "Then who are you? And what is this about?"

His downcast gaze lifts, and when his eyes meet mine, there is indescribable pain etched in the golden flecks. "I told you. My name is Ashton, and I am a literary agent. I do want to represent you, but there's more."

I'm losing my patience, and if I'm not careful, my heart may very well explode right here and now. From fear. From anxiety. From confusion. "Then tell me!"

"Promise me, Esme, not to tell anyone." Ashton stares intently at me from across the small square table, pleas painting his hazel eyes. "This is not public knowledge."

I only pause a breath before I blurt, "I promise." *Whatever it is, I promise. Just tell me the freaking truth. Somebody, please! I feel crazy.*

Ashton grimaces as a sheen of sweat coats his face. He's not entirely sold on my promise, but I see the moment he decides to trust me. On a long exhale, he says, "I believe you're the woman my brother was writing in his—our—novel. One that I haven't had the strength to finish or publish. He's the Ashley in Ashton Ashley." Ashton swallows. "Was."

A swell of justification blooms within me. I knew it! Ashton is Ashton Ashley, and he's the—

Wait.

Brother?

Was?

I feel like that ridiculous meme where all the mathematical equations float around a person's head. What's he getting at? What does he mean by— "Was?" The blood drains from my body.

"He's no longer writing. No longer doing much of anything."

The jet ski accident...

"What are you getting at, Ashton?" A numb darkness scrapes my throat as I swallow. I fight to reach into the black hole in my head, but the strain only makes me dizzy. I'm connected to this somehow, but I can't remember and I'm agitated. I stand, placing my hands on the table for support, and spout, "Did I kill someone? Was I involved in your brother's death in Bora Bora? Is that how we have this weird connection? Did I kill your brother and then use your looks in a novel? That's sick. I'm sick. Oh, my gosh. Am I an accidental murderer? Oh, God. Ashton, I—"

"What? No!" Ashton interrupts my anxious spewing, standing and waving his hands to motion me to stop that train of thought. Sweat drops form on my face as he continues. "Noah's not dead. He's just... missing."

Noah.

The world stops spinning at the mention of his name, and I plop down into my chair, mentally and emotionally spent. "Noah is... *real?*"

"Very real." The corner's of Ashton's eyes wrinkle as he gives me a soft, sad smile. "He's my identical twin, and I think that necklace you're wearing belongs to him."

Hi, sweetheart, Noah appears in my head again after a night of complete silence from him. It's strange hearing my character when I now know that he's real. Out in the world. Existing in this very moment.

My hand flies to hold the silver cross. As my brain computes, firing off at all cylinders and failing to find a foundation of thought, Ashton pulls his phone from his pocket and sits down. Before long, he's showing me a picture of him times two. The two men in the picture are mirrors of one another. Ashton is only identifiable by the half-sleeve tattoo on his right arm while the other man—Noah—has a full sleeve on his left arm. Both wear cross necklaces.

"Your tattoo is a full sleeve now." I note the obvious dumbly as I work to *remember*. Remember anything that doesn't feel like a hazy daydream only meant for me to use in a novel.

The picture disappears as Ashton places the phone down with a mirthless laugh. "Yeah, I expanded it after I thought Noah *was* going to die. He was in the ICU for a week, Esme, after having his throat sliced and battling other internal injuries. I watched you and your family leave the hospital after you woke up after a few days, thinking I might hate you for the rest of my life if my brother died and you survived."

His bitter-sounding words cut me deep and put me on the defensive. "I was in a jet ski accident, Ashton. How could it have been my fault? I think someone would have told me." Then a montage of memories of the past year plays across my vision, and I realize how weird my family has acted every time I try to bring up the accident, and more recently when I've mentioned the Prewitt Publishing or Ashton or my novel.

And finally, I remember that last scene I wrote in my novel. The one where Esme passes out to the image of a knife at Noah's throat. *Oh, God. No. No. No!*

I change my tone, my stomach dipping as sour acid rises in my throat. "What did I do, Ashton?"

Ashton lets out a breath and runs his hands through his hair again. "Before I tell you the truth of what happened, I need you to know that I do not blame you and you are not at fault. The way I felt earlier this year is indicative only of a man on the verge of losing his twin brother. Noah pulled through, and he's alive." He pauses, and I stare wide-eyed at him until he continues. "Promise me, Esme?"

"I can't make promises that I don't know if I can keep, Ashton. But I will try to remember that you believe those words to be true. Now please tell me before I throw up right here in this spot from this sickening anxiety."

But instead, a young waiter approaches the table. I'm in a blind daze as Ashton orders, and when the waiter turns to me, I simply mutter, "I just need lemon water, please."

"You're not getting food?" Ashton asks.

"I can't stomach it right now."

"Right." A flash of uncomfortable sorrow streaks across his face. Ashton dismisses the waiter and turns his attention back to me. He fiddles with his fingers. "I don't want to tell you the whole story as it's not mine to tell. And I know what little Noah told me before he went AWOL. You and Noah met while in Bora Bora together. He saved you from a guy trying to kidnap you, and you spent the rest of the week with him. On the last night before you both were set to leave, the guy who tried to kidnap you earlier in the week returned. You both almost died, but while he remembers everything, you walked away with amnesia."

Ashton stares at me, waiting for me to say something. Or to break. Or to scream. Internally, I'm doing a mixture of the last two, but on the outside, I hold my composure. I bite my tongue, sit up straight, and try my hardest not to cry.

But a single tear slips through as I blink.

And then another.

"Ashton, I—" More tears. "I don't know what to say. Are you sure it was me?" Though I know the answer. The nightmares of a horror-filled face, the daydreams of romance, the plot of the novel that wouldn't vacate my brain. My weird desire to write a kidnapping into the story. The proof of Noah's existence is in the photo. His identical twin sitting across from me.

The necklace the nurse gave me before I left the hospital. Because Noah was with me when I lost consciousness, and somehow I ended up with his necklace.

I gasp like a fish on dry land as I try and falter to wrap my bruised and broken brain around everything.

Ashton moves his chair from across from me to beside me as I lose my wits. He pulls me to my feet and wraps me in a tight embrace. My breaths are short and ragged until I'm struggling to take one at all.

"Name five things that are real. Right now. In this moment," he commands, his strong voice breaking through the attack.

I fight through the haze and the feeling of a pounding jackhammer on my chest, choking out the first word that comes to mind, "Wood. This whole building is wooden." I search for more breaths. "The smell of catfish."

"Three more."

I inhale again, this time catching a faint whiff of Ashton. "You smell like coconut." He laughs, and I continue to focus on my breaths. The sun pours in through the window and warms my skin. "The sun." Ashton feels rock solid against me, his arms wrapped around my waist in a snug, warm, safe embrace. "You. It's really you."

My breathing starts to slow, and the fog slowly clears from my head. Through it all, Ashton continues to hold me and talk to me. Reminding me we are real at this moment and to hold on to that. He's grounding me.

No one has ever done that for me before.

When my breaths come even, Ashton whispers in a raspy voice, "I'm not Noah, Esme. I know you've written a novel about a man who looks like me, and while I do share a lot with Noah, we are not the same person. You fell in love with him, not with me."

"I know, and I'm sorry," I say, leaning my forehead on his shoulder. I'm too tired to be embarrassed. I choose to focus on the panic attack instead of my body attempting to recognize Ashton as the man from my novel. "That hasn't happened in a while." It's partially true. It happened last night when I tied all the strings together in my head. Or, at least, thought I had. Ashton isn't my male main character, but his twin brother is.

Noah is real. The man I thought I created in my head—the perfect man—is real. Is he really perfect?

You know it, Meme, he says, his tone cocky. But I don't have energy to deal with the voice in my head right now.

I continue to take deep, calming breaths. I used to get panic attacks all of the time when I first woke up in the hospital. They continued for months until, one day, I accepted what had happened to me, and I started to move on with my life.

"I shouldn't have told you so much at one time," Ashton says, releasing me. "That wasn't the brightest move on my end. I had to help Noah through his panic attacks often."

"You're hurting, too." I recall his tortured eyes as he told me the truth of what happened that fateful night. I couldn't imagine almost losing Ethan. I would've felt the same way that Ashton did if roles were reversed. "Noah." I taste his name on my tongue. I associate him with mangos. At least, that's what I've written about in my book. *What's real and what's fiction?* "You said he's missing?"

Ashton grimaces and nods. "I think he lost hope that you would remember him, and well, it drove him mad. Your parents wouldn't allow him to contact you."

Frustration flares in my chest at the mention of my parents. They lied to me. Mom, Dad, Ethan, and even Sam. They all told me I was in a Jet Ski accident when the reality was that I was almost taken. Murdered. And a man I had supposedly fallen in love with almost died protecting me. Then I went and hit reset on my brain.

How could they? How could they do this to me and Noah? I don't remember him like I should, I think, but I feel a sense of righteous anger on his behalf. In my head, he's been with me for a year. It's like I *do* know him in some sense of the word. How much has he suffered because of my memory loss? If we were genuinely in love, then what pain must he have been in?

I'm recalling every scene I drafted in a new light. Seeing red and not giving a crud if this makes my family mad, I stand straighter and look Ashton in the eyes. "What do I need to do?"

Ashton raises his brows in question.

I clarify. "Let's find your brother. Let's find Noah."

Chapter Seven

MY ONE CONDITION ~ EARLY JULY

I sit side-by-side with Ashton on my tiny but bulbous burnt-orange couch inside my camper as we thumb through my heavily marked-up manuscript. He followed me back home after we ate. Or *he* ate, I should rephrase. I stole a few french fries and a hushpuppy but couldn't stomach much else. The rest of the lunch, we worked on a game plan to try and find his brother, who has seemingly fallen off the face of the earth.

According to Ashton, Noah is not on social media. He's never liked it, and their sister manages their marketing (who turns out to be the Branda lady he mentioned being on the phone with at our first meeting). When Branda Prewitt stumbled upon my reel about my book, she showed Ashton, and, well, the rest is history, as they say. But by that point, Noah had already left. He had left a note explaining he needed to get away for a while and recollect himself.

He had left his phone, laptop, and keys by his bedside. The only thing he had taken with him was a bag of clothes, his notebook, and his favorite pen. He virtually left himself untraceable, though judging by the coming anniversary of the day I lost my mind and forgot him, we have an idea where he might be.

"As I said, there's a solid chance he's back in Bora Bora, Esme. Are you sure you're willing to go back there with me to try and find him?" Ashton's intense stare makes me squirm, and the thought of flying across the world with a man I barely know is not necessarily comforting, but I owe this to Ashton. I owe it to his family. I owe it to Noah. I owe it to the woman I was while in Bora Bora previously. I owe it to the novel. I owe it to the current version of myself.

"Outside of assisting you, maybe it will make these memories I've written about in the book feel more real. Or completely come back all together." I toss a smile his way, but he still looks wary. I nudge his shoulder with mine. "Relax, Ashton. I said I would do it, and I mean it. Plus, you said you were paying, right?"

Finally, he cracks a smile. "Yes, I'm covering the cost. Noah would disown me if I didn't treat his woman with any less respect."

He's got that right, fictional Noah huffs. Should I tell Ashton that I hear his brother in my head all. the. time?

His woman. I keep the smile on my face to try and hide my discomfort over the phrase. As much as I ship Esme and Noah in my romance novel, I'm not sure about the real-life people. Heck, I wrote Esme as a more outgoing, carefree version of who I really am. Who is to say this Noah guy is exactly the way I wrote him in the book? *Ashton*, my voice retorts. As we've gone through the story together, he's noted how precisely I've captured the essence of his twin within the pages.

But no one is that perfect. Book boyfriends don't magically step out of novels even though I pretend that's the case in my own novel when Esme meets Noah.

I'm confused. A ball of muddled memories blended with fiction.

Ashton clears his throat. "Sorry. Didn't mean to imply the two of you are still together." He stands and grabs his glass of water from the tiny island inside my kitchenette. "When we find Noah," he takes a sip, "please do not feel like you have to continue a relationship with him. The two of you only knew each other a week, and while he fell head over heels for you, it does not mean that you both are the person you were a year ago. So much has happened, and—"

I stand and cut him off, placing a hand on his forearm. "I know, Ashton. Please stop tiptoeing around me and fretting. I know what I'm getting myself into, and I am fully on board." No one gets permission to treat me like I'm broken and fragile anymore. I might be swimming in befuddlement, but I know one thing: the real Noah is the key to clarification. "We will find your brother, and whatever happens after that will happen. But first, let's put our energy into the search."

Ashton cuts his eyes to where my hand rests, and I drop my arm. I was mooning over this man when I first saw him, and I definitely developed a crush. But that is long gone. Not when I know there is a real-life Noah Ashton in the picture. Or, Noah Ashley Prewitt, as Ashton informed me.

I step back and stare at Ashton's profile as he sips his water, Adam's apple bobbing as he swallows. He resembles Noah so much it sends a pang through my soul that I was, at one point in my life, destined to belong to him. But as I study Ashton—those dark curls, hazel eyes, full lips—a dawning begins. Something that once was fuzzy starts to clear.

Esme Samantha Prewitt. There's a familiarity to it, as if I've said it before. Or perhaps someone has said it to me. "In the book," I say slowly, steadying my breathing as the image in my memory crystallizes. "In the book, Noah proposes to Esme before they leave."

Ashton rolls his lips, rocking back and forth on his heels, averting his gaze.

"Ashton," I growl in a low warning. I've been on an emotional rollercoaster today, and I'm ready to tip the cart.

He throws up his hands in defense. "He had texted me and told me he was bringing you home and that he wanted to marry you. I'll show you the text messages between us, but I don't want to feed too much into the narrative. I think that's something you and Noah should discuss together. He never told me if he actually asked you or if you agreed."

My knees shake as my head grows light. I sit down, placing my head between my legs while trying to unravel the idea I might have been engaged to Noah Ashley Prewitt.

How do I even begin to process this? I don't know what's real and what's made up at this point. I glance down at my bare ring finger. I don't remember having a ring when I woke up from the coma, but those weeks that followed are still a little hazy.

My camper door flies open. "Esme!" a shrill voice calls. The camper rocks as my mom, with her brown but graying hair and frantic expression, steps through the door. My dad, with his thinning gray hair and a tired posture, follows. My parents' eyes bounce from me to Ashton.

Ashton, surprising me once again, steps toward them and greets them by name using a clipped tone. "Melina. Gregory." He holds out his hand as I sit stunned on the couch. "Ashton Prewitt. Noah's twin."

Mom stands slack-jawed while Dad cautiously shakes his hand and responds with firm politeness. "It's good to see you again. Heard you're signing my daughter on as your client."

Again?

Ashton doesn't even attempt a smile. "That's the plan."

I stay silent because there are too many things happening inside my head. I'm angry with my parents for their deceit, shocked that they somehow know Ashton, reeling over the existence of Noah, and now, I'm wondering if this whole thing with the book is even legit. Does Ashton truly think

I'm a good writer, or does he just want my help finding Noah? And if he does think I'm a good writer, then is this a one-time thing? Am I only writing this story well because it's an actual memory? At least part of it? Would I be able to completely make something up and write it well?

One thing at a time, Esme. And first things first...

I stand, fisting my hands on my hips. "You lied to me. Both of you."

My parents' eyes snap to me, their faces draining of color. Dad clears his throat and moves to stand beside Mom. He whispers something to her, and she nods mindlessly. Dad speaks first. "Esme, honey. We never wanted you to find out this way." My stomach drops. Up until this moment, I think I was hoping it was all some elaborate "gotcha!" type of hoax. But it's not. Everything Ashton said—*it's true.*

I don't miss how Dad's gaze flattens and shifts to Ashton. That somehow angers me more. Ashton is the only one brave enough to be honest with me around here.

I cross my arms and cock my hip out like a petulant child. "You mean you never wanted me to find out. Period. No 'like this.'"

"Baby," Mom begins, but I cut off her pitying cry.

"No, Mom. You don't get to 'baby' me. You lied to me. Both of you." I cut my narrowed eyes to Dad before bringing them back to Mom. "And Ethan and Sam. You all said I was in a jet ski accident! All of you colluded behind my back and blatantly chose to lie to me. The very people I'm supposed to trust. The people I couldn't even lie to about fake-dating Ashton because guilt was eating me up! I relied on you to tell me the truth about the three years' worth of memories I'm missing. How could you?!" I throw my hands up in exasperation.

"Esme, let us explain," Mom says, stepping toward me with an outstretched hand. I step back as if she's a snake poised to strike. Mom swallows, drops her hand, then continues. "We were trying to protect you. You were in such a fragile, unstable state. Imagine hearing that truth when you woke up. Imagine hearing you had met a random stranger that you wanted to continue seeing when you got back home. That's not who you are. It would have placed an unnecessary burden on you."

"No, Mom! I'm not fragile. I wasn't then, and I'm not now. I can handle the truth. You hid something so important to me that my psyche is bringing back the memories in a fictional format. Whatever happened on that island, I'm going to figure it out. I'm going to learn the truth. And whatever I did or didn't do, whether what this Noah guy and I had was real or not, it's my choice to make. Mine!"

I'm heaving, my throat raw from raising my voice. I can't think straight; I'm furious. A hand rests on my elbow as if holding me upright, but I jerk away from Ashton's touch and collapse onto the couch. "Go. Please go. All of you."

Silence ensues for several moments until I hear shuffling feet and feel the rhythmic rock of the camper. Dad whispers something I can't hear.

"I'm sorry, Esme," Mom calls out through broken tears. I don't meet her eyes. I don't remove my face from my hands until the camper door closes. Anger burns through my veins, lighting me up from within.

"Well, I guess I'll—"

I growl in frustration. "When do we leave for Bora Bora?"

Ashton blinks once, then twice, as if I've caught him off guard. Then I remember I told everyone to leave. I sigh and stand. "I'm sorry, Ashton. I didn't mean for you to leave. Just them. I need space to figure this all out. I need to get away." A derisive laugh escapes me, a tad unhinged and laced with disbelief. "I'm sorry you had to witness that. I swear I've never combusted like that in my life."

And secretly, it felt good.

It felt good to not cave. To stand my ground for once.

To speak my true feelings instead of trying to coddle someone who hurt me like I did when Lane broke my heart. That night he broke it off with me, and then I thanked him for teaching me the truth about romance... It still haunts me, and I loathe myself for trying to spare his feelings while I shattered into pieces.

Ashton is quiet for a beat, his face contemplative as his dark, bushy brows knit together. Finally, he says, "Your parents told us before you all left the hospital that we shouldn't try to reach out. Melina said she would have you reach out if you remembered, and only if you wanted to. She said the doctor recommended not adding any more trauma on top of what you'd gone through." Now it's his turn to laugh with a cutting edge. "Noah, once he was healed, tried to contact them several times. The last time he tried, Gregory told him that he would file a restraining order if Noah didn't stop trying to get in touch with you. It was a nail in the coffin to solidify my brother's deep dive into depression. He respected your parents' wishes, but no one seemed to think twice about the trauma and heartache he'd experienced."

I'm dumbfounded. Speechless. But I'm a writer, so I find words even if they're only first-draft worthy. "I am so sorry. They've always been the hovering type, wanting to make sure Ethan and I made what they perceived as the right and sensible choices in life. But this open deception? That's new. And it's not okay, Ashton. How they've handled every-thing... It's not okay."

"It's not," Ashton agrees, moving to sit beside me on the couch once more, our arms brushing one another. He mirrors my sullen state. "But it is what it is. Nothing left to do but continue to clear the air and learn the truth."

"Which means we need to find Noah," I state. Ashton is silent, but he nods.

"Are you sure he's in Bora Bora?" I ask, rubbing my tem-ples.

"Not at all," Ashton says through a deep breath. "But I think it's a solid guess. Noah likes to travel—liked to travel. Since Bora Bora, he hasn't been the same. I feel like I don't know my other half anymore."

What Ashton means to say is that his twin hasn't been the same since *me*.

"Ashton." I take his hand and look him dead in the eyes, mustering all the confidence and sincerity I can in a situation like this. "We will find him. I will do whatever it takes. I want to know the truth as much as you want to find your brother. And I can't stand the thought that there is someone out there who might have loved me and is now be suffering because of me." I am determined to correct this mess my family made. Indignation motivates me. Acrimony guides my path.

Oh, God. I am mad and resentful over this. I'm going to feel it because You know I don't have any other option right now, but please, help me to move past it. Eventually.

"Love. It's not a 'might.' It's not a past tense. Noah loves you, Esme. You need to know that loud and clear before we go tracking him down. Are you okay with that?"

So many unspoken things pass between me and Ashton, but what else can I do? I want to know what really happened in Bora Bora, and the only one with the answers I desperately seek is Noah Ashley Prewitt.

I firmly nod.

Chapter Eight

Follow You Around ~ mid-July

"I don't remember the last time I've left state lines. Or went anywhere outside of central Mississippi for that matter," I state as Ashton parks the truck in front of a pump at a Chevron gas station. We crossed the Alabama state line not too long ago. The moment the "Welcome to Sweet Home Alabama" sign flew past, a heaviness covered me like a weighted blanket.

I'm really doing this. I'm embarking on a journey to locate the man of my dreams and the character who has spoken loudly to me over the past year, directing my story as I've typed word after word. The guy I used to show the world that real men can be just as good as fictional men.

Through my own fictional novel, of course.

I've yet to prove that a real man measures up, which is why what Lane told me still stings. And apparently, Bryan had told me something similar based on the way he apologized to me at Gunnar's. Am I really that delusional? To believe a bookish love can exist in the real world?

Not at all, sweetheart. Keep on believing. Don't lower your standards, Noah says, and my heart warms. Then I once more remember he's real and get a little freaked out by the voice in my head.

Surely not...

Ashton tosses a mischievous grin my way as he opens his door and hops out of the brown lifted truck, responding to my comment. "Probably because you lost three years of memory. Maybe you were a grand explorer during the time you lost your mind."

I scowl, but I can't hold the false expression long. A smile breaks across my face, and I laugh. "Touché."

"Too soon?" Ashton asks, scratching his tattooed arm. "To joke like that? It's been almost a year."

"Not at all," I remark, talking to him through the open door as he approaches the gas pump. "It's refreshing, actually. People typically look at me as if I've lost my mind when I make dark jokes about losing my mind."

I can't fully see Ashton as he pumps gas, but I hear his throaty, rich laugh. It sounds just as I imagined the Noah from my book did. I guess the real Noah probably has the same laugh. Or something very similar.

And it's a sound I could bottle up.

Noah's real. The thought hits me once more. It's been doing that quite often during this drive to Ashton's house. Once we made the arrangements to go to Bora Bora in two days, and Ashton mentioned telling his family, I made the spontaneous request to do it. To meet his family—a group of people who I've unknowingly hurt through their missing son. Mostly, I wanted to immediately create space between my family and myself. But honestly? Meeting Noah's family is something I need to do to start to make up for the emotional harm my parents' verdict toward Noah caused. So, I'll spend the next two days in Tuscaloosa, Alabama, with the Prewitts, praying they don't secretly harbor hate for me. Ashton says it's the opposite—they've wanted to meet me. They want to know the woman Noah messaged home about, saying he was going to marry her.

But who is that woman?

Yes, she's me. But who was that version of me that fell in love in a week and potentially decided to marry a man she'd just met? I'd like to meet her, too. I'm not completely the woman I was before the accident—er, attempted murder—but I don't think I'd fall in love in a week with an unknown man, either.

Gah, I have to figure out the truth.

If any aspect of what I've written is genuine, then this man is one of my wildest dreams—passionate, living without abandon. He is flirty, kind, and loving. The perfect man. We must have had one whirlwind of a week together.

He loved me.

Protected me.

Because he apparently wanted to *marry me.*

Will he still feel the same way? Ashton thinks so. But me? I can't say I love him. I can't say I want to marry him now, nor do I know if he even proposed to me on that island as I've written in my novel. I love him as a fictional character, but he's just that—fiction. Not real. At least, he was. He's becoming more real with every passing moment I dwell upon him. Is he truly as great as I wrote him to be? Can someone that perfect for me exist on earth?

Regardless, I feel like an enchantress. I made this man fall in love with me then I forgot about him.

"Penny for your thoughts?" Ashton says, pulling me from the topsy-turvy process of figuring out my inconsistent and ambiguous emotions. He shuts the door and cranks the truck, pulling out of the gas station.

I fiddle with the necklace, refusing to meet his eyes. "I feel guilty."

He drives out onto the highway, and we're off again, only the rumble of the tires against the pavement as I wait for him to respond. "Over what? Noah?"

"Yes but..." I trail off, trying to formulate the right words. "I feel guilty that I don't remember him like I should. He's fiction in my head, but he's real to you. I should know him. Remember him as more than a character in my story. I'm so sorry that I don't, Ashton. If I did, maybe all of this could have been avoided. My parents wouldn't have lied. He wouldn't be depressed, as you say, and he wouldn't have disappeared on you. And I should really give this necklace back to you." Panic settles in my chest as anxiety over the situation comes swinging like a wrecking ball to my life. That heavy weighted blanket feeling from earlier cloaks me further. I'm running away with a man I don't know to find another man I don't know because my family lied to me. I'm crumbling, collapsing, caving.

I reach to unbuckle the necklace, but taking it off feels like losing a part of me. It's been a physical reminder of survival. Of hope.

Why, God? Why did I have to get amnesia? What's the purpose of this confusion and chaos? What am I even doing here? I don't know him. I don't love him. What help can I even offer?

"Stop, Esme." Ashton says, his fingers gripping my hand. "Keep the necklace."

I drop my hands into my lap.

Conversational silence envelops us as Ashton drives. The rumble of the road grows louder and louder with every passing second. I fear I might have spoken too honest of thoughts when he says, "Esme, you have nothing to apologize for. Life happened the way God meant it to happen. It sucks, yeah. But you're not to blame. Noah's a grown man struggling. He's doing whatever he needs to do, but as his twin, I couldn't sit on the knowledge you were remembering him even if you didn't realize you were remembering him. He deserves to know, Esme." Ashton grins, immediately shifting the mood with him. "I'm glad you willingly agreed. I might have had to kidnap you."

Why would God mean this to happen? What's the purpose of it all? Great. I'm becoming upset with God over my amnesia again. I thought I had dealt with that many months ago.

Just push it away for now, Esme, I tell myself. *Deal with it later.*

"Ashton," I groan, covering my face with my hands, but the building anxiety begins to ease at his playful tone and my decision to forcibly change my mood. "Not the right thing to say at this moment."

"Saying the right things is my brother's specialty, not mine. He's the one with all the game."

Preach, my brotha! Noah shouts. I hold in my laugh, deciding I'll bring this up to Ashton later. It's just... weird.

"You've got some game," I note incredulously. "Confession time. I developed an immediate crush on you when I first met you. You're obviously hot; you know that. But the way you stood up to Bryan for me, *wow.* That was something. Real winner, game-like material right there."

Ashton rolls his eyes, but I don't miss his smile as he looks ahead at the road. "Don't let Noah hear you say that."

Already heard, Noah grumbles. Okay. Maybe I'll bring it up now.

I inhale a breath before slowly releasing it and saying, "So, don't commit me to an asylum, but I sort of hear Noah in my head. He speaks to me. All the time."

Ashton arches his brow at me. "Like, your book character, right?"

Chuckling, I nod. "I don't think it's possible that I'm communicating with the real Noah. That's stuff of fantasy novels. We aren't in that genre yet."

"My characters talk to me, too. I think it's natural for writers to live with a commune inside their heads."

I hum, knowing he's right. But my creative mind can't help but think *what if...*

My stomach churns, the coffee I was drinking earlier choosing violence in my gut. Ashton, for sure, is off-limits. There's no way he'd make a move when his brother loved—loves—me. And now that I know what I know, I'm beginning to pick up on subtle differences between Ashton and the man who has been living inside of my head. Whereas Noah (my character, at least) is a bubbly, natural-born flirt, Ashton is more reserved. Noah has a wild, carefree abandoned look to him, while Ashton is certified put-together. *But there's something untamed lurking beneath the surface of Ashton.*

"Are you the older twin?"

"Yep. How'd you know?"

I grin as if I've hit the nail on the head. "You're uptight and take charge. The Noah I wrote about in my book has more of a middle-child complex."

Ashton snorts. "And that's true. Branda is the baby." Then he grows serious. "I meant it when I said you wrote Noah—for everything that he is—into your story. From the way he swings his legs when sitting on a pier to his extroverted ways, such as doing something as ridiculous as volunteering to have a bunch of women paint him shirtless."

"I had so much fun writing that scene. I thought—" I release a long breath, staring out of the window at the wall of green passing me by. "I thought it was a rather creative scene. But I guess it might've just been a memory."

"Maybe, but maybe not. Regardless, you're a great writer, Esme. Don't doubt that. You could write your story down all day long and it still be a load of bull. What you did, however, was bring your story—even your real one—to life." He pauses, the road rumbling beneath the tires in the silence. "Your prose and imagery. The way you utilize figurative language and other literary devices." Ashton meets my eyes for a brief second. "Never doubt your skill, okay?"

Numbly, I nod. My head is achingly full of questions that won't have answers until I meet my mystery man, and even then, it might open a can of worms. I'm not the same woman I was. I'm not the same woman Noah fell in love with. I was probably spontaneous, reckless, and wild while on my honeymoon alone if my book is an indication of the truth about how I acted. I imagine any woman would morph into an uncivilized flirt in need of a romantic escape after being left at the altar by a bland box of crackers. That's why I wrote Esme the way I did, and that's who Noah must have fallen in love with, but I'm not her.

Will I only hurt him worse?

Needing a distraction, I reach for the radio and turn on country music. "Is this okay?"

Ashton's response is to start horridly screeching the words to the song floating through the speakers. Laughing until my belly hurts—until the sound turns to sniffling tears—I know I'll never hear "Take Me Home, Country Roads" by John Denver the same way again. The lyrics snuggle inside my brain and wrap themselves up in a blanket, prepared to stay awhile.

Where do I belong?

Who am I now?

Chapter Nine

In My Room ~ mid-July

"I love your place, Ashton." I kick off my light blue Blowfish slip-on shoes in the doorway as Ashton slips out of his tennis shoes. We step out of the entryway and into the small house he shares with Noah. Behind me, Ashton's keys clink together as I take in the living space, narrating what I see. "The plants, the sage accent wall, the neutral tones thrown in for balance. Oh!" I dart to the dining area. It's not quite closed off from the kitchen, but there is a wall that serves as a barrier between the two rooms. I like how it's a closed floor plan, but it's not closed off enough for me to miss the sparkling chandelier in the dining room. "I love the chandelier. You are one classy guy, Ashton."

The various stones glitter in the sunlight, pouring through the floor-to-ceiling windows and reflecting onto the walls and my skin. It reminds me of my stained-glass lamp in my bedroom back at the camper, though these colors are softer. Reminiscent of a setting sun. Hues of daydreams and heaven.

"Noah picked it out," Ashton says as I trace the cacophony of colors projected onto the off-white walls. He clears his throat. "They're fake. Not real rubies, sapphires, diamonds, emeralds."

"There's beauty in the illusions of life." I run my fingers along the matte black, rectangular wooden table before tracing more of the refracting colors along the wall as I make my way into the kitchen. There's beauty in the brambles. The phrase ricochets in my thoughts. Ashton didn't have that phrase on his tattoo when he showed me. Does Noah?

I tuck the thought away for when I find him. Because I *will* find him.

You got that right, my little author. I'm waiting.

I gasp at the monstrosity of vibrant red walls, all-black shiny appliances, and a black-and-white marble floor. "Ashton." I turn to face him, and he's biting back a laugh. "You're not a classy guy. You're a contradiction."

He lets his laugh loose, throwing his head back in amusement. "Noah designed this room. He prefers the loud to the soft whereas I'm happy with quiet and small pops of color." He raises his brows. "When he told me he found the love of his life, I got excited. He'd finally move out, and I could decorate this place how I want it."

"Even pre-amnesia me would have hated this." I scowl at the screaming walls as if they've personally offended me. "There's no way I would have been okay with Noah decorating our place like this. Cue conniption fits."

Noah snorts in my head. *I like loud and in your face, remember?*

I face Ashton once more. He looks as if he wants to ask, but something in my expression must deter him. Instead, I ask, "So where are you stowing the runaway for the next two nights until we leave for Bora Bora?"

Ashton swallows, cutting his eyes away from me. "Noah's room, if that's all right."

My heart does a weird thump. "Yeah, no problem. Can you show me the way? I'll grab my bags from the truck after."

Ashton nods, leading down the narrow hallway. It's full of family photos and enlarged framed photos of Ashton Ashley book covers. "You're Ashton Ashley," I state stupidly. I've been so caught up in everything else I forgot I was walking side-by-side with *the* Ashton Ashley. In *the* Ashton Ashley's house. "You're one of my favorite authors." *Because now is the perfect time to remember that tiny fact and fangirl.* I cringe at myself.

"With Noah, yes. He's the Ashley. I'm the Ashton. Though we haven't come public with the fact we are who we are. We like having our identities hidden, so again, please do not tell anyone." Ashton takes my wide-eyed, starstruck gaze in stride as he reaches from behind me and opens the door we've stopped in front of. His coconut smell lingers even after he's pulled away, and I'm met with a new scent. One that stirs longing in my stomach. One of ocean breezes, vanilla, and citrus.

Turning, I take my first look at my supposed fiancé's room.

Pristine and put together, the room, though sonorous as if I can hear the contrasting colors ringing in my ears, elicits a well of joy. The bed is by far the largest item in the room. It's king-sized, topped with sunset orange quilts on top of light gray sheets. There are lamps on either side of the bed; journals upon journals that he must have filled are stored in one of the light wooden nightstands. The walls are a cloudless blue, smoothly blending with the pops of yellow, orange, and pink. His room is the sky, and I'm floating within it.

See? You like my brand of loud, Meme.

I walk around and peek into his closet. It's a mess in there with clothes haphazardly placed in wooden cubbies and shirts falling off hangers. There's a desk facing the window, and it's almost as if I can imagine him hunched over it, writing in one of his notebooks as if he'd run out of time. Suddenly, as if someone held a flashlight up to my eyes and clicked it on just to immediately turn it off, I picture Noah hunched over a desk in a bungalow, scribbling a note down before briefly looking back at something with a mischievous grin.

My heart clenches and my knees grow weak, but before I collapse to the distressed gray wooden floor, Ashton catches my arm. "Esme, what's wrong? Are you okay?"

Breathless with a racing heart, I cling to his forearm. "I think I just had a memory. A real one. Of Noah writing at a desk. At the resort." I stare dazed at the wooden floor, transposing the memory to a certain scene I wrote in my book. "He's real. It's all real."

And then I shake loose of Ashton, take three steps into Noah's room, and crumble onto his bed in a heap of harrowed sobs. The braveness from today loses all sense of existing. I cry because I've forgotten him. I cry because I desperately want to feel what I'm supposed to feel—in love. I cry because I've hurt this very real man by not knowing him. I cry because I have no idea what's going to happen when we find him, and I don't want to hurt him further.

I cry because I have no idea what I'm doing here despite my initial haze of enmity and guilt in which I made this decision. Did I, in the name of standing up to my parents, fall into my usual trap of people pleasing to appease Ashton and his family?

"Hey, hey," Ashton says in a hushed, soft tone, sitting down beside me. Or so I assume because of the way the bed shifts. "Do you remember how you feel about him? Like, do you actually remember him?" The hope in his voice cuts like a serrated knife.

"No," I wail. In between heaving cries, I manage to get out, "That's the problem. It was just a glimpse."

I don't miss the stifled deflation in his voice as he says, "That's good, though, Esme. It's a good sign. Maybe you'll remember more. Especially while we are in Bora Bora."

"I don't," hitch, "want," hitch, "to get," hitch, "my hopes," hitch, "up!"

Ashton is quiet, but I think he gets the memo that I need some space because the bed shifts as he stands. "I'll just go get our luggage."

Then a door closes, and I'm left to break down alone in the bed of a man who loves me. A man I don't remember.

The guilt is suffocating.

God, how do I move forward when there's a missing chunk of me?

***

Crusty residue from salty tears makes it impossible to open my eyes. Rubbing at my face, I yawn and stretch, desperately wishing for a gallon of water to soothe my parched throat.

When I clutch the comforter that's certifiably not my olive green Turkish cotton quilt, I jolt awake, remembering where I'm at.

And why I'm a tear-stained mess with a developing headache.

With a groan, I sit up and examine the room. It's like I'm inside the sky, and oddly enough, I love it. Pre-amnesia me would have hated all the color. I was a neutrals person, like Ashton. But ever since I woke up a year ago, I've fallen in love with the colors of the setting sun. Vibrant. Rich. *Alive.*

I think a part of my newfound love of color is that I'm glad to be alive.

Even before I knew the truth of why I ended up in a coma, I still had a renewed appreciation of life. It's why I shook some of my uptightness and perfectionism. Sure, I still struggle with those things, but then I remember I'm alive, and God has a reason to keep me awake on this earth. It gives me a sense of purpose.

To write, I think to myself, though I can't deny I'm doubting that now. Would I still be able to write effectively when it comes to something I totally make up?

Ugh. I need to eat something to satisfy my growling, grumbling stomach.

I hope Ashton keeps snacks here. Judging by the darkness outside of the window in front of the writing desk and how heavy my limbs are, it's well into the night. I could check my phone, but I've been avoiding it like the plague. There's not a single person in my contact list I wish to speak with right now.

Standing, I stretch and look around the room one more time. I shouldn't, but I know myself. I'll plunder through Noah's things later under the comforting excuse that maybe something will jog my memory. Sure, guilt tugs at my insides, but it's not like I'm a jealous girlfriend or jilted ex. I'm just a woman searching for herself. And since Noah likes to write and has journals upon journals, maybe there are traces of me within the paper.

The crying jag released a lot of emotion, and though I still don't have all the answers I wished I had, I feel lighter. More intact.

But I want to understand, God. What's Your reasoning?

I wait a beat, but the air around me doesn't speak back.

Even fictional Noah is silent.

I exit the room and am met with the smell of bacon acting as a siren's call, luring me into the kitchen to find Ashton standing in a red apron that matches the kitchen walls and reads, "Kiss the Cook. Tastes Better Than the Food."

He turns as I approach, and I raise my eyebrows at him.

Shrugging, he pops a piece of scrambled egg into his mouth and says, "It's my brother's. He's the real cook between the two of us, but I try."

"Hm." I join him in the kitchen and steal bacon off the paper-towel-lined plate the strips rest upon to drain off grease. I crunch on the crumbly, burnt piece of heaven, sighing. "Breakfast for dinner. I love it."

"It's about all I can cook," Ashton admits sheepishly with a boyish shrug. His hair is more untamed than usual, and I have a feeling he resembles Noah more than usual right now. It makes my heart do a little dance. "I need my brother back simply so that I don't have to eat leftovers from Branda or attempt to cook for myself."

"I can cook," I offer. "Let me make you breakfast in the morning as a thank you for everything you've done and will do for me."

"Will do?" He hitches a brow, holding the spatula up.

"Taking me to Bora Bora, housing me, dealing with my emotional breakdowns as I process everything." My shoulders lift and fall as I crunch on my piece of bacon. "You know, the usual stuff one would do for near strangers."

Ashton laughs, shaking his head. The oven timer goes off, and he silences it before pulling a hot tray of biscuits from the shiny black appliance. "Don't worry. They came from a package," he says, as if he's used to people questioning his skills in the kitchen.

"I'd eat grass right about now." I glance at the clock, noticing it's a little past eight. "It's not as late as I thought."

"I figured you'd be hungry once you woke up from your nap. Thought I'd leave it out in case you woke up after I went to bed."

A warmth spreads in my chest at his kindness and thoughtfulness. "Thanks, Ashton. Truly."

"Oh," he says, pointing the spatula in his hand toward the living room. "Your luggage is in there. Dinner's almost ready, but you have time to put it away if you want."

I nod, steal another piece of bacon, then go collect my things and drag them into Noah's room. That scent of his hits me like a bag of bricks before it settles, and I grow accustomed to it as I organize my bags, fish out my bathroom things, and hunt for my sleep clothes. Once I'm done, I make my way back to the kitchen. Ashton has already set the table, so I join him.

We settle into an awkward silence punctuated with the sound of chewing and clanging of utensils on the ceramic plates. Finally, after I've consumed an entire bacon, egg, and cheese biscuit, I speak up. "So, I'm meeting your family tomorrow. Will you tell me what to expect? Do they hate me?"

Ashton laughs, then takes a sip of his water. "I already told you that they don't hate you. They're thrilled to meet you, actually. They are," he hums, looking away from me and off in the distance, "hopeful."

"Hopeful?"

Still not looking me in the eye, he replies. "Hopeful that you will bring Noah back home. Hopeful that the two of you will reconnect."

"But they don't even know me. Why would they hope that I would reconnect with him?" Uneasiness settles in my chest. Will they question me as if I'm Noah's girlfriend? Or worse, his fiancée? I'm not ready for that. Maybe I shouldn't have agreed to meet the family while we were here waiting for our departure date. I'm acting like Esme from the novel—spontaneous and a bit flighty. That's not me, even if I wish it were. Noah was supposed to be fiction, and now, he's real. It's unnerving, this echoing clash of fantasy and reality.

Leveling me with an intense stare, Ashton slowly says, "You changed my brother. When he woke up in Bora Bora, you were all he was concerned about. The version of Noah who left for Bora Bora, while a good man, was noncommittal and not the dating type. Imagine our surprise when he texted us and told us he had found the woman he was going to marry." Ashton chuckles at that, lightening up.

So Noah's *not* perfect like in my book. He's kind of a rogue it seems, which is great in fiction but doesn't translate to reality in a healthy manner.

I'm silent, so he continues. "He has spent every waking moment since then trying to find a way to get you back without warranting that restraining order your father threatened him with if he so much as showed up in Whitney."

Ire swirls in ribbons of dark maroon at the mention of what my father did. I can't even begin to imagine the pain Noah must have been in. If I loved someone enough to marry him—which I still don't know if that's true—I would be out of my mind if someone told me I couldn't be with him. Love is potent like that. It's the kind of love I've always wanted, but I must've settled for less with Bryan. From what I can remember up to the blank space in my memory, I was the type of woman who settled. Especially after Lane. One good thing came from losing time... I do a much better job at going after what I desire. Or at the very least, staying away from men since my expectations are too high.

You had that soul-rewiring love, something inside of me—not Noah—whispers. *You had it with Noah. I used him to change you.*

But I don't remember it. At least, I don't feel it anymore, I argue back with that still, small voice. The scraping of a chair across the floor elicits my attention. Ashton stands, heading for the kitchen. "Do you want tea?"

I shake my head, not much of a tea person. "If Noah was noncommittal before me, then who is to say he's still not that way? He did run off, after all. Maybe he found someone new and is shacking up. Maybe I was simply a game to him."

Ashton physically chokes in the kitchen. I stand to check on him, but he's got his head bowed over the sink as water drips from his lips. "Not a chance," he says firmly. "One, my brother doesn't 'shack up.' Two, and I don't say this to pressure you, Esme, but I'm positive if you don't end up with Noah, he will be the guy version of a spinster for the rest of his life. He ran off because he kept sitting in his truck every single day fighting the urge to earn a restraining order."

"Isn't that a little toxic?"

"Probably." Ashton straightens and drags the back of his hands across his mouth before turning toward me. "Love is like that sometimes. It sweeps in with raging passion before robbing someone of life." Something in his voice is reminiscent, and I wonder who hurt him. But I don't ask because the pain etched onto his face clearly indicates he's not ready to talk about it.

After a beat of silence, he offers me a soft smile. "But that doesn't have to be the case. I think for some people..." He pauses, looking off in the distance once more. "I think for some people, it inherently changes them. Passionate, reckless love withstands the test of time. Their love never fizzles. Some people are so innately full of love that they breathe life into the dead instead of siphoning it from the living."

But it stole mine, I think to myself. *Three years, in fact.*

Will this so-called passionate love steal Noah, too? Has it already?

"Okay," I say in a high-pitched voice, ready to change the conversation as we sit back down at the table to finish our dinner. "Tell me about your family, please. I don't want to be caught off-guard."

Chapter Ten

A Nice Dress ~ Mid-July

Adjusting the high-waisted, floral-patterned flared skirt and making sure my light orange collared button-up halter top, which compliments my tanned skin nicely, is tucked in tightly, I release a breath. Ashton said his family is chill and low-maintenance, but judging by his put-together style, I have difficulty believing that statement. Maybe it's just an Ashton thing. Then again, I perused pictures of Noah that suggest he was fashioned the same way. Though Noah seems to come with a little wildness painting his spirit. In every single picture, he wears a knowing smirk. Even pictures from his childhood. He's like an imp or a pixie, always up to something mischievous.

After cooking omelets for breakfast, I snuck away into the room to do a little more snooping. I browsed through two of Noah's journals last night before feeling too icky and invasive to continue. I snuck glances at the dates and tried not to read anything that wasn't relevant to me, but I have to admit, I got caught up in his prose over his life. Noah is not one to journal about events; he speaks to thoughts, feelings, and abstract ideas. The way he wrote sentences, even within the privacy of his pen and leather-bound paper, stirred a sense of longing within me. It was reflective of his voice in the novels he writes with his brother, and I wonder if Noah is in charge of the prose while Ashton is in charge of the plot. Or maybe they each contribute to both. Though, admittedly, Ashton seems like the more sensible twin from what I've gleaned. He would be the one to focus on structure while Noah went off script, describing the way golden sunlight caresses his cheek with a gentle hello as it dances through the leaves of a tree.

My heart soars, and I talk it down from the clouds. Noah's becoming so much more than a book character in my head. I have to tread carefully; I can't blend fiction and reality. I can't assume the Noah from my book is the same one I will find.

But we are one and the same, my little author. I shudder as Noah's voice across my senses. *Why do you think you can hear me so clearly? It's because you know me, sweetheart.*

A gentle knock sounds at my—Noah's—door. "Esme? You ready?"

The present voice sounds eerily like the one in my dream last night, but there's a slight difference in inflection than the one in my dream and in my head. I think it was another memory. In the dream, I had woken up in Noah's arms as he whispered my name against my ear. The whispers became a symphony of laughs, kisses, and carefree entanglements. While it's safe to say I woke up this morning hot and bothered and desiring something that I shouldn't with a man I don't actually remember, I'm simultaneously concerned that I may have lost my virginity to my dream man in real life. Though I didn't write that into my story because it's a Christian closed-door novel, I now can't help but wonder. And if I did, it signifies I truly was off my rocker that week in Bora Bora, because I planned to wait for marriage. I haven't had a lady exam since the accident, and I am due for one, but I'm terrified to find out the truth.

It's one thing to forget a guy I met on my un-honeymoon.

It's another thing to forget about having sex with said man.

Glancing at myself one more time in the mirror, I note the few flyaways around my face and neck. I quickly smooth and tuck them into my bun, fiddle with the orange, pink, and white skirt once more, and then move to the door. I slowly open it to find Ashton standing out in the hall wearing mid-thigh khaki shorts and an orange linen button-up shirt that matches mine.

"Hey, we match," Ashton says with a twinge of suppressed happiness in his voice. Gone is the man who looked tortured and hurt while talking about wild loves last night. In his place is the guy who seemingly wants to crawl out of his shell but has a hard time doing so.

His hazel eyes flecked with green snap to mine, and we laugh at the coincidence of our outfit choices. I give him a playful nudge as I pass through the door. A couple of meetings and a night spent at his place, and I already feel like he's my best friend. Especially because he's the only human on this earth that I trust at the moment. My thoughts slip to my parents, Ethan, and Sam, and I have to fight the fury stirring in my heart and mind.

As if he can read my thoughts, Ashton questions me as we leave the house. "Have you contacted your parents to let them know you're still alive?"

I shake my head, my face hardening as I grind my teeth.

Have they contacted me?

Absolutely.

I turned my phone off last night because Sam wouldn't stop messaging me. Ethan wouldn't stop sending me Snapchats. Mom and Dad took turns ringing my phone.

"Esme, you need to contact them. Just to let them know you're alive." Ashton's voice is concerned with a touch of fatherly chastising.

"Okay, Dad," I retort. He ignores my scowl as he opens the door of his truck for me. After I slide into the lifted monstrosity, I begrudgingly fish my phone from my little white purse.

> **Me:** Ashton says I should let you all know I'm alive. I'm going to meet his and Noah's family. Then we are going to Bora Bora to look for Noah. Please stop harassing me. I will talk to you when I'm ready.

Mom's message is immediate.

> **Mom:** I'm so sorry, sweetie. Thank you for the update. We love you. Please, even though you're angry with me, send me your itinerary for Bora Bora.

I thumb up the message and lock the screen just as Ashton begins to pull out of the driveway.

"Happy?" I ask, reaching for the radio.

Ashton rolls his eyes. "You know? With that attitude, though I understand it to some extent, I think you and Branda will get along nicely. Though that might mean living hell for me and Noah."

I toss him a cheeky grin as some Kenney Chesney song starts to play, though my smile is a front. My stomach is churning, my heart is beating a little too fast, and sweat is causing my tucked-in shirt to stick to my back.

Ashton assures me I'll be well-received, but I wonder...

Do I deserve to be welcomed in?

Will they attempt to force me into something with Noah? Ashton says they are *hopeful*, whatever that entails.

Or were they lying to Ashton about wanting to meet me? Is it a bait-and-switch tactic, and they will rain fire and brimstone down upon me for forgetting Noah and causing him to dip out of town without a way to get in touch with him?

Before I've climbed my way out of my head, we are sitting in the truck on the paved driveway of their colossal pearly white home. "You weren't kidding when you said you lived close. I'm surprised they weren't at your doorstep last night. Heck, even after our first meeting in Whitney, the rumor mill spread gossip like grass seeds. Did you know we ran off and got married, Ashton?"

He laughs, a twinkle in his eyes, before shaking his head. "I imagine Noah won't take too kindly to that news."

The mention of Noah once more reminds me of what I'm doing here, and my chest tightens. "Imagine not," I mumble, staring at the house in front of me and half-expecting the Noah in my thoughts to speak. But he doesn't.

"Hey," Ashton says, placing a hand on my shoulder. "It's all right. They're going to love you."

"I think that's what I'm afraid of," I respond, slipping out of the truck and into the humid mid-July morning heat before Ashton has a chance to come around to get the door. We meet in front of his truck and stand staring up at the white three-story house. It has Roman-style columns out front, and though it's not an old antebellum house, it signifies this family comes from money. *No wonder Ashton can afford to fly me to Bora Bora on a whim.*

The dark brown front door swings open, and a young female whose sharp facial features strongly resemble the aging man beside her steps out.

"You're here!" the woman shouts, a broad smile spreading across her face, softening it up. She bolts toward us in her high-waisted ripped jeans and white crop top. Barefeet, chipped, painted toes, and all. Casual, indeed. She juts out her hand to me, a throng of bracelets decorating her tanned wrist. "I'm Branda. The coolest Prewitt sibling. Even Noah's agreeing from wherever in the world he is, right, Ashton?"

I cover my mouth, not knowing if it's appropriate to laugh at that. I look at Ashton, but he shakes his head at his sister while wearing a loving smile. It's as if he's already tired of her antics but loves her and appreciates her too much to comment on it. The older man approaches from behind, bumping his daughter out of the way before I even have a chance to shake her hand.

He's tall and slim with—surprisingly not balding—short salt-and-pepper hair that matches his black T-shirt and white, pleated dress pants. He rolls his sparkling hazel eyes as he reaches out his hand. "Hi, Esme. I'm Lincoln, but you can call me Link. I'm the coolest Prewitt overall." We shake hands, and then he cuts his eyes to Branda and puts a hand to his ear. "Hear that, Branda? That's the sound of Noah agreeing with *me* from wherever he's sullenly run off to."

They all laugh, and this time, I join in, already feeling more at ease as they jest over who is the coolest Prewitt according to the missing Noah.

Dark humor must run in the family, and somehow, I fit right in.

Which is a thought I should not be entertaining.

Finally, Ashton says, "I think we can all agree Noah would say Esme is the best out of all of us."

I blush, but I don't feel quite comfortable to comment. I shouldn't vibe with these people like my immediate response is to. It's not like I knew Noah as long as they did before losing my memories, anyway. I was a blip in his life, but if what I wrote was true, it was the best blip in time.

But what good is living to my best if I can't remember it?

Link and Branda agree, saving me from having to speak.

"Well, let's head on inside. It's hot as blue blazes out here," Link complains, already walking toward the house. We follow him inside.

The air conditioning kisses my face as I leave the sticky July heat behind me. The house is immaculate with its vaulted ceiling, arched windows, spiral iron-clad staircase, and minimalistic color scheme and tones. It's a house that screams that this family comes from money, but it's not ostentatious. This place is a whole other universe compared to Ashton's eclectic home, though I guess Noah had a role in creating the contradicting rooms.

"Can I get you some tea? Water? Coffee?" Branda asks as Ashton and I sit down on the suede brown loveseat.

"I'll take some tea," Ashton comments.

"I was asking Esme. You know where the tea is," Branda quips, then she turns a sweet, hopeful smile on me. "So? What will it be?"

I sneak a glance at Ashton, who nods in encouragement for me to answer. He doesn't look put off by his sister's sass, only mildly amused.

"Coffee, please. If it's not too much trouble."

"Make that two cups," Link hollers from down one of the hallways on the right side of the home.

"Got it, Daddy." And with that, Branda nearly skips across the dining room and into the kitchen tucked away on the far left of the house.

Ashton releases a breath followed by a laugh. "I don't know why I miss her when she's not around."

"Do you want me to make you some tea?" I offer.

"Nah. Just wait. She'll come out here with a steaming cup of peach tea. She just likes to pretend she doesn't enjoy hospitality."

"Does she still live here?"

Ashton nods. "She says someone has to look after Dad and Grandma, and that she's perfectly content being the one to do it. Says she doesn't want to get married. That she's happy in her singleness. She's only twenty-five. Plenty of life ahead of her."

"Hm." Happy in her singleness. I think back to ten years ago when I was seventeen and gearing up for high school graduation. I was so focused on finding a husband that I ran into the first arms that welcomed me. Lane did a number on me with his subtle manipulation and chipping away at my ideas of love. I took a little time after we ended, and I didn't find a man who wanted to marry me until Bryan came along. Safe, bland Bryan. And we all know how that ended up, though I wonder what manipulation I'm missing from my time with him if he actually told me something along the same lines of what Lane told me.

But then Noah apparently popped into my life and was going to give me the happily ever after I'd always wanted.

It wasn't until after the accident—no, the attempted murder—that I woke up with no recollection of my adult life and realized I could chart a new path forward. I was forced to pave new roads. Make new brain connections.

"Esme?" Ashton's concerned voice tips me from my thoughts. He's sitting up and twisting toward me.

"Lost in my head," I say with a weak smile. At that time, Branda walks into the room holding a mug.

"Only because I love you," she says through a smirk, holding the plain black mug out to Ashton. He takes it with two hands, though he glances over at me as if to say, "Told you."

"Coffee is brewing," Branda continues. "How do you take it?"

"Black," I respond, and because I think she will appreciate the lame joke, I add, "like my soul."

A slow grin creeps across her face. "I like you, Esme." Then she bounces back into the kitchen. Literally. It's as if she's walking on those old Moon Shoes.

"I don't want to worry you," Ashton whispers, leaning closer to me so that I can hear him. "But I'm 99 percent sure Branda is going to do everything within that five-foot-two frame of hers to get you and Noah back together after we find him."

I choke on an exasperated breath, coughing a few times before gaining my composure. *That's what I get for immediately bonding with someone,* I grimly think to myself. But would it be so bad? I was attracted to Ashton when I met him. I swoon over Noah's looks according to my novel, and, well, he looks like Ashton, too. Also according to my novel, I immediately bonded with Noah. Maybe I will again? Maybe we will still have some connection that withstood the test of my memory?

And now you're just allowing your whimsical, romantic side to take over. Save it for the novels, Esme. Real life isn't a romance book.

"Esme!" Link appears from the hallway, and I turn to smile at him. An elderly lady with a gray bun atop her head and a shimmering gold shirt highlighted by her white dress pants stands beside Ashton's dad. "This is my mother, Lois. She's excited to meet you."

"Hush, boy," Lois says in a no-nonsense voice, briefly whacking Link in the leg with her bejeweled cane. "I can speak for myself. Now, stand up, girl. I want to look at you."

Scrambling to my feet to accommodate the daunting woman, I make a move toward her, but I accidentally step on the edge of my skirt. The sudden slickness of the fabric under my foot against the hardwood floor sends me careening backward until I'm sprawled on top of Ashton's lap. One of his knees jabs into the middle of my back while the other rests underneath my upper thigh. My head is lolling against the armchair of the couch, and above me, a mug of tea held in a firm grasp floats across my vision.

"Thanks for not spilling the scalding liquid on me," I say through a groan masquerading as a laugh. "Those are some cat-like reflexes you've got there."

Ashton's amused face comes into view as I lie there contemplating if facing Lois is something I am capable of doing
now. "Do I also have a body like a pillow?"

"No," I state without thought. "Your body is like a—" I
pause, remembering where I am and who I'm with. This
man is *not* Noah, and regardless of the slight attraction I
once harbored for Ashton, it's no longer present. Ashton
is, however, quickly becoming a confidant. A friend. And
friends don't comment on the chiseled, perfectly sculpted
condition of another friend's body. Embarrassment blos-
soms through my veins, and I slowly close my eyes. In a
whisper I pray Lois is too old to hear, I say, "You can just
pour that tea on me now. I'd like an excuse to leave and
save a morsel of my dignity."

"Dignity is overrated, girl. Now are you going to keep
using my grandson—the wrong one, mind you—as a lawn
chair or are you going to get up and let me get a good look at
you?" Lois's words are sharp, but not unkind. She's just like
Grannie Bertha—blunt, truthful, and sarcastic in the best
of ways. And for some reason, I really want to impress this
woman.

She's got that energy that demands respect and cooper-
ation.

Get off my brother's lap, Noah growls.

As I start to haul myself up, Ashton uses his free hand to
act as leverage against my back. Within awkwardly silent
seconds punctuated with my heavy breaths, I'm back on my
feet and lifting my skirt, walking with renewed confidence

toward the thin, mouthy woman. I'm a good half a foot taller than she is, but her steely gaze makes me feel like I'm nothing more than a toddler. Still, I drop my skirt, square my shoulders, and jut out my hand. "Hello, I'm Esme Jenkins. It's a pleasure to finally meet you. Ashton—and, er, Noah, in the past it seems, spoke highly of you." I vaguely recall a moment in my book where the characters discuss their families, and Noah's character loved his grandmother deeply.

I'm surmising it was a real conversation.

"Hmph." Lois and her bejeweled cane walk three circles around me as she eyes me up and down, occasionally grunting or harrumphing. Finally, she stops in front of me, looks me dead in the eyes, and gives me the biggest dentured smile. "It's so good to meet you, sugar. When Ashton said he'd found you and that it seemed you were gaining your memory back, I told that boy he'd better bring you to meet me. Noah spoke so highly about you in his text messages and writings, and now that he's run off, you'll be the one to bring him back to us."

The loading wheel above my head spins and spins as I reconcile the doting woman with the one who circled me like a vulture moments earlier.

"Well, go on now. Say something." Lois pokes me in the thigh with the bottom of her cane.

I clear my throat and say the first thing that comes to mind. "I'm sorry you lost him because of me."

"Nonsense, girl." Lois pokes me again, but then Link gently lowers the cane and tosses me an apologetic smile. "The Good Lord has a reason for everything. And my grandson is acting how he feels he needs to in order to cope with his darkness."

I open my mouth to apologize for being the source of his pain, but Lois cuts me off with a whack of her cane against my thigh. "And don't you apologize for his depression. You are not the source of that, either."

Overwhelm sets in as this seemingly loving family looks at me with hope and expectancy in their eyes as if I'm their savior, as if I am the only one who can bring Noah—a man I don't remember, or, well, barely remember I guess—back to them. My brain is spinning and my chest is tightening, my breaths coming short and labored.

"Will you all, uh, give us a minute," Ashton says, and I barely register him placing his hand on my back and pushing me somewhere that's not the living room full of hopeful Prewitts.

"Five things, Esme," Ashton says.

I look around our new location. It's a room full of trophies, sports jerseys, and childhood photos. Like a memorial room of sorts. "You and Noah playing football," I say, noting a framed photograph hanging on the wall. "Soccer trophies. The smell of burnt rubber." I scrunch my nose, and Ashton laughs.

"That's the workout mats in the room next door. Dad just had them recut."

I nod, the pressure in my chest easing. Ashton presses his hand into my lower back, stabilizing me. "Two more things, Esme."

"A chill." I shiver, looking up to find the source of the suddenly cool air. "The condensing vent."

"Now what's got you panicking?"

I sigh deeply, my shoulders drooping. I walk to the large twelve-drawer dresser and pick up one of the trophies that I couldn't tell what sport it belonged to. It's a reading award from elementary school, awarded to Noah Prewitt. I smile despite my current mood. "There's a lot of pressure on me to get your brother home," I finally state, placing the trophy back on the dresser. I turn to look at Ashton, who's still standing by the door of the room with a soft expression on his face. "What if I can't? What if he doesn't want to come back once he realizes I'm not the same girl he met in Bora Bora? Or what if I don't end up liking him like that? How is one supposed to tell in one encounter, anyway?"

Ashton's expression morphs into blankness for a second before a smile splits across his face, and he laughs. "Really, Esme? Do you think we expect you to show up in front of him and be head over heels in love with him?" His laughter grows, but he continues to speak, "That's absurd! We're just hoping the notion you know he exists will be enough to light some kind of fire within him. He might flip a switch and begin a hot pursuit of you, but you have free will to tell him to back off or to invite him in. Up to you. We don't expect anything from you. We are just glad you're willing to help us reach him."

I stare enigmatically at him, processing his words as he belly laughs, making off-hand comments about mail-order brides or something. "You promise? You said Branda would work hard to get us together."

Ashton's laughter dies down, and he says through a smirk, "Oh, she will. And to be frank, I will, too. We know how much Noah loves and cares about you, and we think that you could grow to love him back in the same way. But we aren't going to force anything, and we definitely don't expect it to be a love at first sight thing." His smirk deepens. "I think it would be a thing of great cinema to watch my brother go out of his way to earn your love. I've had the privilege of watching women flaunt themselves like peacocks for him, but I've never watched him lend himself to the chase."

"I fell in love with a playboy?" I ask rhetorically, exasperated. Then I laugh, Ashton joining in. It feels good to let the emotions and tightness out, to accept the truth of the matter. "I really went and fell in love with someone I barely knew. A man notorious for wooing women."

"You did," Ashton agrees through his boisterous laughs. We spend a few more minutes attempting to calm ourselves, but any moment we make eye contact, a new wave of laughter erupts. Something tells me Ashton needed this as much as I did. We've both been tense, and I can only imagine how stressed he's been for the past two months since Noah's been gone.

When we finally can breathe, I say, "So what's this room for?"

"It's Noah's old room. They turned it into a trophy room of sorts. My old room is now the home gym, which is the room next to this one."

"Hm," I comment, sweeping my eyes around the space once more before we exit. When we make our way back into the living room, Branda is the first to talk.

"I'm sorry if we overwhelmed you, Esme. We are just so excited to meet you." The wide sincerity in her hazel eyes softens my spirit. She's inviting, and I know I can speak honestly with her.

"I think I got it in my head you all expected me to still be in love with Noah, the real one and not my fictional one," I confess. "Like I was already a part of this family."

Because you already love me, sweetheart, fictional Noah coos.

I mentally roll my eyes. *You're fiction.*

Ashton steps beside me. "But like I told her, we don't expect that at all. We're just glad she's willing to help us find him, right?"

"Of course, Esme." Link reiterates Ashton's sentiments. "Our Noah is a great guy, but just because we love him doesn't mean you're inclined to. Though never be a stranger to us, okay?"

I swallow and nod.

"I think she'll fall for him again, don't you?" I hear Lois not-so-subtly whisper to Branda. I pretend I don't hear Branda's response.

"She's here, isn't she?"

Chapter Eleven

SEE THE END ~ MID-JULY

"Welcome to Prewitt Publishing," Ashton says as he holds open the sleek glass doors to the old brick building in downtown Tuscaloosa. I walk through, looking around at the cream walls, cherry wooden floors, and sunlit entryway. Plants line the walls and countertops, almost hiding the bubbly-looking receptionist, whose nameplate reads *Kimber Daniels*.

I wave hello after Ashton introduces me as his potential new client, leaving anything to do with Noah out of the interaction, which I appreciate. But then, a tall, slender-built man pops his head out of the door across the room. He's got reddish-brown hair, light eyes, and a friendly face, giving nerdy boy-next-door vibes.

"Esme," Ashton says, gesturing to the man who has fully entered the room. "This is my best friend, Vance Ladner."

"Nice to meet you, ma'am." Vance shakes my hand, his accent thicker than Ashton's. "Heard a lot about you."

I glance suspiciously at Ashton, and he shrugs, his hands deep in his pockets. *Heard about me from Ashton or Noah?* I click my tongue and shake my head before turning my attention back to his friend. "It's nice to meet you as well."

Branda walks in from outside, and before I turn to greet her, I don't miss the way Vance's green eyes soften and sparkle when he looks her way. I almost ask Ashton if they are a thing, but then I remember he said she was single. *Hmm.* If she ends up attempting to play matchmaker with me, maybe I can do it right back. An eye for an eye and all that.

"Oh, good. You're here," Branda says in a quipped tone toward Vance, not giving him the time of day as she power walks past him. When she sees me, she stops in her tracks and smiles widely. "Hi, Esme! Glad Ashton decided to show you the place. Can't wait to have you on board." She pulls me in for a quick hug before clicking away in her bright green heels and yellow pencil skirt, dark brown hair bobbing in its high ponytail. I guess she and Noah share the same eclectic taste. She pauses halfway into the hallway and looks back at us. Vance bites back a smirk when Branda barks, "Vance Ladner. Get your butt back here. We have a book cover crisis to address. One that you caused. *Again.*"

Branda turns on her heel while Vance looks back at me and Ashton. He shrugs and openly grins, waggling his brows. "Boss lady calls."

I flick my eyes to Ashton after Vance disappears, and Ashton answers my unspoken question. "Branda is head of marketing and design, and Vance is her new assistant. By choice." Ashton grimaces as he speaks that last phrase.

"He is smitten with her," I comment. "I know you said Branda was single, but is something going on?"

Ashton sighs, rubbing a hand down his face. "I don't know. I don't think so. Branda is set on being single, and Vance knows that. They've known each other for a lifetime because Vance was always over at the house hanging out with me and Noah."

"Hm."

"I just don't want to see Branda crush his heart beneath her colored heels. He's even softer than he looks."

I laugh despite the seriousness in Ashton's tone. I've known Branda for one day. We hung out all day yesterday, playing games, touring Tuscaloosa, and helping make and eat homemade pizza for dinner at the Prewitt's place. I ended the day teetering on a dangerous highline of hope and sorrow. Hope that maybe something will click, I'll regain my memories, and I'll fully understand what happened with me and Noah. Then, I could become a part of this family that makes me feel right at home. The sorrow... Well, that originates from the anger and sense of betrayal I feel over my family. I've always been close with my parents and Ethan, and now, the rift dividing us is dark and deep. Logically, I know we will come to an understanding, and all of this will one day be water under the bridge. But right now, it hurts. Like water filling my lungs.

Changing the topic, I peruse the front room once more.

"It's decorated like your chosen rooms at your house," I note. "This whole building is saturated with your earthy style."

"Noah didn't get his hands on this place." Ashton opened his arms wide. "He only wants to be one of the authors. He was never interested in the business side of authoring. Just the creative process."

I snort. "After all the research I've done to publish independently, I can wholeheartedly say it'll be much easier on me to have an agent. When you reached out, I nearly had a heart attack of relief."

"Speaking of agenting and stuff, do you want to go see the back?"

Nodding, I follow him through the door Vance and Branda disappeared through moments earlier. It's a long hallway with photos of books they've published and authors they represent lining the light brown walls. Several doors are on either side, and Ashton leads to the very last one on the left. The golden plate on the white door reads: *Nikhil A. Prewitt, CEO*.

"Fancy," I comment, touching the sign.

He grins and winks. "Yep. And because I'm an important and busy CEO," his voice laced with self-deprecation before his features shift into seriousness, "I only personally take on authors I genuinely believe in."

My heart leaps. Not a romantic thump, but one of happiness. But I have to ask. "Or is it a repayment of sorts for helping you locate Noah?"

Ashton shakes his head, crossing his arms over his chest. "I hope you start believing in your talents soon, Esme. I like my clients confident in their work."

"Fine," I feign annoyance and sigh dramatically. "I guess I'll start believing you."

He laughs, then messes with my hair as if I'm his younger sister. "There you go."

If I'm being honest with myself, these past two days with Ashton have been healing in many ways. He's told me the truth, has been a shoulder to cry on and an ear to confide in, and lastly, has been patient with me as I process. I'm nowhere near done processing everything, but this is a start. And going over a book contract with him is making younger Esme shout for joy.

If only for this moment, I'm just Esme. No amnesia. No teaching gig to go back home to. No family drama. No lost and forgotten potential fiancé.

Just Esme.

Better yet, just Lorraine E. Jenkins.

Romance writer.

Too open and honest for her own good.

Finally basking in her hidden, lifelong dream.

Tomorrow, I'll search the depths of the blank space in my brain for answers as Ashton and I travel to Bora Bora.

Chapter Twelve

I Thought Heaven ~ mid-July

I stare at Sam's text message, trying to decide if I want to respond.

Per Mom's request, I've updated her and sent her my trip itinerary. Ashton and I just landed in Bora Bora, and the first message that came through was from my best friend.

> **Sam-I-Am:** I love you. I love you. I love you. And I'm sorry, Meme. Please talk to me. This is self-ish, but I need you. I really need you.

She isn't attempting to guilt-trip me into talking to her; Sam is not like that. Besides harboring the secret alongside my parents, she's never once lied to me or manipulated me. Something must be going on, and so I begrudgingly decide to set aside my anger.

> **Me:** Just landed in Bora Bora. Talk tonight?

I don't bother to factor in time zone differences. If she needs me that badly, she can talk to me when I'm available. It's harsh, I know. But I don't have the energy to go out of my way for someone who lied to me. I'm practicing standing my ground and not giving over to appeasement tendencies.

> **Sam-I-Am:** Yes! Text me when you're ready for me to call. <3

Despite my frustration at Sam, I smile at the old-school heart emoticon. She has always preferred to use the millennial emojis rather than the new and improved emojis.

"Ready?" Ashton asks, grabbing the empty seat in front of him.

The flight attendants start motioning for us to exit, so we stand, grab our bags from overhead, and exit.

"Flying first class through all our flights was quite nice," I say after we leave the tunnel and enter the Bora Bora Airport. It's small, especially compared to LAX, where I wanted to encase myself inside a bubble while we waited out our three-hour layover time. We quickly make it through the space and step outside to a high, hot sun and a balmy wind.

"Like we never left the South," Ashton comments, breathing in the wet, salty air. "Well, with the exception of salt in the air. We both live too far inland for that."

"And crystal clear blue water, green mountains in the distance, and the smell of citrus wafting through the air." I inhale deeply, focusing on my senses, willing myself to remember. *Nothing.* I release my breath and carry on, following Ashton as he leads us to the boat ready to take us to the island and Forever Summer Resort.

Add more of these details into your novel, my little author. Stay focused and take notes. It'll enhance your scene setting, fictional Noah says in a business-like tone.

He's right, naturally.

We pile into the boat along with other happy vacationers, newlyweds, and friend groups. With every step, I'm silently pleading with God for something to happen to cause me to remember.

After a fifteen-minute loading time and a fifteen-minute trip, we exit the boat onto Mute Island where the resort staff are waiting to greet us. After getting a rundown of the resort, safety instructions, and a few pamphlets, we are set free to explore, find our bungalows, and start our "vacation of a lifetime" according to one exuberant employee.

"So, what's the plan?" I ask Ashton as we stand in the main room of the resort while everyone else disperses. "How do we find Noah on this huge resort?"

Ashton scratches his head, looking around. Finally, he lets out an exasperated laugh. "Is it bad I kinda thought we'd arrive here and just... see him?"

I cover my mouth to hide my snicker. "Yes, Ashton." But I can't completely fault him. I contributed to our lack of planning too. With all my emotional spiraling and conflicting feelings, that is. "I guess let's start with getting our stuff in the bungalow, then maybe we just start asking around. See if anyone has come across a man that looks like you."

We meet each other's incredulous gaze and burst into laughter. "Okay, yeah," Ashton swipes his hand through his hair, and a flicker of *something* flashes in my head. "Bungalow first, then harassing poor souls after."

"Does your brother run his hands through his hair a lot?"

Ashton raises his brows, dropping his hand and staring at it. "Yeah, we both do. Habit, I guess."

I follow Ashton as he leads us down winding boardwalk paths, attempting to come up with a more reasonable game plan until we stop outside a large bungalow sitting on stilts atop the glistening ocean. I take in the view with a sense of awe and wonder. Regardless of why I'm here, I'm glad I am. It's as if the ocean is calling me, beckoning me to take a swim in its cool warmth. The sun acts as if it's welcoming me to a place of retreat and healing. The mountains in the distance wave hello, asking me if I've missed them.

Missed them?

I think a little harder, and an image of me sitting on top of a rock on the edge of a mountainous cliff flashes across my vision before disappearing.

Shaking my head clear, I walk into the bungalow after Ashton. Our luggage awaits us by the door. Ashton lets out a low whistle as he roams around the large, open space. "I regret not coming here with Noah last year. This place is heaven on earth."

"I'll say." The room leads directly to an outside deck, and I step out, enjoying the sound of the light waves lapping against the bungalow. There's an outdoor table for dining, and tiki torches stand proudly at the two ocean-side corners. Moving toward the edge, I notice a ladder that leads down into the ocean. A school of small, orange fish dart past the bungalow, and I watch them fade into the water as they journey on. "Paradise."

From inside, Ashton calls out to me. "Do you want the room with the connected bathtub or the one with the ocean view?"

"You decide. I don't care," I holler back, mesmerized by the sparkling water. I slip off my tennis shoes and pull off my socks before sitting down on the edge of the deck and dipping my toes into the warm, surface-level water. I'm here to find Noah, yes, but I also want to soak up every ounce of this experience as I can since the last time I was here feels more like a work of fiction than reality inside of my head. And like the character inside my head commanded, I can use this as story fodder.

I've come to terms with the fact that the events I wrote in my book are actual memories. All that is left to do is have Noah verify it for me, but I know what the answer will be. I can feel it in my soul. I feel the memories now, percolating on the edges of my conscious thought.

"Whoa, this is nice." Ashton's footsteps sound from behind as he steps out onto the deck. He slips off his socks and shoes and joins me on the edge of the deck. We sit in silence, listening to the ocean waves and the slight rustling of the palm trees around us.

I want to stay here forever, but we have a purpose.

"We tossed around the idea of visiting the places I mentioned in my novel earlier while we made the trek here. So, do we want to walk the beach? Maybe check the cabanas and umbrella chairs?"

Ashton rolls up his sleeves. "Yeah, let's do that. But first I'd like to change into my swim shorts." He looks over at me and scrunches his nose as if he's thinking of doing something he ought not to do.

Better run, sweetheart, fictional Noah teases.

My eyes widen in terror as I start to creep backward with my pointer finger up and out. "Nikhil Ashton Prewitt, don't you dare—"

My words are cut short as I tumble into the ocean.

***

"Y ou know what they say about payback." I tighten my ponytail as we walk along the hot sand, the setting sun creating a road across the ocean.

"That's why I needed to change into my swim trunks."

I shove him lightly, but it's like trying to move a wall. My stomach growls, and my hand flies to it as if that will make the stridulant noise stop.

"Should we press pause on our search and get something to eat?" Ashton asks. So far, we've found no trace of Noah. We've asked employees as we've passed them, snooped inside of cabanas, and searched the faces of relaxed humans lounging in beachside chairs. Nothing.

I sigh, fanning myself. "Yeah, that's probably for the best."

"Let's check out that restaurant you mention in the book. What was it called?"

I open the pamphlet and find the name of the Mediterranean restaurant I thought I'd made up. "Puaiti Moana."

Ashton opens his mouth, and I peg him with a glare. "Don't do it."

A wicked smile stretches across his face as he starts to belt, "See the line where the—"

"Ashton!" Though I shout his name in flustered embarrassment as my eyes cut to onlookers, I laugh. Seeing him so open and free, as if he's shaken off his responsibilities and burdens, warms my heart. I think that's what I did last year. Shed the uptight version of myself in favor of a go-with-the-flow type of woman. My stomach grumbles again, so I grab Ashton by the forearm and haul him toward the restaurant.

There is only one wall in the building, the rest being floor-to-ceiling windows. Woven branches of wood meander around the columns that support the building with lights interspersed throughout. It's a romantic, dimly lit dining area with white Tahitian gardenias serving as centerpieces on the small, meant-for-two, round, wooden tables.

"Wow," Ashton and I remark at the same time as we take our seats and receive our menus from a waitress. We look over the options and make small talk while we wait for someone to take our orders.

"I think I'll have the mango fish tacos," I say with a knowing smile. It's one of the dishes I wrote about in my book.

Ashton runs his finger down the menu before stopping and pointing to a dish he can't pronounce. We thank the waitress, and she leaves.

"Yeah, I'm so jealous my brother got to experience all this without me." That strange, regretful sadness tinges his voice once more. I thought he had left it back on the plane, but it seems something caused it to come creeping back.

I take a sip of my lemon water before asking, "Why didn't you come with him a year ago? Don't the two of you do practically everything together?"

A grimace paints Ashton's face, and he looks away, taking a drink of his water. I don't pressure him. I wait quietly until he turns back to me, sets down his cup, and sighs. "Noah wasn't the only Prewitt to fall into a whirlwind romance last year."

The way he spoke of passionate love only two days ago races into my mind. "Do you want to talk about it?"

Crossing his arms and leaning back in his chair, he knits his brows. "Not really, though Branda says it would do me good to tell someone. I haven't even told my family anything outside of the obvious—that Georgiana and I broke up."

Georgiana. I store the name away to social stalk later. "Branda's right, you know. Lord knows I've dumped my mess on you. Now's your chance for your emotional vomiting payback while you await my ocean-centered payback."

Ashton laughs, letting his hands fall to this lap. He's quiet for a moment before he meets my eyes. "Georgiana Beaufort spun into my life like the hurricane she's named after." He pauses, a smile playing at the corner of his lips. "She's the epitome of a Southern belle. Ever seen *Hart of Dixie*?"

"I love that show!"

"Georgiana is the equivalent to season one Lemon Breeland."

"And you are just sweet ole George Tucker, aren't you?" I snort. But then I remember there is heartache at the end of this story. "No. You're not George Tucker. You're Lavon Hayes."

Ashton folds his hands on top of the table, his thumbs moving circles around each other. "Something like that. I almost wish Georgiana had a secret man lying in wait for her. Instead, she ghosted me after three months together. Happened while my brother was here. Georgiana didn't want me to come here without her. I told her I loved her one night, she said it back, and the next morning, I never heard from her again."

His eyes are distant, and I can tell there's more to the story, but I don't want to push him further and sour his time here.

I reach for his hands and take them between mine. The action is affectionate, but not romantic. Over the past couple of days, Ashton has come to feel like a best friend. A brother.

But you have a brother, my mind helpfully reminds me.
One you're not speaking with right now.

I ignore it, choosing to focus on Ashton right now. "It's for
the best, right?" He nods as if he's unsure, but I continue
talking. "You're in Bora Bora right now. Let's forget about
hurricanes and enjoy this paradise while we're here hunting
your brother."

Snickering at my phrasing, a glow rushes back to Ashton's
face, and I pull my hands away. "Feels like we're *hunting* him
down, huh?"

Our food arrives, and I rush to try the mango fish tacos.
Once I get past the burning sensation from the heat, an
explosion of flavor covers my tongue. Suddenly, I'm back
on the deck, eating similar tacos with a man who looks
like Ashton but isn't him. Noah is laughing, but I'm sitting
cross-armed and staring him down, trying not to show any
hint of excitement. But I *feel* them. The emotions at that
moment—nervous yet comfortable, thrilling excitement,
longing, and confusion—flooded my heart.

"Oh." I gasp through a mouthful of food. I chew quickly
and swallow as a single tear runs down my cheek.

"It's that good?" Ashton raises a single brow, holding
some kind of sandwich to his face as if he was about to bite
into it, but then he saw me.

"Another memory."

We finish our meal and meander back to our bungalow,
but Ashton is spent and retires for the evening while I go
for a walk under the setting sun. Everything about this

place feels familiar, like there's something lingering below the surface of my mind that I can't quite grasp. It's a haze, and when I attempt to grab the fleeting fog, it dissipates between my fingers, vanishing.

It's frustrating.

I kick the sand and stare out onto the beach, listening to the soft waves break against the shore. I've searched the faces of the beachgoers, and none of them resemble Ashton. Some sinking feeling within me says I'm wasting my time, that Noah's not here. But can I trust my intuition?

Groaning, I continue walking up the beach and back to the boardwalk. *God, please?* I plead. *Help me remember. Give me a sign. Anything. Tell me if I'm on the right path or the wrong—*

"Ah!" I scream as my sandal snags on a loose board, and I plummet toward the boardwalk. I break my fall with my hands, but the texture of the splinters beneath my bare thighs are like little lightning strikes to my memory, conjuring a starry sky, guttural screams, and blood. Lots of blood.

And just as quickly as the images appear in my head, they're gone again.

"GOD! WHY?" I holler, uncaring if anyone hears me. I ball my fist as I stand, breathing deeply to calm myself. Then hot tears of anger roll down my face as I clutch the cross necklace. What am I doing here? Noah isn't here. I don't know how I know that, but I do. I watch as a couple walks into a bungalow, realizing it's number twenty-one.

The one I stayed in. With Noah.

My heart speeds up as I realize I'm in the area where Noah and I were attacked. Something otherworldly comes over me, and I frantically search the boardwalk, looking for any traces of blood or nicks in the wood possibly caused by a knife. Hitting my knees, I pull at my hair as I scrape at the boardwalk, looking for *something. Anything.* And I don't stop crawling around like a madwoman until Ashton's at my side, lifting me to my feet, and pulling me into a tight embrace as I sob in his arms. "It's unfair, Ashton. It's unfair."

"I know, Esme."

***

L ater that night, after I calmed down and collected myself, apologizing profusely to Ashton who insisted it's a plenty normal reaction to have, I pull up and stare at Sam's contact, my finger hovering over the "call" button.

Fortifying my walls and mustering my willpower, I press the button on the screen.

Within one ring, a sniffling Sam picks up the phone. "Esme," she cries, drawing out the "me" sound of my name. "I don't know what to do."

Alarm rings through me, and I straighten up in bed, pulling the soft, downy white blankets over my legs. "Sam? What happened? Are you okay?" A million possibilities pass through my mind, all past transgressions on her end forgotten.

I hear Ethan in the background, telling Sam he's going to get her a glass of water. Then, Sam says, "Esme! They are talking about canceling Shakin' Up the 'Speare!"

My heart drops in my chest, though I'm partially relieved she's not dying or seriously injured. But I know how much this theater group means to her. She's worked her butt off to not only help establish it but also to build it from the ground up. Theater has always been her passion, and this was a dream of hers.

"Sam, I'm so sorry," I whisper into the phone. "What happened?"

My best friend speaks in a jumbled mess as I strain to understand her. "We were looking to expand our production down to the coast, and then Bradford, you know, our owner, got tangled up in a lawsuit with the Callahan family. Bradford won't tell me all the details, but he said the Callahans were backing us financially and now they've pulled their funding due to a dispute between one of our actresses down in Willow Bay, Remi Martin, and Johnny Callahan's son, Julien."

"What dispute?"

"I don't know," Sam exasperates. "I'm trying to figure it out, but I keep running into dead ends. Both of their social media accounts are down. There are no local reports mentioned of a feud, though it does seem the two families, the Martins and the Callahans, have a history of going to war with one another."

"Huh," is all I respond with. While Sam says something to Ethan, I think over everything she's said, trying to make sense of it all. "Honestly, it sounds like a small-town feud that the theater got caught up in the middle of. Kinda rude on the Callahans' part, if you ask me."

"Yeah, that's for sure," Sam scoffs, sniffling again. "And poor Remi. She's just an absolute mess thinking this whole thing is her fault. I'm going down to Willow Bay in the morning to meet up with her and try to figure out what's going on since Bradford's keeping me in the dark."

I find myself nodding along though Sam can't see me. "Yeah, well, let me know what you find out. I'll be praying for you and over the situation."

Silence settles between us for a beat before Sam, in a small voice, says, "Thank you, Meme. I just needed to talk to my best friend."

Tears prickle in my eyes as my heart unfreezes. "Me too. I've missed you."

"I'm so sorry, Meme. This isn't my excuse, but it's my reason. I'm married to your brother, and I didn't want to step on my in-law's toes by going against their wishes. You don't have to believe me, but I promise you, I told them time and time again that they were wrong and that you deserved to know. I tried, Meme. I tried."

She sobs on the other end of the line, and I join in, knowing good and well she's telling me the truth. I can hear the honesty and the heartbreak in her tone. I can feel her presence through this device. And I know it's only a small step in mending what's been unraveled, but I take it. "I forgive you, Sammie. I understand, I do. But I'm still hurt. That's going to take some time to heal."

"I know," she says through her tears. "And Meme?"

"Yeah?"

"I'm proud of you. For standing your ground."

***

The sun shines a little brighter today as Ashton and I head for the paint studio I wrote about in my novel.

"What's got you in a buoyant mood?" Ashton asks as we walk down the boardwalk. Crowds of people are out today, basking in the sun, sipping on drinks, and enjoying life.

"I talked to Sam last night."

"Oh? And?"

Smiling softly as I remember her words—how she told me she was proud of me for standing up for myself—I meet Ashton's hazel eyes and reply, "I forgave her."

"Forgiveness frees the soul, doesn't it?" Ashton throws his head back for a moment as the sunlight pours down upon him.

I think of the hurt and the betrayal I still feel like a week-old wound. "Eh, it's a start."

Ashton laughs, and then we continue to look around for Noah, asking employees as we pass them. We do that until we reach the paint studio, which is currently in the middle of a session as we walk through the propped-open door.

Today, the model is a young, blond-haired man who looks the epitome of a California surfer guy. All eyes turn to me and Ashton, and the director of the studio, an older, petite woman with thick black hair and round glasses, shouts, "It's you!"

Within moments, she's standing before us, her jaw dropped to the floor.

"Hi there," Ashton says. "My name is Ashton, and this is Esme. We are looking for..."

"You're the woman who got attacked last year." Her pin-prick eyes flick to Ashton. "You were our model."

"No, ma'am." Ashton waves both his hands in dismissal. "That was my twin brother, Noah. Speaking of, have you seen him? Another guy that looks like me walking about?"

She shakes her head, the beads to her glasses chain holder clinking. "Dear, how are you?"

"I, uh—" I look to Ashton for help, but he shrugs, leaving me to tell my own story. "I'm good now. I have amnesia from the attack, so I don't remember you. I'm sorry."

A certain air of pity fills her rotund face. "We heard about what happened, and I've been praying for you both. It's nice to see you and get an update." She tilts her head. "And your man? You said you were looking for him?"

Now Ashton speaks up. "Yes, my twin. He's been missing for two months, and we thought he might have run off to come here. It's the anniversary of the accident."

The woman frowns. "I'm sorry, sincerely. I wish I had information. I..."

As she continues talking, I sweep my eyes around the room, taking in the open windows, canvas, and paintbrushes. The countertops around the walls of the room are full of paint and splatters. The walls boast artwork, one particularly catching my attention.

I break away from Ashton and the woman, and as I get closer to the bright orange painting that snagged my gaze, I realize it's Noah. In orange shorts and a bright orange cape with NAP written on it. My knees buckle beneath me as I take in the intricate tattoo on his arm, and finally, in the corner, my initials: ELJ.

Not allowing myself to think through my actions, I grab the painting off the wall and hold it behind my back as I turn toward Ashton and the woman, who is still in conversation. Keeping my front side to her, I stand beside Ashton and interrupt. "I'm not feeling well, Ashton. Can we go back to the bungalow?"

He narrows his eyes in confusion as he studies me, and I try to keep my face as innocent as possible. Thankfully, he decides to play along with me versus questioning me. We say our goodbyes to the woman and thank her for her time, then I spin on my heel, moving the canvas and pressing it against my stomach.

"Is that one of my—" the woman begins, but I break into a sprint.

Ashton catches up easily as I run through the crowd, clutching my painting. "Why are we—what do you have there?"

I keep running just in case she sent anyone after me. "My painting. Of Noah. I found it!"

"And you stole it?"

"Just keep running!"

After a few minutes of running and consistently looking back to make sure we aren't being followed, we slow to a walk, catching our breaths.

"Can I see it?" Ashton asks. I hand him the painting.

"Don't judge my skills too hard."

He snorts, and I watch him as he examines the photo, his eyes misting over.

"Is it that good?" I smirk, repeating what he told me after I took a bite of the mango fish taco yesterday evening and had a flash of memory return.

"Har har." He comes to a stop right in front of our bungalow. "Actually, the painting isn't bad at all. You did a good job of capturing my brother's arrogance."

I chuckle, taking the canvas back. "If I had any smidgen of doubt that my book was anything less than memories, it's banished. This painting... It's real. Down to making him the superhero of naps."

"I don't think he's here, Esme. I think we would have found him by now. Unless he's on the top of a mountain somewhere."

Grimacing, I nod in agreement. "Yeah, me either. I just have this intrinsic feeling he's not here."

"Is there anywhere else?"

I search my brain for what I remember from my novel, for what I remember from snooping in his journals. But I come up blank. "I don't know, Ashton. I'm a little too overwhelmed right now, I think."

"Do you want to stay here for the remaining few days we booked, or do you want to cut out early?"

As much as I'm loving this place, I long for home. I want to hug Sam. I want to talk to my parents face to face. I want to start making everything okay again. I want to find Noah and hear from him exactly what happened to us a year ago. I still don't understand why God has done this, but I'm not feeling so out of sorts about it anymore. The more I pray, the more I feel that God is telling me to go home. *Keep trusting me. Take the path home.*

"Let's go home. But for now," I trail off, keeping my eyes glued to the painting instead of looking over the edge of the boardwalk and into the ocean. "It's time for payback." I throw myself into Ashton, watching him flail over the edge and into the water with a tremendous splash as he yells my name.

Atta girl, the masculine voice in my head praises.

Where are you? I ask it back.

Chapter Thirteen

I Can See ~ mid-July

I despise confrontation.

But I love the smell of homemade lasagna, my favorite dish. It's the first thing to hit my senses as I walk through my parents' door and into the house. I arrived home from Bora Bora late last night, and ever since I woke up this morning, I've been preparing myself for this talk.

You can do this, Esme, I mentally motivate myself. *You used to despise confrontation. This new you, however, can handle it.*

I glance at Ethan, who sits on the recliner with an exhausted-from-traveling-all-morning Sam in his lap, watching some ultimate frisbee competition on the television. A wave of frustration washes over me at my older brother's lack of caring. It's not that I expect him to go out of his way to apologize and beg for my forgiveness for the wretched lies he took part in, but the seeming lack of remorse on his end rattles me.

Sam notices me in the doorway, crawls off my brother, and runs to bear hug me. "I've missed you, Meme." The smell of lasagna mingles with her floral perfume and apricot shampoo. I wrap her up, snuggling my face into her blonde hair.

"I've missed you too, Sammie."

"Mmm." We give each other one last squeeze before my mom pushes between us.

"You're back, sweetie." Mom holds me tight, and I return the action even though there's still much to be discussed between us. She's my mom, and I love her more than anything.

We pull apart, her hands moving from my upper back to my biceps as she stares at me with water-filled eyes and a sad smile. The wrinkles in her forehead and the black circles under her eyes cause my chest to ache. Coming out of my initial anger, I feel terrible that I put her through this past week of absence, only allowing her to know I was safe and alive.

I remember the hazy weeks after I woke up from the coma. Mom mothered more than I could ever remember her doing. She's always hovered and spoken her opinions, but this was a whole new level. She attended to my every suspected need, rarely leaving my side as my ribs, lung, and head healed. She fretted over my food and water intake, and any time I got a small ache in my head, she'd make me lie down and stare at the wall until it passed. Dad stopped her on more than one occasion from dragging me to the hospital over it.

A couple of months later, I found my voice. I had started writing, had gone back to work, and finally decided to move into the lightly used camper I had bought off the Hillsdales as soon as I heard they were selling it. Bless them, they gave me a supermassive discount. I think the whole town felt sorry for me because Mom wouldn't let me go anywhere without her. While I was at work, she would call me during every class transition and break.

That conversation rings loudly in my head.

"Mom," I had snapped. "I need my space! Quit smothering me!"

The stunned, confused look in her eyes as we talked underneath the magnolia tree standing erect on the side of the house almost had me backtracking. Almost.

"What do you mean? I'm only trying to make sure you're safe and healthy, sweetie."

"I'm twenty-six, Mom." I had fought to keep the fearful quiver out of my voice. "I can take care of myself, can look out for myself. I don't need your hovering and fretting."

Mom had opened her mouth. Closed it. Huffed. Tugged at her jean shorts. "I love you, Esme. I don't want to see you dead." Her voice had raised, and she crossed her arms. "Is that not allowed? Is a mother not allowed to worry about her injured daughter who almost died while halfway around the world?"

"Of course you're allowed to worry," I had said, attempting to work around her straw man argument. "All I'm saying is that I'm an adult, and I have to stand on my own two feet and get my life back on track."

She was quiet for a minute before she dropped her hands to her side and nodded her head, letting out a long-winded sigh. "You're right, I'm sorry. I just—" She sniffled. "You scared me, Esme. I didn't know if you'd wake up. You were texting me and saying you were safe and having a good time, and then you missed your flight home and we got a call from the police."

Her pain was palpable, so I wrapped her in a tight hug as we cried together. From then on out, she slowly loosened her hold on the metaphorical leash she had around me.

Maybe I would have understood better if I had known the truth of what happened in Bora Bora and why she clung so closely to me.

Shaking the memories from my head, I smile at Mom. "It's good to be home. Lasagna smells amazing."

"Made it just for you, sweetie."

"Hey, baby girl," Dad pronounces, walking around the wall that divides the living room from the kitchen. "Glad you're back. How was Bora Bora?"

Though his voice is upbeat, and there is a smile on his face, I can see the relief in his eyes and, like Mom, the dark circles underneath. Guilt over greatly worrying my parents nestles deep into my bones. "It was bright. Hot. Humid."

"So not that much different than Mississippi, huh?" Dad jokes.

I hug him, my arms not quite fitting around his rotund belly. "Nope. Not really."

"Well, lunch is ready. Y'all come on to the kitchen." Mom unties her apron as she shuffles across the tile floor of the kitchen, Dad and I following behind her. Ethan and Sam enter from the other side. It's a small space, but we have just enough room at the round table for all five of us to sit comfortably. We load our plates with lasagna and sit down. Dad makes Ethan say a prayer over the food, and then we dig in. In the awkward absence of speech, the metal forks clang against the glass plates, the sounds of chewing drive me up the wall, and Ethan, in his boyish grossness, farts.

It does, however, break the silence.

Mom smarts. "Ethan Marshall Jenkins! You know better, son. I didn't raise you to be a heathen at the dinner table."

Sam's expression matches Ethan's smug face, though she does have the decency to elbow my brother. When Sam looks my way, I roll my lips into my mouth to keep from smiling.

Just like old times, I think to myself. It's then I realize my brother is doing what he does best—just trying to make me laugh. That's his way of apologizing, even if it isn't the most emotionally mature way to handle things. Like me, he doesn't like it when there are disagreements and fights within our family unit, even if he's the source of over half of them with his reckless spending.

To save him from further chastisement, and to get this over with, I clear my throat. "So, let's talk about the elephant in the room, shall we?"

Mom sets down her fork while Dad shoves another bite into his mouth. Sam wipes her face, and Ethan looks down at his plate, chopping up his slab of lasagna.

After a beat of silence, Mom speaks. "We just didn't want to mess up, Esme. The doctor said you should discover the forgotten memories on your own. He said we risked implanting false memories if we attempted to fill in gaps we had no knowledge of. So, we came up with the idea of the jet ski accident because it would cause less trauma than telling you that you were almost kidnapped, attacked, and watched a man almost die."

"We thought Noah would die," Dad adds. At the horror on my face, he quickly says, "We were relieved when we heard he survived, but by that point, you were starting to get back on your feet. We didn't want anything to set back your healing."

Surprising me, Ethan speaks up, a tinge of bitterness in his voice. "And face it, Esme. How were we supposed to know that Noah wasn't the guy who got you into that mess in the first place? Dad was just trying to keep you safe by turning him away."

Oh. Oh. My brother has blamed Noah this entire time.

Sam visibly shrinks.

"Look," I say, looking each of them in the eyes and mustering as much appreciation in my tone as I can. "I get it. I do. I understand. But it doesn't excuse the deception. What if my memories would have come back with the truth? What if it's been too long, and even the truth won't set them free?" My voice cracks over the last word, and I shift my gaze upward to keep tears from spilling over.

Mom stands and moves to place a hand on my shoulder. "Sweetie, we are terribly sorry. I'm sorry. We shouldn't have lied regardless of the situation."

"Please forgive us, Esme," Dad tacks on. "I wish we could take it back, but the only thing we can do is move forward."

I want to believe them. I do. Something still bothers me, however. "Why would you keep a man away from me when you've shoved the importance of stability down my throat all of these years? Wouldn't getting married help provide stability?"

Mom blinks at me a few times while Dad whistles low. "That's yours to tackle, Melina."

Mom gives Dad an odd look. Then, to me, she says, "Of course I want you to get married one day. And to have stability. But Esme, I don't want you to just marry any ole man off the street. Marriage is sacred. You should only marry someone when you know *that you know* that person is your forever. It's why I had my qualms about you marrying Bryan."

"You didn't want me to marry him?" My jaw drops at this revelation.

Mom wipes a tear from her eye. "No, not really. He gave all of us a bad vibe. But we weren't going to interfere. It's your life."

I want to laugh at the hypocrisy, but I don't. Because Mom only tried to control my life when I was still trying to figure out what happened to it. It dawns on me that she was simply a terrified mother unsure of what was going on. Just as I was attempting to figure things out, too. She wanted to protect me, and while I still don't like how she went about it, I think I understand. But all this time... I've thought she was ready to push me out of the house and hitch me to the first man she saw. But no. That was a false reality I concocted in my head. A motive I assigned to her without questioning it.

The tears push their way out as I stand and hug Mom. "I'm so sorry for worrying y'all over the past week. I just needed space."

"We know, sweetie." Mom silently cries onto my shoulder. "But did you really think I wanted to marry you off quickly in the name of stability?"

I nod, sniffling.

Mom whispers against my ear as she hugs me close. "Sweetie, I need you to know that I want you to have a marriage full of love and romance and friendship, just like I have with your father. Stability is important, but who you marry is the most important decision you can make outside of giving your life to the Lord. When the Lord brings that man into your life, you will know it. Just as I knew your father was the one for me."

Dad joins the hug as I break into heavier sobs, and before we know it, he squeezes us tight and picks us both up. "I love my girls."

We break into tearful laughs, and when my feet are planted firmly back onto the floor, I narrow my eyes at my brother.

"Ethan," I drag out his name through my ragged breaths. "Get over here."

He rolls his eyes, but I don't miss the smile hiding behind his bearded face. Sam pushes Ethan out of his chair and drags him to the hug pile. I stand there, surrounded by my family, feeling a little more whole than I have in a while. It's true what they say—fights bring family closer together. When you can trust someone enough to fight with them, beautiful bridges are built to bury all of the nasty water under it.

Ethan mutters against my ear as his brown beard scratches my cheek. "I'm sorry, Meme. I just don't ever want to see you unconscious on a hospital bed again. You hear me? And no more forgetting years of memories between us."

Tears spring free once more, but this time, they're ones of completeness and healing. I sometimes forget that my infirmities impacted those closest to me. We all have mountains to overcome together.

"And for the record," Ethan adds, "I did try to talk you out of marrying Bryan. You got hot mad at me and Sam over it."

"Well, thank you, I guess. And sorry for getting mad."

Ethan steps back and shrugs while Sam laughs.

"Mom," I say, breaking free from the huddle. "I wrote in my book that you pushed me to go on my honeymoon to find someone new. Is that true?"

"Well, I said that, yeah. But mainly because I wanted you to go out and experience something your father and I have never been able to afford to do. I didn't really want you to meet some stranger on an island halfway across the world."

Sam giggles as we all move back to the table and sit. "Oh, but that's exactly what you did. And I, for one, am proud of you for that."

"So, if I find him," I look to Dad, "you aren't going to try and put a restraining order on him, are you?"

"No, baby girl. Not unless he hurts you." He pauses for a second, then adds, "If your book is true, then I need to shake that man's hand, look him in the eyes, and thank him for saving your life."

***

Rubbing my sweating palms onto my jeans, I take a deep breath. *In. Hold. Release.*

"Chill out, Esme. Lucy May's not gonna bite you."

I'm sitting beside Ashton in a quaint coffee shop-slash-bookstore called Books and Beans in the Lucy May's hometown of Juniper Grove, Mississippi. My all-time favorite author. Ashton picked me up on his way through, and we drove nearly two hours north to attend The Sweet Tea Writers Association's quarterly in-person gathering.

"Esme." Ashton waves a hand in front of my face. I snap to attention, pulling my gaze off the flourishing bird-of-paradise plant sitting on the windowsill by the door.

"I've read all her books, Ashton. I'm nervous. She's like a legend to me."

Ashton folds his arms across his dark green Henley shirt. The color pops nicely against his tanned skin and brings out the green in his hazel eyes. The familiarity of him eases me, and once more, I'm awestruck that I found a friend in him so quickly.

My said friend, however, is scowling at me. "You only fangirled for a half of a second when it came to me. And that half of a second was an hours-long afterthought."

I raise my eyebrows. "Really, Ashton? You told me you had a twin who apparently wanted to marry me before I lost my memories and that we both almost died because of some kidnapper. But no, I was supposed to focus on the fact that you're one half of *the* Ashton Ashley."

"He's always had a bit of an ego when it comes to his stories," a feminine voice retorts from beside us. My mouth opens and closes like a fish out of water as a curly-haired redhead with hazel eyes and a tremendous amount of freckles on her face stretches out her hand, a toddler wrapping himself around her leg. Lucy May acts as if she doesn't even notice the boy. "Hi. I'm Lucy Harper. It's so nice to finally meet you, Esme. Noah went on and on about you. I'm sorry about the memory loss. That sucks."

Swallowing the starstruck lump in my throat, I grab her hand, and in the process, knock over my coffee, which proceeds to spill all over the table. I yank my hand back, squealing a string of apologies as I hunt down napkins to clean the mess. *Where are the napkins in this place?*

Just as I move to go check the front counter, the blonde barista walks over carrying a towel. "I got it!" she says, setting to work easily cleaning up my mess.

When she's done, she kisses Lucy on the cheek. "Good to see you again, Luce." The barista bends and ruffles the blond hair of the boy still attached to Lucy's leg. "And good to see you, too, Mr. Andrew Harper. Where's your twin?"

Andrew roars like a monster as he hollers, "Daddy!"

Lucy laughs, shaking her head. "Patton's with Stone heading to Dasher Valley. We divided and conquered today. I'm leaving to join my boys after our meeting. Speaking of," Lucy motions me over. I feel like the Tin Man as I force my joints to work. I'd been standing back, watching the madness unfold with a slack jaw. "This is Esme Jenkins. She's joining our writing group."

My heart thuds as I shake the barista's hand. "Hi, it's nice to meet you. Sorry for the mess."

The woman waves me off, her bright smile infectious. "It's no big deal, girl. I'm Emma Jane, by the way. The owner."

Mortification doesn't begin to address the feeling that implodes through me. The owner of this place cleaned up after my mess? If this had happened back at Main Street Coffee, Katie would have thrust a mop into my hands and told me to get to work, relishing in the role reversal where she could boss her former teacher around. "Again, I'm so sorry," I hurriedly state.

Emma Jane waves me off again and then tells Lucy May that she'll watch Andrew. Lucy thanks her with a hug, and then Emma Jane pries Andrew off his mother's leg. "Whew, what a start to the meeting," Lucy says, taking her seat across from me.

"I just watched from afar," comes a masculine voice from behind me. "Y'all didn't even see me come in. That was chaotic."

Lucy and Ashton, at the same time, shout, "Chase!" and jump up. Lucy hugs him like a brother and then Ashton does the bro-pat on his back. I stay firmly seated to not cause any more messes.

"Meet Esme," Ashton says. I get a good look at the tall, chiseled, lean man. He's got honey-blond hair and gorgeous dark blue eyes. "Esme, this is Chase Hayes. Also known as Rac—"

"Stop it!" I shout before he finishes as I connect the dots, going over the mental list of Mississippi authors I keep in my head. I cover my mouth with both hands. Everyone laughs as I stare wide-eyed at yet another one of my favorite contemporary romance authors. I drop my hands, making the decision that I couldn't possibly embarrass myself further. "You're a guy?"

He shrugs with a smirk, then walks with Lucy to sit across from me and Ashton.

"I feel like I'm in the presence of romance royalty," I say, still dumbfounded. Emma Jane returns and sets a new iced caramel latte down in front of me before rushing back to a mischievously giggling toddler.

"Never a dull moment when we all meet up," Ashton says through a wide smile. "Where's Katy, though? I thought she was flying in."

"Oh! She texted me this morning and said she woke up late. She said she's going to sit this meeting out but will join our Zoom one next month." Lucy shows us the message from Katherine Newcomb.

"Is she published?" I ask.

Chase nods. "Katy is a natural disaster journalist. But on the side, she's writing a mystery romance novel. It will be her debut into the world of fiction."

"I remember your debut into fiction two years ago," Lucy comments. "I'm glad you decided romance was worth writing in the midst of your bland political analysis books."

Chase bristles a bit, but he quickly regains control and smirks. "Your twin loves them."

"That she does." Lucy laughs. "Speaking of, I need a signed copy of your new one before you leave. I'm traveling to Korsa for Lorelei's family-only baby shower and can give it to her then. She'll like a book more than another noisemaker for baby Estelle. Finley will also be pleased not to deal with an overstimulated and hormonal wife."

It dawns on me that Queen Lorelei Andersson is Lucy's twin. I remember hearing about the marriage four years ago. Every woman in Mississippi wanted to be her.

Who are these people, and how did I find them?!

"Speaking of husbands and wives," Chase comments, fixing his gaze on me and Ashton. "You've returned from Bora Bora, but Noah isn't present."

I want to ask how that has anything to do with marriage, but Noah must have told them that we were—I swallow—engaged. Guess it's true, then. My palms start sweating again.

Ashton saves me the pressure of responding. "He wasn't there. We're going through Esme's manuscript to try and find where he might be. We were hoping to get y'all's help today."

"Do you remember anything, Esme?" Chase asks. Ashton shoots him a glare.

"A little," I respond truthfully, once more rubbing my palms onto my jeans. "I've started having little glimpses. Emotions. Remembering smells, sounds, and specific moments."

"And do they align with your book?" Lucy May asks, leaning on the table toward me.

"Yeah, so far. I guess." Outside that one glimpse where I seemed outwardly closed off to Noah, that is.

She grins. "Then let's dive in. I want our Noah found. This group ain't half as funny without him."

Ashton mocks offense, but we laugh (me uncomfortably, of course).

This table of all-star romance authors is about to read my incomplete manuscript. *Mine.*

"Hey," Ashton whispers against my ear. "They're going to love it. And any feedback will be constructive and polite, I promise."

Nodding once, determination taking over, I reach into my backpack and pull out my laptop and my printed manuscript. "Here. Dig away. I'm going to go throw up now."

Lucy laughs, but I slide out of my seat and head through the bookstacks to the bathroom. Once inside, I take a moment to collect myself and not think about the authors I love reading my book. My phone buzzes in my back pocket.

Ashton Prewitt: Don't hide away, Esme.

"Pft. Easy for you to say." I shove my phone back into my pocket and grab a paper towel to blot the sweat from my face and neck. As much as I love Mississippi, sometimes I really wish I could live somewhere cooler. Somewhere that had an actual winter and more mild summers. Like Alaska or something.

I toss the paper towel into the trash, daydreaming of snow.

Alaska.

Honeymoon.

Crescent Cove.

There it is, sweetheart. Come find the real me, the deep voice living inside my head purrs.

I plow through the door, tripping over my feet as I announce to the entire coffee shop in a breathless voice, "I know where he is!"

Chapter Fourteen

Getting Good Now ~ Late July

Two days later, Ashton and I find ourselves once again on a plane, but this time, our destination is the wild expanse of Alaska.

I had an epiphany in the bathroom of Books and Beans.

Noah and I were planning to honeymoon in Crescent Cove, Alaska, a part I completely skimmed over when reviewing my book with Ashton before we left for Bora Bora. We had only talked about it, never made official plans. But something in my gut tells me that's where we will find him.

The character inside my head tends to agree.

How we will hunt him down in the quaint small town, I have no idea. But we've got to try.

The lights flicker on, and the pilot announces we've begun our descent into Ted Stevens International Airport. I raise my right shoulder up and down, causing Ashton's head to bounce. "Wake up, sleepy head. We're landing soon."

"Mm." Ashton groans and stretches as much as the room on this plane will allow him and his long limbs. We are flying first class again, but first class on Alaska Airlines is much different than on our previous flight to Bora Bora. "How long was I out?"

"Long enough to drool on me." I point to a wet spot on the shoulder of my sweatshirt.

A sheepish look passes across Ashton's face. "Sorry, Meme."

I raise an eyebrow. "Meme? Who told you my nickname?"

"You use it for your Esme character in the book. Figured you went by it."

"Do you have a nickname?" I ask as we give our trash to a flight attendant.

Ashton shakes his head, but he's hiding a smile.

"Yes, you do," I excuse. "Tell me or I text Branda to find out."

He groans, rubbing a hand down his tired-looking face. "Ashy. It's stupid. Don't ever call me that."

"Does Noah have a Branda-given nickname?"

Ashton smirks. "She just likes to call him by his middle name, Ashley, because she thinks it's strictly a female name. It's why he chose to use it for publishing. Just to stick it to her."

We continue chatting about family nicknames and things we did with our siblings when we were younger as the plane bounces onto the runway. Once we come to a stop, we grab our bags and once more, set out into another airport in order to track down Noah Prewitt.

"Oh my," I say just as Ashton states in astonishment, "Wow."

We are staring at taxidermied polar bears inside of a glass display.

"I think I might like it here," Ashton hums as we continue to find our way around the airport. We pass by more animals in display cages—moose, brown bears, and a musk ox.

We pick up our rental vehicle, and then we're heading to find food before starting the three-hour drive down the peninsula to Crescent Cove, Alaska.

"Anchorage was more crowded than I expected," I note as we merge south onto the Seward highway. Ashton agrees, and then we fall into mesmerized silence. I stare in awe out of the window at the mountain ranges around us and the high noon sun shining through an overcast sky. The air is crisp but warm as we ride with the sunroof open and windows cracked, and I already know I want to come back to this place after I leave. The roads wind, a cliff on Ashton's side with the Turnagain Arm on my side. When the sun breaks through the clouds, it causes the water to sparkle like deep, solid, blue diamonds. Where the water in Bora Bora was see-through, this water is a block of sea blue. I can taste magic in the air, if such a thing exists.

After we've been driving for about an hour and a half and my bladder is on the verge of exploding, I ask, "Where is the nearest bathroom? There's like nowhere to stop."

"How should I know?" Ashton retorts. I look at my phone for the millionth time, checking for signal, and squeal when I see two bars and LTE. I quickly search for restrooms along Seward highway and find a place called Caveman's coming up soon in Cooper Landing.

I set the GPS to take us there and memorize the photo of the wooden building with eclectic-looking signs out in the front of it in case my phone loses signal again.

Once we're heading out from the convenience store that also happened to have delicious ice cream, Ashton comments, "We'll be there in a little over an hour. Are you ready?"

The ice cream sitting heavy in my stomach churns. "I guess I have to be." I pause, then add, "Will you see him first? Whenever we find him? If we find him?" Though my gut tells me he's here, there are still seeds of doubt. My soul knows the Noah of my book. I've written him in perfect detail. He yaps in my head all the time, and I wonder if my memory of him merged with fiction to create the character who talks too much.

Rude, he says, interrupting my thoughts. *You like my yapping.*

Proving my point, I smart back.

Ultimately, Noah still feels like a fantasy of sorts. He's real, no doubt. But I want to set my eyes on him, to see the truth of him. To see if I got him right.

But I want Ashton to take the lead because I'm terrified and nervous.

"Of course," Ashton responds as we take tight curves slowly, evergreens all around us with the Kenai River flowing quickly off to the side.

"So," I take a deep breath, "we are going to visit different stores and restaurants in Crescent Cove and ask if anyone has seen another you." The plan is weak, just like Bora Bora, but it's all we can do when there is no way to digitally track Noah.

I fight the anxiety rising as we eventually pass a sign that reads "Welcome to Crescent Cove" with mermaids hugging either side of the distressed, gray, wooden sign. A faint longing for magic and folklore glitters around me. And as we enter the town, I gasp.

"This is much more crowded than I expected." People walk down the sidewalks in packs wearing waders and carrying poles, ice chests, and large nets.

"Fishing and dip netting season." Ashton grimaces. "It's the height of tourism here."

Just great.

"Should we park somewhere and walk around? This traffic is atrocious."

Ashton nods, and we make our way into the parking lot of Crescent Cove Park, which sits on the edge of the Kenai River.

Bad choice. This is where all the fishermen are parked.

We find a spot after ten minutes of looking, lock up the vehicle, and begin walking underneath the cloudy, evening sky. Though you wouldn't be able to tell it's approaching five in the evening, the sun is still high in the sky, hiding behind light gray clouds. The light wind coming off the river is cool and invigorating, kissing my face. We walk around the small town for an hour, asking cashiers at stores, waiters at restaurants, and random people on the street until we meander into a dive bar called The Siren's Call. It's a small place with only a few other people frequenting it right now. A couple plays pool while a group of elderly gentlemen sit at a table, shooting the wind and drinking beer. The whole vibe of this place is centered around the ocean, sirens, pirates, and sailing, and I'm starting to think much of this town is steeped in mermaid-esque mythology. Collapsing on rickety barstools, we both release exhausted sighs. My feet ache from walking, my skin is drying out quicker than a drop of water on hot Mississippi asphalt, and I'm feeling a headache coming on.

"What will it—" The bartender, a tall native man, stops in his tracks as he enters from the back of the bar room. "Noah? Back already? And with a friend and a haircut?" The bartender smiles warmly at me, his white teeth standing out against his tawny skin.

The aches are long forgotten.

Ashton looks at me before snapping his attention back to the man and stretching out his hand. "Hi, I'm Ashton Prewitt. Noah's my twin. He's been here?"

"Big Bear," the man says, clasping Ashton's hand and shaking it heartedly. "Yeah, your brother's been here. Nearly every day with Nick, though thankfully, Noah's stopped drinking so much. It was rough when he first got here."

My heart races in my chest as my palms begin to sweat. Noah is here. In this town. Has been in this very place. *Has had it rough. Because of me.* "Where is he now?" I butt in. Then remembering my manners, I introduce myself. "I'm Esme Jenkins."

Big Bear's smile falls. "Do you remember him? He told me everything."

I knit my brows together. "No. Yes? I don't know. I wrote a book about us and apparently it's real, though I don't necessarily remember it not being fiction and—"

"She's on her way." Ashton interrupts my rambling to this perfect stranger. I'm too out of my mind for this. "Do you know where my brother might be?"

Big Bear nods, wiping a glass dry with a towel. "Probably at Nick's. He's been staying there for the past month after they met here and became friends bonding over their," he smirks, "romantic woes, despite what Nick likes to tell himself."

Ashton and I exchange glances, then he asks, "Where can we find this Nick guy?"

"Nick Lancaster lives down Holiday Avenue."

"Is there an address I can plug into my GPS?" I ask.

"Outsiders." Big Bear shakes his head, but then he gives us the address of Nick Lancaster. We thank him, then make the five minute straight-line walk to our rental car.

Once buckled up and pulling out of the Crescent Cove Park parking lot, Ashton gives me a tight smile. "Ready?"

I press the route button on the GPS, and the woman's voice announces our destination. Ten minutes away. My head is spinning once again; blood swooshes in my ears.

"I think my blood pressure's rising," I state, twirling my thumbs in my lap. "Sky high, Ashton. Sky high. I'm about to meet the real version of the man I wrote about."

He chuckles humorlessly, and I press my lips together. He's just as nervous as I am.

I ramble on, more to myself than to Ashton. "I wrote him so perfectly in my book. Is he truly the perfect man?"

Ashton responds anyway. "I hate to be the bearer of bad news, Meme, but my brother is far from perfect. But—" Ashton throws me a small smile. "—I think he might be perfect *for* you." It sounds like Ashton mutters something about shock over Noah and drinking, but I'm too on edge to listen coherently.

We ride in silence until we exit the highway onto a dirt road. Fireweed blooms high in the ditches, a perfectly pink pop of color against the evergreens. "I'll go first, Ashton!" I blurt as we pull into a short driveway where a wooden cabin with a green tin roof sits at the end.

"Why the change of heart?" He shuts off the car after we park.

I have no earthly idea. I shrug.

Because you're on pins and needles to see me, the flirty man in my head says.

"Are you sure? Based on what that bartender said, I'm worried about what we might find." Ashton opens his door, but I stay inside the car, staring at the house. Noah's in there. Right there. Steps away.

"No. I've got this." I steel myself.

Ashton knocks on my window and motions for me to unlock my door. It snaps me from my haze and I do as he says. He opens the door and I slip out, once more locking my eyes onto the light brown door of the cabin. As if in another trance, I take step after step until I'm standing on the front porch by a stack of firewood. I stare at the door as if it might bite me if I touch it, but at the same time, I'm drawn to it. I raise my fist and knock. Three nervous raps that sync to the beat of my heart.

I can't wait to lay eyes on you again, my little author. My stomach clenches at the thought of fiction and reality heading for a crash course collision.

All is quiet around me except for the soft sounds of Ashton's breathing next to me, and then, shuffling feet coming closer and closer to the door. My heart rate rockets as the door knob turns, and I'm eternally thankful for the overcast sky, light breeze, and moderate temperature so I don't turn into a sweating pig. My blood continues to rush in my ears as I fight off dizziness.

The door gets stuck on something, then it's yanked open and a tall man who is certainly not Noah, though he looks to be around our age, steps out. "Sorry about that," he says with a slight Midwestern accent. "It gets stuck every now an—" The man stops talking as soon as he looks up. But he's not looking at me. He's looking at Ashton.

"Ashton Prewitt?" the man asks, eyes wide and a muddied brown. He runs a hand through honey-blond waves, disbelief crossing his sharp features. "Are you Noah's brother? Man, the two of you look just alike."

Beside me, Ashton swallows. "Yeah, that's me. You must be Nick Lancaster. We ran into a man calling himself Big Bear who said Noah might be with you."

Nick grins, and if I'm being honest, it's charming. He has a boy-next-door vibe. "He's here. Inside reading." Finally, Nick shifts his focus to me. "You must be the woman who drove him here. The one who forgot him."

I laugh nervously, fiddling with my oversized sweatshirt. Now that I know Noah Prewitt is on the other side of that door, I'm regretting my choice of leggings and a Whitney High School sweater. "That's what they tell me."

"Come on in," he says, gesturing to the door. "I was heading out anyway. My house is yours."

Ashton and Nick shake hands, talking about Noah in some capacity, but I find myself moving toward the door as if some invisible string is pulling without my consent.

I push the door; it's cold against my sweaty palm. After it doesn't budge, I lean into it, and it creaks open.

Hi, sweetheart.

"Who is it, Nick?" Noah says in a deep, resounding voice that makes my nerves quiver, and my feet glue themselves to the old wooden floor of the cabin-style home. How could I have ever thought Ashton's voice was the same as *this*?

Noah is lounging on what looks to be a worn plaid couch with quilted blankets thrown across it. He looks oversized in such a small space, but his tanned skin and dark, mussed, curly hair nearly blend into the ambient low light of the lamp on the opposite end of the couch. He's wearing gray sweatpants and an orange hoodie. The thin-framed reading glasses resting on his face have my bookish soul kicking itself for ever forgetting a beautiful man such as the one who has yet to look up from the Bible resting in his lap.

Using an orange pen, he underlines something.

When I don't answer his question, opting to stand plastered to the floor with my lips parted in a silent gasp while my nerves hum in tune with the electricity sizzling and popping within the crisp air, Noah finally looks up.

The world ceases to spin...

Gravity loses all sense of existence...

Oxygen is sucked from the atmosphere...

When his eyes meet mine.

"Esme." Hearing my name on his lips is vastly different than what goes on inside my head.

A poetic dance of heartbreaks and happily-ever-afters twists and twirls at the breathless tremble in his voice. In the slow blink of an eye, Noah is towering over my frozen frame, his large hands cupping my cheeks as wonder lights the gold flecks in his hazel eyes. *Just as I'd imagined them to look.* "Esme, sweetheart. Are you real? Am I lost in reverie again?" His thumbs brush featherlight across my cheekbones, and I find myself raising my hands to cover his.

Sweetheart.

"Noah."

The biggest smile I've ever seen inches across his face.

The world resumes...

I fall back down to earth...

Oxygen fills my lungs...

As my head explodes in a myriad of shattered pieces of memory of this very smile.

"Noah." My limbs feel as if I'm floating, my vision fading in and out. My eyes flutter closed. My knees give out. Strong arms hold me close against a warm chest as my sense of self evaporates.

***

H ave you ever had the best sleep of your life?

The kind of sleep that, as you start to wake up, you're perfectly happy, content, warm, cozy, and at peace?

Stretching, my hands slap against something.

No, not something.

Someone.

I startle from my dreamlike state, struggling to untangle myself out of whatever I'm wrapped so snugly inside of.

"Hey, hey, hey," a deep, familiar voice whispers quickly. "You're safe, sweetheart."

Noah.

Alaska.

We found him, the Noah inside my head celebrates.

The montage of his smiles flickers to life in my head as a film reel. I play it on repeat, wondering what was the cause of each one.

My eyes fly open, and Noah kneels beside me as I lie on that raggedy couch I found him on when I walked through the door. Hints of golden sunlight shine around the edges of the window, but thick curtains block most of it out. I must not have been out long.

Noah smiles so brightly and genuinely, though I can tell he's been crying. His hazel, gold-flecked eyes are red, and his face is puffy. I memorize every detail of his expression. His wide eyes, the wrinkles of his smile line, the sharp contours of his nose, his high cheekbones. Perfection. Every inch of him.

It terrifies me.

"Where's Ashton?" I ask.

Noah's brows scrunch together. "He, uh—" Noah runs a hand through his hair and blows out a breath of air. "Nick and Ashton went to the store for groceries."

He stands and takes a few steps back from the couch. "Do you remember me, Esme?" The hope in his voice cuts me like a knife, and then I remember Ashton told me he *was* cut by a knife. Stabbed by a knife. Beaten and broken and bruised. *For me.*

Readying myself, I drop my gaze to his neck, but I can't see anything due to his hoodie and the low light of the room.

Clearing my throat, I sit up and look around the cabin. It's on the smaller end, looking like it's two bedrooms. The living room is connected to the dining area and kitchen, and the fireplace is doing a wonderful job at keeping the place warm.

"Esme?" he asks again, hope undulating in his voice.

"A little," I confess, not brave enough to make eye contact. "I've remembered glimpses of things, but I—" I exhale, hating myself for not remembering everything when the joy I felt at his smile came rushing back. "I remember your smile. And that it made me happy."

Startling me, Noah throws his head back and laughs. It's a crazed sound, as if he hasn't laughed in years and is trying out the action again. "My best feature. It cost my parents over five grand, so I'm glad it's memorable."

Finally, I lift my face toward him while tucking my legs underneath me on the couch. I tug the blanket around me tighter as if it's a shield. "When will Ashton be back?"

Noah's laugh stops abruptly. A worried and conflicted expression crosses his face. "He'll be back soon, I promise. Do you want me to call him?"

"No, that's not necessary," I state, taking a deep breath. Noah looks like Ashton, but he's not Ashton. And I know Ashton whereas I don't truly know Noah. But I trust that Ashton wouldn't leave me alone with a man who would hurt me.

Gosh, what am I thinking? This is his twin brother. And there's something about Noah that's familiar, outside the fact that he and Ashton are copied and pasted. But it's that golden thread of familiarity that's scaring me and putting me on edge.

A pregnant silence sits in the room as we find ourselves in a staring contest. I have a million questions, but I don't know where to start. I simultaneously feel like I know this man, yet, I know I don't. Not really. He's not a fictional character. This man in front of me has not talked to me over the past year. He's not lived in my head.

Noah Ashley Prewitt is real. Right here.

He chuckles awkwardly, running a hand through his hair. "You're the last person I expected to see walk through that door. I didn't have time to prepare."

"I think that was the point," I reply, attempting to smile to put him at ease. As uncomfortable as this is for me, it must be for him too. I take a moment to really look at him. While I slept, he must have styled his hair and changed into jeans and a T-shirt. "Are you okay?"

Noah snorts, and I briefly wonder what about that question he finds funny. But then I recall that his family is loaded with people who find humor in unfavorable and uncomfortable situations.

His unhinged-sounding laugh moments ago makes more sense to me now. I'm not the only one coping in this moment.

Noah gestures to the couch, already moving my way. "Do you mind if I sit down beside you?"

I nod, scooching over to make plenty of space between us. Noah sits on the farthest end of the couch while I hole up at the opposite end.

Noah twists to angle himself toward me, so I mimic his actions. Finally, he says, "I'm okay. I wasn't for a while, but I'm back on my feet. I don't want you to worry about it. How are you, Esme Lorraine Jenkins? I've had a million conversations with you in my head, but here you are. How?"

That captures my attention. Talking to one another through our heads is one thing I can relate to.

"I could say the same," I state, a small smile flickering on my face. I watch as Noah's shoulders relax, and that small action paves the way for me to take my first deep breath. He gives me room to continue explaining. "I wrote a book, and, um," I close my eyes and exhale, "I think it was about us. At least to some extent."

Noah is slack-jawed for a moment before he shakes his head clear. "You wrote a book? That's amazing, Esme!" He stands, bringing his hands to his head as he paces. I trace the width of his shoulders with my eyes, and a little shiver runs down my spine. Noah is a big guy. Maybe even more built than Ashton. He takes a few steps back in my direction, and I twist on the couch to face him. He kneels onto one knee in front of me, a brilliant smile on his face. "That was your dream, and you did it. I'm so proud of you!"

Noah takes my hands in his, and I'm overcome by how they swallow mine and how warm they feel. I pull away, shocked by how much I like it.

"Oh, sorry." Noah clears his throat, taking his place back beside me on the couch. I notice he sits a little closer this time, and I also notice that I don't mind it.

"No, it's okay," I say, mustering sincerity in my eyes. He's in the same boat I am, both of us jostling for the role of captain. Except neither of us expertly know how to steer around the wreckage of my missing memories. "And thank you. I'm still in awe that I did it. And that Ashton's offering me a book deal."

"He forgot to mention that earlier," Noah says, his thick brows furrowing together. But then he shakes away whatever thought held him hostage for a second, and he plants his smile back in place. "That's awesome, Esme. Truly. When can I read it?"

My eyes widen, and Noah hurriedly says, "If you want me to, that is."

I nod. "Of course I do. It's, uh—" I stop myself from saying it was the whole reason I wanted to find him so that he could sort out my reality, but that's not entirely true, and that would hurt him if I said that. "I just don't want to bother you with a newbie's novel."

"You could never be a bother, Esme." Noah's fingers twitch as if he's fighting not to touch me. That thought causes my heart to jump, but the jury is out if the reaction is out of desire or skittishness.

No, it's a hung jury.

"I don't have my laptop with me. Or my printed manuscript." I look down, fiddling with my thumbs. "I do have it on my phone, though. If you want to read it there on our way home." *Be brave, Esme. This is why you wanted to find him. He has answers.*

"Home?"

I snap my eyes to his. "I didn't mean to assume you'd come back with us, but I—" I laugh nervously and give a little shrug. "I was hoping you might."

"Of course I'm coming back. I was planning to go back at the end of the month, anyway." Once more, Noah's fingers twitch. I roll my lips into my mouth and place my palms face up on my lap. Noah stares at me, hitching a brow.

A blush creeps across my cheeks, but I will myself to stay strong. He's just as new to this situation as I am. And I think he needs the contact. "You can take my hands. If you want." And then as if I needed to justify myself, I tack on, "Maybe it will help me remember everything."

A wicked grin spreads across Noah's handsome face, and I don't know if I want to play with fire or run. His voice lowers an octave as he whispers, "Sweetheart, I will hold your hands until you remember every." He leans in. "Single." Our faces are inches apart, and my breath hitches. "Moment."

I gasp, taken aback by his bold flirtation, but before I can formulate a thought, the door swings open.

"Put a sock on the knob next time," that Midwestern accent comments.

Noah meets my eyes, joy blending with an air of sadness shining through as he smiles. He stands and greets Nick and Ashton, who take up way too much space standing in the small entryway.

Noah offers his hand to me, and I take it as he helps me off the couch. I'm still feeling a little weak, so I reason with myself. If I don't want to fall over, I should lean into Noah's side. For support. That's all. Not because even though I have no idea why, I like the feel of his hand in mine. Even if it freaks me out a little.

Okay, a lot.

It's like my body and soul recognize him, but my brain hasn't caught up yet.

I need a dose of comfort. "You're back!" I slowly slip my hand from Noah's and walk across the room to greet Ashton. He gives me a weird look, but I think he reads the storm of confusion raging behind my eyes.

After I take a grocery bag from Ashton's hand, I dare to glance back at Noah, knowing that the abrupt exit must have hurt him. He wears a tight smile, and a sinking feeling swirls in my stomach. I don't want to hurt Noah, but I need a moment to sit with his existence in front of me and process.

Noah, however, casually strolls toward us and introduces me. "Nick, this is the woman who decided it would be a fun time to forget me." His eyes crinkle in the corners as he grins wider, but there's still something dark swimming underneath his expression. "And she still doesn't remember everything, but she remembers my heart-melting smile."

Ashton rolls his eyes as Nick sighs dramatically before responding. "How fortunate. I saw Windsor when I took Ashton out to Safeway. She didn't even look at me. She actively stuck that little nose in the air and walked right on by."

"It was quite funny," Ashton comments, holding one handful of groceries since I took one bag from him in a hasty action to make it seem like I rushed to help Ashton instead of taking a breather from the intensity that is Noah Prewitt. "She acted like he didn't even exist."

Nick shrugs. "I don't *like* her anyway. It's just fun to rile her up."

Noah snorts. "Whatever you say, buddy."

"Windsor?" I ask. "That's her name?"

Nick grins, tilting his head. "It's my name for the Princess of Crescent Cove."

I narrow my eyes in confusion, but Nick doesn't offer to elaborate, obviously lost in some sort of vision of said princess.

Once the guys come inside and put away the groceries, Nick sets to work cooking some kind of secret dish he says we'll love while Ashton, Noah, and I sit around the campfire in Nick's backyard. I'm a wallflower while the guys talk, but I'm enjoying seeing Ashton's pure elation at being with his twin again. It's as if a weight has crumbled from Ashton's shoulders.

I was wrong earlier when I thought I hadn't slept long after passing out from the overwhelming sensation of that stupid montage that didn't help me remember much of anything. I had slept for four hours while Ashton and Noah caught up. It's ten at night here, but the sun says it could be five in the evening with how brightly it's shining since the clouds have disappeared.

Part of me wants to continually stare at the blue sky. It moves differently here, creating the illusion that I'm standing on the edge of the world.

But Noah is real, and I can't rip my eyes away from him as he laughs at something Ashton says. I'll never read my book the same way again, and there are so many new layers and depths I want to add to the story and to Noah's character. The way he masks his deep-seated sadness with humor. The way he's been avoiding talking about anything too heavy with Ashton. I think he's trying to protect me, but I wish he'd just open up. I'm the last person who would judge him. Or maybe he thinks I'll beat myself up if he starts to talk about just how much my memory loss impacted him.

I can't deny he's right about that, but I still wish he wouldn't tiptoe around me with humor and flirty comments.

It's *our specialty*, fictional Noah states.

"And then Branda took off her heel and threw it at me." Ashton laughs as he finishes telling Noah a story about yet another time Branda got peeved at him at the office.

Noah laughs, shaking his head. His curls bounce, and I want to run my fingers through them to see if they feel as silky and smooth as I wrote them. "Don't worry," Noah says. "I'll get her back for you when we get home."

"So, you're coming back?" Ashton's voice quivers lightly as he casts his gaze down.

"I honestly was planning to come back at the end of the month." Noah, apparently reading the raging emotions in Ashton's eyes, just as I did, stands and walks around the fire to where Ashton sits on a log. Ashton stands, and the brothers hug. Tears spring to my eyes, and I can't help but smile at the wholesome picture in front of me. From over Noah's shoulder, Ashton mouths, "Thank you."

I give him a nod as I wipe a tear from my cheek.

"Man, Noah," Ashton says after a beat of silence where we listened to the crackling fire while they embraced. They pull apart, beating each other on the back like men do. "I haven't seen you this happy and light in months."

"Haven't seen him at all in a couple of months," I helpfully remind Ashton with a smirk. Noah turns around and meanders back to sit on the wooden bench beside me.

Ashton grimaces, which matches Noah's current expression perfectly.

Not the right thing to say, Esme.

"She's right." Noah exhales and places his hands on his knees, his fingers gripping the fabric of his jeans as if he's uncomfortable. "Ashton, I'm sorry. I know I shouldn't have disappeared like that. The pain, it was—" He cuts himself off, looking at me with hesitation. "Well, it hurt. A lot."

Guilt washes over me. "I'm sorry I don't remember you, Noah. I promise, I wish I did. And I'm trying. But it's been over a year, and so chances are low that I will ever recover all the memories."

Noah grabs my hand, and I reel over his touch again, but I don't pull away. "I don't want to talk about it right now." Noah sighs deeply, bringing his head to rest on top of mine. I go still as a statue, but he needs this, and well, I can't say I don't like this hot live wire he infuses in me. Because I do. Very much. "I just want to enjoy you."

"I'm going to see if Nick needs help in the kitchen," Ashton comments, standing to his feet and speed walking across the small yard, up the back deck, and through the sliding glass door. I watch my anchor disappear, but unlike when I first woke, I'm more at ease.

Noah lifts his head and releases my hand.

"You've got an amazing brother. You know that, right?" I move to straddle the bench to face Noah. A softness ripples over his face.

"Don't tell me you fell in love with my twin while you looked for me?" Noah quips, but he's smiling. I see through it, though.

"I thought he had somehow stepped out of my novel for a minute there, but no, Noah. I didn't fall for your twin." He doesn't need to know the truth of that first encounter with Ashton or how I attempted to reason with myself that it would be a good idea to date my literary agent. Despite the initial physical attraction, there's nothing romantic between me and Ashton. He's like another brother I didn't ask for, a new best friend I didn't intend to make.

Noah stares at me in silence, that sense of wonder from when he first saw me claiming his face. "I've missed you so much, Meme."

"You know my nickname."

"I probably know a lot about you that you've forgotten you told me." He reaches out to cup my face, but I lean back instinctively.

"I'm sorry, Noah. I—"

"No need to apologize," he huffs out, running that same hand through his hair and looking at the fire. "I remember you, so please forgive me if my instincts attempt to go before my brain sometimes." He looks back at me and smiles. "That's something we were working on before everything happened, anyway."

I offer him a smile even though he's not looking at me and I'm freely examining each curl as it moves around his fingers. His hair is thicker and more untamed than Ashton's. *Just as I imagined it.* "It's okay. Seriously. I get it."

Noah shakes his head as if he's trying to understand something. "I still can't believe you're here. I thought I—" His pretty eyes shine with wetness when he turns them back to me. "I thought I'd lost you forever, Esme."

"I'm sorry, Noah. I'm so sorry."

"Don't apologize, sweetheart. It's not your fault." His expression clears a little as he gives me a lopsided grin. "It just hurt my pride to know I was so forgettable."

"Except your smile," I jest back, though he's attempting to hide his pain through humor. Maybe I just have to play along for now. Allow him the time he needs to open up. "I have a vision board of cutouts of moments you smiled at me montaged in my head."

He laughs a little easier, and so I add on, "I remember you hunched over a desk in the bungalow, writing. I remember us sitting atop a mountain. I remember—" Heat flames at the base of my neck. "—painting you." I don't admit to stealing the painting and hanging it in my camper in my bedroom.

Noah waggles his brows. "I was the most handsome muse Bora Bora has ever seen."

"So, that's definitely real?"

Noah nods, and I gasp through a dawning realization. "Crap, Noah! Your brother read detailed make out scenes that could have very well been real." It was one thing for it to all be fiction and for Ashton to read it, but it's obviously not all fiction, and I *wrote about his twin!* "I'm not going to be able to look him in the eyes," I mutter, my hands over my face.

"I really want to read your book now, sweetheart. To see if you captured my immaculate kissing skills correctly."

"So conceited." I chuckle, easing my hands from my face. Then another thought hits me. *What if he kisses that way?* The heat deepens in my face, and if he decides to point it out, I'm blaming the fire that I refuse to look away from. *His hands in mine felt like I'd written about...*

I let out a long, emotion-filled exhale, an important question dancing around my head. Might as well get it over with. "Ashton said you wanted to marry me. That you texted him that while we were still on the island."

The masquerading lightness in Noah's expression fades as the stalking darkness that was lingering beneath the surface makes its grand appearance. His voice is dry and gravelly as he chokes out, "He told you that?"

I nod as Noah swallows and continues talking. "You utterly captivated me, and when you said yes to continuing to date me once we got back to the States, I knew I wouldn't date another woman ever again. I knew you were the one my heart and soul needed, but you had a sour taste in your mouth when it came to marriage. So, yeah, I told my brother that I found the woman I wanted to marry, but I never asked you. That would have been completely insensitive of me." Noah smirks a little. "I was going to wait until a few months after we made it home. I needed time to make sure my seduction efforts were effective."

I snort, relief washing over me that we were never truly engaged. But the fact remains: Noah Prewitt wanted to marry me. Is that where he still stands? I shove the thought away for now and focus on the one thing we both did on that island. "How did we do it, Noah?"

"Do what?"

"Fall in love in the span of a week?"

Noah releases a slow breath, pondering his answer. "I've asked myself that question a thousand times. From the moment I watched you take down that man who tried to run off with you, I—"

"What?" I bark out, flabbergasted. "I took down the kidnapper?"

Noah stares at me incredulously. When he realizes I'm seriously asking him, he runs his hand down his face as if he's shocked I didn't remember that. "Yes, Esme. A middle-aged bald Hispanic guy tried to take you. I was about to intervene because you looked really uncomfortable with his arm around you, but right as I moved to take care of it, you spun out of his grip and punched him square in the nose. He ran off, and I swooped in to check on you. You mentioned he had a knife, but he'd disappeared into the crowd so we called the police and gave them everything we knew."

I soak in every word, attempting to unravel the threads between fiction and reality as he tells me the tale of what really happened when a man tried to take me away in Bora Bora.

Our real meet-cute.

A *punch of a thousand Bora Bora suns...* I throw my head back and laugh in disbelief. "I can't believe I fought him. I'm usually one to freeze in high-stress situations." *Way to go, me!* I mentally pat myself on the back.

Noah arches a brow and crosses his arms. "You? Afraid? That's not the woman I remember. You were a grumpy firecracker on that island. Mad at the world while trying to prove to it that you were fun, flirty, and free. Once I wiggled my way through your defenses, we had the time of our lives." He winks.

That sobers me up. *Not the woman he remembers.* Just as I was afraid would be the case. Island Esme was, in fact, much different than the person I am.

"Noah," I lead, nervously picking at my fingernails. I bite the inside of my cheek before meeting his eyes. He needs to hear this. Maybe it will change his mind about me, and he can stop feeling hurt over losing me. Because I was never the woman he thought I was from the offset. "I'm not that woman. I never was. The girl you met in Bora Bora was going through a difficult time, as I imagine getting left at the altar would do to someone. I'm not fun, flirty, and free. I'm a little timid, though I'm working on being bolder. I prefer plans and schedules to spontaneity. I have anxiety and get nervous easily. And flirting, well... I have no game. Not like you do, as I'm told."

Noah's enigmatic expression has me on pins and needles. After seconds pass, I blurt, "Say something."

And he laughs. *Belly laughs.* Teeters on the edge of falling off the bench because he's laughing so hard. A *genuine* laugh.

"Noah Ashley Prewitt," I scold, catching myself by surprise. Did I really just use his full name like I'm his mother? But why in the sweet stars above is this man laughing at me?

"I'm sorry, Esme. I—" He breaks into another round of laughter that lasts minutes as I stare incredulously. Finally, he gets out, "I'm sorry. I haven't laughed like that in a while."

My frustration diffuses. Of course he hasn't. He's been depressed over a woman who doesn't truly exist.

Noah breathes deeply and smiles softly, his eyes sparking. "May I put my hands on your face so that I can make sure you hear every word of what I'm about to say?"

Confused, I nod.

He stands, straddles the bench, and sits, his knees knocking into mine. Warmth from his large hands settles on either side of my face as he stares into my soul. "Esme Lorraine Jenkins," he breathes my name, his breath smelling like mint toothpaste. "I know just the sort of woman you are. You freaked out when I asked you to continue dating me when we returned home. You were going on about how I didn't really know you and that I might not like you when we were off the island. I'll tell you now what I told you back then." He clears his throat. "You think I couldn't tell that you are timid and anxious and settled? You hardly made a decision that week because you went along with whatever I suggested, huffing and puffing through climbing a mountain with me and everything. I picked up on the cues that told me when you didn't really want to do something. I identified your plastic smile and what set it apart from the genuine one. I saw your planner. I noticed the way you got nervous in large crowds and preferred quieter environments. And most importantly, you opened up to me about your past with Lane and Bryan. You told me how they said your romantic expectations were too high and that no man could ever meet them."

My hands fly to cover my opened mouth. Noah removes one of his hands to gently move mine away from my face. He doesn't let go of it as he continues. "And then I told you that they were emotionally unintelligent boys who didn't know what to do with a woman like you. A brave, intelligent, beautiful, meek, and kind woman."

Tears run down my cheeks, and Noah gently wipes one away with the pad of his thumb. I'm at a loss for words, so he fills the silence. "And also like I told you that day... I know I have so much more to learn about you, so please, take me to school, Miss Jenkins, because I want to learn. I want to do it every day by your side. I want to learn your soul." I'm a statue as Noah gently places his hand over my heart. I should swat it away, but I can't. I won't. "Your heart." He moves his hand to stroke my oily, airplane hair. "Your mind."

I know what comes next. I wrote this scene. *Real.*

Noah asks permission with his eyes when they drop down to my lips and back up to me. I should say no.

When I drafted *Forgetting My Vacation Fling*, I never imagined he was real. I wrote about instant love because I believe it exists and is beautiful, but I never imagined it was something that could happen to me because of my personality.

But it did. And as my title suggests, I forgot about it.

A little string in my soul tugs as if it's telling me he's the one. He's it. *He's the one who I've searched for. Waited for. Longed for. My missing person. My missing memories.*

I close my eyes and lean toward him involuntarily.

Does he kiss like I imagined?

His lips press featherlight to mine. A breath, and then he pulls away, a small reverent smile lifting his full cheekbones. "And eventually, one day when I finally coerce you into marrying me, every inch of your body."

"Real," I murmur out loud, swiping my thumb across my bottom lip where it still feels the imprint of his soft mouth against mine. I should feel off-kilter for a thousand other reasons than the one currently taking precedent.

Noah makes a humming sound. "Very real."

At that moment, Nick calls for us, saying his moose lasagna is ready. I'm shaken out of my stupor and jolt back from Noah.

What am I thinking? I just met this guy!

You've known me for a while, my little author, fictional Noah states.

Real Noah flinches at my sudden movement, but to his credit, he doesn't show his disappointment or sadness.

"Noah, I—"

He holds up his hand. "You don't have to say anything, Esme. Let's just focus on being in Alaska right now, and we can figure things out later."

I swallow the anxiety in my throat and nod.

We stand, and Noah takes my hand. "You don't have to date me right now, Esme. Or ever, for that matter." He says the last phrase with a tinge of sourness in his tone. "But, if you're willing, I'd like for you to give me a chance. Don't answer me now. Think about it. We can make decisions back home."

Home. The word feels so close yet so far away.

"Thank you, Noah. I know this isn't easy for you, but I can't tell you how much it means to me that you are willing to put yourself through—" I search for what I'm looking for, but I let it fall because I don't actually know what I want to say. I squeeze his hand before dropping it. "Anyway, thank you."

"I'm just glad God saw fit to bring you back into my life, even if it's just in this small manner. Him and I went rounds over you." Pain flashes through his eyes, and I know he's trying hard to believe that.

Nick hollers again, and we start making our way to the cabin.

I scrunch my nose. "Lasagna is my favorite dish, but I don't know about this moose business."

"When in Crescent Cove, Alaska..."

Chapter Fifteen

You All Night ~ late July

T he plane is dimly lit and quiet as the world sleeps around us, but Noah and I are head to head, scrolling through my manuscript on my phone. I'm against the window while Noah occupies the middle seat. Ashton sits in the aisle seat, begrudgingly. We weren't able to secure first class seats for this unplanned flight back to Jackson, Mississippi, after hanging out for another day in Alaska. We went on a small hike yesterday, and the entire time, Noah and I swapped life stories. We held hands a few times, and he was flirty, which I've come to realize I captured perfectly in my novel. But he was respectful and not once did he try to kiss me again or take conversation too deep. It was like three days worth of dates rolled into one, and if I'm being honest, I couldn't get enough time with him.

He's funny. Charming. Obviously hot.

He's also considerate. Kind. Thoughtful.

A venus fly trap. Already sucking me in.

"This absolutely did not happen." Noah snorts as we read a scene in my book where fictional Esme and Noah make out on a jet ski. I eye him suspiciously because he seems like the type to, well, make out on a jet ski with a woman. "I'm serious, Meme. I tried to make out with you, but you shoved me off and drove the jet ski away. Left me bobbing in the water with sharks until you circled back around two minutes later."

I stifle my laugh. "There it is."

He bumps against my shoulder, and our eyes meet under the dim blue light of the plane. It isn't the first time electricity has shot from our eyes and into each other's souls throughout this close quarters flight, and it won't be the last. Memory retention or not, Noah has already proved exactly why I was attracted to him. He has an easygoing laugh, beautiful smile, and a body hotter than a desert. But outside the obvious physical intrigue, Noah is also kind, respectful, and funny. He hasn't tried to initiate contact with me outside little brushes and bumps, and he's letting me set the pace when we talk about the past.

Like right now. I thought a plane ride where we're sitting shoulder to shoulder was the perfect time to read the book I unknowingly wrote based on me and him. Not my best idea.

I clear my throat and release a cooling breath before I look back at the document on my phone as he continues to read. After a few minutes, he stops and swallows. "That happened."

I scan the scene I wrote from Noah's point of view where he's lying next to Esme as she's falling asleep post-amnesia. Fictional Noah plays with fictional Esme's hair and whispers, "I'm going to marry you one day."

"How? You were—" The words *in the* ICU fall off my tongue.

Noah shakes his head. "It didn't happen at the moment you wrote in your book. It happened the night before everything happened." He gives me a soft, sad smile. "You mumbled 'yes' before you drifted off to sleep. It gave me the courage to text my brother that I'd found my future wife."

My breath catches as a memory of Noah and me snuggling in a hammock flashes through my mind. "Did we have a hammock?"

"Oh, we did," Noah says, waggling his brows, his flirty nature overtaking his soft seriousness. "It didn't like us very much as it dumped us on our butts nine times out of ten."

"I remember it," I state plainly. I coax the memory to take a fuller frame, but it runs and hides instead. I sigh with building frustration, looking back down at the story. "I wish it'd just all come back at once instead of in these little snippets."

Noah clicks my phone dark. "I think that's enough for now. You should probably get some rest."

Ignoring him, I continue blabbing in a hushed tone. "I mean, why did God allow this to happen to us, Noah? What's the point? What's the purpose in this?"

Silence envelops us, the hum of the engines taking up space. I take deep breaths, trying to tame the anxiety rising. The full weight of reality crashes down on me. All the emotions I've stuffed down since the moment I laid my eyes on Noah are bubbling to the surface in the quiet, small space, and I have a litany of questions for God that He seemingly doesn't want to answer for me. Hot tears burn down my cheeks as I stifle my short, breathless sobs.

Noah slips his arm awkwardly around me and pulls me into his side. The armrest between us jabs into my side, and I squeak in pain. Noah mutters a curse before lifting the armrest and pulling me once again into his side. He whispers against my ear as his fingers trail up and down my arm. "Tell me three things you see, sweetheart."

I force my bleary eyes open. It's dark, but I can make out a few things in my area. "A screen. The chair." I look out of the window into the clear night sky. "Stars."

Noah adjusts us so that my back is leaning against his chest. His arms wrap around me, and I know he can't be comfortable in this tight space. But he whispers again. "Two things you smell."

I inhale, though it's hard to smell anything with how stuffy my nose is. But I'm able to make out Noah's scent. "Citrus." My chest aches as choppy breaths fight for release.

I inhale again. "That's it." *Hitch.* "All I can smell," *hitch,* "is you."

"One thing you feel."

The answer comes immediately as I press against him. "You."

"I'm right here, Esme. Right here. Breathe with me."

His chest rises.

I inhale.

His chest falls.

I exhale.

Keeping the pace with the rhythm of his breaths, my breathing begins to mellow out as my tears slow.

"I had them, too, you know. Panic attacks," Noah whispers against my ear, his voice gravelly and deep. His breath is warm and inviting, and despite how we're mashed up like sardines, I lean further into him. "Every time I thought about how the only woman I'd ever loved forgot me, I could have just died right then and there."

"Ashton helped you through them?" I ask, though really, it's a statement. Noah nods.

"Do they still happen?" I press on.

"Not often," Noah says. "But sometimes, yeah."

I take stock of that. I want to help him if I'm ever around and it happens. But then something else he said catches my attention. "The only woman?" I ask breathlessly. "Really?"

Noah's voice softens. "Yes, Esme. Sure, I've dated a lot of women." I bristle, and he chuckles. "Let me finish."

"Fine," I respond, unsure why I'm bothered by the fact he's dated a lot of women. He's not mine. Not really. Even though his fingers rub slow circles on my stomach. *He's not mine. He belongs to an Esme who doesn't exist.*

He thinks he knows me; he doesn't. Not really.

Though this panic attack is a great way for him to start.

"I've dated a lot of women, yes, but I never loved any of them. You got that angle right in your novel, though my novels have sold very well, thank you very much." Noah smirks, a bit of Ashton's headiness coming through. "But unlike the playboy vibe you give me—thanks, by the way—I didn't lead them on. Once I realized it wasn't going to work with a woman, I'd kindly tell her and we'd go our separate ways. But with you, it was different. From the moment I saw you sulking on that beach, drowning your sorrows in mimosas and kicking sand as if it personally offended you, I thought to myself, 'I've got to know her,' and I started formulating a plan to talk to you. I watched as you removed the pink umbrella from your empty drink and accidentally poked yourself in the cheek when you attempted to put it behind your ear. I was smitten, and I had my move ready. I was going to pluck that umbrella from your fingers and smoothly tuck it behind your ear. But that's when that bald guy stepped in."

Unbidden laughter leaks out of me. "Really? You saw a broken woman on her honeymoon alone and thought 'yep. I've gotta talk to her'?"

I feel Noah's shrug from behind me and laughter vibrating in his chest. "Then I saw you deck a man in the nose."

I laugh aloud now. Drying my face, I sit up and face him as we both stretch out. "Every man's dream," I mock.

"You know, I actually spent that first night outside your bedroom door, keeping watch for you. I didn't tell you that earlier, but I think you should know just how much I care about you—and have from the start. You were shaken over the attempted kidnapping, and I couldn't bear to let you sleep alone in that bungalow knowing the criminal was still out there. We didn't kiss that night, didn't spend the night talking or laughing. I didn't want to be too forward after what you went through, even though that's how you wrote me." Noah side-eyes me, and I look away, a smidge guilty. What can I say? Readers like a romantic rogue.

If we didn't spend that first night how I wrote it, then I wonder... "When did we kiss? Did that scene ever happen?"

Noah gets a reminiscent look on his face. "The next morning. You came out of your room wearing an oversized T-shirt and sleep shorts, and you found me a bit delusional due to sleep deprivation. I said, 'I'm glad you made it to tomorrow,' and you said, 'No more wasted chances.' I couldn't blink before you were grabbing my face and kissing me senseless before making more mango fish tacos for breakfast. I didn't even care that neither of us had brushed our teeth."

My stomach swoops and soars. I'm definitely adding *that* into the final draft. "You truly are a superhero."

Noah laughs, rolling his eyes before continuing, "Then I really got to know you. I watched you cycle through anger, acceptance, and then back to anger. I watched your walls fall hour after hour when we were together. You started smiling and laughing, and I was—am—mesmerized. You opened up to me, and you trusted me. And you were a safe place for me to land."

I perk up. All this time, I thought I was the only one between us who had issues. "Why did you need to land?"

Noah leans back in his seat, tilting his head back and staring at the top of the plane. After releasing a slow breath, he lowers his voice, turns to me, and says, "It sounds dumb compared to what you had been through, but I needed a place where I didn't have to be happy and perfect all the time. You showed me I could be real with my feelings and didn't need to masquerade them behind my smiles and laughs. Maybe you can add that into your novel's final draft." He snickers. "You may have written me a little too perfectly. Give me some flaws, because trust me, I have them."

"That's not dumb, Noah."

He scoffs and rubs a hand down his face, an action so similar to Ashton's. "I've always been the one in the family to hold everyone together. After Mom died, I needed to be the one to make sure Branda had a space to fall apart in. To make sure I reminded Ashton that he didn't have to carry the weight of it all on his shoulders. To make sure Dad got up and at least walked in the sunshine every day."

"So you took the weight of it on your shoulders in the name of lightening the load for everyone else." I raise my brows, and Noah smirks, holding up a hand.

"I know, I know." He sighs, leaning his head back once more. "That's why I came to Alaska. I didn't want them to see me fall apart. I'd already shown them too much sadness and distress as I held out hope you'd remember. But after about nine months, and I still hadn't heard from you, I broke. I quit working out for a while. I quit eating. I quit doing much of anything because numbness cloaked me. So I ran."

My heart beats hard against my chest as he lets me into his psyche, but he doesn't continue. He smiles up at the roof of the plane for a full minute before turning to meet my eyes. "And now, here you are."

"Here I am. And here you are, coaxing confessions out of me just like you did back in Bora Bora. You're so easy for me to talk to, Esme. You're my landing pad, even with miles of memories between us."

His sweet smile and heartfelt words melt me to my core as he looks back up, and though I have a lot more questions and a lot more fiction and reality to sift through, I know there's one thing I want for certain.

"Noah?"

"Hm?"

When I don't immediately answer, he sits up and looks at me with a gaze that says he cares about me and would move mountains for me.

A look I only ever imagined from my fictional men.

"When did you fall in love with me?"

He doesn't miss a beat. "You didn't write about that moment in your novel, but I knew I had chosen to love you our second night together. You were sitting on the outside deck, kicking your feet in the water and gazing at the stars. I slid the glass door open, and the moment you heard the sound, you looked back at me with the sweetest smile I've ever seen. The moonlight danced across your face, and I was awestruck. It was as if God whispered, 'She's the one.' I finally understood the phrase 'when you know you know.'"

I let his words wash me from the inside out, and I sit in his confession bath until I'm waterlogged. Crawling out of the metaphorical tub, I'm renewed. Like being dipped in the fount of youth. I tug the necklace from underneath my sweatshirt. "Is this yours?"

Noah looks at the cross between my fingers, his breath hitching. "Yes. You still have it?"

"Obviously," I jest. "A nurse gave it to me before I left the hospital. She said it was a reminder to always cling to my faith. But I wrote in the book that the necklace was yours, and it came from your grandpa. Is that true?"

Noah nods. "He gave me and Ashton these necklaces when we were eighteen. He said they belonged to him and Grandma. Ashton has hers. Grandpa said the cross was specially forged to always lead us in love."

Just as I wrote it...

"Here." I go to unclasp it, but Noah places his hand over mine, a look of pure love shining in his eyes under the dim plane light. It scares me, but also, it stirs a sense of wonder.

"You keep it safe for me, Esme. If you want."

The question lingers. The answer could very well insinuate we will continue to see each other when this plane lands. The past couple of days getting to know him have been perfect. I want to know him more. The journey to this moment—the book, Ashton, learning more about Noah before I even came face to face with him—has filled a gaping hole I didn't fully realize was present until *him*.

My mind is made up.

"Yes."

"Yes?" Noah questions.

I take his hand in mine and intertwine our fingers. His hand swallows mine, and I love the way we fit. "I'd like to date you. I know you have a head-start in this relationship—" He laughs, and I notice his eyes misting over. "—but I'd like the opportunity to catch up to you. To," I swallow over my next words, "fall in love with you again."

Chapter Sixteen

Of This Town ~ early August

Noah and I stare down at our entwined hands, and I pray he can't feel the way my palms are sweating. We sit on my parents' couch, waiting for them to get home from the store. The television shows baseball in the background, but we aren't watching the game. Thankfully, Ethan got called into work this weekend, so he's one less person I have to worry about.

It's been a week since we returned from Alaska.

A week of dating the man I forgot, though we've only been physically together for two days this week. He had returned to Tuscaloosa with Ashton when we got back, but he drove down yesterday and is renting a room at Grannie's Inn. Not prepared to have Noah face the entire town, Grannie agreed to keep Noah's presence here hush-hush until he talked to my family. So, I spent half the day and into the wee hours of this morning tucked snugly away in the vintage floral- wallpapered room with him. He even brought me a bouquet of his favorite books to read. *Books!*

We talked about our pasts, our favorite things, and our ambitions. We pored over the rest of my book, and Noah helped me separate reality from the fiction. And not once did he pressure me into physical contact or speak about how he loves me. He had done that once on the phone earlier in the week, and it freaked me out the way he casually mentioned it. But like the look in his eyes on the plane did, it also conjured up desire. Like I *want* to love him.

And all of this still feels way too good to be true, which terrifies me more than anything. It's like I'm waiting with bated breath for him to realize I'm not the one he truly wants. Every conversation we have, I'm drawn deeper into his orbit. He's perfect, just like a book boyfriend, which is said to not exist.

So when will the other shoe drop? When will I find a reason to demand more romance out of him? One week? A month? A year down the road?

I glance over at Noah as he squeezes my hand. He mentioned last night how he was nervous to meet my parents again as the first time didn't go over well. I had laughed and told him that was understandable, but I encouraged him that I had spoken with my parents, and they were ecstatic to meet him.

The door knob turns, and Dad steps through. Noah shoots to his feet, yanking me along with him. Without saying a word, Dad does exactly what he said he wanted to do. He shakes Noah's hand, hugs him, and says, "Thank you for protecting my daughter, son. And I'm deeply sorry for the way I treated you. Please know you are always welcome here."

Mom, in a heap of tears, bear-hugs Noah who returns her strong embrace in stride. "Thank you," she finally says after a minute and lets him go.

"Mr. and Mrs. Jenkins," Noah says, a grand smile on his face, "the pleasure is all mine. I'm glad to meet the people who raised such a kind, intelligent, talented, and beautiful woman." Noah slips his arm around my waist and smiles dotingly at me.

Mom flicks her eyes from Noah to me, her eyes brightening. "Are you two going to get married now?"

I choke and cough, and Noah patiently pats my back until I regain my composure.

"Not until she's," Noah smirks at me before turning his attention to Mom and then landing on Dad, "caught up to where I'm at. I've been ready to marry her for a while, but she needs a little time." Noah Prewitt. Bold in his assessments and statements. I like that about him, his blunt honesty.

My parents look at each other, confusion crossing their faces. I bite my tongue to stop from laughing. "Well," I say, dragging Noah down to the dark brown couch. He adjusts the khaki shorts he's wearing and tugs at the collar of his white shirt. He resembles Ashton right now because he wanted to impress my parents, but his hair is still curly and disheveled, his eyes colored wild, and his entire aura inviting. "Why don't we get the game of Twenty Questions over with."

"You know me so well," Dad says, laughing. They sit down on either side of us on the recliners, and Noah holds my hand for dear life.

***

"**W**ell, guys. Should we get ready to head to lunch?" I ask, shooting to my feet to save Noah from any more questions about marriage and grandchildren and hunting.

Mom claps her hands together, standing. "Yes. Oh, and Ethan and Sam will be meeting us at El Mariachi."

Great.

My brother and best friend will meet Noah in front of the entire town. Okay, not the entire town, but El Mariachi is always hopping on the weekends. I tug Noah to his feet. The mountain of a man stands, never releasing my hand. "Awesome. We'll meet y'all there. I want to show him my home."

"*This* is your home, sweetie," Mom comments, insinuating once more that my camper isn't a real home. I give her a flat, warning look that says: Do not start this with me. If I've learned anything over the past year, it's that I can stand on my own two feet. I can speak up for myself. I can say no. I can create the life I want to live. One moment—one second—at a time.

"See y'all later, Mr. and Mrs. Jenkins."

Dad walks over to shake his hand. "It's Gregory and Melina, son."

My heart grows three sizes as I watch Dad's blue eyes shine with appreciation. This has been a hard journey of healing for us all, and though we all have a long way to go, I trust God to see us through.

We say our "see you laters" and exit the house into the hot, humid August heat. I lead Noah across the yard until we stand at the steps of my camper. Suddenly nervous, I drop his hand and face him, rocking back and forth on my heels. "So, this is where I live. I know it's small, but it's cozy and mine."

"I already love it, Esme." But then Noah smirks, a wicked gleam sparking in his eyes as he crosses his arms over his Prewitt Publishing T-shirt. He'd lost that collared shirt as soon as he took a bathroom visit in the midst of the parental interrogation. "Think I'll fit inside?"

I choke on a breath, doubling over as a coughing fit takes over. Noah pats me on the back. "Joking, sweetheart."

Catching my breath, I straighten and quirk my brow at him. "I wrote about your wicked humor in the book."

"Only when it comes to you." He boops my nose as if he didn't just turn me inside and out. Those comments... They are Eve's apple. Delicious and sinful. Promises of things to come when this man is all mine.

But that's not the case right now.

Which means I need to put a stop to it.

Nerves hum, but I know I need to get it out. "Noah? I love your humor, I do. But it takes my mind places it doesn't need to go right now."

I brace for him to get mad at me, to say I'm immature and need to grow up. But his face softens. "Of course, Esme. I'm sorry; I was joking. I tend to not think before I speak sometimes. I can't promise it won't happen again, but I will try my hardest to be more careful because I respect you and this relationship, and I don't want to cause you to stumble."

And then, as if he didn't just say all the right words and make me fall even harder for him, he steps up to my door and opens it, walking inside like he owns the thing. I'm flustered and left standing on the grass as I stare into my camper at the man who is taking up so much space in my home and my life.

Though we've been working to sort fact and fiction, I still have Noah innately entwined with the version of him that I wrote, and it scares me. The things he said to me back in Bora Bora, the promises he made me... There's a year of soul-wrenching heartache between that moment and today. But yet, he still is my perfect man. He is somehow better than I wrote him to be in the novel. That fictional version of him I fell in love with as I drafted line after line of his character doesn't hold a flame to the real man. And something whispers that I don't deserve him. That he's not real.

Maybe you should kiss him and find out just how real he is to you, fictional Noah suggests, and I choke on my spit as I contemplate the action. Of course my character is going to egg on the real-life romance.

Butterflies take off in my stomach at the thought. Can I? Is it too soon? We kissed once back in Alaska, but it was the gentle pressing of lips. A featherlight touch. I want to *kiss* him.

"You coming inside? I promise there's room for the both of us even if we have to squeeze on the couch." Noah winks, motioning me inside my own place. His innuendo and double entendres can use some work, but I'd never ask him to stop flirting with me. I clear my head and smile, remembering the way Ashton and I were smushed up on the couch only about a month earlier. Being smushed up against Noah is going to feel a heck of a lot different.

I step through the doors, immediately calmed by the cascade of colors. The camper decor is desert chic with its brown, green, orange, red, pink, and white color scheme. The houseplants tie the vibe together.

Sneaking a look at Noah as I sit down on the couch, I smile. He plunders through the kitchenette, looking in all my cabinets. He moves to all the storage spaces in the main area next, reaching above me and looking through my small book collection. He pulls down one of his novels and smirks. "Well worn, I see."

I snatch my copy of *Days in Dothan*—a contemporary romance about a couple who reunite in their hometown of Dothan, Alabama, after being apart for eight years—from his hands. Noah chuckles and sits down next to me as I hold my cherished book in my hands. "This book is my favorite Ashton Ashley."

Noah leans back, manspreading as he wraps one arm around my shoulders. His smells of citrus and vanilla, and I now know that his scent wasn't just an island thing. "Why's that one of your favorites? It's one of our earlier ones."

Noah and Ashton have written way more books than the three I gave fictional Noah. But one thing remains: these Prewitt boys write in tune with the music of my soul.

"I love second chances and think most people deserve at least one second chance in their lives." I snuggle close to his side as I flip through the paperback book. "I like how Vance... Wait, did y'all name this character after y'all's best friend?"

Noah's fingers play with my hair. "You met Vance?"

"Ashton took me on a tour of Prewitt Publishing. The day after I met your family."

The hum in his chest vibrates against my shoulder. "They're on pins and needles to see you again," Noah states. "To see us together."

Together. Images of how together we could be right now flit through my head. Should I do it? Should I try to kiss him? I don't want to do anything else, but I'm dying to know what my boyfriend tastes like. If it's anything like what I wrote about.

We have an hour before we need to head to El Mariachi, so I woman up and make a move to initiate. "We're together. Right now." Okay, that was bad. But I warned him flirting wasn't my specialty.

"We are," Noah remarks. I sit up and twist to face him, adjusting the strap of my jean overalls while I play with the one that dangles. But he turns the conversation back to books. "I was writing a book about us while I waited for you to remember me. But I burned it before I fled for Alaska."

I freeze, looking him dead in the eyes. "Why did you do that, Noah?"

He laughed derisively. "Because I didn't want any reminders of what we could have been. It hurt too much. It scared me that I felt so strongly for a woman who could never return the feelings."

Soaking in his words, I try to think of how to respond. I would have loved to see Noah's point of view, written in his beautiful prose, of the events that happened on Bora Bora. Then, an idea occurs to me. "Noah? What if we wrote my book together? We could revamp some chapters to be in the male point of view, and you could draft those. We could write our story."

He stares at me in silence, searching my eyes. Noah opens his mouth to speak, but then he snaps it closed before shaking his head. "I can't do that to you, Esme. This is your debut novel. I want all the focus on you."

I continue playing with my strap as I bite my lip, a small flush blossoming across my cheeks. "I want you to write this with me. It's just as much your story as it is mine. It'll be a good way to bond." I don't know why the thought of reworking my book with Noah feels so... intimate. But I want it.

I want so much from this man; it scares the mess out of me. Every moment with him, whether in person or on the phone, is a blessing. A gift that was withheld for far too long.

Noah follows the motion of my fingers fiddling with the hanging strap, and so I drop it and bring that hand to my lips. As I hoped, his gaze follows. "Yes, Esme. Let's do it." He drags his eyes to mine. "But right now, you're killing me, sweetheart. I'm trying to take physical contact slow, but—"

"Did we have sex in Bora Bora?" I blurt, remembering that I had questions about that based on... dreams... I've had.

Noah's pupils dilate, desire flickering within their depths. But he swallows. "No, ma'am. We were going to wait until we were married."

"But you wanted to?"

He sighs deeply, his head lolling back and a smile pulling at the corners of his mouth as he stares at the ceiling. "Esme, sweetheart. I'm only a man. And you are the most stunning creature I've ever laid my eyes on." Noah releases another breath. "I'm a virgin. We had this talk back in Bora Bora, but I want to reassure you once more in case it's one of those memories you forgot: I've always wanted to wait until marriage, and I'm still clinging to that." He smirks. "Even if you read smut."

I roll my eyes. "So, did *those* conversations really happen?"

He chuckles, eyes brightening. "Yes. All jokes. But you left out some important dialogue."

"Hm?"

Fire ignites between us as he whispers in a throaty voice. "I told you that I didn't want you reading smut because I want my wife's thoughts to be utterly consumed with me."

"I wrote something similar—"

Noah places his finger on my lips. "And," he continues, his voice lowering to a sultry depth, "whatever *my wife* and I do in bed will make a smut reader blush."

Tingles run up my arms and into my stomach, rippling down my legs. At my heated face, Noah starts to say something about how he believes in the sanctity of the marriage bed, but I drag his lips to mine before he speaks further.

He's startled at first, still as a statue, but then he sighs, sinking into me. Noah wraps one arm around my back and pulls me flush against his chest, deepening the kiss as he coaxes my lips apart. He hums against my mouth and nuzzles my nose with his. "I'm glad you're still willing to make out with me, though."

My body reacts at the explosion of emotion coursing through my veins as he captures my lips once more. Kissing Noah is like tasting the sun—hot, chaotic, and energizing. My hands find their way to his hair, and I relish in the smooth texture, tugging gently on the hair at the base of his neck. He groans, his hand splaying across my lower back as he holds me tighter. *I know him, I know him, I know him,* my soul sings on repeat, filling me with awe and wonder at the familiar way he feels against me. I move my lips to his jaw as his breaths become labored. I trail down until—

The faint scar across his neck jars me, and I pull back.

A question I should have asked so much sooner dawns on me. "How did you survive the attack? I remember," I swallow. "I remember the knife at your neck before I lost consciousness. I wrote about it, as you know."

Noah's eyes flicker from dazed to haunted as he straightens. "I elbowed him and attempted to spin out of his grasp. It worked, but the knife had already done its damage. I had just enough strength to jump on top of him, knock him down, and bang his head into the boardwalk. Over and over. Until he was passed out. Then I crawled to you."

Tears stream down my face, my heart swimming with emotions. I look at the scar running across his neck, proof of his love for me. I trace it with my fingertips before my hands move to his cheeks, one slipping into his hair.

My eyes flick back up to his, and regardless of the jumbled knot of emotions within me, one perfectly strong strand stands out in a golden flame, but I can't believe it. Not yet. People don't fall in love in a week, regardless of what I wrote. That was fiction. This is *real*. Raw, beautiful, and real. "Thank you for saving me."

"I would save you again and again and again, sweetheart."
He claims my mouth once more in a gentle manner, wrapping one hand behind my neck while the other slips behind
my back, pressing against him in an awkward position on
this little couch. The kiss is slow, hesitating, as if he's still
unsure if it's okay for him to initiate.

I break the kiss and straddle him, pushing back against
the cushion. A thin, angry line, slightly lighter than his skin,
runs from one side of his neck to the other. Rocks gather
in my throat as I try to speak, but no sound can move past
them as I stare at the evidence of Noah's love for me. Men
often say they'd take a bullet for their woman; Noah took
a knife across the throat for me. Was stabbed in the side.
Beaten and placed in the ICU for a week. He pushed me out
of the way and put himself in danger for me. For a woman
he'd only known a week.

"Noah Ashley Prewitt," I manage to get out in a gravelly
voice. Then I lift his chin with one hand to get a better
angle. Dipping to bring my lips to his neck, I pepper the
light scar from the shallow cut with soft kisses. Each one a
well-overdue thank you and apology.

"Thank you for saving my life." Kiss. "I'm sorry this happened to you." Kiss. "Thank you for protecting me." Kiss. "I'm
sorry I forgot you." Kiss. "I'm sorry I forgot our conversations and our kisses and our memories."

Noah groans, leaning his head further back as I continue
to kiss across his scarred neck. A shiver runs through him,
and he pushes me back before pulling my lips to his, his

fingers gripping my hips for dear life. We kiss and laugh and cry, sometimes all three at once, as emotions I never thought possible swirl to life within me.

I'm so lost in the rightness that is Noah that I don't notice my door opening until it's too late.

"Ope. My bad," a familiar voice calls, and I detach my lips from Noah, but I don't move to get off him. It's only Sam.

"Yes, your bad," I growl, not even looking away from a dazed and red-faced Noah. "I was being thoroughly kissed by the man who saved my life."

Noah laughs breathlessly, coming back to his senses. He looks around my shoulders as I roll away, though not leaving his lap entirely. "You must be Sam. Hi, I'm Noah." He holds out his hand, while I play with his disheveled curls.

Sam reaches around me to shake his hand. "It's good to meet the man of my best friend's novel." Noah smiles, but Sam continues, "However, I suggest switching your position because Ethan's gonna be coming in any second."

"Not like you don't use my brother as a chair in front of me," I murmur, but I jump to my feet anyway, knocking my head against Noah as he stands at the same time as me. "Ouch," he says. "Hard head."

"That she is," Sam agrees, laughing. "Glad you've already caught on."

The camper shakes as Ethan walks up the three stairs and through the door. "Did someone say my sister has a hard head?" His voice is deeper than usual as he spreads his legs and crosses his arms. He shifts his attention between me and Noah, no doubt noticing our frazzled and unkempt states. I run my fingers up and down Noah's arm.

"She does," Noah bravely says, holding out his hand once more. "Noah Prewitt. Heard a lot about you, Ethan."

Ethan waits a total of three seconds before grabbing Noah's hand and giving it a firm shake. I want to roll my eyes at my brother's dramatics. He and I both know if Noah really wanted to, he could wipe the floor with Ethan. But I love my brother and his feigned protectiveness. What else are older siblings for anyway?

"I thought you two were meeting us at the restaurant?" I ask.

"Got off early," Ethan states. "Dad said you two were in here, and well, I figured we'd get introductions out of the way before the entire town watches and dissects our every move at lunch."

"Well, would you look at that," I joke, clapping my hands and getting Sam and Noah to join in without telling them why. "That's about the smartest thing I've ever heard coming out of your mouth."

Everyone laughs except Ethan, of course. I place my hand back on Noah's arm.

After a few minutes of mindless chat, Ethan clears his throat and says, "Thank you, Noah. For saving my sister's life last year."

My lips quiver as tears threaten to push their way from my eyes once more, and I wish Mom wouldn't have given me her "cry at the drop of a hat" gene. Ethan and Noah do one of those bro-hugs, and the tears find their way out. *Thank you, God,* I silently pray. *Though I don't understand, and I likely never will, thank You for bringing beauty to our brokenness.*

There is beauty in the brambles, fictional Noah reminds me. I drop my gaze to Noah's tatted arm, and the words are there, woven around a cross like a beacon of hope.

I catch up with Sam and the theater situation, which has only gotten worse over the past few weeks. Remi Martin's and Julien Callahan's parents and friends are at each other's necks, and it's as if the entire community of Willow Bay has taken sides over something to do with the theater, but Sam still can't figure out exactly what the issue is. Apparently, the theater owner, Bradford, is talking about sending Sam down there to the coast as a liaison for a while to help smooth things over.

Ethan and Noah go outside to throw a football and talk, and when my parents join them outside, getting ready to leave, we all hop in our vehicles and head to El Mariachi.

"Okay, Noah." I state as I park my truck at the restaurant. "Listen carefully. Paulo is the owner. He likes to give us free cheese dip because I worked here when I was in high school. He may question you. Also, my grandparents will be here: Larry and Veronica. Pawpaw is the pastor of our church."

"I remember you talking about them back on the island. You mentioned if you ever married that you wanted him to officiate since your last dud of a guy didn't want to let your Pawpaw officiate," Noah interjects.

I nod, that familiar uneasy feeling that Noah may up and disappear back into my novel manifesting. *Oh, but kissing him was so very real.* "Yes. But let's please not bring that up this afternoon."

He grins and winks. "One day. Soon."

A blush creeps up my neck, but I remind him we're dating right now. That's all. Then I add, "There's also no telling who else will be here. Judging by the parking lot..." I look around at the gazillion vehicles. "I think word got out."

"About what?"

"That I have a man in town."

"Yeah, you do." Noah waggles his brows then kisses me on the cheek. "Calm down, sweetheart. I can handle your town."

"They will harass you, Noah. Are you sure you're prepared?"

He unbuckles his seatbelt. "You underestimate my charm."

"You underestimate this town," I murmur, getting out of the truck. Noah meets me on the sidewalk and takes my hand.

"Yer let 'er drive yer here? And didn't get 'er door?" Crazy Colt stands by the door to El Mariachi, holding it open as my parents, Sam, and Ethan walk inside.

"Colt, mind your manners. I wanted to drive him," I bark out.

"And she got out the truck before I could get the door for her," Noah tacks on, shooting me a wicked smile. "Little Miss Independent."

I mouth, "That's Crazy Colt."

He holds the door open for us and mutters, "See. This is whatta real man does," as Noah passes through. I catch Noah's eye, and he's completely unbothered. *Hmm.* He's already encountered Crazy Colt, and he's taking it like a champ. But there's still—

"Oh my gosh." The entire town is here tonight, I swear it. And my grandparents sit in the middle of the dining area, where the rest of my family is taking their seats. Everyone's eyes are watching us, the silent atmosphere thick with gossips waiting to take notes. I swallow, squeezing his hand. "I'm so sorry, Noah,"

Noah, to my utter surprise, leans down and kisses me right on the lips. Murmurs float above the crowd, intermingling with a few high-pitched whistles. Noah straightens and announces, "Hi, everyone. My name's Noah Ashley Prewitt. I'm from Tuscaloosa, Alabama, twenty-nine years old, have a steady but flexible career, and I'm willing to relocate to Whitney so that you can keep your Esme close. I love her. She's my world. I promise to cherish her, protect her, and take care of her until the Good Lord sees fit to split us apart." Then under his breath, he sighs. "Again." But his large smile doesn't falter as he leads us through the hawk-eyed citizens of this nosy town and pulls out a chair for me to sit in. I sit down, flabbergasted over his words. It's something a man in a book would do—stand in front of the town and declare his love for a woman. I couldn't even get Lane to say "I love you" over text before we went to bed.

"See, Colt? I'm a gentleman," Noah shouts, scooting my chair into the table, and my heart helicopters right out of my chest. Then, he bends down and whispers into my ear, "Until I get you alone later. That kiss from earlier ain't going to resume itself, baby."

A shiver runs down my spine as I fight the heat rising to my cheeks. Satisfied, Noah sits down beside me and introduces himself officially to my grandparents. After Pawpaw shakes his hand and tells him how excited he is to meet him, loud chattering resumes around us.

I lean into Noah's side, a huge smile spreading across my face. "Noah Ashley Prewitt, who even are you?"

He kisses my forehead and takes my hand under the table. "I'm yours, sweetheart. All yours. And if you come with this town—including a guy who calls himself Crazy Colt—then so be it."

I grin, squeezing his hand before lifting my other to cup his face. "Crazy Colt, though a nuisance, is someone we all try to look after," I mention in a whisper, eyeing the white-haired man sitting off to himself in a corner booth. "He lost his wife, and he hasn't been the same since."

Noah presses his lips together, a distant look haunting his eyes. "I can begin to imagine the pain."

I fiddle with his hair before moving back to his cheek and then down to his shoulder.

Grannie Bertha hobbles up to me and Noah. I stand to greet her, and Noah follows suit. "Hi, Grannie."

"Always a pleasure to lay eyes on you, handsome," she says, patting his arm. I have no doubt Noah is noticing the same tone and inflections used by his actual grandma, Lois. We've discussed the uncanny similarities between the two women multiple times since he's staying at Grannie's Inn.

He smiles and looks down at her cane. "Tell me, Grannie. Have you ever thought of bejeweling your cane? I know a fine lady who'd help you out."

"Well I'll be," Grannie says, eyeing her cane. "I haven't thought of it, but now that you mention it, that's a grand idea."

"I'll get you in touch with my grandma, Lois. She has one, and I know she'd love the chance to show it off."

Grannie pats my arm next. "I sure do like him, Esme." She leans in close, and Noah and I bend down to hear her whisper, "I knew God would bring you two back together. He told me He would."

Then, to me, she tsks. "You're in love." I scrunch my nose, but Grannie continues, a twinkle in her eyes. "You're pettin' him."

Noah's Novel Notes

Chapter One ~

For starters, if this is how everything went down when Bryan left you, he better pray he doesn't run into me. I have zero respect for the Bland Box of Crackers (Ashton told me that's what we call him).

Okay, now onto constructive (and very loving) criticism.

While you set the scene of Juniper Grove (and Book Esme's –hereby referred to as BE- external conflict) up well, I would like to see you dig deeper into the internal conflict of BE. You tell me about her heartache, her anger, and her confliction over Ryan's abandonment, but I'm not feeling it for myself. Try to get rid of words like "feel" and "'think" and drop strong verbs. Instead, describe it. Utilize the five senses to coax your reader deep into the warring emotions of BE.

You're doing great, sweetheart.

Chapter Seventeen

TAKE ME DOWN ~ MID-AUGUST

A knock on my camper door startles me from my book world.

Yawning, I make a mental note to make another pot of coffee to try and pound out the last few chapters of my novel. Ashton messaged me yesterday and said he and Noah were coming back into town this weekend, which is only a few days away, to meet with me about a timeline for publishing. On top of that, school starts back next Monday, which means I only have these last few days to achieve my goal of finishing this first draft. Noah has already written his chapters.

I tug at my messy bun and tuck the loose strands in my face behind my ears as I take the few steps to my camper door. I'm so tired these days because Noah and I have talked for hours on the phone every single night. He never fails to call me at eight p.m., and we talk until the wee hours of the morning about everything under the sun. Last night, we conversed about how we came to adopt our faith as our own outside of our parents and Bible Belt culture.

And you know what?

I've never clicked with a person like I do Noah Prewitt, and it still astounds me he stepped right out of my novel.

The knock on the door comes again right as I go to open it, and the door knocks into whoever is on the other side.

"Oof." A loud, masculine groan floats through the air as the door bounces back toward me from the force of hitting the man. It's Noah. I know because I'm now all too familiar with that baritone from talking to him every single day since I brought him home from Alaska.

I ease the door back open to find him lying on the grass. Heat that has nothing to do with August in Mississippi overcomes me. "I'm so, so, so sorry, Noah!" I bounce down the three steps and reach out my hand to help him up. He laughs as he stands, brushing grass off of his flamingo-pink shorts and yellow Hawaiian shirt. Though the clash of colors hurts my eyes, this man makes it work.

"Not how I expected to be greeted," he jests, then he looks at the ground where a bouquet of sunflowers lies. My stomach dips then soars as he picks them up, gives me an easy breezy smile, and holds the slightly mangled arrangement out to me.

I take them, step toward him, place a hand on his chest, and rise to my tiptoes to kiss him. As if it's as common a thing for me to do as breathing.

Noah grins against my mouth as his arm slides around my back. He presses me into him, not letting me back away. "You know," he says. "You could kiss and make better the places I hurt where I fell. If you want."

I laugh, though the images conjured in my head are not fit for the dating stage. Battling between loving that comment and his obvious show of desire—but knowing I can't act upon it and need to throw a barrier up to crash my train of thought—I playfully slap his chest and push away from him. "You rake." And then it dawns on me he isn't supposed to be here until Friday. It's Wednesday. "What are you doing here?"

Noah runs his hand through his curls, which fall right back into a haphazard state that simply works for him. Then, as if he's nervous, he rocks back and forth on his heels and folds his hands in front of him. "I hope you don't mind the intrusion, but I'd like to take you out on a surprise date."

My heart leaps like a ballet dancer. A *surprise* date? Planned for *me*?

"Intrude away!" I state, elation leaking through my voice. I look down at the beautiful bouquet of flowers in my hand and then remember I'm dressed in a day-old-sweat-pants-and-sweater combo that boasts coffee stains and reeks of exhausted, over-caffeinated author. "Crap. I need to change. How should I dress? I should probably shower. And I need to do my makeup and—"

Noah silences me with a long, delicious kiss. When he pulls away, leaving me begging for more, he says, "Be ready at five, sweetheart. I'll come pick you up. Wear something you feel pretty in." He plants a kiss on my forehead, the sweetest action I could even imagine, and leaves me speechless as he walks across the yard, gets in his dark blue truck, and leaves.

"What in the romance novel?" I ask myself aloud as I watch him drive down our dirt road. He honks the horn three times as he gets to the stop sign, then he pulls out onto the highway. He disappears behind a wall of oak trees, and I'm left once again wondering how this man is even real.

Once I'm back inside my camper, I check the time and realize I have three hours to get ready. My heart's beating a little too fast, my skin is a little too clammy, and I'm a lot too distracted to focus on writing. Instead, I call my best friend.

"Sammie? You busy?" I ask as soon as she answers.

"Just doing laundry. What's up?"

"Noah kinda just showed up on my doorstep, and I about knocked him out, but that's not pertinent to the story. Point is, he gave me flowers and told me he was taking me out on a surprise date tonight and to wear something pretty and be ready at five."

A beat of silence, and then, "Be there in fifteen."

Thirty minutes later, Sam finally arrives. She's throwing my clothes everywhere as she digs through my small closet at the end of my bed, looking for only God knows what. I told her I wanted to wear a simple sundress, but she said that wasn't going to cut it.

"Seriously, Sam. This is Whitney. Where in the world could he take me that I need more than a simple sundress?" "He could take you to Jackson. There are fancy places in the city."

"He said 'pretty,' not 'fancy.'"

Sam stops, her hands grabbing one of the felt hangers. She drags out a mini black dress, one that I haven't worn since, well, I don't remember. It belongs to the three-year memory hole.

"I've never even tried that on," I state, crossing my arms like a child.

Sam waggles her brows. "Yes, you have. You wore this bad boy on your first date with Bryan." She frowns. "At least the first one after you told me about him."

I scoff, throwing my hands up. "Then I definitely don't want to wear it out on my first official date with Noah."

"But you don't remember that date, and you didn't have a good time with Bryan anyway."

That catches my attention. "Sam, why did I even date that man? I have my assumptions, but did I ever confide in you about them?"

Sam drops the dress onto my bed and sits down as I stare at her from the bedroom steps. She sighs, fiddling with her short blonde hair. "You were pretty closed off in that relationship, which is why we haven't told you more information about it. You weren't in love with him; that's for sure. We could all see that from a mile away. Like I've told you before, I think you were settling. When you finally told me about him, you said he was sensible, had a decent income, and was kind, to which I replied that you needed more than sensible and kind. I told you that you needed romance and passion." She scrunches her nose. "Then you told me that romance and passion were only meant for heroines."

I soak in her words as I move to sit next to her on my bed, a defeated slump in my shoulders. "In that time, did I ever tell you what Lane once told me? I know I didn't tell you before I lost my memories, but did I ever open up about it?"

Sam shakes her head.

"Before Lane dumped me on Valentine's Day, we had been doing a lot of arguing. He had started going full days without talking to me, never planned dates outside of me going to his apartment and watching movies, and a bunch of other things like not telling me he loved me or not even bothering to get me little gifts like he had used to. Of course, I noticed it all. But when I brought it up to him one day, he laughed at me and told me that we were past all of that. The romance. He said I was his, and he was mine, and that was that."

"What a fusty, barren-spirited, abomination of a man."

"Okay, Miss Shakespeare." I laugh, then continue my story. "Determined not to believe that, I kept bringing it up. I was kind, gentle, and respectful in my approach, but no matter, it always ended in him ghosting me for a few days until I ended up practically begging him to talk to me and kept telling him how sorry I was for even mentioning it again. Then, when he broke up with me, he told me that my expectations were too high and that I wanted a fictional man, not a real man."

Sam curses, her fists clenching at her side. "I never liked that guy."

I laugh at the truthfulness of the statement. If only I would have listened to her warnings about him sooner, maybe I would have saved myself from a lot of heartache and self-doubt.

"Judging by what you all tell me about my missing years, I don't think I fully healed from what he said. When I woke up from the coma, it still all felt too fresh. But I woke up, you know? I had a new appreciation for life, and well, I wanted to try and believe that passionate love could exist. That it could exist for me. I think it's why I wanted to write the book so badly. It was a place for me to pretend that Esme could find a reckless, passionate, all-consuming love."

"And then it became real," Sam says slowly, catching on to where I'm headed.

"Then it became real," I reiterate, pursing my lips and nodding. Tears push against my eyelids as I confess the truth to Sam. "And I'm scared, Sammie. Because my brain has been effectively manipulated into believing that kind of love is not real, yet there's a real Noah. With a real love. And a real big heart. Full of romance. He makes me feel all the things, Sammie. Every night when we talk on the phone, I'm giddy with butterflies over what new thing I'll discover about him. He sweeps me away even when he's not actually here. I like his *voice*, Sam. I hate Bryan's voice."

We laugh, and the tears find their way through. "I just," I continue through the stuffiness setting into my nose, "I like him. A lot. And I think I might love him. But that's impossible because I've only known him for a couple of weeks. I've only been in his presence for less than that. And we haven't even gone on a real date."

Sam is quiet for a while, letting me lean into her side as she strokes my gross hair that's in need of a serious washing. Finally, she says, "Love isn't about how much time you spend with someone or the amount of dates you go on. Love is impossible to put into words. It catches you off-guard and defenseless when you least expect it to. Love makes sense of things previously unclear while muddling things you once thought you understood." Sam laughs, pulling me closer into her. She smells of lavender and lemon; I can tell she was cleaning before she came here. "You know my story with Ethan. We were engaged one month after we started dating."

"But the two of you have known each other y'all's entire lives."

"Never once did I look at him as anything romantic until he did that play with me on a dare. But Meme, when Ethan put his hands around my waist, pulled me close, and locked eyes with me, completely breaking character, I knew. Right then and there, I knew I'd marry him. I know it's cliche, but it's also true. When you know, you know. And you don't know until you know."

Do I know? Noah seems to know. I seemed to know when we were on the island. But now?

YES!

The word is shouted in my head like a crazed fan screaming at a Taylor Swift concert. But it's not fictional Noah talking. It's me.

Tears sober up fast. "Hypothetically, if I did *possibly* know I *potentially* wanted to marry him, how do I overcome the fear that, one day, he'll stop putting in effort and I'll expect too much?"

"You can't know the future, Esme. But do you think the Lord will lead you to a married life full of blandness and boredom when you're a woman whose heart and passion overflows more often than the Mississippi River?"

I don't know, I want to say. Because if I say no, that's admitting the Lord wasn't responsible for Lane. I was. I chose to stay with him even when all the Holy Spirit told me to do was run. I chose to stay even when my family said they didn't like him.

Instead of answering, I stand and pick up the black dress. It's a sweetheart neckline number with a cinched waist and flare skirt made of rayon. Classy, feminine, and gorgeous. I hold it up to myself as I face my mirror.

"Sam?"

"Yeah?" She stands and looks toward the mirror.

"What shoes should I wear?"

A slow Grinch-style smile crawls across her face. "I think we'll go with those glittering pastel orange strappy heels you bought on a whim and never wore. Since you like that color now and all."

Noah's Novel Notes

C hapter 7 ~

Esme. Lorraine. Jenkins. Baby, you are bringing the heat! I was blushing reading through that first kiss. I wonder if that's how you really felt when we first kissed on the island. Do you still feel that way when I press my lips to yours? When I run my fingers down your arms? When I whisper how much I adore you into your ear? When I—

Okay, I paused to video call with you, so when you read this note, remember I stopped in the middle to call you and tell you how much I miss you right now.

On to the notes!

This chapter was a pivotal moment in BE's arc. She wavers back and forth on whether she should have this fling with a perfect stranger (thank you, my very real Esme, for deciding to, by the way), ultimately deciding to go for it. It shows her emotional instability due to the external conflict present in her life, which is great. BUT. I fear many readers may not like my character and will surmise he is taking advantage of a heartbroken girl. To work around this, I suggest adding in internal thought and dialogue between the two characters that presents a different side to BE. Lean into the underlying character arc that BE didn't truly love Ryan and that, while she is hurting from the embarrassment of the situation, she isn't actually hurt by the loss of him. Does that make sense?

You're doing amazing work, sweetheart. I am so proud of you!

Chapter Eighteen

AT THE SUNSET ~ MID-AUGUST

"Bye, now. Love you. Have the best night ever." Sam continues to blow me kisses as she walks out of my camper. Once she's gone, I stand in front of my mirror once more, making sure I'm perfect.

The black dress sits about mid-thigh, hugging my upper body while giving flare to my bottom half. The heels are striking against the black, and though I feared I'd look too much like Halloween with black and orange, the color is soft enough to give a playful vibe to the look. Paired with gold bow earrings and a matching bracelet, my hair shiny and in a loosely curled high pony, I'm a vision if I do say so myself.

I live in the South, so I'm forced to care about my image. But I rarely get this dressed up, and as I continue to take in my reflection, I wonder if I should find reasons to dress like this more often.

Being Noah's just might be the answer to that.

I shake the thought, not wanting to start the date off with any more nerves and doubts than necessary. No. I'm going out tonight with an open heart and an open mind and a—

Knock. Knock. Knock.

My heart jumps right out of my chest as I wobble on my heels, careening backward off my bedroom steps. I grab the sides of the small doorway and steady myself as the knocks repeat three more times.

I check the time as I click down the steps. He's five minutes early.

Though I don't want to, I can't help but compare him to my last real relationship—that I fully remember anyway. Lane was always at least fifteen minutes late. Most of the time longer than that.

Readying myself and patting any flyaways down—not that they exist, thanks to the excessive amount of hairspray Sam used—I breathe in. Out.

And pull the handle of the door, leaving Noah to open it as I wait for my moment. You know the one. Where the man first sees the woman dressed up nicely for him. I tried for Lane, but he never showed any indication that he cared if I put on sweatpants or a sundress for him.

Noah, however, does not disappoint.

He's standing there at the bottom of the steps with yet another bouquet of flowers—this time orange and pink wildflowers—and wearing fitted black dress pants, a light orange collared button up tucked into his waist, and an expression that has me wanting to twirl for him.

So I do.

And when I make it back around, his jaw is still hanging open, eyes bugging out of his head, and he's still yet to find words.

"Hi," I whisper, averting my gaze and clutching my little white purse. I don't know which is making me melt more: how recklessly hot he looks or how he takes every inch of me in before clearing his throat and rubbing his hand down the bottom half of his face.

But his voice is rough and breathless when he finally speaks. "Esme Lorraine, you might just be the most beautiful thing I've ever seen." He holds out his hand to me, and when I slip my fingers through his, my world clicks right into place. Noah guides me down the steps, and when my heels are digging into the grass and I'm pressed against him, he kisses my cheek. And I thought the forehead kiss was the sweetest thing...

"For you, my lady." Noah hands me the flowers, and I take them, my fingers brushing against his. Those sparkling hazel eyes are dancing as his gaze bounces from my eyes to my lips. But instead of kissing me, he whispers, "Ready to go?"

I nod, not trusting myself with words. He chuckles and starts leading us across the yard, but my heels keep digging into the dirt. "I'm sorry," I rush out, yanking my heel from the ground. "I shouldn't have worn these things."

"On the contrary," Noah says, a lilt in his voice. He drops my hand, and before I realize what's happening, he swoops me into his arms, bridal style. The widest grin overtakes his face. "Now I've got a good reason to sweep you off your feet, sweetheart."

A girlish giggle escapes my lips as I wrap my arms around his neck. He kisses my forehead and stares into my eyes, a look of love that has my stomach tumbling. The words are on my tongue, *I love you*, but I bite down. The fear that this will all fade away one day is a weight on my chest, and until I can lift it off, I have no business telling this man I think I've chosen to love him forever.

Enjoy the date, Esme. Just enjoy the date and feel things out.

I sway to the rhythm of his gait, my fingers playing with the edges of his hair, until we stop in front of his truck. He sets me down on the gravel, opens the door for me, and even helps me in. Through it all, my brain is battling between *this is real* and *this is not real*.

This is princess treatment, and while many say these are basic expectations for a woman to hold for a man, I've never been cared for this way by any man besides my dad when he took me out to show me how a man should treat me. Didn't work, of course, because I then ended up clinging to a man who played with my mind and emotions, making me believe I wasn't worthy of this. *Or that it was even real.*

Noah gently closes the door before walking around and hopping into the driver's side. The truck roars to life, and in the evening summer sun, another memory flashes across my vision. This one is of us swimming underneath a setting sun, kissing and touching and whispering I love yous.

It's the first time I remember telling him that. Feeling love for him.

I'm breathless when I come out of the memory, and Noah is staring at me with concern in his eyes. "What's wrong?"

Centering myself and focusing on the present, I give him a soft smile. "Another memory resurfaced."

"Tell me." Noah throws the truck in drive, and as we roll over the gravel and to the stop sign at the end of the driveway, I tell him about the memory.

Everything except the I love yous.

I hold that in, and I ponder it, and I sit with it all the way into Jackson, which is where he told me we were headed after I changed the subject off my memory. I guess Sam was right to dress me up more than usual.

An hour later, thanks to potholes, roadwork, and traffic, Noah drives into the parking lot of Inkwell's, a small independent bookstore Sam and I like to frequent. But it's after six, and they're closed.

"Why are we stopping here?"

A smile forms on his handsome face. "This is our date."

I wrinkle my brows, questioning him with my eyes. But he doesn't answer. Instead, he hops out of the truck and rushes around to my side to get my door. He offers me his hand to help me down, and then we walk with our fingers intertwined into the dark bookstore.

A bell above the door rings, and past the stacks and stacks of books, into the back room I've never entered, are dimmed lights and candles. My breath hitches as we near the faint glow and I see a table set for two with a rose in a thin, glass vase and two candles on either side as a centerpiece. Twinkle lights hang from the tall ceiling, giving a warm, romantic hue to the space.

"Noah," I gasp his name as we enter the small room that is most definitely the back office of this place. But you can't readily see the desks, papers, and boxes pushed up against the walls. Instead, I'm drawn to the steaks, potatoes, broccoli, and basket of bread rolls on the table. And don't get me started on the massive slice of chocolate cake begging me to eat it first. Tall glasses of what looks to be sweet tea sit on the table, condensation rolling down the sides of the glass. Noah lets go of my hand only to move his to my lower back. I turn to look up at him. "You did all of this? For me?"

His thumb rubs up and down my spine, sending a shiver to meet the movement. "For us, sweetheart. I remember you didn't quite like my adventurous dates like hiking back on the island. I thought I'd try something quiet, romantic, and soft. A date fit for my introverted and a little anxious woman. My friend Kade owns this place, and he helped me set it all up earlier."

"Well tell him thank you for me."

My knees are noodles as I fight to not swoon. His steadying hand on my back as Noah guides me to my seat is the only thing keeping me from tumbling to the ground.

Because truth is, I don't just love this man.

I *like* him.

There's a huge difference.

And the liking him just might scare me more than the loving him.

I fell out of *like* with Lane within a few months, but I stuck around because he'd made me believe he was the best I'd get. I believed the transposed idea of what I desired over what I was actually getting.

But this?

No man has done this for me. I don't remember Bryan, but I'd venture to say he didn't measure up to *this*.

"Meme? Are you going to take your seat?"

I jolt from my head and quickly land in the chair as Noah scoots me into the table. He takes one step and sits down across from me, a hesitant smile on his face contradicting his earlier smirk.

"Are you okay?" I ask, lifting a brow.

Noah nods, though I don't think I buy it. He clears his throat. "Let me pray for us."

Heaven, take me now...

"Dear Heavenly Father, thank You for Your consistent grace, Your unwarranted mercy, and Your everlasting, eternal salvation through Your son, Jesus. Father, I can't thank you enough for bringing Esme back to me. All those nights

I screamed, cried, and begged. All those nights I thought You'd given up on me." Noah's voice breaks, and I open my eyes to find his hand taking mine as my tears drip onto my steak. "Well, God. You heard me and saw me. And in Your timing, though I'll never understand on this side of eternity why we had to take this journey, You brought the woman I want, the one I need, back to me. So, thank You, God. And please bless this meal to our bodies and our bodies to Your service. In Jesus's name, amen."

I squeeze his hand before letting go, and his teary eyes meet mine. We smile with broken sadness at one another. "Noah," I manage to say as I wipe at my wet cheeks, hoping my mascara didn't run. "What really happened during those months?"

He releases a breath, leaning back in his seat. "I felt like what I imagine it would feel like if I lost Ashton. Like half of me was missing. You bolted into my life like lightning, Esme, and I knew I'd never be the same again. And then just as quickly as you struck, you were gone. Worse, you weren't dead. You were alive, but you didn't remember me. Us. And I couldn't for the life of me reconcile that twist of fate." He laughs mirthlessly before continuing. "I was so mad at God, Esme. But through it all, He was still good to me."

My steak is probably too salty to eat with the amount of tears puddling on it, but I don't care. Noah laid himself open and showed me a non-perfect side to him. A side that questions and gets mad at God. And well, it makes him even more perfect in my eyes. "I've been there," I finally respond, drying my eyes with the back of my hand. "When I woke from the coma, I was so mad at God for causing it to happen. Heck, I think I've been mad at God for a lot of things that I've done and placed the blame onto Him."

"What did you get mad at Him for outside of the coma?" Noah sniffles and blots at his cheeks. My heart breaks at the sight of his vulnerability.

Now it's time for me to be honest.

With him, with God, and with myself.

"I was with a man for a while—Lane."

Noah tenses. "Yeah, you told me about him back in Bora Bora."

I laugh lightly. "Well, I know you told me that I said similar words to what I'm about to tell you now, but I don't remember that moment. I had to learn the lesson twice, I guess. But I blamed God for Lane when in reality, I chose to stay in a situation I knew wasn't right for me. He made me believe I wasn't deserving of romance and passion. In fact, he led me to believe no real human man would measure up to the fictional ones. I still don't know the full picture of Bryan, my ex-fiancé, but I think it was a similar story." *Maybe darker than I want to know,* I think to myself, remembering the weird memory that surfaced when I was last with him. I shove it aside and focus on Noah.

"I thought Lane was right, you know?" I clear my throat and hold Noah's gaze as I enunciate my next words. "Until you."

If a man could melt into himself, Noah Prewitt did. And the sight of the affection and love in his softening eyes has me coming undone.

"I love you," I blurt. I drag my hand to cover my mouth, staring at Noah with trepidation. *What if this is what he wanted? What if he was waiting to make sure I loved him, and now he's going to switch up on me and stop being romantic and bringing me flowers, and then tell me I expect too much when I ask him just to text me at least once throughout the day to let me know he's alive.*

Noah stands, his face giving not one single thought away as he moves beside me and kneels down. No, no, no. I'm not ready. "Esme, I'm not proposing to you. I told you I'd date you until you're ready, and I don't think that you confessing you love me—which has sent me over the moon, by the way—" He can't stop the smile that stretches across his face no matter how hard he tries to keep an enigmatic expression at the moment. "But I want you to know that I value your love, your choice to love me. I will not take your love for granted. I promise to keep our love alive. *Always.*"

I swallow the lump in my throat as he caresses my face. "I love you, Esme Lorraine Jenkins. And my love for you will never falter or wane. Everyday, I will wake up and choose you."

Fear is still present. I still have doubts. But one golden thread of hope is perfectly clear. "I choose you, too." I smile through my tears. "I love you, too, Noah Ashley Prewitt. Superhero of naps."

His curls bounce as he throws his head back with laughter. "I saw the painting in your camper." A dark brown brow quirks up. "Right in front of your bed."

"Where it shall live forever to fuel my fantasies." I boop him on the nose as he once did to me after making a roguish comment, and satisfaction rolls over me in waves when I watch his eyes darken and his body shudder.

"Double standards," he tsks, and guilt pools in my stomach. But then he adds, "The student has become the master."

"I shouldn't have said that. I guess when you really have it bad for someone, your tongue loosens. I get how it can just slip out now." I hang my head. Experiencing desire for a man—this loud, screaming red—is something I'm still getting used to. Learning the boundaries of us both in our dating relationship. "Your picture is there to remind me that I once lost an epic love—a love I've always longed for. I'm determined not to lose it again."

"It's okay, sweetheart." Noah stands, then he pulls me to my feet and tugs me into him. "There is beauty in the bramble. Our mess is ours, and it's my favorite." My hands naturally float to his chest as his wrap around me and press me into him.

Noah's forehead touches mine, his lips breaths away. "I have it bad for you, too, love." Unhurried, he licks his top lip as his eyes bore into mine. I whimper, and his mouth twitches upward. Then without a warning cue, he traces the tip of his tongue along my lips.

I implode.

My hands fist his shirt as I drag his lips down to mine in a fiery kiss full of desire. But just as quickly as it started, it comes to an end, replaced with long, slow, sweet kisses as Noah tells me how much he loves me without a single word.

And I crumble into him, telling him right back.

"Our food's gonna get cold," I mention in a break from the kiss.

"There's a microwave," he mumbles incoherently.

I giggle and push him away, taking my seat and leaving him standing and flushed and thoroughly kissed.

What a beautiful sight.

"Come eat. You prepared all of this for us."

He begrudgingly sits and huffs a laugh of disbelief. "Don't ever tell me you can't flirt again. You, sweetheart, are an enchantress."

His words cause me to preen like Ares, Sheriff Hodges' K9, when he's done a good job. "Only because it's you."

And I'll be danged.

Maybe I did have a playful and flirty side in me after all. I needed the right person to call it out of me. And now I need to discover where the new boundary line is for *my* flirty mouth.

"After we eat," Noah says as we take our seat, "pick out as many books as you want. It's on me."

Noah's Novel Notes

Chapter 13 ~

Wow, love. WOW. The chemistry these two have is off the charts, but I adore the way you've brought in the deeper emotional aspects in this chapter. BE has gone from grumpy, closed-off, and simply enjoying her fling to caring about BN, opening up to him, and thinking about the possibility of a future outside of the island. Well done!

The only loving criticism I have is that I would like to see a little more action in this scene. Middles in novels are complicated, and if you're not careful, they can fall flat and cause readers to become disinterested. What ideas do you have that can connect with my next chapter? What adventure can we send these two insta-lovebirds on while they have these deep, emotional conversations?

I love you, Esme. Can't wait to see you tonight ;)

Chapter Nineteen

HE'S SO BAD ~ LATE AUGUST

"I see you've found the correct grandson's lap this time." Lois Prewitt fixes me with a knowing stare as she folds one hand over the other on top of her signature bejeweled cane. My face flames hotter than the sun high above us as I sit halfway on Noah's lap. I didn't intend to sit this way, but when I went to sit beside him on the edge of the hourglass-shaped saltwater pool, he tugged me close and wouldn't let me go.

Naturally, I didn't put up a fight. Look at him! He's golden and glistening from the water. He smells like sunshine, salt, and citrus. Like happily ever afters are real.

But Lois's comment has me inching away, and Noah lets me this time, though my hand stays firmly locked with his.

Lois and Link weren't out here earlier when he plopped me down like he was my personal throne.

This is the first time I'm seeing the Prewitt family after finding Noah, and I fretted as I drove all the way here, wondering if they would fully accept me into their family.

I had feared for nothing.

The moment my old truck pulled into the driveway, Branda was racing to open my door, pulling me into a tight hug as her bangled wrists dug into the bare skin on the backs of my shoulders. "We're, like, sisters now!" she'd shouted. I couldn't fight the smile off my face if I wanted to as she had led me toward the door where Noah had stood with crossed arms, pouting about how he was supposed to greet me and not his sister.

Noah's deep voice brings me back to the present. "Is there something I need to know about?" I don't turn around to see his eyes, but I surmise they're bouncing back and forth between me and Ashton, who is setting the water volleyball net up with Branda's and Vance's help.

"It was an accident, Ashley. Chill," Branda retorts, using his middle name as she often does when she wants to pick at him.

"I second the statement," I say, raising my eyebrows at Lois who simply shrugs and hobbles over to take a seat in one of the white reclining chairs under a huge tan umbrella.

Beside me, Noah rises. From my seated position on the pool's edge, I watch as he stretches, momentarily entranced by the way his muscles ripple. My eyes flick down to a barely visible scar on his side, a faint white color against his sun-darkened skin. A swell of gratitude blooms in my chest, the same one I get every time I remember what he did for me over a year ago.

God, help me remember it, I pray silently. But I know that even if I never fully remember my time on Bora Bora, Noah is helping me trust that it's probably for the best. While I wrote the attack scene fairly accurately, Noah says it was much darker than the hazy images my brain conjures when I attempt to recall the moment. But he still won't tell me the details; he only shudders, kisses my forehead, and says that it's best I don't remember.

We are still working on getting him to stop taking others' burdens. It's a slow process. His ability to care for me and others with such a huge heart is part of the reason I've fallen in love with him.

But then I hear Ashton, in a cautious warning, say, "Don't you even think about it."

Noah looks down at me, wearing a mischievous smile that says Ashton isn't going to like whatever is coming to him in a moment. Burdened to help my friend, I place my hand on Noah's calf, capturing his attention. "Leave the poor man alone. It was my fault. I tripped and fell on top of him."

"But she lingered," Lois pipes up, wearing a wicked smile.

And this is how I know I've been fully accepted into the family.

Noah's lip twitches before he bends down and swoops me into his arms. His drying black curls hang loosely in his face as his hazel eyes twinkle. "I can't let you off the hook, now can I?"

"Noah Ashley Prewitt. Don't you—"

He kisses my forehead and chucks me into the water, the second Prewitt man to do so. It kisses my hot skin before warming around me as I kick my way to the surface, preparing to find Noah and... Well, I don't know what I'm going to do. Maybe I'll bide my time.

Good choice, my little author. We can seek revenge in the confines of our book, fictional Noah states. He doesn't talk to me much these days; it's bittersweet.

As I break the surface, I'm met with a monster of a splash. In front of me, Ashton and Noah are wrestling, creating a maelstrom in the water as they go round and round. Vance decides it's a good idea to join them.

Definitely will seek my revenge at a later date.

I swim away to the shallow end where Branda looks upon her brothers and friend with disdain. She sighs as I stand beside her in the chest-deep water. "Every time they want to play water volleyball, this happens. And I'm left with setting up the net all by myself."

"Hey, I'm here." I bump her shoulder. Branda's dejected look instantly shifts.

"I'm so glad another woman is in the picture."

I comb my fingers through my hair, pushing the soaked brown strands out of my face. "Put me to work, boss."

Within minutes, we finish setting the net up and exit the pool as the men continue to go at each other playfully. I can't lie; it's a sight that warms my heart. Being here, sitting next to Branda and Lois under this giant umbrella, while Link grills under the pavilion across from the pool, is like being home. Like I found people who were never supposed to be mine but, somehow, they are.

"I'm so glad you found my boy," Lois says as she stares at the brawling group. She tsks and continues. "He scared me."

"I'm glad we found him, too. I know it wasn't easy for you all. Did he tell you his reasonings?"

Lois shakes her head. "He didn't, but he doesn't need to. He broke and needed to disappear."

"He needs to let us in," Branda comments, aggression in her tone. "I wish he knew he never has to struggle alone."

"I think he knows that." I take a sip of sweet tea then set it down inside the cupholder. "Ashton might technically be the oldest, but Noah is right there with him. They're twins. Ashton handles burdens differently than Noah, I think. Ashton holds things close to his chest, while Noah masquerades with humor and levity. He carries the burden of making sure you all are well."

"But Esme, we never asked him to do that." Branda sits up as Lois removes her sunshades. All three of us make eye contact, and I know this conversation is headed somewhere only Noah can provide the ending to.

I release a breath. "I know, Branda. My brother is the same way. He's the oldest, keeps his true emotions to himself, and looks after me even when I don't need nor want him to. My brother is more stoic than Noah, even more so than Ashton, but it's still the same concept. It's just a thing older siblings do, and I know it would be hard for Noah to shake that feeling of responsibility."

"It just—" Branda pauses, her brows scrunching together. "It hurts. That he doesn't trust us enough to be by his side in his pain. He's always there for us. I want to be there for him."

Lois replies, "I don't think it's a trust issue, dear."

I nod. "And I think it would be best if you spoke to him about it. His story—his doubts, fears, and burdens—aren't mine to tell."

A few minutes of silence pass between us, and I fear I may have made a mistake. But the guys finally call truces, and Noah saunters my way, breathing heavily with droplets of water rolling down his cheeks, his jaw, his chest...

"My eyes are up here, sweetheart," he jests, moving to stand beside me before leaning down and kissing my forehead. I catch Branda's overthinking, concerned gaze, and make an impromptu decision.

"Lois, would you mind showing me all the flowers in the front garden? There were some I've never seen before and would like to learn about them."

Smart as a whip and intuitive to a fault, Lois catches what I'm throwing and slowly works herself up to her feet, cane in tow. "I'd love to show you my marigolds. Are you allergic?"

"No ma'am," I reply, rising to my feet. I stand on my tiptoes to hug Noah and whisper in his ear, "Talk to your sister about what happened. You have to let your family in."

I pull away, take in his furrowed brows, kiss his cheek, and follow Lois across the grass and around the side of the huge white house. Whatever is going to happen is going to happen.

"You're good for him," Lois says as we approach the sprawling garden full of every color imaginable. It's nestled between the edge of the front porch and an ancient-looking magnolia tree. The sunlight streams through the leaves, giving the shaded garden enough light for the flowers to bask in the golden glow.

"He's good for me." I tug at my swimsuit cover-up, which is clinging to my damp high-waisted two-piece underneath. "I think he's slowly showing me that good men who want to love a woman well exist."

"His grandfather was the same way." Lois smooths the sides of her silver hair as if it wasn't still in a perfect, tightly wound bun, not a strand out of place. "His name was Ashley, you know?"

I palm the bud of a red rose. "No, I didn't. Could you tell me about him?"

Lois's eyes light up, and for the first time, the put-together, sassy yet stoic grandma looks on the verge of tears. "I'd love to tell you all about how Noah is a replica of my late husband. Starting with that necklace you're wearing around your neck. It was a gift from an Alaskan alchemist, or so the legend goes..."

For the next twenty minutes, we check flowers, talk about her beloved, and brainstorm business ideas for bejeweled canes (as I promised Grannie back in Whitney). Lois reminds me so much of Grannie Bertha back home, and I hope to introduce the two of them soon. In fact, I want the Prewitts to meet my entire family. I want joint-family cookouts and vacations and parties.

The thought startles me.

In the past, I tried to keep Lane away from my family.

Bryan's parents obviously know mine, but Mom has told me before that they didn't do much with us, and even then, I kept Bryan away from them except on special occasions.

Why did I do that?

I guess I won't fully know unless my memories return, but as for Lane...

I kept him away because I was embarrassed of him.

Embarrassed of the way he treated me. Embarrassed that I let it happen. Embarrassed that I was settling even though I didn't want to admit it to myself.

"Burgers are ready!" Link calls from around the house, and Lois and I make our way back there to see Branda and Noah hug, Vance slap Noah's back, and Ashton remaining off to the side with a faraway look on his face. As we all come together to help Link set the table under the pavilion, Noah meanders toward me, carrying a jar of pickles, and whispers, "Thank you, Esme." Then he bumps my shoulder, almost dropping the jar in the process.

"Careful," I say through a laugh as my hands wrap around the jar to steady it. "It'd be a shame to lose the pickle."

Noah, in all of his roguishness, waggles his brows. As soon as he opens his mouth to comment, I nail him with a warning glare. He swallows the retort. "Right. I'm working on not letting my sexy inside thoughts out until we've said our vows. Sorry, sweetheart." He kisses my cheek then goes on about his business.

I stare after him, taken aback that he shifted gears so quickly. And with respect and sincerity. When I used to address Lane (because I guess I have a thing for the flirty rakes of society), he would brush me off and say that I needed to grow up and not be such a prude. He didn't respect the fact that his sexual comments turned me on and made me want things that I wouldn't allow myself to have until marriage due to my morals.

But Noah?

He's respecting me. Cherishing me. Showing me just how much he loves and cares for me by honoring my requests.

Snapping out of my comparison monologue, I rush to where he's cutting the pickles into circular slices. I wrap my arms around him from behind and rest my face against his back. "Thank you, Noah. Now let me go help Branda whip up the Orange Julius. It's still your favorite drink, right?"

Noah grins a megawatt smile. "Indeed. It's almost as sweet as you."

I roll my eyes, but the blush coating my cheeks over his cheesy line follows me all the way inside.

Noah's Novel Notes

C hapter 17 ~

Esme, sweetheart. *Chef's kiss* I love how perfectly you show the two of them back home in their typical environments, bonding and connecting. It's sweet, gentle, and precious. Branda is going to be thrilled that we decided to include her into the story. And she's going to die over the fact that we named her Annie. She's always hated that name. Dad would use it as a shortened version of her middle name, Annison, when she was getting in trouble. So, thanks for letting me use that name for her character. I'll take the heat from her if she comes after you about it.

I want to see you develop the town of Juniper Grove a little more. What are the quirks of the town? Does BE have a favorite place to hang out there? Does she run into people she knows when she's out and about? It's time to start connecting the beginning back to the ending, so get creative and breathe life into the town. Maybe we should explore it together soon? It'd be fun to check in on Lucy May while we're there if you're down.

All my love, your Noah Ashley Prewitt, superhero of NAPS! (P.S. – let's cuddle soon?)

Chapter Twenty

As It Begins ~ mid-September

O ne month of dating.

One entire month of officially being with the man who stepped out of my novel, and I still can't comprehend how I wrote a perfect relationship into existence.

Except it's not perfect, which makes it all the more real and wonderful.

We had our first scuffle a week ago; I grin as I recall it.

"I won't make it to Gloria's cooking class tonight, Esme. We have a deadline to meet at work, and I'm not going to be able to get away in time. I'm sorry." Noah sounded stressed on the phone, but I couldn't stop my initial reaction. My heartbeat picked up, and all I could think about were the hundreds of times Lane bailed on our plans to hang out with his friends instead of spending time with me.

"But you promised me, Noah. You said we'd attend her first class together to support her."

Noah sighed over the phone. "I know, sweetheart. And I'm truly sorry. I wish I could get out of this project, but I have to finish these edits or Ashton will have to take on extra work. He needs my help."

My heart sank as I tasted bile in my throat. I tried to remind myself that it wasn't an excuse. That Noah wouldn't do something like that to me. That it was my relationship trauma speaking. But in my anxiety, I blurted anyway, "Oh? So you'll be there for Ashton and not me?"

Silence stretched between us, and I begged God to open the earth and swallow me whole. I shouldn't have said that. What was wrong with me? Noah was a good man, and I was punishing him for the color of pain a past lover had painted me in. "Noah, I—"

My words were cut off as he started talking at the same time as me. "Esme, I don't appreciate being talked to that way. What can I do to help you trust that my words are true?"

Tears beat against the back of my lids. "Noah, I'm so sorry. I do trust you. I know you wouldn't make up an excuse to bail on me." Liquid fell from my eyes as my chest was set aflame from shame and embarrassment. "You're a good man, Noah. I spoke out of fear. Please forgive me." I could barely manage to get that last phrase out around my sniffles.

More moments of stillness passed between us before my phone buzzed. Noah was video calling me. Wiping my eyes, I accepted the call. "I'm sorry," I said again.

"Love? Look at me." His voice was calm and gentle, and so I reluctantly turned my face from my lap and toward the phone screen in front of me. And Noah was... *Smiling?* "Hey, beautiful. It's okay. All is forgiven. I have a few moments. Do you want to tell me what lies your fear was whispering into your ear?"

The burning in my chest eased at his steady show of love as he sought to understand.

God, I love this man, I thought to myself.

Still grinning over the memory, I sneak a look at my handsome guy sitting next to me in my brother's truck. Every single day, he makes me feel safer, more secure, and stable, which is crazy for me to think about because the man is the extrovert to my introvert, routinely secondhand embarrasses me in public, and is always trying to do spontaneous things with and without me.

But tonight isn't spontaneous, and it's something I've written about in my novel. In fact, it's the last scene I wrote. And while I know tonight won't go exactly how I wrote it, I'm excited to see what happens. In the realm of reality.

"You ready?" Noah asks as we pull into the crowded parking lot of The Wild Whitney.

"You know it, babe." I wink and take him in. Noah Prewitt should always wear old Wrangler jeans, cowboy boots, and a tight white T-shirt.

I match him in my short cut-off jeans, white tank top, and bedazzled boots.

"I love the way you look in those jeans," I comment as Noah gets out of the truck. I've gotten better at openly complimenting him because he is always saying how beautiful, hot, smart, kind, and talented I am. Noah receives love through affirmations and words whereas I am more action-oriented, and we are learning to speak each other's language.

"Gross, Esme," Ethan retorts as he climbs out of the backseat with Sam. I ignore him because it's not like he didn't just comment on Sam's—and I quote—"fine-as-white-wine legs."

A familiar truck pulls in as we're all piling out of the truck.

"Ashton!" I shout with giddy excitement when he rolls up to The Wild Whitney. "And Branda!"

I run to hug the two of them, and then I make quick introductions. "This is my best friend, Sam, and my brother, Ethan."

Ethan adds, "And I'm married to this beautiful woman." He wraps his arm around Sam, tugging her close and kissing her. The two of them already had a drink back at the house, which is why Noah—probably a little offended by Crazy Colt's earlier comment about not driving me—drove us four over here tonight. His truck is as lifted and decked out as Ashton's, except Noah's is a deep blue color to Ashton's brown.

"What are you two doing here?" I ask, grabbing Branda for another hug.

"Noah said something about going to the town's raucous nightlife, and we couldn't pass up the opportunity to join."

"Two hours for The Wild Whitney," I hum. "It'll be a letdown for sure. I'm sure y'all've got fancier clubs in Tuscaloosa. In fact, Noah took me out to one last weekend." And yeah, the anxiety was real, but I powered through. We take turns tagging along with what the other wants to do whether we necessarily like it or not. It's getting me out of my comfort zone, which I think is what he's trying to do.

Ashton shrugs. "But the people we care about are here." And in a mock whisper, pretending that he's not letting Branda hear, he says, "Branda and Vance got into a huge fight, and the girl needs to blow off some steam. I came to pawn her off on you two."

Branda elbows her brother, smiling sweetly. She's a scary one sometimes, that's for sure. *Poor Vance.*

"Well," Sam slaps her arm, "let's get inside. It's hot as hell's kitchen out here and the mosquitos are getting me."

"They like sweet things," Ethan coos, and I groan. These two will be relentless tonight.

Noah throws his arm over my shoulders as we walk into The Wild Whitney. It's a ratchety old place that has been, and will always be, a town staple. The lights are dim, and there's a trace of cigar smoke wafting in from the smoking quarters off to the side of the building. Mikey, the aging bartender who's been working here for as long as I can remember, waves us over. Ethan and Sam are first in line for drinks, Ashton and Branda behind them, and finally, me and Noah. Country music pours from the speakers.

"I don't want to drink," I tell him as I rub my hand up and down his arm. Noah doesn't drink, so I rarely do unless I'm having a girls' night with Sam or an occasional weekend brunch with Isla. "I want to remember every moment of dancing with you tonight. You do dance, right?"

Noah smiles brighter than the neon signs, adjusting his grip to take my hand and lead me out to the small dance area. At that moment, the music shifts, and "Head Over Boots" begins to play. "What kind of Southern man would I be if I couldn't spin my old lady around a dance floor to Jon Pardi?"

A lightness lifts me and carries me around the dance floor as Noah guides me in a swing dance. *Just like in the last chapter I wrote.* The couples on the floor part the way for us, but I'm so lost in Noah's eyes and his smile that everything and everyone else begins to fade away. He spins and dips me all around this joint, pushing out then pulling me in. Kissing me, pressing against me, and swaying to the music with me.

The bridge slows us down, and Noah pulls me close, our foreheads touching as he mouths the words of the bridge and then into the chorus that follows. In this little bubble of ours, I kiss him. Applause erupts around us, hoots and hollers and whistles interspersed throughout. Noah and I break the kiss, but we cling to one another as if there's never a possibility of letting go. I touch his face, his hair.

I can't stop myself, and I realize Grannie was right: I pet Noah. For a girl who doesn't necessarily enjoy physical touch, I need it like I need air when it comes to this man.

My will to hold out breaks, crumbling like an eroded statue. "Ask me, Noah."

He processes for a second, a loading wheel spinning above his head. Then, when it dawns on him, his entire body lights up. It's as if joy are beams of light shining from within him. "Ashton!" he hollers over the music, never taking his eyes off me. I wrinkle my brows in confusion, but Ashton stumbles over to us with the help of Isla.

"Yes, my dear brother?" Ashton slurs a little, but it's the smile on his face as he looks at Isla that takes me by surprise. Noah whispers something in Ashton's ear while I compute the age difference between Isla and Ashton. Eight years? She's eight years older than him, I believe. *Interesting.*

I wonder if he knows.

Isla throws me a pleading look that makes me think he doesn't. I wink at the slender, redheaded curly-haired woman who's got her arm wrapped around Ashton's waist. If anyone deserves a night clinging to a Prewitt brother, it's her. She's the sweetest, most gentle soul I know. Though I always thought her and her best friend, the sheriff, would end up together.

The music cuts off, and Noah loudly clears his throat as people start to gather around us. He gives me a nervous smile before sliding down onto one knee and opening a black ring box. My heart beats wildly in my chest as my breaths stop.

"Esme, when I saw you standing in Nick's house back in Alaska, I had just underlined this piece of scripture from Lamentations: 'The Lord is good to those who wait for him, to the soul who seeks him.' I'd been studying the book, trying to make sense of why God does the things that He does. I concluded I will never understand the mind of God, but all that matters is that He is God and He is good. Even if I never got the chance to see you again." Noah sniffles, pushing back tears. "Then there you were. Standing in front of me. The answer to my most desperate of pleas." He shakes his head, a look of wonder and amazement shining through his handsome face. "I've been carrying this ring with me since I made it back to Tuscaloosa after Bora Bora. Even though you forgot me, I kept this ring on me at all times, waiting for this moment. I had to have faith it would happen. And," he shakes his head breathlessly, "here it is. Marry me, Esme, sweetheart. Pencil me in with Sharpie."

"Yes!" Laughter bubbles out of me as I offer him my hand, accepting the proposal he ripped right from my book. He slips a gorgeous silver ring on my finger, but instead of a diamond at the center, there's a sunset orange imperial topaz.

My story ends here, my little author. Congratulations. I'll let you relish in the real, fictional Noah whispers, and I want to cry.

Noah kisses the ring on my finger. "A little birdie told me you were now a fan of orange." A whimper escapes as he kisses my neck. Tears push through my eyes, but I'm not sad. I'm happy. Elated. Content. I once thought I didn't deserve a passionate, fiery love; I thought I deserved sensible and secure.

But I don't want sensible and secure and bland.

I want passion and romance and the unexpected.

I want Noah Ashley Prewitt forever.

The entire room claps and applauds. Branda drags Noah to his feet, bear-hugging him before throwing herself at me. My brother and Sam are next, and finally, Ashton.

He pulls me into a tight, drunken hug. "Esme, taking a chance that you'd help me find Noah is the best decision I've ever made." He releases me from the hug but doesn't drop his arms. "I'm so happy for you, sister." And with that, he winks and stumbles into Isla's arms.

I arch a brow at her, but she smiles timidly, shrugs, and mouths, "Congratulations" before walking back to the dance floor with Ashton.

We continue to dance, drink, and sing in a mass celebration, and as word of our engagement got out, the entire town has found its way here, including Sheriff Hodges, who busies himself keeping Crazy Colt's drinking in check while Branda busies herself ogling the law enforcement officer. Isla and Ashton dance, but I don't miss the way Isla keeps glancing at Sheriff Hodges. *This town might get a little more interesting...*

Once Noah and I slip out the back to get some fresh, humid air, I throw my hands up. "You knew this would happen tonight!"

He wears a boyish guilty grin and shrugs. "Like I said, I've had that ring on me or near for a long time just waiting for you to catch up with me."

I laugh with disbelief before pointing my finger into his chest and backing him up against the outside wall. "You weren't lying when you said you were a little too impatient the other night when you were apologizing for getting frustrated at me that I got lost in my book and ignored you for most of the day."

He grabs my hand and spins us around until he's holding that hand above my head and pressing his sweaty body into mine. "I go after what I want, and I want you. Forever."

"You have me," I say breathlessly as he runs his fingers down my raised arm. "Forever. And again, I promise to try really hard to escape my reverie in favor of real life with you."

"Because I'm better than the fictional version of me you wrote, right?"

I grin and mean every word that I say. "Noah Prewitt, there isn't a fictional character around that measures up to the reality of you. Lane lied to me. A real man is better than a book boyfriend, not the other way around."

"You got that right, sweetheart."

And then a thought occurs to me as I get lost in thoughts of marriage with Noah. "Where will we live?"

"Here, if you want. I'm a writer. I can work from any-where. I will gladly live in that camper with you, though I'd prefer if we relocate it. All the rocking that will happen after I marry you might not sit well with your parents." He winks and moves to trail kisses down my neck and onto my shoulder. I didn't realize the night could get hotter. But I'm talking to Noah Prewitt, so who am I kidding?

And now... I'm engaged. His roguishness is hitting a little differently. A little more, how do I word this? Expectantly.

Not married yet, Esme.

I push the thought aside.

"What about buying a place here in town? Would you be interested in that?"

"Absolutely, sweetheart." Noah kisses along my jaw. "We can start looking tomorrow after church."

"When do you want to get married?" I ask, closing my eyes to deeply feel his lips against the other side of my neck.

"As soon as you'll let me, Esme." He pulls away and catch-es me off guard with his serious expression. "We can go to the courthouse or we can plan a big affair."

"As much as the courthouse sounds preferable, this town will skin me alive if I don't give them a wedding."

Noah laughs. "You still have a little people-pleaser streak in you, don't you?"

I shrug. "It's okay in healthy amounts. And plus," I wrap my arms around his waist and pull him back to me, "I want that with you. To have a man who loves me fiercely to be waiting at the altar for me. I want to walk down the aisle to you while wearing a white dress. I want to exchange vows with you in front of the town."

Noah shivers as I slip my hand under his shirt and run my fingers down his spine. "So, we'll plan a wedding," he rasps out. "And it's gonna be the quickest planning anyone has ever seen."

I chuckle as I kiss his jaw. One hand moves to cup his cheek, and I catch my ring glittering like a sunset in the low lamppost light above us. "So, who told you I like orange instead of pink now?"

"You sent my twin an orange heart and said you loved the color. Imagine my jealousy when he showed me."

"It reminded me of you," I state, bringing my lips to his. "My fictional dream guy come to life."

Noah smiles against my lips. "Oh, but sweetheart. This is *very* real."

Noah's Novel Notes

C hapter 23 ~

You did it! Esme Lorraine Jenkins, you have drafted your first novel. And I stand in awe at your talent, my love. I fear my POVs will be drastically overshadowed by you, but I am not complaining. I will rise to the challenge. I pray we make each other better for the rest of our lives. It's been an honor to write this novel alongside you.

The ONLY suggestion I have here at the end is to consider a circular ending to really drive home the theme of the novel. As you have it now, with BE and BN getting married and honeymooning in Bora Bora, is fantastic. But, I think we can elevate it. I've heard chirpings in the book world that readers are tired of stories ending with engagements or weddings, so why don't we fast forward through those things and show the characters doing a small part of life together? How do they interact with each other now that they are married? What glimpse can you give to show that BE has embraced her true nature and is romancing her reality? Drive that home since it's a central theme. As my mom used to say, there is beauty in the bramble. Show me the characters' beautiful life, even in the bramble.

I know our bramble is beautiful.

I'm typing this as I sit next to you while you read, and now I think it's time we put the book down and cuddle. I miss your touch, my love.

Epilogue ~ One Year Later

NOAH • JUNE

I watch through the window painted with blueberries outside of Main Street Coffee as my wife creates trenches, pacing around the tables set up for the book launch event. She tugs at the ends of her straight brown hair, worry coating her face as she bites her bottom lip.

I've been standing here for over a minute, and I should have entered and put her at ease by now, but she's adorable when she's fretting. When she stops in her tracks and leans against the table like she's about to vomit, however, the doting husband side of me resurfaces, and I push open the glass door. Esme spins on her sparkling orange heel, her off-white skirt fluttering around her. Her tense shoulders drop as relief washes across her tanned face.

"You're late," she says on an exhale, but we meet each other in the middle of the room, and she wraps her petite arms around my waist. I kiss her on the forehead while relishing in her floral, feminine scent.

"And you're a strung-out mess." I stare into her soft brown eyes, fingering flyaways out of her face and tucking them behind her ear. She is so beautiful; it stuns me every time I gaze upon her. *Thank You, Lord,* I silently pray, *for bringing her back to me.* Aloud, I say, "But I come bearing a gift."

I reach into the back pocket of my white linen pants and pull out an orange Sharpie. But not just any orange Sharpie—it's a specific sunset orange hue that matches our book cover perfectly. I've been searching for two days for this specific color simply because my wife wanted one last-minute.

My wife. I still can't get over those two words. Meeting her in Bora Bora was nothing short of God's perfect timing, but losing her to the intricacies of the human mind was pure hell, the darkest moments of my life outside of losing my mom. I shake the thoughts, not wanting to put a damper on this day.

"You found one?" Esme's eyes widen as she snatches it from my hand. She stares down at it as if it's a relic worthy of protection, and then she throws herself into my arms again, causing me to stumble backward a few steps until I gain my footing and wrap my arms around her, lifting her off her feet and spinning her. She lets out a squeal, and I can't stop the smile sweeping across my face at her joy. I live for every smile. I would scour the ends of the earth for every sunset orange Sharpie if she wanted me to. If it made her this happy. *After all we've been through to get to this moment...*

"You're the best, babe," Esme says as I set her down. She kisses my cheek, her eyes sparkling.

"Better than fictional Noah, *my little author*?" I quip, raising an eyebrow and tracing circles on her lower back. She once confided in me that a fictional version of me, the one she wrote about in the book, often talked to her. She said she thinks that's when she started to fall in love even though he was somewhere between the real and the reverie.

She winks and steps out of my grasp. "Always."

"Even when I'm late?" I grab her hips and pull her back into me as she half-heartedly tries to squirm away. It's impossible not to touch her when she's near. I had trouble keeping my hands to myself when we first met, not to mention when we reunited and started dating. Now that we're married? Yeah, no. I choose to be that annoying handsy couple. I want the world to see how much I love this woman.

"You're better than fiction because of when you're late." Esme boops my nose while wrinkling hers. "Being with you has taught me that real life is better than fiction *because of* the messiness."

My heart thumps wildly at her statement. She does this now and then. Stares at me as if she's contemplating life itself, and then says some statement about how I'm so much better than the version of me she created in her head. I think she tends to forget that the version she crafted of me came straight from her memories, with tweaks here and there. Finishing this book alongside her has been a godsend. It's allowed me to dig deep into her brain and her heart under the guise of work. Her chapters have been a step-by-step guide on how to romance her and love her well. She's taken notes on the chapters I've written, too, and puts my scenes into practice.

What a glorious year it's been. Especially after that season of utter darkness and depression.

I drag her lips to mine, relishing in the taste of her mango lip gloss while my mind is swept away to memories of Bora Bora and mango fish tacos and our very first kiss. Esme playfully pushes me away, saying, "Okay, babe. I've got to make sure everything is perfect for this evening."

"Breathe, sweetheart. You don't need to have a panic attack before your big night." I slip my arm around her, massaging her hips. My body hums with the contact, and I have half a mind to find a closet in this coffee shop.

Esme grabs my hands and drags me behind her as we check the table set up in the corner. It's long with a white cloth that has Prewitt Publishing's logo—a rising sun over an ocean—on it. There is a sign with information about me and Esme, and then three stacks of *Reveling in Reverie*.

Written by Lorraine E. Jenkins and Noah A. Prewitt. It's her debut and my debut under my real name, as a solo author instead of with my twin. I've known for a while Ashton was ready to step back from writing, but I kept pushing him to continue because his worldbuilding and plotting are unmatched. A perfect pairing to my prose. But he saw the opportunity to tell me that he wasn't going to write any more novels when Esme invited me into writing alongside her. There was nothing I could say or do to dissuade him. He's made up his mind to stick strictly to the business side of publishing, and I wish he'd tell me why instead of the stupid excuse that he's tired of writing. I've watched him sit at his laptop and draft stories that he refuses to talk about. I've seen the fire in his eyes as he types away. There's something he's keeping from me, but I can't push him. Just like he never pushed me when I realized I'd lost Esme for good.

Which wasn't the case, thanks to my meddling, amazing brother. I can never pay back the debt I owe to him for being bold enough for both of us. To go against Esme's parents' wishes and contact her on my behalf while I tried to piece my life back together in Alaska. Looking back, I wish I would have fought harder for her. But the pain of her forgetting me was crushing. I was drowning in black waves of despair, and when her dad, Gregory, threatened the restraining order in his attempt to protect Esme, it was the tsunami that took me out.

I shake my head clear, remembering now is not the time to visit that faraway place once more.

Esme loops her arm around my waist as we stand in front of the book table. She leans her head against my shoulder, and I hear a quiver in her voice when she says, "We did it, babe."

I spin her to face me, and sure enough, there's liquid gold in her eyes. "I'm glad we get to share our story with the world." I kiss the top of her head as she buries her face into my chest. "Now everyone gets to know just how head over heels in love with you I am."

Esme pulls back, a smirk on her face. "As if you haven't declared it to the town ten times over." She places her hand on my chest, and I entwine my fingers with hers. I lift our hands and kiss her knuckles.

"I will never tire of letting you know just how loved you are, sweetheart."

The door flies open, and Esme jerks away from me, but then as if she remembers she is perfectly allowed to be wrapped up in me, she steps right back to my side, once more slipping her arm around my waist. I rest my arm across her shoulders as we greet the owner of Main Street Coffee.

"Y'all ready to get this shindig started?" a spunky woman with sass and attitude for days asks as she struts inside. Danica Carnes wears a pink leopard-print cross T-shirt that matches the pink streaks in her cropped ash-blonde hair. Katie McBride, Esme's former student, follows in behind her.

"Yes, ma'am," Esme shouts, though I feel her grip on my orange linen button-down tighten. We set to work to put the final touches on the coffee shop. Katie curated a special menu for the night, full of orange, mango, and other beachy flavors. Sam and Ethan show up, followed by Branda, Ashton, and Vance. They help set up games and tables outside on the town green off to the side of the coffee shop because we expect overflow tonight. Vance and Branda did a phenomenal job promoting the book, even if they bickered their way through it.

Before we know it, the sun is setting and the town green is popping. I expected everyone in Whitney to come out and support Esme, and they didn't disappoint. It's almost as crowded as the Blueberry Jubilee held in the area last weekend. Or the Founder's Day parade held the weekend before that. I swear there is always something going on in this one-red-light town. But as I watch Esme laugh with Sam, Branda, her mom, and other women from the community, I know there's nowhere else I'd rather be.

"Well, Son." Dad approaches from behind, clapping me on the back. I embrace him with a full-on hug. "Proud of you."

"Thanks for coming tonight," I say as we pull apart. Grandma Lois hobbles up beside me, and I hug her next. "Hey, Grandma."

"Sorry we're a little late," she says, holding up a bedazzled cane that matches her own. "I forgot this at home and we had to turn around. Now where's Bertha?"

I point across the town green from my position against the red brick wall of the coffee shop. Bertha—who we all call Grannie—is tossing a cornhole bag while leaning on her original bedazzled cane. I hope to be that spritely when I'm her age.

Esme looks back at me from her circle of women, and when she sees I'm with Grandma and Dad, she walks over to us.

"Hey, Link! Lois!" Esme hugs them both, and they congratulate her on the book release, which she blushes her way through. We are still working on her ability to fully accept compliments.

I pull my wife by my side, tucking her close despite the humid June heat, as she catches up with my dad and grandma. I love how easy it was for her to blend into my family and me into hers, once they realized I wasn't a villain in their story, that is. "This town really loves you," I whisper into her ear during a lull in conversation.

"They love us," she responds, leaning her head on my shoulder as kids rush past us in a game of tag.

Grannie hobbles our way, meeting up with Lois and receiving her new bedazzled cane with Southern flair—lots of "Oh, honey, you didn't!" and "Bless my soul, Lois Marie."

I don't know if the women planned it or not, but they are mirrors of one another with their gray hair in buns, black dress pants, and sparkling orange shirts that match Esme's heels. We will need a family photo tonight; we are all in various shades of orange, white, yellow, and pink.

I hug Grannie before passing her to Esme.

"Your title is still smutty, dear," Grannie says in Esme's ear, though it's loud enough for me to hear. I can't help the snort that erupts from me.

"It is not!" Esme proclaims before turning to me. "Noah, tell Grannie our book title is not smutty."

I smirk, shrugging. "Reveling?"

"All reveling means is to enjoy oneself, particularly in a lively way," Esme retorts, folding her arms across her chest.

I raise a brow, meeting her challenge. "Quite a connotation it has, doesn't it, Miss English Teacher? Connotation is sometimes more important than denotation. Have you heard the version where it means to get great pleasure from something... *or someone?*"

Esme groans, covering her face. "Why did you let me choose that title then?"

I cup my hands to her ear and whisper, "Because I *like* reveling in reverie with you, sweetheart." I bite her lobe for good measure, and when I pull back, her face is flushed a pretty pink. Checking my watch, I say, "It's time for the author to read a chapter from her book. Are you ready, Meme?"

Grannie lets out a loud, piercing whistle, and the crowd snaps to attention. Grandma proceeds to shout, "It's time for a reading!"

Beside me, Esme trembles. I grab her hand and squeeze it three times, letting her know I love her and I'm here. She steels herself when our eyes meet and nods her head. I guide her to the sound system set up between the coffee shop and the town green as applause erupts around us.

"Thank You, Jesus," Esme whispers as she steps onto the small, black stage. I take my place by her side, where I will reside forevermore.

"Glory and honor to Him," I add. Esme smiles up at me.

Sam approaches with a copy of the book, and I take it because Esme's hands are still shaking. I turn to Chapter One, which is written from Esme's perspective.

She stares down at the words before clearing her throat.

I understand how important these words are to her. She told me once that they were the first words she thought when she awoke from her coma two years ago. She never understood what they meant until we found each other again, and she learned the truth of the night we were attacked.

Esme glances up at me one more time for reassurance, and I smile at my wife. The woman I knew I wanted to choose from the moment I saw her drinking a mimosa and glaring at the sand and the sun as if they were Enemy Number One. God whispered, "That's her," and when her heart stopped on that deck in Bora Bora, while I rested my head on her still chest after crawling to her, I begged God to let me join her on the other side. I ripped my necklace from my neck and folded it into her hands as I lost consciousness.

And for a brief moment, God answered my prayer in the most unique way. A way that led me to believe in quantum entanglement, because who's to say God didn't create us that way? In a way I'll never utter to another being. She doesn't remember our souls touching as we looked upon our beaten and bruised bodies, the medics who saved us both, but I do.

"If death soldered our souls, I'd die a thousand times over."

"If we shadows have offended,

Think but this and all is mended:

That you have but slumbered here

While these visions did appear.

And this weak and idle theme,

No more yielding but a dream,

Gentles, do not reprehend."

William Shakespeare, A *Midsummer Night's Dream*

AUTHOR'S NOTE:

Reverie is the first novel in the *Daydreams & Disasters* series. This book ties into stories I have previously published and ones that are on the horizon. Please keep in mind that I am building a world out of all my stories, so if there are frayed ends at the end of each book, that's why. Series cross over, genres blend, and there is so much more to come! <3

***

Stay tuned for more love stories from the town of Whitney, Willow Bay, Crescent Cove, and the rest of The Sweet Tea Writers Association!

Read President Darcy Marshall's story in *The Politics of Love*

Read Lucy May's story in *The Designated Date*

Read Emma Jane's story in *Emma Jane's Guide to Matchmaking the Mayor*

Read "Windsor" and Nick's story in *Chasing Kensie*

And stay tuned for more romances / urban fantasies / political thrillers coming your way...

Book Club!

Below are discussion questions to contemplate and talk about with your book club! <3 If you ever want to invite me to chat, just send me a collaboration request through my website, www.drewtaylorwrites.com

1. So, Esme's writing a book about herself—sort of. How did that whole story-within-a-story thing hit you? Did it make her journey feel more real or just a little wild?

2. Esme feels called to write stories that show God's love through romance—real, flawed, beautiful love. Do you think fiction can be a ministry? Why do you think God might care about stories like these?

3. Esme lost three years of her life and somehow found a whole new one. What do you think this book is really saying about memory, identity, and getting a

second shot at life?

4. Faith plays a quiet but steady role in Esme's choices. How did her relationship with God shape her growth, and did anything about it resonate with your own story?

5. Let's talk about Noah—fictional and maybe-not-so-fictional. Did you love the blurred lines between Esme's imagination and her real life, or did it leave you with questions?

6. Poor Esme's trying to juggle everyone's expectations—her family, her town, and let's be honest, her head. Where do you see her breaking free, and where does she still hold back?

7. Esme talks about God with a lot of honesty—sometimes clinging to Him, sometimes questioning Him. Did anything about her spiritual journey feel familiar to you?

8. This book doesn't shy away from romance tropes like insta-love and whirlwind flings, but also kind of pokes fun at them. Did it work for you, or were you side-eying some of the swoony moments?

9. Grannie and Sam are an absolute riot, but they also drop some wisdom bombs. Which side characters stuck with you, and why?

10. Writing becomes Esme's way of healing and figuring herself out. Have you ever used creativity (or something else) to process life like that?

11. What did you think about that last scene with "real" Noah/Ashton? Coincidence, divine intervention, fate with a capital F? Spill.

12. There's this undercurrent of divine timing and calling—Esme's accident, her writing, even meeting "Noah." Do you believe God works like that in real life? Why or why not?

13. Okay, last one's personal: if you were writing a story starring you, what parts would you keep and what would you rewrite? Be honest.

Bonus Activity:

Invite each book club member to write (or brainstorm out loud) a short alternate version of Esme and Noah's meet-cute. Maybe they bump into each other in a bookstore instead of Bora Bora, or he's her new neighbor who knocks on her door holding a mango pie. Keep the tone flirty or faith-centered—whatever feels right. This activity plays off the novel's love of storytelling, imagination, and second chances at life. It also invites everyone to step into Esme's shoes as a writer and explore how small changes shift a story's tone or direction.

LOVED THE STORY?

***

Consider leaving a review on Amazon and Goodreads!

Acknowledgments

Reverie came to me in a whirlwind idea, and I must admit, this is the first time I've felt like a real author. My other books are so close to me, but this one is different. While I was writing it, I felt like I was weaving a tale from the depths of my imagination. I could see this story clear as day, and that has never happened before. It was a beautiful, overwhelming experience.

First of all, I must take time to thank Samantha Oglesby for coming alongside me for the entirety of this book. Thank you for the countless late night and early morning video message exchanges and hours upon hours of voice notes. Thank you for brainstorming unhinged ideas with me, for talking me down when I felt like burning the manuscript, and for KEEPING NOAH ALIVE. That's right, friends. Noah was supposed to die. Esme was supposed to fall in love with Ashton. Sam (who graciously lent her name to Samantha Prewitt), saved Noah. You can send her a message thanking her now. Sammie, your friendship is so dear to me. Keep staying beautiful and spreading goodness in this world. You are an inspiration.

Next, I need to also say a special thank you to Latisha Sexton for also coming alongside me during the drafting of this book. Like Sam, you also listened to countless voice notes as I tried to nail down all the ins and outs of this wild ride of a novel. Your advice is invaluable to me, and your friendship is even more precious to my soul. Thank you for the constant encouragement and support, girl. I have so much love for you! Keep being a rockstar.

To my brilliant and funny and talented editor, you are irreplaceable. Leah, I absolutely love your wisdom, your humor, your unhinged theories document, and your joyous encouragement. With every book of mine you edit, I learn more and more about the art of storytelling. You said this book was near perfect when you got your hands on it, and I can only say that it's because I've learned so much from you over the past few years. You are a gem, and I couldn't do this authoring thing without you, love. <3 Stay amazing!

Melody, thank you so much for creating an absolute VISION of a cover for this book! You were so pleasant to work with, and I'm excited for what's to come with the rest of this series. Alicia, thank you for making sure this book's final draft was tight, polished, and clean! I'm so grateful you were available to proofread for me last minute. You're amazing!

Ally, you sweet and beautiful soul. Thank you for being the best PA for this launch that the world has ever seen. You are the glue holding me together most days in the midst of this chaotic author life. I'm thrilled to see where our partnership takes us beyond Reverie. So much love for you, friend.

To my alphas and betas—Beth, Amanda, Lizzie, Anna, Hannah, and Audrey—thank you all for your input and for making sure this novel became the best novel it could be. To Abby—thanks for always coming in clutch with last minute formatting and grammar mistakes! I'm extremely grateful to have you all on my team!

To Drew's Crew—the core members of the Taylor-verse—and my ARC readers: thank you for everything you've done to make sure this book received all the hype it could get. Every day you all show up for me, and I pray every book I give back to you is worth it. Writing a book takes a village, so thank you for being a part of mine. I couldn't do this without each of you <3

Dear reader, thank YOU for picking up this book and giving it a chance. If you made it this far, please know I love you and—from the bottom of my heart—I appreciate the heck out of you.

Mama, thanks for listening to me develop this idea. And for always being my biggest cheerleader. I love you to the moon and to Saturn.

Jesus Christ, my Lord and Savior, I'm humbled every time I remember that this gift of writing could be taken away from me. So, thank You for giving it to me, and I pray I always use it to bring You glory and honor. I pray every story finds the right readers and helps people to reflect on life, the world, sin, struggles, grace, redemption, and most importantly, Your love. Life is messy, but You make beauty out of our bramble.

Also By Drew Taylor

Sign up for my newsletter where you will receive access to bonus scenes, additional chapters, extended epilogues, and much more! New content added at random!
Scan the QR code or click on the link to learn more about Drew Taylor's books!
www.drewtaylorwrites.com

Drew Taylor writes modern closed-door chick-lit romance stories from a Christian worldview. She believes faith-based romance can be full of heart, humor, healing, and hope while showcasing the reality of our fallen human condition. Her redemptive and engaging stories point to the One who embodies true love–Jesus Christ. Drew lives in the great state of Mississippi where she teaches high school English. When not teaching or writing, she enjoys reading, baking, researching conspiracy theories, and spending quality time with the people who mean the most to her.

***

Follow Drew:
Instagram: @authordrewtaylor
Facebook: Drew Taylor, Author
Pinterest: @authordrewtaylor

YouTube: @authordrewtaylor